The Hypothesis of Giants

Book Three: The Control

By

Melissa Kuch

ISBN: 1979403317
ISBN 13: 9781979403313

For my mom: *My love for you has no beginning and no end...it will always be.*

"I alone cannot change the world, but I can cast a stone across the waters to create many ripples."

— Mother Teresa

Chapters

Chapter 1

The Nightmare

A gunshot rang out to signal the start of the Independence Day of the Last Straw parade. Participants marched with great pandemonium and pomp and circumstance. Batons twirled and the High School marching band blew trumpets and trombones with the steady heartbeat of the drums leading the pack. Onlookers proudly waved the orange and indigo flags inscribed with the slogan "IDEAL for Unity" as Common Good soldiers, clad in those same colors, marched in rhythm with the pounding drums. The parade was making its way down the side streets of Candlewick and toward Main Street where the Candlewick Government Building rose high into the sky like a beacon of hope and fear.

Jake Fray stood tall and proud riding in an opulent float at the tail end of the parade alongside the leader of this young nation,

Inspector Herald. Jake observed neighbors and students he had gone to school with eye him with admiration and envy, saluting him and the Inspector as they rode past. Jake was honored to represent the Common Good Army as the First Lieutenant, the highest honor bestowed by Inspector Herald and the IDEAL. An honor that came with great responsibility. The badge with the crisscrossed swords, the symbol of the First Lieutenant, was proudly sewn onto his uniform sleeve and a tattoo of the same symbol was burned into his skin beneath the fabric.

The float was making its way past his childhood home on Wishbone Avenue, where his younger sister Mary stood on the front stoop. He still pictured her as the annoying baby sister who tended to follow him around and annoy him when he was preoccupied with training for the Common Good Army. Now at fourteen, she was like a stranger to him with cropped black hair; dressed in indigo jeans and a white tank top exposing a rose tattoo on her shoulder blade. Her big owl eyes glared back at him, mad that he had missed her birthday party earlier that week. She didn't understand, nor his parents, how important it was for him to be First Lieutenant. None of them understood or were happy for him in his new role. All of them wanted to carry on their Jewish faith and customs. They were lucky he didn't turn them in, more for fear of how it would reflect on him to be associated with believers. He cursed under his breath as Mary clutched a Star of David necklace in her hands, exposing it just so he could see it, having completely ignored his warnings.

Beside Mary stood his mother, standing tall yet fragile, clutching onto Mary and staring at her son like she didn't even recognize him. She mouthed the words, "I love you" but he marched right past, head held high, not daring to show weakness in front of the Inspector. The Common Good was his family now, drilled into his brain through the countless missions he had mastered. He was now the Inspector's right hand man- and he wouldn't let him down.

Inspector Herald patted him on the arm protectively and whispered to his young protégé, "This is our world now. No one will stand in our way."

The drums beat on as Jake stole a quick glance back at his mother and sister, but they were gone! A pool of blood was where they once stood. The parade vanished and the Inspector tore the First Lieutenant badge off his uniform and flung it into the pool of blood, pointing the gun at him.

"Traitor!"

Jake awoke, shaking and shivering, catching his breath. He rubbed his eyes, awakening to a different kind of nightmare. He was no longer outside on Wishbone Avenue but instead a prisoner of Candlewick Prison. He wrapped his arms around his decimated body, being allowed only meager rations to keep him alive – barely. Inspector Herald didn't want him dead – he had made that very clear at their last encounter a month before – when everything had changed.

He tried to stand up but his leg was still healing and a sharp pain shot up his femur when he put pressure on it. His makeshift splint from the plank on his bed was giving it the support it needed to heal, but it would never be the same. Nor could he be the same again.

His mother was dead, killed at the hand of Inspector Herald right before Jake's eyes. Her final words to him saying "I forgive you" continued to haunt him. If only he could forgive himself for not saving her when he had the chance. Instead he was unmasked as the traitor, stripped of the First Lieutenant title, deemed enemy of the state, and was now wasting away at the Inspector's bidding within a prison cell. Now his only hope was to save his sister Mary who was imprisoned out west and still at the mercy of the Inspector. If she wasn't already dead...

The alarm for his cell beeped and he scrambled to the far corner of the cage, shielding his eyes from the light as the door slowly slid open. A shadowy figure walked in and the door slammed shut behind it, the alarm re-activated. He looked up to in disbelief as a lone lantern illuminated the features of the eighteen-year-old beautiful journalist Analise Jones. She was dressed like she had just come from a TV interview, wearing a maroon pant suit and the red ruby necklace, the gift from the Inspector, hung loosely down her neckline. Her cropped black hair had grown in the past month and was now tied back in a short ponytail, and he couldn't believe this young woman was once the pigtailed, tomboy friend he had grown up with on Wishbone Avenue. She appeared nervous and Jake felt responsible for putting Analise's life in danger, convincing her to work undercover as the media spokesperson for the Common Good. Her deep auburn eyes stared at him with such pity that he had to turn away from her gaze.

"So, you are alive."

She said it so abruptly that he had to laugh breaking the uneasy silence.

"Nice of you to check in on me. Or were you hoping I was dead?"

She proceeded with unpacking the bag she had brought with her. "The camera that is spying on you…the feed is being monitored by Miss. Thompson. She manipulated the feed for the next 10 minutes so that we can meet without the Inspector knowing. The guard, Johnson, is a friend of mine who brought me down here in secret. But we don't have a lot of time."

She handed him a thermos of warm soup and their hands touched. In that momentary interaction, Analise felt emotions run through her. Jake quickly opened the thermos and drank heartily, welcoming the warm broth. The warmth from the container alone brought feeling back into his fingers.

"A lot has changed since you were arrested," she said, rubbing her arms from the damp coldness and scrutinizing Jake's accommodations with horror. "Henry Stockington, Boreas's father, is now the first advisor. No one has yet been selected to take your place, or more likely the Inspector wants to keep your role vacated… for obvious reasons."

Jake wiped his mouth. "Because I tried to kill him."

Analise nodded. "That took a lot of courage to turn on him."

"Courage!" Jake laughed darkly, throwing the thermos against the wall where it emitted a loud clang before bouncing wildly on the concrete floor. The guard Johnson rushed to the the door and Analise called out that everything was fine. She glared at Jake who didn't answer for his actions, slumping off into a corner, putting his head in his hands. She walked over to his feeble form, wanting to touch him, hold him, but instead just sat next to him, hoping her presence would help give him strength.

He took a deep breath and wiped his eyes. "I failed, Analise. I had to watch my own mother die."

"I'm so sorry, Jake," she said slowly.

"I had the gun on Herald. I had the chance to end this, to end him. And he played me. He knew there was no bullet in the gun he handed to me. He knew I was the traitor."

Analise took a deep breath. "Herald and the Common Good Army killed your mother, my father and countless others. We can't let him take any more lives."

Jake tried to stand up but then crumpled to the ground once more as his leg faltered. "There is no fight in me… not anymore."

Analise leaned in close so that her lips were nearly against his ear. She whispered, "Don't give up on me. I'm still on the inside, as is Miss Thompson. We are recruiting more day by day, secretly of course. We are going to save you."

Jake shook his head, "There is no saving me! I already watched my mother die. I will not watch my sister die. I have to do what Herald wants to keep her alive."

Analise handed him a cup of water, holding it to his lips until he gulped it down. She couldn't believe this man before her used to be the First Lieutenant, the second most feared man in the United States of the Common Good. A man who was a killer and a leader of hundreds of soldiers was now like a crumbling edifice, defeated and empty. She couldn't believe that there was no fight left in him. She couldn't believe that he would give up on their cause.

"I came down here against my own better judgment to warn you that the Inspector believes he knows where Aurora and Boreas have been hiding this past month. Somewhere up in the Catskill Mountains. He is going to force you to gain their trust and then betray them. But you can't do it, Jake.

"I have to."

"He is never going to live up to his side of the bargain. You know him well enough to realize that. Mary is probably already dead."

Jake stared down at the empty cup shaking in his hands. "No! Herald wouldn't kill the only leverage he has against me if he wants to force me to help him. And the only reason he kept me alive is because he wants to stop the prophecy and he knows he needs me to do that."

Analise stood up abruptly, facing the wall, not wanting to face the man she had believed so strongly in. The man who had just 3 months earlier recruited her to be the Common Good Media spokesperson, a role that brought more danger than she had anticipated. She clasped her hand around the ruby red necklace and wanted to tear it off her neck and throw it at the man who had gotten her mixed up in this crusade to begin with. She whirled around to face him. "If you turn against Aurora and Boreas, more people than just Mary are going to perish! You know that the Geometric Storm is coming!"

Jake looked up and, for the first time since being reunited, Analise saw a glimmer of the Jake she knew buried deep down in his pain – that there was still fight left in his soul.

"Storm or no storm, one thing is certain," he said fiercely. "Mary is going to live, even if that means Aurora and Boreas have to die in the process."

Chapter 2

Running Away

Aurora ignited an orange tear-drop match in her hand, the fire dancing whimsically with the wind. She watched as the fire took hold, and withered, crinkled, and incinerated her carefully constructed pile of dried out leaves and twigs, then cursed as a strong cold wind extinguished the flame with one strong breath. She stood alone outside of the Safe Haven and crisscrossed her arms over her chest trying to keep herself warm in that brisk, autumn night. She looked left and right making sure that she was not being watched and then cleared her mind. She pointed her shivering hand at the concoction of dried leaves and timber that she had assembled. She cleared her mind and her hand stopped shaking and suddenly a spark flew out from her fingertip and caught the edge of the timber wood, charring and smoldering and growing until a fire blazed in front of her that no wind could extinguish.

She sat beside the fire and pressed her still warm fingers against the skin of her face. She gazed down at her hands with a mixture of fear and awe, still in disbelief of this power she possessed. The fire crackled and Aurora looked at her shadow reflected off of Storm King Mountain. Just then another shadow, larger and more ominous, loomed higher and higher above her own. Aurora jumped up in attack mode, but quickly sighed in relief when she recognized the giant shadow as none other than that of her 30-foot friend, Otus.

"Aurora, I'm so glad I found you!" his ears wiggled in delight like they had just been playing some game of hide and seek.

She defiantly turned her back on him. "Leave me alone, Otus," she demanded.

His bulky silhouette stood stark still watching her but then stomped ruthlessly on the fire until it was completely snuffed out. Aurora jumped up, whirling to face the giant who was coughing as smoke filled his nostrils, rubbing his watery green eyes.

"You can't hide from this!" He cried out in between coughing fits.

"Hide from what?"

Before she could blink he scooped her up with his mammoth-sized hand raising her high into the air.

"Testifying."

Despite her protests and threats he placed her in his denim blue overalls chest pocket. He took off climbing up the solid rock wall formed by the glaciers thousands of years before. He climbed over the jagged slabs of stone and Aurora's teeth chattered as they ascended to higher elevation, providing a 360 degree vista of the moon hovering over the Catskill Mountains and its shimmering reflection in the Hudson River. Otus stood on the peak of Storm King Mountain and turned slightly toward his right where, to the naked eye, it appeared to be a dead end with only the frozen water lurking beneath them with a 1000 foot drop. This illusion helped prevent the Common Good Army from locating the secret entrance to the Safe Haven. Otus leapt, appearing as if he was jumping off of the cliff to their deaths but he landed safely on a sturdy piece of glass suspended in mid-air. Otus then crossed through the shadowy entrance that led deep into the hollow interior of the mountain.

Aurora knew there was no escape for her once they entered the Safe Haven of Plymouth Incarnate.

Two cloaked men emerged who were guarding the opening and called out in unison, "Did you find her?"

Otus patted Aurora on the head. "Found her."

The guard nodded in approval and replied, "Report to the High Magistrate immediately."

Plymouth Incarnate was the name of the Safe Haven, a country within the glacier rocks that resembled a glittering coal mine. As Otus worked his way down the long wooden staircase, the walls sparkled with dazzling rock crystals. Aurora peered down at people of all religions working together to build this wondrous world, founded by the High Magistrate, Fawn Stockington. Plymouth Incarnate was hidden away from the tight grip of the Common Good establishment, which was run by Inspector Herald and the IDEAL. Under the United States of the Common Good, these people lost their freedom to worship freely. Despite the demolishment of many of their religious structures following the Last Straw protest, which took place 15 years earlier, Fawn and her followers had grown to greater numbers and were resolute on defending their beliefs and their freedom together.

They entered the great chamber whose center housed the great religious books that were salvaged from the tragic destruction of the first rebellion country, Plymouth Tarturus. Plymouth Tarturus had been an underwater castle that was destroyed by the bombs of the Common Good Army and had killed many people, including Aurora's friend, Eileen O'Hara.

Beside the great books stood Fawn Stockington, the High Magistrate. Her long black hair was hanging loosely down her shoulders and a shell clip was secured in her hair. She wore a white dress and a silver cape that nearly touched the floor. Next to Fawn stood her eldest son, Jonathan Stockington, who towered above her at a height of 6 feet 2 inches with long honey blond hair tied back in a ponytail. He had an athletic build being the captain of the football and basketball teams back in Candlewick High School and had big turquoise eyes that made Aurora melt every time she gazed into them.

Fawn glared at Aurora with those enigmatic hazel eyes…the same feature she shared with her younger son, Boreas. At the thought of Boreas, Aurora's throat clenched tight like it was caught in a vise. Boreas was going to be on trial today and they wanted Aurora to testify against him.

"Thank you, Otus for finding her," Fawn's voice echoed in that room of solid stone.

"Found her safe and sound," Otus beamed and lifted Aurora gently out of his pocket and onto the ground in front of Fawn.

She brushed herself off and crossed her arms defiantly as Fawn stepped down gracefully from the altar.

"Don't you realize that Inspector Herald and his army are out there looking for you as we speak? That they know about your powers? What made you do something so foolish as to run away?"

Aurora didn't answer, looking instead at the large grandfather clock with its pendulum rocking back and forth. Each swing of the pendulum was another second closer to the trial where she would have to face Boreas again.

Fawn followed Aurora's line of vision and immediately stood blocking the grandfather clock but couldn't block the sound of the tick tock that emanated from it.

"Don't you realize that this is hard for all of us?" Fawn sighed, crisscrossing over to the Great Books and putting her hands on them for support. "Boreas is my son. But we cannot deny the fact that he tried to turn both you and Otus over to the Common Good. And he tried to kill Jonathan."

"He wasn't acting on his own accord," Aurora yelled. "The Inspector injected him with the Soul Extractor serum! The Inspector was using Boreas to get to us."

"Boreas was acting on his own accord," Jonathan rebuked with vehemence. "The Professor said that the Soul Extractor will only intensify evil in a person's soul if it is already there to begin with. Boreas could have stopped it if he truly wanted to."

Aurora shook her head, not convinced. "There is good and evil in all of us. Isn't that what those great books say that you are protecting? That people need to choose? The Soul Extractor doesn't give you that option. If Boreas could have chosen, I believe he would not have turned us in. He would rather have died than..."

"Boreas is a coward and a failure!" Jonathan kicked a chair, sending it flying across the chamber. "He has always been one and you can't change that."

"Enough, Jonathan!" Fawn put a hand on her son's shoulder and then faced Aurora. "Boreas will be put on trial and I am sorry but you will need to testify about what happened. You had a first-hand encounter. Let the jury decide. That's what a democracy is all about. If Boreas is innocent, God willing it will be found out."

Aurora marched out of the chamber and slammed the large engraved stone doors shut behind her. She ran across the glittering corridor until she reached her room, a circular enclave in a corner of the mountain. She slid the velvet blue curtains shut to block any eyes from watching her, which she knew they did. They watched and judged her ever since she returned to the safe haven. Word spread like lice and before they had locked Boreas in his cell, everyone in Plymouth Incarnate had heard that Aurora was the Goddess of Dawn and that she had gotten her powers by stopping Boreas, who had betrayed them. But she really had used her powers to save him.

It wasn't the first time she had tried to save Boreas. When they had been thrown together on this quest with Otus back in July, they had found themselves running from Inspector Herald and discovered Plymouth Tartarus beneath the Atlantic Ocean. Boreas got caught kissing Babs O'Hara and arrested for violating the law of kissing an engaged woman. Fawn was going to sentence her own son to 10 years imprisonment but Aurora had intervened. She convinced Fawn to spare him, but no one anticipated the Great Secretary was going to try to slit Boreas's throat.

Boreas survived that knife attack, as well as survived being captured by the Common Good Army. He had survived a lot those past 5 months, but now Boreas was on trial for his life. How was Aurora going to prove his innocence amongst a country who already deemed him guilty?

She had to see Boreas before the trial, even though she was forbidden to do so. She knew that if she didn't speak to him then they would need more than a God to save him from his fate.

✡ ✡ ✡

Aurora dashed into the classroom where Mrs. Xiomy was teaching a Biology class. There was a podium at the center and in front of her lined in pews were teenagers, many not much older than her fifteen-year-old self, who had never had a formal education. Mrs. Xiomy volunteered to teach them in order to educate them with knowledge of the outside world. Some were newcomers who had been under the clutch of the Common Good and were freed when Fawn and Mrs. Xiomy infiltrated Candlewick Prison. Many were still ill and malnourished from the treatment in those cells. Despite popular belief, criminals were not entitled to trial by jury and were suffering for crimes consisting of religious rituals and customs. If one family member was caught practicing religious beliefs or customs, then the whole family suffered. Also, if anyone was found with books not deemed appropriate by the Common Good, then they suffered the same fate. Aurora still could not believe that all of this transpired in her hometown of Candlewick. She, and so many others, had believed the lies the media had told them; that these were hardened criminals and traitors of the Common Good. No one had ever thought to question their judgment, since it was easier for the people to believe that what the IDEAL said was just. The Common Good had to be trusted to keep them safe and secure.

"How naïve I was," Aurora thought bitterly as she stood in the midst of this classroom looking at the fragile faces of the children and teenagers. They now faced her with looks of shock and bewilderment and awe. She even saw one girl with blond messy curls nudge the nearly bald boy next to her and whisper, "That's her. The Goddess of Dawn."

Mrs. Xiomy was still lecturing, oblivious to the interruption in her classroom. "And this microorganism is an amoeba... wait... is anyone paying attention?"

She whirled around, and lifted her purple eyeglasses to the tip of her pointed nose, smiling when she made out Aurora through her glass frames.

"Class dismissed for today. For your homework, please read chapters 2 and 3 on water organisms and cell structure for your next exam."

The class groaned, slammed their books shut and ran out the door past Aurora, each staring at her intently as they left. Aurora felt completely self-conscious as they eyed her up and down as if she wasn't real but another foreign organism from their textbook. When the last student left, Aurora closed the door behind her and walked up to Mrs. Xiomy who embraced her, the scent of chalk dust and rose petals resonating off her skin.

"Aurora Alvarez, don't you ever run away like that again!" Mrs. Xiomy hugged Aurora tightly against her chest cutting off Aurora's air supply.

"Mrs. Xiomy... I can't breathe," Aurora gasped and Mrs. Xiomy released her hold, her long blond curls wafted gently to the side of her neck, though some grey strands were just peeking out at the scalp. She was wearing an indigo dress that was cut right above her knee and her sleeves resembled wings that nearly hid her long pointed fingernails.

"I won't give you a lecture," Rana Xiomy said, packing up the papers on the desk. "I'm sure Fawn already talked your ears off, like she does to everyone. I don't know how I was ever friends with that woman."

Seventeen years earlier, Rana & Fawn were best friends and involved with the rebellion to sustain religious freedom in the country known as the United States of America. They both fell in love with the leader of the rebellion, David Xiomy, also known as IMAM. David, against all odds, united people of all different faiths and together they started a peaceful protest movement. He ended up falling in love with Rana and they were married. Fawn had been so distraught that she had walked away from the rebellion and settled down on Wishbone Avenue, marrying Henry Stockington. Two years later the rebellion was still in full force but during the final protest, both Rana and David Xiomy were arrested in New York City at what was known as the Last Straw Protest. Rana had been coerced to give up details about the rebellion to Inspector Herald believing that doing so would save her husband's life. The Inspector had not kept his end of the bargain and executed David anyway, believing that it was for the betterment of the Common Good. The details that Rana Xiomy provided, in addition to the death of their leader, brought about the end of the rebellion and the IDEAL was able to rule along with the Common Good government over the newly founded United States of the Common Good.

Fawn, after hearing of David's death, realized her mistake in abandoning him and the rebellion and faked her own death. She started a new country called Plymouth Tartarus many leagues beneath the Atlantic Ocean, determined to carry on where David had left off. She gained followers from all over the United States of the Common Good. She never forgave Mrs. Xiomy for turning against the cause, but Mrs. Xiomy had been forced to make a choice and she had chosen to try to save the man she loved over the cause itself.

Aurora was playing with a piece of chalk in her hand. "I can't believe they are going to make me testify against Boreas. It's not fair."

Mrs. Xiomy fixed her glasses and exclaimed, "Is that why you ran away? You thought you were going to help Boreas by running into the hands of the Inspector?"

"What happened to not being lectured?"

Mrs. Xiomy bit her tongue and sat on one of the desks, crossing her legs and swinging her purple heel back and forth like a seesaw. "Fine. So why did you so rudely interrupt my class? Water organisms is one of my favorite topics, well almost. I love fungi."

"I need to get into the jail and speak to him for just five minutes."

Mrs. Xiomy laughed outright and put her hand over her mouth to muffle the sound. "You have got to be kidding me! You are never going to get close to him. None of us have been able to see him for the past month. They definitely want to keep you away from him before the trial."

"You think I don't know that?" Aurora wailed. "I have not been able to forgive myself, since the last time I saw him, when he saw me and Jonathan almost kiss... I mean, not that I care that he saw that or anything, and we DIDN'T kiss... anyway, I just need to talk to him."

Mrs. Xiomy smiled gently and put her hand on Aurora's shoulder. "Look, I more than anyone know your relationship with Boreas has been a... challenging one. I know that you are torn between him and Jonathan."

"I am not torn," Aurora cried out defiantly. "It has always been Jonathan."

"Then why do you care that Boreas saw that *almost* kiss?"

Aurora stared down at her hands. "I don't know. I don't know how I feel about Boreas. Some days I wanted to kill him, and other days... I feel like he's the only one who really knows me. I mean I can't forget that even before this quest and even before we were friends, he distracted people at the Spring Formal to stop Hattie and her gang from making fun of me."

"He sounds like he's always cared for you. But if that's the case, why did he pursue Babs and not you? After Machu Picchu they were boyfriend and girlfriend."

Aurora bit her lip. "I turned him down at Machu Picchu... and at the barn in Australia. I honestly believed that we couldn't be anything more than the answer to the prophecy."

"Because of Jonathan."

Aurora nodded. "And this past month Jonathan and I have gotten closer... not romantically, but I have gotten to know him as opposed to staring at him from across Wishbone Avenue like some lovesick puppy."

"And..." Mrs. Xiomy urged her on.

"And... I am still not sure if I love Jonathan or the idea of Jonathan."

Mrs. Xiomy shrugged, "Aurora, I wish I knew what to say to help you but don't take love advice from me. I had to compete with my best friend for the man I loved. Fawn still hasn't forgiven me for pursuing David, even after I knew she cared for him. That was never easy for him to choose me over her. He did care for her, I know that. But he chose me. And for that time we had together, as tumultuous as it was during the protests and the running and even after losing him, I know that our love is stronger than any war and any fight here on Earth – stronger than death itself. I hope you will find that with whomever you choose.

Aurora gave her teacher a big hug. "David would be so proud that you joined the fight again."

"I hope so," she wiped a tear from her amethyst eye. "But enough about me. It's almost the Sacred Hour and the trial will be starting soon."

Aurora was brought back to reality and jumped to her feet. "That's why I need to speak with Boreas."

'Look I know you think that will help but think about it, if you did get in and you got caught, then your testimony would be null and void and you are the only one who can really help Boreas."

Aurora sat down helplessly looking at her hands, begging them and her powers to tell her the answer. "If only I could prove that my powers brought him back to the light."

"There's no evidence to prove that though. If only you could get your hand on the Soul Extractor serum and we could do a case study, but that would take weeks. And who would be crazy enough to inject himself with it?"

Aurora snapped her fingers and exclaimed, "I have a plan. But we need to find the Professor. We're running out of time."

Chapter 3

The Trial

The Sacred Hour struck — the hour between dusk and dawn that was the mandatory curfew of the Common Good. While the rest of the world was adhering to the Common Good's rules and sleeping soundlessly, Plymouth Incarnate was wide awake and waiting anxiously in the Great Hall for the trial to begin. The Great Hall resembled an amphitheater with the front part elevated. Two long pews were divided by a central aisle and the right side was marked for the defense and the left side marked for the prosecution. At the center stage stood a high bench made out of granite for the judge to preside on and beside it was a wooden witness stand where a lone candle stood lit and blinking ominously. Beneath the stage were rows upon rows of pews where people were filing in to witness the long awaited trial. Above the masses stood a Juliet balcony where the perimeter of the box was lined with candles flickering in the otherwise dark hall. A staircase spiraled down from the balcony and slithered around and around like a snake leading back to the main floor.

Aurora sat agitated on the side of the Prosecution, fidgeting with her hands, eying her unpainted nails and missing such modern conveniences as a manicure. After her talk with the Professor, she had showered and changed and was wearing the only fancy dress she owned, or actually borrowed, that just fit. It was a navy blue dress and some ugly, but appropriate, black heels that were digging into the sides of her feet. She took them off and made sure that no one noticed as she bent down to massage her ankles having not worn heels since the gala 5 months earlier. Her wavy golden-brown hair was hanging loosely down her shoulders and how she wished she had it up in a ponytail.

The Prosecuting attorney, Wilfred Hopkins, was schmoozing his way up and down the stage, shaking hands and putting on a show. He was a mousy looking man with big ears and a receding hairline and he had been a prosecuting general back in Candlewick for many years. He was not a deeply religious man but had high morals and believed in the justice system. He was tested when he was appointed to be the Prosecutor for a case regarding an elderly woman who had held a secret Catholic funeral mass for her husband of nearly 80 years. Realizing the injustice of the case and that it was heavily rigged by the Inspector, Hopkins tried to fight the ruling even after she had been found guilty. Instead of getting heard by the judge, he found himself locked up for ten years in Candlewick Prison. He managed to escape during the mass prison breakout.

Babs O'hara ran swiftly down the center aisle, her long auburn hair tied back in a braid, her legs gracefully sailing past the crowd of people gathered for the trial as if she was doing ballerina lunges through the air. She was wearing a short navy blue dress that hugged her thin figure and freckles were speckled over her cheeks. She had naturally rosy red lips that stood out over her pale white complex-ion. She squeezed through the people lining the center pew and hastily sat down beside Aurora. She was out of breath but there was not even the hint of a bead of sweat on her brow, which Aurora could hardly believe since she had run the entire length of the courtroom without stopping.

She turned to Aurora and exclaimed, "All of Plymouth Incarnate is here in the Great Hall. It's complete chaos! They almost didn't let me in. Fawn had to tell the guard that I was a witness for the prosecution."

Aurora turned to see Fawn speaking with the defense attorney, Herberta Rochester. She was a middle-aged woman with short spiked hair and a pig snout for a nose and was wearing a plaid suit with mismatched heels. She had high cheekbones and baby pink lip-stick smeared over her lips and most of her front teeth. Aurora feared that if her appearance was a representation of her legal skills, then Boreas was in trouble.

"Are there any witnesses for the defense?" Aurora asked, con-cerned and stretching her neck to see if anyone was sitting in the opposite pew.

"I think Otus is speaking for him. Didn't he tell you?"

Aurora shook her head in disbelief just as the room split to allow passage for Otus to flounder down the aisle. The floor vibrated with each footstep, like Otus was a shifting tectonic plate. He was being extra cautious to not step on anyone, but Otus being extra cautious meant that he was extra clumsy and a group of people immediately ran to avoid his large footsteps. He found a spot against the wall and gave Aurora a thumbs up signal thrilled that there were no casualties.

All of a sudden, boos rose up from the crowd. Aurora jumped up to see two armed officers leading Boreas into the courtroom. His legs were chained and his wrists were handcuffed and yet he held his head up high with his ebony hair combed with a slight strand hanging over his left eye. Facial hair had sprouted over his cheeks and upper chin and Aurora almost didn't recognize him. His eyes were tired and blood shot and he looked weak and lanky, so much older than his 15-year-old self. Mrs. Rochester ushered him into the pew as if she was on a strict schedule. He stood awkwardly, his chains clanking against the wooden pews.

"Hope he gets what he deserves," Babs muttered under her breath.

The bailiff told everyone to rise as Judge Littlefoot entered the court room. He was in his mid-forties with black braids hanging down his shoulders and bright brown eyes that took up half his face. He wore a black robe that covered his rotund stomach and his large hands with manicured fingernails banged the gavel on the wooden bench to silence the murmurs from the assembly. Though he had tight closed lips he possessed a big booming voice that was heard throughout the entire room.

"Thank you, Bailiff. We are present today for the trial of Boreas Stockington against the people of Plymouth Incarnate. What does the defendant plea?"

Mrs. Rochester cleared her throat and said, "The defendant's plea is not guilty."

"Guilty," Boreas's voice rose from the pew and immediately the crowd murmured amongst themselves as Judge Littlefoot banged the gavel on the bench.

"There seems to be some confusion. Mrs. Rochester please take a minute to review this with your defendant."

"There's nothing to review," Boreas declared, his voice stoic and reserved. "My plea is guilty. Mark it down, Judge, for the record."

Mrs. Rochester stood up, whimpering and then said, "Can I please have a quick recess, your honor? I apologize for this outburst from my client."

"Your client?" Boreas laughed. "I haven't seen you until right now. This trial is fixed and I won't have any part of it."

"You don't have a choice, young man," Judge Littlefoot snapped. "If your plea is guilty then we don't have to go through the motions of a trial and we will move to sentencing."

"His plea is NOT GUILTY." Otus's voice boomed out like a chord from an organ.

Everyone turned to the giant who was standing at his full stature and Boreas looked up at Otus with shock plastered on his face, as if he had thought that Otus was against him. Aurora felt so guilty, sliding further down into her pew.

Boreas mouthed the words, "Not guilty." His chains rattled as he collapsed down in the seat.

"Ok, now that we got that covered, let's proceed with opening statements."

Mr. Hopkins stood up and proceeded with an eloquent opening speech about how Boreas had been a loyal friend to both Aurora and Otus and had been chosen to go on the mission with them to save the world from the Geometric Storm. At being captured by Inspector Herald and the Common Good, he chose to side with them and betray his friendship and bring them to the Inspector by fabricating a lie that the Inspector held Aurora's parents in Candlewick Prison. He drugged Otus and would have killed his own brother if Aurora had not intervened and saved him from committing this act. The Inspector and Common Good Army were prepared to take them all into custody when Fawn Stockington and Mrs. Xiomy, acting under the orders of Aurora Alvarez and Babs O'Hara, infiltrated the prison and managed to fight off the Inspector and help Otus escape along with the others back to the safe haven.

"I will prove that Boreas was acting under his own will and judgment to betray his friends in order to grant himself clemency from the Inspector. He was willing to sacrifice everything they had fought for, in order to save himself."

The room fell silent as Mr. Hopkins returned to his seat and Aurora thought his ears were twitching in jubilation. She watched as Mrs. Rochester stood up, her plaid suit was irritating in that light as she stood in front of the crowd.

"My client is innocent and I am here today to prove that. Thank you."

She resumed her sitting position and Aurora stood up in aggravation about to scream out when Babs pulled her back down.

"Get a hold of yourself," Babs whispered.

"She didn't mention anything about the Soul Extractor. She didn't mention…"

"She's the lawyer, Aurora. Not you."

Aurora slid back into her chair feeling antsy and her mouth was parched but she was too aggravated to drink any water. She watched as Mr. Hopkins called Babs as the first witness for the defense. Babs walked up to the stand and swore an oath pledging that she would tell the truth, the whole truth and nothing but the truth, so help her, God. She then took her place inside the stand, looking as radiant as ever in the candlelight.

"Please state your name for the court."

"Babs O'Hara."

"What is your relationship with the defendant?"

She cleared her throat and drank some water. "He was my boyfriend."

Mr. Hopkins waited for the crowd's *oo's* and *ahh's* to die down before proceeding. Aurora realized that many of them remembered the incident at the gala 5 months earlier.

"And what happened to you about a month ago when you were alone with the defendant?"

Babs closed her eyes and then started speaking, "We had just rescued Boreas who had been taken prisoner by the Common Good Army."

"And where did you find him?" Hopkins interjected.

"Underneath a bridge back near Lake Champlain. He said he had escaped from the Inspector and that Aurora's parents were in trouble and that we needed to return to Candlewick."

"And you were suspicious?"

"More about his behavior than what he actually said. He was being very controlling, especially when I was speaking with his brother, Jonathan. I didn't like it and told him that we needed some space."

"So what happened next?"

Babs turned bright red and her voice was shaking slightly as she continued, "We were looking for Fawn and the safe haven and I kept telling Boreas that we were broken up. He thought I was after his brother, that I liked Jonathan and not him. I told him he was crazy but in a jealous rage he grabbed my arm, twisting it and I screamed out for help. Luckily Aurora heard me and came to my rescue. She held him off with a gun and I ran for safety."

Aurora remembered the fear that they both felt, when she had looked into Boreas's eyes as if he was a demon. She found herself shudder at the thought of it and Mr. Hopkins allowed Babs to regain her composure before asking her the final question.

"I am so sorry that you had to re-live that horrible day in this courtroom, but we need to know for the record, Miss O'Hara. Are you certain that Boreas was acting on his own free will? That he was the one who attacked you, and not someone forcing him to do so?"

Babs stood up and opened her eyes wide so that they glared into the eyes of Boreas, like her stare was laced with venom.

"I have no doubt that Boreas attacked me. Even if he was under the Soul Extractor serum he would have fought it if he cared for me."

Aurora stole a glance over at Boreas who shrunk back in his seat like Babs's testimony had sealed his fate.

Judge Littlefoot asked Mrs. Rochester if she would like to cross examine the witness, but she shook her head, and continued chewing on the eraser of a pencil. The Judge dismissed Babs who stepped down from the bench and walked past Boreas with her head held high and resumed her spot in the pew. Aurora offered her a tissue but Babs refused and stood there gallantly though her face was still pale, her lip quivering from the aftermath.

Mr. Hopkins next called Jonathan to the stand and he jumped up and hastened over to the bailiff pledging his oath to the court, resembling more of an Armani model than a witness. He was wearing a navy blue suit and Aurora couldn't help admiring his muscular body as he walked swiftly toward the bench.

"State your name."

"My name is Jonathan Stockington."

Hopkins proceeded with the questioning, jabbing a bit with him first. "You got mixed up with this after a library incident didn't you, Mr. Stockington?"

"Yes. My brother got in some trouble with the Candlewick police and my Father and I were entrusted by the Inspector to trap him if he fled to our upstate cabin."

"How did that work out for you?"

"Well, we caught them. But Boreas impersonated me and so they arrested all of us. We managed to escape, but Boreas stayed behind to buy us more time to escape through the tunnel."

Mr. Hopkins smoothed his clean shaven chin with his hand.

"Tell us what happened after you rescued Boreas."

"Boreas had been acting weirder than usual and more jealous of me than he normally is. I mean he has always been jealous of me back in school and knowing I was Dad's favorite. But this time it was more than that and we got into a few fist fights even prior to leaving for Candlewick Prison. Anyway, Aurora and I were in Candlewick Prison and had disabled the electricity and were freeing the prisoners. We tried to signal to Otus and Boreas but they never answered."

"And what happened next?" Hopkins asked, his ears flapping like an elephant.

Jonathan cleared his throat and said, "Aurora received information that Boreas had turned against us, we dashed to their location and sure enough Otus was drugged, face down on the grass and Boreas was pointing a gun at us. Aurora distracted him and I attacked Boreas, knocking the gun from his hands."

Mr. Hopkins held up a gun from the exhibit table so that everyone in the courtroom could see it.

"Can you verify that this is the gun that he used against you and Aurora Alvarez that night outside the Candlewick prison?"

Jonathan looked at the gun and nodded. Mr. Hopkins proceeded with requesting to have it entered into evidence and Judge Littlefoot nodded his assent.

"Jomathan, what happened after you knocked the gun from Boreas's hands?"

Jonathan cleared his throat and continued. "We fought for about 5 minutes and he trapped me, strangling me and then there was a strong ray of light. Boreas was knocked off me and I never saw anything like it in my life."

Jonathan's eyes scanned the room until they rested directly on Aurora. With a slight crack in his voice he said, "She saved my life."

Chapter 4

The Revelation

Boreas sat with the chains handcuffed tightly around his wrists, cutting off his circulation. His lawyer, Mrs. Rochester, was preoccupied filing her nails as Jonathan was giving his testimony. He leaned back and closed his eyes, not believing that this was happening. He was going to be proven guilty and his friends and his brother were testifying against him. Not that he could blame them after everything he had put them through.

Jonathan stood on the stand looking cocky and self-assured as he relayed the events of that night in Candlewick Prison. The memory of nearly killing his own brother felt like a nightmare to Boreas, one where you think you are going to wake up, but you can't. As much as you scream at yourself to wake up, you fall victim to the fate of the characters in your mind, except that he really had strangled his brother, the character within him had taken control and he had succumbed to the evil within.

The defense attorney shook her head when the judge asked if she would like to cross examine and continued filing her nails. He heard someone cry in an uproar from the prosecution's witness stand, but he couldn't make out who it was. It almost sounded like Aurora, but that was impossible. She was probably raring to testify against him and make him suffer for everything he had put her through. If only he had a chance to speak with her, he could have explained himself but all he was able to tell her before being locked away was that he had been injected with the Soul Extractor serum. He seriously doubted that she believed him and it was only her powers that had saved him. If she hadn't then they all would have been killed by Inspector Herald.

Mr. Hopkins called Aurora to the stand and Boreas's face shot up. She looked beautiful with her hair flowing down her shoulders, the navy dress hugging her curves as she stepped forward. She looked different, like she had a natural glow about her, as if a fire was burning within her. He thought hearing Babs's testimony was going to tear him to pieces, but this was going to be too much to bear.

The judge silenced everyone with a raise of his hand and the bailiff proceeded with asking Aurora to pledge the oath. She looked nervous and yet he didn't understand why she would be since she had nothing to hide.

"State your name for the court."

"Aurora Alvarez."

"And what is your relationship with the defendant?"

She looked directly into Boreas's eyes, piercing through his as if wanting him to read her thoughts. "He is my friend."

"You say that as if it is present tense," Mr. Hopkins continued, pacing a little more hurriedly. "But can you explain how Boreas worked against you and plotted to turn you and Otus into the Common Good?"

"Boreas didn't turn me or Otus in. I believe that Boreas never would have done such a thing."

Boreas sat up, his mouth open in pure shock and the stunned crowd rose in an uproar. The gavel banged repeatedly onto the bench and after about five minutes the crowd settled down. Mr. Hopkins, for the first time, wiped sweat from his brow, his ears wiggling uncontrollably.

"Miss Alvarez. Why do you believe that Boreas didn't do these things?"

"Boreas was injected with the Soul Extractor serum."

Laughter erupted from the audience, egged on by Mr. Hopkins' expression of disbelief.

"When you say that he was injected by the Soul Extractor, how do you know this?"

"He told me right before he was put under arrest."

"And yet, as per both Babs O'Hara and Jonathan Stockington's testimony, the defendant lied to you about escaping from the Inspector, about your parents being arrested and sentenced to death in the Candlewick Prison, he held a gun at you, drugged Otus AND tried to kill his own brother, right in front of your eyes."

"I know all those things happened, but you don't know Boreas. Throughout all this time, ever since we found him under that bridge in Lake Champlain, I knew he was not the same person. I know the real Boreas and that was not him. When I hit him with the powers of dawn I knew that I was conquering whatever control that serum had over him and brought him back to the light."

Boreas was sitting on the edge of his seat, not sure what to think. Even his lawyer was awake for this testimony. Mr. Hopkins smiled slightly and clapped his hands repeatedly over and over again.

"Aurora, you ran away today to avoid testifying against your friend. Can you deny this?"

Boreas watched as Aurora shook her head sullenly. She ran away? No one had told him anything about that. For the entire month in prison, he had believed that both Aurora and Otus hated him. How could he have doubted them?

"Are you just making up this Soul Extractor story to save him from his fate?"

"No I am not. I..."

"And are you worried that if we have him arrested, Boreas won't be able to continue with you and Otus on your mission to the Aurora Borealis?"

"That is not true. Are you not listening to me?"

"Aurora, please just answer one question. Did Boreas, this man in front of you, betray you and make you believe that your parents were being put to death at Candlewick Prison?"

Aurora froze and looked up for some sort of sign but nothing was given.

"Yes or No, Aurora," Mr. Hopkins leaned forward so that his face was nearly touching hers. She swallowed and turned toward Boreas and she mouthed the word, "Yes."

"And if the real Boreas was in there, wouldn't he have stopped you? Wouldn't he have warned you?"

"I don't know."

"Exactly. You don't know. Because even if Mr. Stockington did have the Soul Extractor serum, wouldn't he have been able to fight it if there was still good in him? Everyone in this room knows Professor Gassendi's account of when the rebellion leader David Xiomy was injected with the Soul Extractor serum. He was able to fight it every time because he was a pure soul. Boreas, I am afraid, has evil in him and therefore the Soul Extractor serum brought out his true nature. We cannot allow a man like this to be free and jeopardize your mission or our lives again."

Mr. Hopkins turned to a huge applause from the audience. Mrs. Rochester, who had recently fallen asleep, awoke with a start to the applause, shouting, "I object" to deaf ears.

The crowd died down and Mr. Hopkins said that the Prosecution rests. Judge Littlefoot asked Mrs. Rochester if she wanted to cross examine and she shook her head in the negative. Boreas wanted to smack her, but then again he didn't have anyone else jumping out of their chairs to defend him. Aurora was dismissed and slowly got down from the witness stand but hesitated as she walked past Boreas. Boreas watched as she continued to glance over at him as if she was pondering something and was playing it out in her mind. She stood paralyzed in mid-step and waited as Mrs. Rochester stood up and said in mid-yawn, "The defense rests."

"No you don't," Aurora spit out and she ran over toward the defense table. As a guard charged at her she pointed her hand at him and hit him with a ray of light and he fell backwards into a domino effect knocking over the other guards as chaos ensued. She rushed over to the Defense table and knocked Mrs. Rochester out of the way and knelt down beside Boreas.

"Tell them that you want me to represent you."

"Aurora, what the hell are you doing?"

"Just tell them that you want me to represent you. Boreas you have to trust me. Please."

A guard grabbed her from behind and started to drag her back toward the Prosecution when Boreas jumped up and shouted, "I wish for Aurora Alvarez to represent me as my legal counsel."

The judge smacked the gavel against the desk so hard that the head split off, went sailing across the room, hitting Mrs. Rochester in the head and knocking her unconscious. The judge cried out over the noise, "If there are no objections?"

Mr. Hopkins opened his mouth to object, but Aurora pointed her hand in his direction and he immediately sat back down.

"Fine, good,"The judge whimpered and the bailiff handed him a new gavel. "Who is your witness, Miss Alvarez?"

She walked over and stood beside Boreas. She cried out in a loud voice, "I call Professor Gassendi to the stand."

The Professor refused any help from the guards and slowly stood up from the wheelchair and using his cane for balance, hobbled toward the witness bench. He was still suffering from temporary blindness, the goggles that he had designed and now wore were helping, but the Multiple Sclerosis was wearing away at his body.

The bailiff recited the oath.

The Professor pledged in his gruff voice, "I don't believe in a God, but I swear to the leaders of Science that I will tell the truth."

The judge nodded, accepting that pledge and the Professor hobbled up onto the stand and placed his cane roughly beside him.

Boreas whispered into Aurora's ear, "Do you know what you're doing?"

She turned toward him and whispered, "Just what I learned from my Dad."

He smiled nervously. "I hope your Dad was a good lawyer."

She smoothed out her dress, approached the bench and said in a clear loud voice, "Professor Gassendi, you invented the Soul Extractor serum, did you not?"

"You know fully well I did and if anyone else takes credit for it, I swear I will knock them over the head with my cane so hard…"

"Thank you, Professor. No one is denying that you invented it. Now, you worked for the Inspector 16 years ago in the court when David Xiomy was first incarcerated, did you not?"

"Yes, I did. Never did I meet a better man in my life. It still pains me that I did not try to save David Xiomy when I had the chance."

"And you were instructed to inject him with the Soul Extractor serum as a test subject, correct?"

"Yes," he adjusted his goggles and his cold blue eyes stared blankly into hers. "It never took though. His will was so strong, that he fought it every time."

"All the sculptures of David Xiomy down here and even in Plymouth Tarturus has his arm with a mark on it. A greenish tint that was found on his body near where the forearm meets the elbow. Is that because of the Soul Extractor?"

"Yes, it leaves a green mark on your vein where it is injected."

Aurora turned toward Boreas. "Boreas, please stand up and lift your shirt sleeve so that we can see your forearm."

Boreas stood up and rolled up his right arm sleeve where there was a greenish mark, though slightly faded, still visible where the Inspector had jabbed him with the needle. The audience reacted in shock and the judge hit the gavel again and screamed louder for the audience to be silenced.

Aurora thanked Boreas and he sat back down. The Professor immediately shouted, "That doesn't prove anything and you know that, Aurora. There's evil inside him and that's what the Inspector used to make the Soul Extractor work. Focus on the evil and the demons within and that's what gets triggered inside of his body. Those demons are still there and he could change even without the extractor."

"That might be so, but the question is whether Boreas Stockington had a choice. Was he able to choose right or wrong once he was injected?"

"Yes, most definitely. I saw it in David Xiomy. I saw that a pure soul could fight the demons even once injected."

Aurora smiled slightly and her heels clip-clopped over to the Prosecution's table where she leaned over slightly and pulled her purse out from underneath the pew. Boreas watched Aurora not sure where she was going with this testimony. If anything she was proving the Prosecutor's case even more. He thought she should just give it up while she had the chance but she pulled out a long thin object from her purse and he froze at the sight of it. It was a needle and a glass vile containing a green serum. Aurora was holding the Soul Extractor.

"Professor, I am holding up a vile of the Soul Extractor. Please confirm that before this trial you gave me and Mrs. Xiomy this for exhibit B. Can you please verify that this is it?"

She handed him the vile cautiously and he sniffed it and felt it with his fingertips. He agreed that it was the serum. Boreas felt a coldness sweep over him as he stared at that green vile that had turned his life upside down. Something that appeared so innocent had caused him so much destruction and the burned face of the Inspector loomed before his eyes. Boreas's arm still ached from where he had struck him so forcefully over a month before, as if the memory was causing him physical pain and that the vile proved not only the existence of a soul but that evil truly did exist in him.

"Now Professor, I need you to answer honestly the next two questions I ask. Am I a pure soul?"

"The purest soul I have ever seen. I mean you are the Goddess of Dawn for heaven's sake."

"And do you think I have fight within me to destroy all demons from my past?"

"If anyone can fight them, you can."

She nodded, apparently pleased at where this line of questioning was heading, but Boreas sat anxious and agitated, unsure as to what the hell she was getting at.

Aurora took the vile out of the Professor's hand and pointed it up toward the audience and especially at Fawn. Boreas turned slightly and saw his mother standing up on the top of the balcony, candles surrounding the ledge and illuminating her face as she peered down intently at the sight of the needle. Boreas quickly turned away, not bearing to look at her, his own flesh and blood who hadn't visited him once while he was in prison. She was doing what she did best and forgetting that he ever existed, watching these proceedings from afar.

"This must be really getting to her", he thought, grimacing and wondering why the only time he could capture his mother's attention was when he was arrested. Mrs. Xiomy would probably diagnose him as crying out for affection.

Boreas turned back to the woman with his life in her hands. Aurora playfully waved the needle in front of the audience making sure everyone was able to see it as if this was a game she was playing with all of them. She continued, "So Professor, if I inject myself with this Soul Extractor, are you saying that I should be able to prevent the dark side of my soul from taking over?"

The Professor's eyes grew wide and he fumbled with his goggles. "Wait, I didn't give you the serum for that!"

"Just answer the question, Professor."

He blinked nervously and fumbled with his goggles so that they fell out of his hands and thumped onto the stand. Aurora removed the tip from the needle, but Boreas couldn't believe that she was actually going to go through with this. She was going to stop. She had to. Aurora continued to edge the needle closer and closer toward her arm and he couldn't stand it any longer and jumped up and cried out, "Aurora, Stop!"

"Guards, please silence the Defendant," Judge Littlefoot said.

Boreas tried to knock the guard out of the way using the hard part of the shackle, but the guard avoided the attempt and punched Boreas across the face until he fell back into the seat. Dazed, Boreas felt a pain escalate from his wrists as the guard chained him down forcefully. He tried to move, but his arms wouldn't even budge. He looked up quickly and watched horrified as Aurora lifted her sleeve and held the needle up close against her forearm.

"Professor, you enjoy experiments. Let's prove that the Soul Extractor will not work on me. That based on your testimony, I should be able to fight this. Here I go."

She started to tap her skin so that she was making the vein more visible and started to puncture her skin. The shadow of the needle stretched and the green liquid started to swirl upwards and Boreas felt his heart in his throat wishing someone would intervene. That someone would stop her.

The Professor shouted out into the air, "Fawn, I can't hide it any longer."

Aurora immediately stopped and put the needle down as all eyes diverted towards Fawn who was standing up, her face pale and rigid.

Aurora squeezed the Professor's arm slightly so that he knew that she hadn't injected herself. "I am fine, Professor," she reassured him. "Now tell me, what can't you hide any longer?"

He put his face in his hands and then confessed, "I lied. David Xiomy did fight the serum, more than I ever saw anyone fight in his life. But he gave in one night. He gave in one night."

The Professor buried his face in his hands and Judge Littlefoot turned to Mr. Hopkins to inquire if he wanted to cross examine the witness. Mr. Hopkins just shook his head and Judge Littlefoot dismissed the Professor who hobbled down from the stand and with his cane, tapped his way back toward the pew where he had been sitting. Boreas turned 180 degrees and found himself spellbound, eying his mother who now pivoted and started down the long, winding, red carpeted steps of the balcony and made her way toward the stand. She walked past him, not even turning to look at him. The white gown and ivory cape was like a train as she walked, her footsteps a rhythmic metronome. Fawn walked past Aurora, not waiting for herself to be called, and took the stand, pledging to the bailiff, and then settled herself in the witness booth.

"My name is Fawn Stockington and I am the High Magistrate of Plymouth Incarnate, and the Defendant's mother."

This chain of events was unexpected for everyone, including Judge Littlefoot who was watching these events unfold before his eyes. He nodded to Aurora to proceed and she caught her breath, about to interrogate Boreas's mother on the stand.

She turned back toward Fawn and her voice shook as she asked, "Can you elaborate on the one time that David Xiomy couldn't fight the Soul Extractor? The night he gave in?"

Fawn nodded, pinching the candle flame so that the flame extinguished against her flesh. A shadow settled over her face, as if she preferred this part of her testimony to happen in the dark.

"I had left the rebellion after David chose to marry my best friend Rana. I was heartbroken and had married Mr. Stockington and had a baby, Jonathan, by him. I was content, until I found out that David had been arrested. This was the first time Herald arrested him, months before the Last Straw Protest. I spoke to the Professor, who I knew from the university and he managed to get me clearance to see him one night in Candlewick Prison. The Professor had warned me that he was working on an experimental serum with David, something to control him so that the Inspector would have a reason to hold him, but that it wasn't taking. He told me that most likely they would release him once the experiment was finalized. I didn't heed the warning however, and snuck in one night to tell David that I was sorry for leaving the rebellion. To tell him that I still cared about him."

She paused and looked directly at Mrs. Xiomy. "That night, he made love to me."

The rosy complexion drained from Mrs. Xiomy's face in an instant.

"He seduced me, Rana. I'm sorry, but he did. And I gave in. I thought that in prison he had a change of heart. I thought that he realized I was the one he wanted to be with after all. I was and always will be in love with him."

She paused and her eyes squinted upwards as if fighting back tears. She looked deeply distressed but took a deep breath and continued, "I went back to him the following day, but he was not the same man. He was angry with himself for giving in to the serum. Saying that it was the serum not him, that he never would have betrayed his love for Rana. He never would have slept with me. Rana, you have to believe me."

Mrs. Xiomy had her head in her hands and there was such anguish over her face.

Aurora looked like she was about to end the line of questioning when Fawn held her hand up, as if ready to confess one more bit of evidence before her courage failed her. She sat up and looked directly at Boreas, her eyes glittering and shining as tears welled up beneath their lids, one released and slid down her face until it rested on the tip of her mouth.

"And then I found out I was pregnant."

The room fell silent as the candle lights flickered menacingly on the walls. No one attempted to take a breath as Boreas stared blankly at his mother, not comprehending the words she had just spoken; not wanting to comprehend.

"I'm sorry, Boreas. I never wanted you to find out. I never wanted you to know."

Judge Littlefoot was flabbergasted and he raised his gavel and yet couldn't put it down. It fell from his hand and collided against the bench. He cleared his throat and proclaimed to the masses, "Due to new evidence in this case, I find the defendant, Boreas Stockington, not guilty."

The room remained silent and nobody moved, except for Mrs. Xiomy who stood up and ran at Fawn with every ounce of strength she had within her and slapped her hard across the face.

"Damn you!" she cried out.

A guard grabbed her and despite her kicking and screaming, led her away. Aurora hurried over to Boreas and ordered the guard to unchain him. Boreas didn't move. Not even once the chains were released. He just continued to stare at his mother as the words settled in against his will.

Chapter 5

Ray of Light

"I must have known," Mrs. Xiomy whimpered, sitting on the edge of the bed, pillow in hand and her face pressed firmly against it as if wishing to suffocate herself. Aurora stood there holding a glass of water and a pain killer that Mrs. Xiomy refused.

"I must have known all along and was in denial. I mean, how could I have not seen that Boreas is David's son? Boreas has David's countenance, his smile, his voice."

She stuffed her face once again into the pillow. "I just couldn't face the truth. I couldn't."

Chaos had ensued following the court verdict. Boreas had been ambushed by reporters and Aurora had tried to fight them off, each of them trying to get a firsthand interview of what happened. Otus had come to the rescue, had picked Boreas up and carried him safely out of harm's way and Aurora had been stuck picking up the loose ends, answering questions about how she knew that Boreas's father was David Xiomy.

"I didn't," she admitted, still in shock over what had transpired. What it all meant.

The entire episode played over and over again in her head, but still did not make any sense. How did she know? It was almost as if she had been guided along that line of questioning. All she had wanted was for the Professor to confess that it was possible that not every person of a pure soul could fight the Soul Extractor. She had no idea that Fawn was going to be involved. That Fawn had this big secret that was finally revealed.

Mrs. Xiomy relented, took the pill from Aurora's hand and swallowed it with a big gulp of water. It helped calm her hyperventilating and she took easier breaths. Her hand went over her heart.

"My heart hasn't been broken like this since the day I found out he was dead. When I found out that despite everything I tried to do, all my efforts to save him, he was dead. That he wasn't coming home to me; that I wouldn't kiss his lips or hold his body again. I was alone. And I got used to it. For 15 years I got used to it because I put him and his legacy on a pedestal. Like everyone did. The great man who had fought against the Common Good and united people of all beliefs together. That was the freedom he gave to everyone. And yet, after all that I knew he fought for, all I wanted was for him to come back to me. To have chosen me for once! To have chosen me and not try to save this world that couldn't care less about him. And now I just feel so angry! Angry because how can I justify him now to my heart? Knowing that he betrayed me, how can I live with myself? How can I continue to justify that I made the right choice in trying to save him?"

Aurora put her arm around Mrs. Xiomy who sobbed on her shoulder and continued to hold her until Mrs. Xiomy cried herself to sleep. Aurora snuck out to let her sleep and get away from the torment she was faced with, and made her way across the Great Hall. Aurora felt exhaustion kicking in and she too needed to get some rest, but her mind was racing as she climbed the long rickety wooden steps that stretched upwards for what seemed like a mile toward Boreas's room. Yet, as her feet climbed up each step, she started to lose momentum. She didn't know what she would say to him. She had saved him from a lifetime in prison or even death, but at what cost? To find out that everything he had ever known was a lie and that his true father was a man who had sacrificed his life for this cause. Would Boreas have the same fate? Would she have the same fate since they were both now following in David Xiomy's footsteps?

She sat on the edge of one of the steps and looked down at the winding world that spun downwards like a vortex beneath her. One misstep and she would fall downwards into that abyss and all of these worries would vanish in a heartbeat. She looked down, her head getting dizzy and she closed her eyes, yet it continued to spin as white specks flashed in her mind where darkness should have been. She continued to keep her eyes shut and rested her head on the banister, tracing the grain of the wood with her fingers. Footsteps descended toward her but she ignored them. If it was another reporter she might be tempted to throw him or her off the staircase. She was pondering this option when the footsteps stopped and she felt a presence behind her. She opened her eyes and turned to see Jonathan sitting there facing her. His eyes were swollen and his honey blond hair was out of its neat ponytail and hanging loosely down his shoulders. His suit jacket was draped over his left shoulder and he had unbuttoned the top button on his white dress shirt, exposing some loose blond chest hair. He put his hand into hers and she grasped it tightly.

"I don't know whether I should be thanking you or hating you," he said coarsely.

She laughed nervously and squeezed his hand more than she should. "I thought that would be something Boreas would say to me."

He nodded, wrinkling his nose as they sat together on that staircase high above the action transpiring beneath them, like white noise.

"I don't know what to believe anymore." He stood, glancing down into the dark abyss below. "I mean none of this feels real. This place, Otus, you, none of it falls into the realm of reality for me. Not what I was brought up believing. I was taught that my mother was dead. That giants don't exist and girls can't make sunlight stream out of their fingertips!"

He paused leaning farther down over the banister. "What's next? I was taught people can't fly. I bet I could if I jump off this staircase. I bet I would fly."

A bunch of children scurried down the staircase and Aurora watched their pitter-patter of feet flying past them and hurrying toward the dining room where breakfast would be served. Aurora couldn't believe that she hadn't slept all day and that it was already the Awakened hour. It was so hard keeping track of the days with no natural sunlight exposed in this dark secluded prison. The outside world was too dangerous and yet there was no escape from evil or lies or deceit. They find a way to sneak through the crevice of any country or any hole. She thought about what her father had told her once. He had told her there will always be wars on Earth and that as long as there were humans on this planet, they would find some way to kill each other. Peace was a dream that would always be unreachable.

Jonathan watched the children and scribbled an autograph for one who had seen him during the trial. He asked for Aurora's, but she shook her head slowly. The boy shrugged, unfazed, and chased after his friends waving the piece of paper in his hands like it was a trophy.

"It feels like yesterday that was me, having won my baseball championship trophy and gloating to Boreas," he laughed, cracking his knuckles. "I mean just tell me this has all been one big nightmare and I will wake up in Candlewick with my father and Boreas, all of us still one family. One big happy family. As if nothing has changed."

He paused and looked up at the carved statue of David Xiomy in the rock, staring down at all of them.

"But nothing will ever be the same anymore. Will it?"

Aurora stood up and gave his hand a reassuring squeeze and rested her head on his shoulder as they gazed up into the eyes of the man who had passed the torch to them. To her, to Jonathan, Boreas and Otus. He had paved the way and it was their turn to fight back.

She raised her hand into the air toward the dark ceiling above, sunlight streamed out from her fingertips until a huge ball of sunlight stood suspended in mid-air over the statue like a glimmer of hope. The children paused in their tracks below and looked up to behold the sunlight that they had forgotten and it shone brightly — overpowering the darkness.

He took her hand in his and tenderly kissed her fingers, still warm to the touch, as the light stretched over their bodies. The rocks glistened around them like stars in that enclosed den. He leaned close to her and kissed her softly on the lips, his nose nuzzling against her own. She fell into his embrace, as their bodies intertwined and continued kissing until the sunlight faded and draped over them like fireflies. He pulled away and she felt like her knees would give out from under her; her body was already missing the sensation that he had caused from that simple act; a manifestation of her dreams. He looked once more up at the sunlight that was now just specks of yellowish orange sparklers and then took off running upstairs two steps at a time. She watched him ascend until he was a dark speck in the distance and faded behind a corner where his bedroom was situated. She collapsed back down and took a deep breath, his lips still imprinted over her own. She pricked herself to make sure she hadn't been dreaming. She gleefully enjoyed the pain that escalated from her skin confirming once and for all that Jonathan Stockington had kissed her. Nothing would be the same anymore.

Chapter 6

Deal with the Devil

*J*ake stood shivering on the balcony of the Candlewick Government building, staring down at the armies flying in from across the country for the invasion of the Hudson. Fighter jets were lined up on the runway with soldiers preparing for battle. Wherever Aurora and Boreas had gone it was going to be a slaughter, with innocent civilians paying the price.

"Preparing to jump?"

Jake's blood curdled at the mere sound of that voice and he turned and was face to face with Inspector Herald. The Inspector looked as strong and arrogant as ever, not even wearing his gun in its holster as if to say "kill me, if you dare". He stood tall at his 6-foot-7 stature, wearing a long trench coat and black turtleneck. The scars on his face were exposed in the moonlight, a lingering feature caused by the Candlewick Prison fire 10 years earlier. His burned flesh, the Inspector said, was a reminder of what could happen to the country if the rebellion regained strength. He had a moral duty to prevent that from ever happening again.

Jake stepped back, wishing he could end this and just jump, but he knew that the Inspector had brought him up here for a reason. He was testing his will to survive. Everything was a test from here on in, with Mary's life in the balance.

The Inspector looked him up and down and sneered, "It's like the strong man, the powerful protégé I used to confide in, is just a memory. Look at you now. A poor withering and wretched traitor at my mercy."

"You're the one who wanted to keep me around," Jake leaned against the wall for support, feeling the ache in his leg getting stronger. He didn't want to show the Inspector that he was in pain, but the Inspector's gaze went straight to the leg and smiled, his chipped front tooth glistening.

"You mended it yourself, I see. So glad I taught you to be resourceful."

"Among many other things," Jake sneered through his teeth.

The Inspector grabbed Jake by the throat and held him up against the wall. "I trusted you with my life. You were one of the VERY few men I counted on and you betrayed me. I could crush you right now with just my hand and no one would mourn your death."

"You would mourn me," Jake spit out, in between gasping for air. "You already mourn the loss of your protégé and can't bring yourself to replace my position. You can't bring yourself to kill me. Using me to get to Aurora and Boreas is just buying you time until you have to act."

The Inspector released his hold and Jake collapsed against the concrete, grabbing onto the telescope for support to get back up. The Inspector turned his back on him.

"I had a son once. I don't think I ever told you that. He was only 10 years old. Died when the Towers of Freedom fell. That's when I swore I would do everything in my power to change this world so that no one would have to go through that pain that I went through. I will never stop mourning my son, but you, Jacob, I will get over mourning you in time. But until then, I own you and you will do what I say and go where I tell you to go and betray who I tell you to betray. Because I know that's a skill you do very well."

He flung open the screen door and marched into his office, and Jake followed like an obedient dog with an invisible leash tight around his neck. Jake welcomed the heat as he surveyed the office that was still filled with TVs flickering silent pictures. The room brought an ominous vibe that the Inspector thrived upon. Henry Stockington, Boreas's father, sat in the chair across from the big oval desk, on his phone. A computer screen of satellite imagery sat in front of him as he was working with the patrols in the field to try to locate this Giant who had fallen off the radar.

"A Giant doesn't just disappear!" Mr. Stockington yelled into the phone. "You located footprints, but they led to a dead end. He must be SOMEWHERE. All of them must be. Keep searching!"

Mr. Stockington hung up and then quickly stood when he realized the Inspector had reentered the room.

"Henry, sit down old friend," Herald said, grabbing a brandy and sitting on the edge of his desk. "The traitor and I have just come to an understanding."

Mr. Stockington didn't even acknowledge Jake's presence and Jake was unsure of where he should go, so he just leaned against the wall to ease the pressure off his leg while awaiting his next order.

"What's the latest?" the Inspector asked, sipping on the brandy.

"They just lost the trail. How could they lose a 30 foot giant? Fawn is smart, but she can't make a giant disappear."

The Inspector bit down on the rim of the glass, "She's outsmarted us before. She built that blasted underwater rebellion headquarters right off of Candlewick in the Atlantic Ocean and no one - not ONE of my officers noticed for 10 years. She would be able to find a hiding place in any of these natural wonders."

"But you can't go blowing up the entire eastern coast line."

Jake who was standing quietly in the corner felt his blood run cold, fearful that the Inspector would resort to just that option. Immediately, he started to think of a way to prevent that outcome.

The Inspector was scrutinizing the map, licking his front tooth in mid-thought. "Mark off this perimeter. If we bomb this area, they will come out."

Jake coughed, "If you want my opinion…"

"No one asked your opinion, Traitor." Henry snapped. "I still don't know why Herald is even enlisting the likes of you after everything you put him through."

The Inspector put his hand up. "Henry, be nice. Jacob and I have an understanding, don't we? Now, what is it?"

Jake took a bite of stale bread, but it was better than anything he had down in prison. In mid-bite he said, "He is going to come after you."

Mr. Stockington scoffed, "Prison has warped his brain. Who would dare go after the Inspector…besides you and we know how great that turned out."

Jake leaned back in the chair, "Mr. Stockington, it is your son who is going to come after the Inspector. He is going to find a way to separate from the group, because Aurora won't betray her mission. He is going to come after you, possibly alone, but maybe with or without his powers."

"Boreas is not going to get powers," Mr. Stockington cried out. "He is nothing special!"

"You're wrong about that. He will get powers, just like Aurora did, if this prophecy is true. And you can't deny that Aurora has the powers of dawn. We all saw them first hand during the attack at Candlewick Prison."

The Inspector snickered, unconvinced. "I know the way that boy's mind works. I saw it when I injected him. He doesn't have a murderous bone in his body."

Jake folded his arms over his tattered shirt and looked the Inspector dead in the face. "You saw the Boreas before you turned him with the Soul Extractor serum. You took everything from him... his self-worth, his control over his emotions, his mind. He is going to want revenge. You created a murderous prototype in Boreas... like you did to me and so many other young men. Except this time, you have a young man who is going to be the God of the North Wind."

The Inspector took another long sip of his brandy. "Well then, we'll have to make sure we capture him before he gets his powers. Proceed with the attack. If he's planning to kill me, let's give him a little motivation to want to kill me sooner, rather than later."

Jake stood up, mad that his plan had backfired. He had hoped the Inspector would have called off the attack, but no such luck.

Mr. Stockington looked up and this time his stare was colder than anything Jake had ever felt before from the Inspector. His glasses were glued onto his nose but the bright blue eyes were those of a father ready to risk it all for his son.

"My sons are not to be harmed, Traitor. If you hadn't interfered the last time, we could have captured all of them and put this whole episode behind us."

"And what about the Geometric Storm?" Jake couldn't help but point out. "What are your ingenious ideas for getting us out of that mess after it hits? Or are we all to be killed, to end this misery?"

Mr. Stockington and the Inspector both froze and Jake felt like he was the odd man out in this party.

Mr. Stockington shook his head, "I told you this is never going to work. He knows too much."

Jake laughed, "Newsflash! I was the First Lieutenant. I know everything."

The Inspector stared out the window at the pilots and the armed forces mobilizing. "He doesn't know everything. And neither do you, Henry. The Geometric Storm is going to help us cleanse this country. All those loyal to us, and we know who they are from their social media and online history as well as those with no record against us and the IDEAL, will be ushered into a bunker that is being built by a compatriot of mine named the Siren. The Siren has been working on this for the past 3 years in Alaska near the Arctic Circle. It will hold up to 500,000 people. That's enough for us to continue on, emerging more victorious than ever before. Those people will idealize us. We will be the future, with no past to hinder us. No more protestors and people like Fawn and her rebellion to fight against us and our ideals. It will be a brand new start for us."

Jake stared at him wide-eyed as the Inspector said all this with an eerily calm voice. "So you want to annihilate 90% of the country?"

Inspector Herald stood, towering above him. "Of course new measures will need to be put into place for even the most loyal could turn against you. A system like the one we have now could never sustain itself. As we have seen from history, eventually something will overthrow us."

Jake stared at Mr. Stockington who only nodded at this rationale. The Inspector watched Jake curiously as this new information registered.

"The Geometric Storm is upon us. I know the date of the storm. A code that I saw from Boreas Stockington's mind when I injected him with the Soul Extractor. A code that I don't think they even understand yet, nor the professor whose mind is too scientific."

Jake felt his whole world crumbing around him as the weight of this mission and his role in it hit him. He was enlisted into this mission, always had been enlisted. Was Mary's life worth millions? He kept seeing his mother's face, her eyes beseeching him to change. Mary was the only family he had left. She was his world now.

"If I still help you, even knowing all this, I need you to swear that Mary will be in this bunker. That she will make it to this brand new world you are creating."

The room fell silent as the TV screens blinked, their screens like eyes judging Jake and what he had become.

Inspector Herald poured two glasses of brandy, "If you do as you're told, and your precious Mary survives, then yes she can have a spot in the bunker. You on the other hand will have no place in this bunker."

Jake took the drink from the Inspector, "I think we both know how this plays out. I know my story doesn't have a happy ending. Either you will kill me or the Giant will. But Mary will survive."

The two men toasted to their murderous pact and Jake drank swiftly, the alcohol burning as it was swallowed, fitting, since he had just made a pact with the devil. "It wouldn't be the first time", he thought, as he went further down the rabbit hole.

Just then the elevator doors flew open and in raced Officers Woolchuck and Pelican scrambling over each other's feet. Officer Woolchuck rammed his huge, burly self onto his smaller, yet still muscular female partner as they raced forward like a Three Stooges routine.

"So sorry to interrupt!" Officer Pelican cried out.

"What the hell is he doing out of the prison!" Officer Woolchuck demanded, spotting Jake Fray drinking a brandy on the couch in the Inspector's office.

"It is not up to you to ask questions!" The Inspector growled, clearly not happy that he had been interrupted. "Why aren't you two facilitating the march on the Hudson?"

"It's hard to get good help these days," Jake slyly said, taking another sip.

Officer Woolchuck stepped forward, "Be careful, Traitor, or I'll have to break your other leg."

Jake jumped up but the Inspector put a hand on his shoulder to stop him. Herald licked his chipped front tooth and his coal black eyes didn't blink as he stared down the two officers.

"Jake is going to be working undercover, if for some reason our mission to overthrow Fawn Stockington and her evil supporters doesn't succeed. And with you two being up here, I am doubting your ability to complete this mission and I am getting angrier by the minute!"

"We got the DNA results back from the Stockington boys." Officer Woolchuck butted in and stepped in front of his partner.

"Who cares about those results? How is that going to help us find them?"

The Officers turned towards each other awkwardly, like they were waiting for the other to speak.

"But one of them doesn't match," Pelican stammered, fixing the cap over her hair.

"What are you talking about?" Mr. Stockington cried out.

"What she means," Officer Woolchuck interjected, "is that one of our DNA samples for Boreas Stockington on file was fixed. The real Boreas Stockington, who you interrogated, his DNA doesn't match the computer."

The Inspector was growing impatient and grabbed Officer Woolchuck by the uniform collar, lifting him off the floor until only the tips of his toes touched the ground. "What are you getting at?"

Officer Woolchuck squealed, "Boreas is Fawn Stockington's son but that man is not his father!"

He pointed assertively at Mr. Stockington who nearly dropped the iPad that he was carrying.

"What are you talking about?" Mr. Stockington cried out angrily. "Who is his Father?"

Officer Pelican nervously handed Mr. Stockington the results. He ripped the document out of her hands.

One look at the name and he crushed the paper in his grasp.

Chapter 7

Mark of the Father

Aurora dashed to her room and hurriedly peeled off the navy dress that was sticking to her body. She hummed to herself as she remembered what happened that evening. Jonathan had kissed her, and it was everything she had hoped for. Sure, he ran away from her as soon as he pulled away, but that wasn't the worst thing that could have happened after a first kiss? Was it? She began to overthink things after she looked into her box of belongings. Her few outfits were unflattering clothes she had brought from Candlewick for their journey and the navy uniform-like clothes the seamstresses from the safe haven made for her. She tore each of them out of the box with disgust. Nothing looked good on her, most of her clothes now too baggy for her frame. But when she looked at her naked self in the mirror she still saw a girl too fat to be seen with Jonathan Stockington. If she was going to be his girlfriend, she had to look the part and be like or better than Hattie Pearlton. That was the type of girl Jonathan Stockington dated, not the frumpy girl in her reflection. She tried to be positive but was too busy eyeing flab in places they should not be. Her breasts were perky and that was a plus, but were they too big? Or not big enough? She tried to remember what size Hattie was.

Aggravated, she threw her clothes across the room and slumped down on her mattress. What was she thinking? Jonathan Stockington could never fall for someone like her. He must have kissed her because of the turmoil of the day with the confusion and mixed emotions he was feeling. He just needed someone to hold him and she had been there for him. If it had been Babs on the staircase, or anyone, he would have kissed them too. *Shut up, Aurora*, she thought, *he didn't kiss Babs; he kissed me. So just enjoy it!* And soon that goofy smile was back on her face.

She heard someone tap at the black curtain hanging in the doorway. She jumped up to answer it and quickly realized she was only wearing her underwear. She cried out that she would be a minute and grabbed the first outfit she spotted on top of the pile, blue jeans and a navy sweater, and stuffed herself into it.

"Come in!" she called out.

Otus stuck his head through the curtain, not able to fit through the doorway. Aurora felt a brief dismay, having hoped it would have been Jonathan, but forced a smile across her face.

"Oh Otus, isn't it a beautiful day?"

Otus stared at her in astonishment as Aurora whirled around the room like a ballerina. She then went and kissed Otus on the cheek and ruffled his already unruly hair. Otus grabbed her before she could twirl again and lifted her outside of her room and high into the air.

"What has gotten into you? I have been with Boreas for the past 2 hours and you have been nowhere to be found. Have you been prancing around in here all morning?"

She sat on his palm petulantly, upset that he was spoiling her good mood. "Can I not be allowed five minutes of happiness, Otus? Do I have to be miserable like everyone else?"

"These miserable people you are referring to are your friends. Mind you, one that just got freed from prison, thanks to you, and also found out that his father is not his real father, thanks to you. After all that, you didn't think you should check on him?"

Aurora sat down and the trial came back to her in a montage of flashing images. Jonathan's kiss had erased all sense of obligation and sense of propriety. She blew a strand of hair out of her face and let Otus lift her to the top of the steps where Boreas was resting in his mother's room. She felt uneasy as Otus pushed her forward, but she tapped on the hanging curtain and waited for him to call her in. There was no answer, but she lifted the curtain tentatively and peeked her head inside. She heard his gentle breathing and slowly stepped forward into the room, closing the curtain behind her. She tiptoed over to where he lay beneath a plaid comforter in the fetal position. He had cut his hair so that it hung just beneath his ears and shaved so that his face was smooth once again. He looked more like his old self and was resting so peacefully that she dared not wake him. She took a seat beside him on the bed, fixed the blankets over his shoulders and smoothed his hair with the back of her hand.

He whispered, "I wondered when you would come."

Startled, she snatched her hands back, putting them quickly into her lap.

"I thought you were sleeping."

He opened his eyes and gazed up at her. He sat up, leaning against pillows for support. "You should think about becoming a lawyer. You did pretty good out there."

"Yeah," she laughed, eyeing the room around her, observing the sink and cushioned bed, all the comforts of home...everything he had been without for the past month while he was sitting in prison as an innocent man. "Boreas, I am so sorry."

"Shut up," he said closing his eyes forcefully. "That's my line."

He grabbed her and held her tight. She tensed up at first but then relaxed, allowing him to wrap his arms around her and squeeze her tightly. She put her hands on his back as their hearts beat as one.

"I thought you and Otus hated me." He said, pulling himself away. "When you both stood up for me, I knew that even if I lost the case... at least I hadn't lost you. You knew I would never choose to betray you."

He looked up at her and for the first time she saw what Mrs. Xiomy saw. Though his eyes were so much like his mother, the rest of his face revealed the countenance and facial structure of the chiseled statue of David Xiomy. He was looking right back at her.

Aurora stood up, feeling like she was suffocating in that room. "Boreas," she said slowly. "God, there's so much to tell you. But the main thing you need to know is that I didn't know that Fawn was going to confess about your father."

He lifted the covers and hung his legs over the side of the bed. He rose to his feet holding onto the bedframe for support and walked over toward the antique styled water basin and rinsed his face. His torso was bare and she could clearly see his rib cage popping out of his skin. She couldn't believe how sickly he looked.

"David Xiomy is not my father," he sternly rebuked after splashing another handful of water onto his face. "It must have been some ruse Fawn and Professor Gassendi made up to get me acquitted."

She handed him a towel and he patted it over his father's features that she now couldn't help but seeing. He couldn't see the truth. He didn't want to see the truth.

"So you are just going to forget about it? Don't you think you should talk to your mom...?"

He squinted his eyes, glaring at her, "No…I'm not talking to *Fawn* because there's nothing to talk about. Besides, I am leaving. I met someone in prison who is going to help guide me back to Candlewick."

Aurora smirked and crossed her arms. "Now you are going back to Candlewick? What for? And what do you mean you met someone in prison? So you have replaced Otus and me with hardened criminals?"

He shrewdly looked up at her and chided, "And I see you have replaced *me* with my brother."

Her mouth dropped open in shock and she declared, "*Replaced* you? You were never first to begin with!"

"Keep telling yourself that."

"Besides, Jonathan and I are just friends."

"Now that you are the Goddess of Dawn, I am sure he wants more than that."

He caught a glimpse of her blushing and he forced a smile though his eyes were uneasy. He grabbed a shirt off a hanger, slid his arms through the sleeves and started to button the front. "Jonathan does like a challenge. Lives for it, actually. But I don't think he'll get much of a challenge from you, since you have worshipped him all your life."

Aurora smacked him across the head with a pillow.

"If you aren't careful, Boreas, I am going to kick you back into that jail cell of yours and throw away the key."

Boreas wrestled the pillow out of her hands until little white feathers busted through the seams and floated around them, landing on their heads like snow. Aurora started to laugh and Boreas followed suit, blowing feathers in her direction as Aurora watched him and smiled. She hadn't realized how much she had missed him and knew that, for some reason, the universe still had them intertwined. Boreas laughed so hard he collapsed on the bed and let the feathers flutter down onto his face. She picked one up that was stuck to his cheek and rubbed it between her fingers, the feather soft to the touch.

His sleeve had risen to expose the green mark that stained his skin. She let go of the feather and went to put her hand over the mark when without even looking, he grabbed her hand and held it tight.

"Don't," he cried out hastily, his eyes closed and body rigid. "Don't try your powers on it."

He released his hold on her wrist and brought his shirt sleeve down, covering the mark once again. He stood up facing the mirror with his back to her.

She stood up, put her hand on his shoulder and gave it a reassuring squeeze as Boreas's anguished face stared back at her through his reflection. A strange feeling escalated through her body, like electricity pulsing through her heart as he looked at her.

"You're better off with Jonathan," he confessed, sadly. "There is evil in me, Aurora. Your powers couldn't erase the fact that the Inspector played off that evil to turn me. It's still in me and I fear it always will be."

All she could say was, "We're in this together, Boreas."

She headed toward the door, looking back briefly to behold Boreas wincing as he looked at the green mark that encircled like a parasite over his vein. He bore the same mark as his father.

Chapter 8

The Feast

"Fawn, I am just saying lie to him. You are used to lying to him."

Aurora was chasing Fawn around the Great Hall as Fawn was hurrying to get everything assembled for the big Thanksgiving feast.

"He knows the truth now. I am not going to go on pretending." She bit her pinky nail and closed her eyes trying to gather her thoughts. "I never wanted him to know. Or anyone. But it was the only way I could save him."

She tried to scurry past Aurora, but she blocked Fawn again. "He thinks it was a ruse that you and the Professor came up with to get him out of prison. He doesn't want to admit the truth."

"That's up to him."

Fawn pouted into the mirror, putting her long black hair into a high bun and securing it with a conch shell. She then put her hand on Aurora's shoulder and said tenderly, "Look, I can't thank you enough for stepping in and saving my son. But now Rana hates me and I fear may try to kill me, and Boreas already hated me and I just gave him one more reason not to trust me. I can't lie to him anymore."

They headed into the dining hall where people were assembling for the Thanksgiving feast. The dining hall was decorated with long flowing gold curtains that draped over the rock walls and, for added elegance, a huge chandelier hung in the center of the hall. Long tables filled with an assortment of food formed a square with people seated on the outside of the square. Turkey, mashed potatoes, green beans, squash and meat abounded. A fountain of red wine flowed. The children were filling canisters, bringing them back to the tables and filling the goblets for each of the adults.

At the head of the table, Fawn raised her goblet and everyone quieted down, raising their goblets towards her in return. Her voice addressed the commune:

"Hundreds of years ago, pilgrims landed on Plymouth Rock and befriended the Native Americans. They feasted in harmony despite their different backgrounds, beliefs and cultures. Today we do the same in Plymouth Incarnate. All of us were persecuted and prevented from standing up for what we believed to be right or even from exercising our beliefs. That was the freedom that the Common Good took away from us. Whether you believe in a God or believe in the right to assemble peacefully in honor of what the first pilgrims celebrated, let's say thanks for good friends and pray for freedom for all. Happy Thanksgiving, everyone!

"Happy Thanksgiving!" Everyone toasted, the room erupting in a cacophony of clanging metal goblets while the music started with a harpsichord and flute duet played by Father Thomas and the new Great Secretary, Rabbi Eli. Aurora walked to the melodious beat as she searched for an empty seat amongst the guests. She waved at Otus who was devouring turkey leg after turkey leg and drinking from a huge goblet the size of 20 standard goblets. He raised his goblet to her and gulped down its contents, turning the same shade of red as the wine that warmed him. He started tapping his foot to the music and Aurora laughed giddily as the tables shook from the vibrations. She spotted Jonathan in a magenta shirt and his eyes brightened when they spotted her. She hurried over to his side of the table and slid in beside him. He handed her a goblet and raised his own to her. She clanged his happily, some wine spilling out onto the table. She felt so clumsy for spilling it, and quickly cleaned it up.

She wasn't sure what to say, smoothing her navy outfit and hoping he would complement her hair or dress. Instead he said, "It looks like Babs and Boreas are finally talking again."

He pointed to a far corner near the gold curtains where she spotted Boreas and Babs speaking. It appeared to be cordial, but she knew there was still a lot of anger and resentment on Babs's part.

Aurora asked Jonathan for some mashed potatoes and he served her, putting a small spoonful of potatoes on her plate. She wanted to ask for some more but then stopped herself, looking down at the slight bulge protruding from her stomach that she hid with a napkin.

"What an interesting holiday, Thanksgiving." He took a big bite from a turkey leg, ripping the crispy skin with his teeth. "Father Thomas and his men went through the underground tunnel beneath Storm King Mountain and ended up in town where they have people working for them on the inside. They managed to sneak all of this food for them."

Aurora smelled the sweet aroma of cranberries and gravy and her mouth salivated. She went to take a turkey leg but ended up resorting to only a small thigh. She felt so self-conscious eating in Jonathan's presence, fearing he was watching and judging her intake. She ended up nibbling at the turkey, almost afraid to swallow.

Don't think about food!! Focus on Jonathan!!

Her stomach churned in response.

Boreas bounced into his chair, smelling of fresh soap and wearing a long-sleeve navy shirt, part of the sleeves rolled up. His jet black hair was still wet, like he had just hopped out of the shower and he slicked it back out of his mesmerizing hazel eyes. He no longer looked like the emaciated prisoner who had been on trial days prior. Aurora had to stop herself from gaping at him, focusing instead on Babs, who slid into the chair next to her.

"Are you alright?" Aurora whispered to her friend, knowing the conversation she had with Boreas could not have been easy

Babs gave her a reassuring nod, smoothing out the end strands of her braid that dangled down her right shoulder

Boreas dug into the carving station and began slicing a big juicy piece of turkey off and plopped it down on his plate. He carved another piece and offered it to Babs who took it with a slight smile. He then put another slab of white meat and a glob full of mashed potatoes on Aurora's nearly empty plate.

When Aurora realized she had already finished her first helping she felt so guilty.

"Here, Boreas. You can have mine."

She immediately spooned the potatoes back onto Boreas's plate and his eyebrow raised in surprise. "Are you sure?"

"Positive," she scooped the last piece of potatoes onto his plate.

Boreas shrugged and scarfed down the food and she felt her stomach rumble in hunger. Eating that would mean not fitting into the dress she wanted to wear for Jonathan. Priorities. She didn't need those potatoes. Boreas did.

A hand reached out and tapped Boreas on his shoulder and he whirled around to face the new Great Secretary, Rabbi Eli. He was an elderly ex-General, having served for the army of the United States of America before Inspector Herald's regime began. He became a Rabbi to avoid fighting for the Common Good Army but had to take his followers underground to Plymouth Tartarus when practicing of any religions were abolished.

The Great Secretary put his flute to the side and though his graying hair revealed his age to be in his early fifties, he still maintained a massive muscular build. As Great Secretary, he was the 2nd in command to Fawn Stockington and was her military advisor. He stared at Boreas with his intense eyes and looked like he wanted to devour him for dinner.

Boreas gulped. "Can I help you, Eli?"

"That is Great Secretary to you. I know about your brief encounter with my predecessor."

Boreas pointed at the scar along his neck. "As long as you don't try to slit my throat, I think we'll get along just fine."

The Great Secretary almost hit him over the head with his flute, but then put it reluctantly to his side. "You are very lucky, aren't you, Stockington? First the gala and now the courtroom. You are getting a lot of 2nd chances. The Inspector won't give you a 2nd chance. I hope you know that."

"Are you threatening me?" Boreas jumped up, knocking his plate over. Jonathan instinctively jumped up too, ready to break up a fight if needed.

The Great Secretary smirked at this juvenile act.

"I'm offering a friendly warning," The Great Secretary thrust a newspaper into his chest. "Someone from the outside brought this to me along with the food for this feast."

Aurora watched as Boreas unfolded the newspaper article and there in black and white was his picture with the headline, "Son of David Xiomy-- menace to the Common Good. Must be stopped at all cost!"

Boreas threw down the newspaper clipping like it was plagued with a disease. Aurora quickly snatched it before anyone else could see it.

"Who else saw this?" Boreas whispered urgently.

"Down here? I only showed it to you and the High Magistrate. But up there, the Inspector knows. How he knows is beyond me? But what is clear is that he can't let you live now that he knows the truth."

Father Thomas summoned the Great Secretary over to play a duet and he made his way back to the stage with flute in hand.

Aurora straightened the article so that both she and Jonathan could read it, her heart doing hiccups in her chest.

"Boreas Stockington, the fugitive from Candlewick who attacked two officers in the Common Good Library, has been identified as the long lost son of the infamous rebellion leader, David Xiomy. Xiomy was against the Common Good's mission to save the world from hatred and wars caused by religious differences. He fought against the IDEAL and ended up killing many civilians in the process. He was captured after the Last Straw Protest failed and was put to death to rid the country of this unstable and dangerous radical. Boreas is following in his father's footsteps and needs to be captured before any more innocent lives are taken. The Inspector has said that he must be caught at any cost. In the Inspector's words: 'He needs to be made an example of so that we will never again suffer for the injustice that religious strife has caused us. Religions divide, but the IDEAL unites all!'"

They all sat there in silence, contemplating what they had just read and the shock settling in.

"It was from the DNA sample," Jonathan realized. "They took one when we were captured by the Inspector. They must have seen that our DNA was not the same and compared yours, Boreas, to others they had on file."

The chair legs screeched as Boreas jumped up, grabbed the article, and ran out of the dining room without looking back. Aurora took off after Boreas but when she opened the golden curtains and gazed out into the Great Hall, there was no sign of her friend anywhere. Aggravated, she zigzagged her way through the various corridors, but she found only an eerie silence since everyone else was still eating in the dining hall. Finally she spotted the dungeon door ajar and realized there wasn't a guard stationed outside the entrance. She approached the door and could hear faint voices within. She snuck inside the opening and found herself in a dark corridor with only a green, hazy light visible at the far end. Her heart was beating nervously in her chest again as she headed down the corridor, expecting the missing guard to pounce on her for intruding. She cautiously inched toward the voices and when she reached the end she recognized Boreas's voice. And another voice. A voice that was vaguely familiar.

Boreas whispered, "We need to leave now. I need your help."

"My help. Boreas Stockington never needs my help."

"Shut up and do this for me. You want me to get you out of here, well this is your only chance!"

Aurora peeked her head out slightly to witness Boreas standing outside of a small cell. Behind the bars she could discern a ragged-looking man in his early 40's with a porcelain-white face. His lips were a purplish/blue hue and his red eyes were wide open, like a baby doll's that blinked only when their head bobbed robotically.

Aurora had to stop herself from gasping. *It was Max Radar- the IDEAL!*

Radar jeered at Boreas, "You know my terms. Can you live with them?" Boreas paused and leaned unsteadily against the bars of the jail, deep in thought.

Aurora moved closer to get a better look, but once immersed in the hypnotic green light she couldn't move! She was paralyzed! She tried to yell for help but nothing escaped from her lips. She was helpless, like an insect stuck in a spider's web.

Radar cried out, "It looks like there's another invitee to this party."

Aurora, seized with a sudden fit of fear, wanted to turn and run but the mysterious green light kept her planted in that same spot. She felt arms grab her and lift her up out of the light.

"What the hell do you think you're doing?" Boreas cried, shaking Aurora until she snapped out of her stupor.

"What happened? What is that light?"

"Hypnotic Paralysis. Prevents people like you from sneaking into this prison and helping poor prisoners escape."

She wiggled her fingers, glad to get feeling back. She looked at Boreas. "But you got through?"

He sighed and closed his eyes, "Let's just say that my body is immune."

Aurora looked down at his arm where his rolled up sleeve exposed the greenish mark. She realized it must be a similar technology to the Soul Extractor, except this time it was meant to make the victims catatonic.

Max Radar sat looking emaciated and pale on the other side of the prison bars. His short and stringy platinum blond hair was nearly as white as his pale skin, making him appear older than his forty-year-old self. His red eyes gleamed as he held his fingers out through the tiny slits in his prison wall to shake Aurora's hand. "We have to stop meeting this way, Goddess of Dawn. Yes… I heard you got your powers. Boreas couldn't stop raving about that light of yours. Let me offer you my congratulations."

Aurora ignored his handshake. "Radar, I thought you were still in Candlewick Prison."

"Lucky for me I escaped during the prison breakout, but unluckily got caught again trying to steal one of the Safe Haven planes. I am stuck rotting in this prison now, but at least it gave me time to catch up with Boreas, here."

Aurora glared at Boreas and nearly pushed him. "This is the hardened criminal you were telling me about earlier? The one you want to go back to Candlewick with? Have you gone mad?"

Boreas sat down against the cold brick wall, "My reasons have nothing to do with you."

"They have everything to do with me if you are going to run off with the former IDEAL and head back into the hands of the Inspector. Yeah, I think that concerns me and Otus quite a bit. What would entice you to go back to Candlewick?" She paused. "Except…?"

She turned to the former IDEAL… now the jailed, weak man before her. His words from Machu Picchu echoed in her memory.

She sputtered, "Boreas, please tell me you're not thinking of killing Inspector Herald."

Radar massaged the iron bars with the back of his hand, his pupils dilated and a bitter gurgling noise escaped from his throat. "Tick tock goes the clock. The Geometric Storm will be here before you know it."

Aurora's patience was running out and she grabbed Boreas by the hand and dragged him out of ear shot and away from the IDEAL's wretched, manipulative clutches.

"Boreas, you have two seconds to explain what the hell is going on here or I'm going to march straight up to your mother and tell her about Radar."

Boreas stuffed his hands into his pockets at the mention of the word 'mother', which Aurora knew would have the desired effect.

"Aurora, it's true. I am going to kill Herald."

Aurora stared at Boreas like he had lost his mind. She hoped it was just the effect of the numbing light that was making her hear these things. There was no way Boreas Stockington was going to kill Inspector Herald.

"I am going to pretend that I didn't hear any of this. I am getting out of here, we both are. Boreas, come on."

Radar clapped his hands over and over again like they were putting on some show and Aurora needed to get away from this madman. She cautiously evaded the green light on her way out of the dungeon, hugging the wall to avoid any contact with it. Boreas walked right through the green spotlight and blocked her retreat.

"You should help us, Aurora."

Radar continued clapping, this time faster and faster and Aurora felt it was in rhythm with her heart. She felt the noise would bring the entire army down upon them.

"Boreas, I just risked everything to get you out of jail. I am not about to get both of us stuck down here. I heard what you said. You want to try to help him escape. Well you'll have to be just as crazy as him to think I would ever help you do that."

She continued inching forward and he slowly moved aside to let her pass. Once she was free of the light he called after her, "Aurora, please wait."

She ran like a wild animal down the corridor, trying desperately to forget everything she had heard and seen. He raced after her, grabbed her hand and pulled her toward him.

"You know as much as I do that Inspector Herald must be stopped. And now that you have your powers, we can stop him for good!"

"Boreas," Aurora whispered. "I am not a murderer and you are not evil. Don't let Radar make you think that about yourself. He is evil. We both know that he is not our friend. He just wants to use you to get out of this prison so that he can take over the Common Good Army. That's what he tried to make us help him with at Macchu Picchu, don't you remember?"

"Yes, I remember," Boreas sighed, watching a rat scuttle past them in the hallway.

"Besides," Aurora continued, "we have been delayed long enough and now that we have you back, I am not about to let any fake IDEAL stop us. You want to leave. Fine, let's leave, but toward the Northern Lights, NOT Candlewick, OK?"

He nodded unwillingly and she didn't let go of his hand until they were safely away from that ghastly prison and back in the light of the Great Hall. She spotted Otus in the center of the room doing a jig of some sort, surrounded by a great circle of everyone in the hall with joined hands, dancing around the giant. Jonathan and Babs were laughing and trying to do the dance along with the others, but tripped over each other's feet time and time again. The Professor was beside Fawn in the center, clapping along with the music as the singing got louder and louder. Otus picked Babs up and placed her on his shoulder and her beautiful voice rang out along with the music.

"There's no place but here and now
No time to run and no time to bow
Just you and me forever in tune
With the lively music in this lively room.
So let us dance in harmony this day
Despite our eyes, yours brown, mine gray
The sun is one that shines above
One heaven; one hell; one life; one love."

The room erupted in cheers galore as Babs finished her solo. Aurora found herself clapping wildly along with them as the words continued to play over and over in her mind. She took a seat at the table and grabbed a drink, catching sight of Boreas hidden by the shadows and away from the crowd. She figured she'd give him some space, trying to forget about what she had heard and seen. Max Radar was a master at manipulation and was the idea behind the IDEAL, the idea that had kept the nightmare above going for the past 15 years. All believed that things would be better following this IDEAL, this thing that never existed. An idea could be stronger than any one person. And down here, these outlaws around her were following an idea of their own. An idea stronger than anything the Common Good's IDEAL could ever begin to imagine. Here there were people from all backgrounds and beliefs celebrating together. This was why Aurora had to save the planet from the Geometric Storm. The world above had to live to learn about this powerful, peaceful idea. An idea that the Common Good feared more than anything else...

Chapter 9

The Vision

Boreas attempted to avoid the dance floor, but was scooped up by Otus who ruffled his hair.

"Otus, put me down!"

"Not a chance!" Otus laughed, jumping high into the air; almost hitting his head on the ceiling. "It's time you had some fun!"

Boreas tried to squeeze out of Otus's enormous fingers, but they would not budge, it was as if they were glued shut. He felt queasy as Otus spun around and around, and the great chandelier above rattled. He closed his eyes to stop the dizziness and stop his stomach from churning, when all of a sudden he was no longer in the hall but outside. He heard a noise and looked up to see a giant shadowy object falling from the sky. It wasn't until it was nearly upon the town that he realized it was a bomb. He tried to yell...to warn the people to run, but they didn't hear him. The bomb exploded, erupting in flames. He screamed louder than he ever had before.

Boreas's eyes burst open, once again in the Great Hall. The vision of the explosion was still raw in his mind. The music had stopped and Otus was staring down at Boreas who was shaking in his palm.

"Boreas, what's the matter?"

Boreas cried out, "The Common Good is here!"

Chaos erupted throughout the room. Fawn immediately made an announcement, telling everyone to continue the festivities as there was no immediate threat. She told them that Boreas was ill and there was nothing to be alarmed about.

Aurora raced over, instructed Otus to follow her to her room and they placed Boreas' struggling body on the bed. His eyes appeared possessed, rolling to the back of his head.

"Boreas, it's okay," Aurora said, forcing tears from her eyes, knowing she had the power to heal him. She took his hand, praying that the seizures would stop.

When the tears dripped down onto Boreas's face, he immediately stopped convulsing. His body relaxed on the bed and his eyes slowly flickered open. They settled on Aurora, her hand encircling his. She gave it a reassuring squeeze.

"Where is my Mom?" his voice wavered as he spoke.

As if she heard him, in marched Fawn. She was followed by Jonathan, the doctor and the Great Secretary.

Fawn closed the curtain behind her and exclaimed, "Why can't we ever get through one celebration without you raising hell?"

Boreas seemed to snap out of his spell at the sound of his mother's voice. He sat up and frantically cried out, "The Common Good Army is coming! They will be bombing this entire area. The Inspector knows we are here."

Stunned, nobody moved.

Boreas banged his fist on the pillow. "Mom, did you hear me?"

Fawn appeared even more stunned at being called "Mom". She turned to the Great Secretary and inquired, "Please check with Master Control and find out if there is anything on our radar."

At the mention of radar, Aurora thought of the prisoner Max Radar and wondered if this fit that Boreas was suffering might be an act. The Great Secretary spoke into his communication device, raised his brows at the response from Master Control and then turned toward Fawn.

"Something just popped up on the radar. Planes are coming into the area at rapid speed. There's a chance that it could be the Inspector's planes."

Fawn blanched as she sat down across from Boreas. "What else do you know?"

Boreas looked haunted, having to relive the nightmare, but he closed his eyes and said, "They are bombing villages. Towns, places near us. A place called Tipanary."

"Tipanary Grove," Fawn jumped to her feet, her son's words resonating truth.

"There is no way to know if it is an imminent threat, High Magistrate," the Great Secretary exclaimed, pointing accusatorily at Boreas, "The boy was having a drunken delusion. And besides, you can't trust him."

Fawn stood by the curtain, her eyes troubled, but she spoke with conviction in her voice. "I will go to Master Control. We need to take immediate precautions and tell the people to retreat to their rooms until the threat can be assessed. Great Secretary, you are in charge, please tell everyone this is just a drill as we don't want to cause a panic. Also alert our people at Tipanary Grove. Inform them that the Common Good Army may attack them as well as any of the surrounding towns. We may be able to save some lives, if we're not too late."

She stormed out of the room before anyone had a chance to counter her decision.

The Great Secretary focused his beady eyes on Boreas's face and exclaimed, "I will follow the High Magistrate's command, but you better watch yourself. I am not as foolish as my predecessor."

He stormed out after the High Magistrate and began to give instructions over the loud speaker for everyone to retreat to their rooms and await further instruction.

Aurora grabbed water from her sink and handed it to Boreas, "How are you seeing this vision? Did you ever see them before?"

Jonathan tapped his fingers against the dresser and said through clenched teeth, "That is if he even saw the vision. He could have alerted the Inspector to our location."

Boreas sat up. "Is that what you think?"

Jonathan crossed his arms over his chest, "Yes, that's what I think. Remember it was just a month ago that you tried to kill me."

There was a commotion behind the curtain as the Professor rolled into the room in a wheelchair. He was yelling at some boy, saying they had taken him in the wrong direction and asking why they didn't have compasses down here in the mountains.

He fixed his goggles and smiled awkwardly. "I just ran into Fawn, who said that the Common Good Army is coming."

"That's what Boreas says, at least," Jonathan mumbled.

The Professor nodded, pleased and excited. "It may turn out to be lucky that you got the Soul Extractor serum, Boreas."

Boreas took a drink of water. "What do you mean by lucky?"

The Professor's blind eyes gleamed. "The Soul Extractor serum connects you to the person who injected you. It's generally momentary, but sometimes that connection can linger."

Boreas nearly choked on the water. "Are you saying that because the Inspector injected me with the serum, what I saw in that vision…that's what the Inspector is seeing?"

The Professor hacked up a lung and took a swig of whisky from his flask. "Too bad they don't have good liquor down here. Only this second rate…"

"Professor!"

"Well I don't know if it's what he's seeing, exactly. It might be what he's thinking. Just like when your father, David Xiomy, was able to read my mind about the prophecy when I injected him with the serum."

Boreas looked stunned as this information took hold. "So we need to stop the attack, if it hasn't happened yet."

Jonathan shook his head, "We are waiting to see if there is an actual threat. We can't give ourselves away."

Boreas jumped out of bed. "Well, we can't do nothing."

"What do you propose we do? Fight? The Common Good Army has had time to mobilize. We only have two hidden planes stolen from the Common Good and 10 submarines and most of the people here are not soldiers. We have to wait it out."

"We have Otus and Aurora!"

"Otus is still not 100% after the Candlewick Prison. Remember he got shot at because of you. Or have you forgotten the day you tried to kill all of us!"

"I wish I could forget it!"

The two brothers looked like they were about to fight so Aurora quickly jumped in between them.

"That's enough!" she shouted. "This is my room, and my rules. And if you want to fight it out, then you have to leave."

Jonathan backed down, his fists still clenched as he slumped down in his chair. Boreas faced away from him, his arm stinging and reminding him of the hate and evil that possessed him. He felt so vulnerable thinking about that side of himself, yet he had to be careful. He needed to channel the hatred he had toward the Inspector. After having that vision and knowing what the Inspector was planning, he wanted even more to stop him.

An alarm blared through the loudspeakers and a robotic voice repeated, "This is just a drill. Retreat to your rooms and await further instructions. This is just a drill..."

"Looks like it's starting," Aurora said, as if the tension couldn't get any worse.

The Professor who was deep in thought suddenly whirled his wheelchair toward them. "The answer is in Hyperborea. Boreas needs to get his powers and become the God of the North Wind if there is any chance of winning a fight or defeating the Geometric Storm."

Boreas felt light headed and sat back down as symbols popped into his head. The symbols were from the book written by Pierre Gassendi, prophesying that he, Aurora and Otus were the only ones who would be able to stop the Geometric Storm- a cataclysmic event that would start in the Northern Lights. The Professor concluded that the coordinates predicting where the storm would hit was in the state of Alaska. They just didn't know exactly *when* the storm was supposed to occur, that code in the book still indecipherable.

Aurora quickly scurried around her room to try to clean it up. "Sorry...wasn't expecting company in here. Otus, anything going on outside?"

Otus peeked his head into the room, "Just helping some kids get to their rooms safe and sound. Little lads were climbing on me like a staircase."

"Get me to Master Control," The Professor barked up to the Giant. "I know the Common Good's strategies better than anyone here."

"I'll help," Jonathan declared, vacating the room after shoving past Boreas. Otus picked them up and transported them across the glittering menagerie that was swarming with people, rushing to get to their rooms. Many were chanting prayers and singing songs of hope, their voices echoing throughout the center of the menagerie. Aurora paused as she recognized one of the songs. Her mother used to sing it to her when she was a little girl, those words and that melody lodged deep within her memory. Aurora listened to the harmonies resound as more people joined in, overpowering the fear in her heart. It was beautiful how fear was erased with love.

Boreas plopped down on the bed, "Well, at least Jonathan is talking to me again."

Aurora laughed, "That's progress."

"Of course that fight was the most we have said to each other since he found out I'm his half-brother."

Aurora went into her bag, grabbed her sweatshirt and threw it over her head, feeling more at ease since Jonathan left. "You are still brothers. Nothing has changed."

"You tell him that. I can only imagine how my father is taking the news." He stopped himself. "I wonder if he always knew. Maybe that's why he always favored Jonathan. Maybe that's why he didn't stop the Inspector from doing this to me."

He pulled up his shirt sleeve and put his fingers over the green mark. Aurora put her hand over his, and once again Aurora felt goose bumps tingle on her arm.

"Let me try to help," she said, catching her breath as he gazed at her, with those hazel eyes she remembered, not the ones veiled with the hatred that the Soul Extractor had created. His eyes were shining back at her with such tenderness that she wanted to take all his pain away again.

"I know how you saved me," Boreas said slowly. "I felt it, when you shone your light on me."

"I was given my powers to save lives, not take lives."

Boreas shook his head, inching his way closer to her. "That wasn't the only thing. You believed there was still good in me. You believed I would come back to you."

Her fingers wrapped in his, they were holding onto each other... they were in this together.

"If I let you use your powers on me…will you let me kiss you?"

Aurora felt her whole body go numb as his words resonated. She gazed deep into his eyes. She was lost in his trance as they leaned toward each other and light emanated from her hand, pouring light down onto his skin, and then....

The whole room shook and Aurora was flung into Boreas as they tumbled to the floor. They heard screams from the hallway as in the room the lone light crashed, glass shattering and drawers tumbled out from her dresser. Boreas grabbed Aurora's hand again and dragged her under the bed, narrowly avoiding the barraging dresser. Huddled together, they waited as more bombs sounded, afraid to breathe, afraid that each moment would be their last.

The waiting and the screams echoing from the corridor was nearly unbearable when all of a sudden Fawn's voice echoed from the loudspeaker.

"The planes have moved North. It appears that the Inspector doesn't know where the Safe Haven is and instead bombed the sur-rounding mountain area. We need every able bodied person to help check Plymouth Incarnate for those injured and transport them to the Great Hall immediately for medical assistance."

Aurora and Boreas crawled out from under the bed as the crowd of people cheered.

"What about everyone else out there?" Boreas cried out, but his voice was drowned out by the cheers.

Aurora didn't know, but was glad they were safe at least. She found herself staring down at the green mark on Boreas's arm. She hadn't been able to use her powers on him. She swatted at the goose bumps still visible on her skin. Those old feelings had returned, or maybe they had never gone away in the first place, hidden deep down inside her, afraid to be summoned and realized. That hidden part of her wished she had kissed him.

Chapter 10

The Bargain

It was near the Sacred Hour and Aurora and Babs were in the infirmary helping the wounded injured from the attack. Babs was in charge, instructing Aurora to get supplies and apply ointments and bandages where needed. Aurora treated Joshua, a friend from Candlewick who owned the Laundromat, for a bad cut from a fallen bookcase. They were monitoring him now to make sure he didn't have a concussion. Professor Gassendi was instructing 3 boys to build a ramp to make the room wheelchair accessible.

"Don't you have anything better to do?" Babs cried out. "You're the only one rolling around in a wheelchair because you're too lazy to use your cane."

"Right now I am the only one in a wheelchair. What about in the future? You've got to think ahead, Babs O'Hara. That's what I'm always telling you."

"And I'm telling you to wheel that chair out of here or I am going to build a ramp on that thick skull of yours."

They both laughed and the Professor admitted defeat for the time being, whispering to the boys to meet him there after hours when the mean Irish nurse couldn't tattle on them.

Fawn came in to offer moral support. She looked like she hadn't slept for the past 24 hours but went to each of the patients one by one to offer them words of comfort and cheer. When she reached Aurora she smiled nervously, handing the conch shell to her.

"I forgot to give this to Boreas. Can you make sure he gets it?"

Aurora took the orange tinted conch shell, the gift Fawn had bestowed upon her son 5 months earlier when they embarked on their mission. This shell when sounded, only Aurora and Otus could hear. All three had one. Fawn had confiscated it when Boreas had been put in jail.

Aurora let the conch shell sit in her palm and she said, "I honestly think you should give it to him."

Fawn looked stoic and exhausted as she said, "I don't think he wants to talk to me."

Aurora took Fawn's hand and led her to the Great Room where Boreas and Otus were helping to sweep and clean up some of the rocks that had fallen during the attack. Boreas was using this chore as a chance to teach Otus how to play baseball and Aurora stopped to watch them.

"It's simple, Otus. First there's a ball, which will be this rock here. I'm the pitcher and I throw it to you and you take that bat..."

Otus held some ridiculously small club in his hand to be the bat and it was difficult for him to wrap his fingers around it. "Like this?" he asked hopefully.

Boreas laughed. "Yes like that. Now you swing when I throw it to you. Ready?"

The rock charged at Otus. He swung the bat too hard and ended up doing circles and falling on his butt, shaking the whole room.

Boreas laughed so hard he nearly knocked over the pile of rocks they had made.

"Be careful, Otus or else the colony will think we're under attack again."

Boreas whirled around at the sound of his mother's voice. He turned back and proceeded to pick up rocks again, blatantly ignoring her.

Otus picked himself up, apologizing. "Boreas here was just teaching me baseball."

"I could see that. I remember when Henry and I taught Boreas how to play."

Boreas dropped a handful of rocks onto the pile, rolling up his sleeves. "What do you want?"

Aurora gave him a look, scolding him to be nice, so Boreas crossed his arms and waited.

Fawn wiped some sweat from her brow and said, "Boreas, your vision has saved dozens of lives. I received word today that the people of Tipanary Grove were able to get to safety in the mountains before the attack. Unfortunately the same cannot be said for the other villages in the area. Many of our friends from the outside have been killed or taken by the Inspector. It is just a matter of time until they reveal our location."

"So we'll have to leave?" Aurora asked.

Fawn nodded. "We knew this was temporary until we could reunite with some of the other protesting groups in the country. We look to you, Otus to see if you can guide us. You had mentioned once that a woman named Mrs. Taboo was your protector and the one who revealed the prophecy. Where can we find her?"

Otus smiled, "She said she would wait for us in Hyperborea, once we were ready for Boreas to get his powers."

Fawn nodded, still avoiding Boreas's gaze. "It sounds like the time has come for all of us to head west to Hyperborea. We will need to fill the 10 submarines and first go to the colony in San Francisco led by Babs's parents. The Professor has shared the coordinates of where Hyperborea is hidden and it is located out west. He says it is a hidden valley called the "Land of Eternal Spring" that is surrounded by mountains. My hope is that the San Francisco colony may be able to offer safe passageway for our people to Hyperborea, if it even exists."

"I should go there first," Otus said. "To ensure Mrs. Taboo is even there."

Fawn nodded, looking at the Great Books again. "We may need to retreat to the waters for now until we hear word that you have reached there safely."

She turned to Boreas who was staring down at the old books, reading them leisurely like he wasn't listening.

Fawn took a deep breath, "I also wanted to give you back your conch shell. That is, if you still want it."

Boreas looked down at the conch shell and took it from his mom's hands. As it touched his hand, it triggered a memory. He looked at his mom as he wiped dirt from his eye.

"When is my birthday, Mom?"

Fawn stared at her son nervously. "Why are you asking...?"

"Because the day you handed this to me, you said that I was an Aquarius. Like you. That we were meant for either greatness or madness. But if my birthday is March 1ˢᵗ, then I'm not an Aquarius. March falls under the fish one. Pisces... I recall Mrs. Xiomy ranting on and on about astrology when we were out in the wilderness. I never put two and two together until now. So tell me, when is my birthday?"

Fawn leaned her head back like she was looking for strength. Her hair formed ringlets down her back. "You are right. I hid the day I gave birth to you. The Professor helped take care of you before the date I told Henry that I had you. He would have gotten suspicious if he knew the true date. Your birthday is in February."

"So you hid the fact that you conceived me a month earlier. You hid me, you hid the date I was born, you lied to my father and me!"

"You were never supposed to find out!"

Boreas grabbed the conch shell out of her hands and threw it against the floor. "I don't want your gift. I don't want anything from you. Let's just pretend I'm not your son. Or Henry's or David's or anyone's."

He stormed off through the maze of rocks, kicking them out of his way until he barged through the infirmary doors and slammed them shut behind him.

Fawn went over to the conch shell and dusted it off. She held the shell in her hand close to her heart.

"I can't blame him for being angry. I was glad Jonathan found it within himself to forgive me, but Jonathan is a very different person than Boreas."

Aurora took the shell from Fawn's hands. "I'll give this to Boreas. I know he really wants it, whether he admits it or not."

She nodded, the stoic expression returned to her face. "I'd better get back to Master Control."

Otus cleared a path for Fawn so that she wouldn't have to stumble through the rocks. She thanked him for his help and Otus smiled at her.

"You're a strong leader, Fawn Stockington. I'm just glad I can offer my services."

Aurora spotted a gap in the wall and went over to go check on it. It was so bitterly cold she was glad she had managed to keep her sweatshirt after all these months.

She looked down to see the squiggly lines on her sweatshirt and she nearly fell over.

"Fawn, wait!" Aurora cried out, stumbling over the bricks as Fawn waited on the opposite side of the hall.

"Aurora, what's the matter?" Fawn cried out as Otus lent Aurora a hand, helping boost her to the other side.

Aurora caught her breath and pointed to her chest. "This symbol on my sweatshirt represents my astrological sign. I'm an Aquarius too."

Otus stared at her. "Did I miss your birthday, Aurora?"

Aurora shook her head wildly. "No... no, but that's it, Otus! My birthday! It's in February. February 1st. Is that Boreas's birthday?"

Fawn took a step back. "How did you know?"

Aurora reached into her backpack and grabbed the book from Pierre Gassendi. She turned to the page with the symbol on it - the symbol that would tell them how they would stop the Geometric Storm. "This symbol, the squiggly lines I knew would help indicate the date of the storm but I never thought about astrology! It is the symbol of the water bearer, the astrological symbol for Aquarius. I think this 16 means that it will be when Boreas and I turn 16. Fawn just confirmed that Boreas and I have the same birthday. We were both born on February 1st."

Fawn stared at her confused. "What does it mean?"

"It means that the Geometric Storm is going to occur on my 16th birthday. So in 2 months' time. Happy Sweet 16 to me."

Fawn nearly collapsed. "Two months. Are you sure?"

Aurora nodded. "I'll ask the Professor to confirm, but I don't believe it's a coincidence that Boreas and I have the same birthdate."

Otus sat down hard, the room shaking. "That's not a lot of time for Boreas to get his powers and for us to get to the Northern Lights.

The Bargain

Fawn took a deep breath, "That's enough time. It has to be."

☆ ☆ ☆

Aurora was searching everywhere for Boreas to tell him the news with the conch shell clutched in her hand. She was surprised to spot him emerging from the prison. She called after him and he turned around with a huff, annoyed that he got caught.

"Were you speaking with Radar again?" she demanded.

"It's my business who I speak with. But while we're on the subject, I didn't appreciate you ambushing me in the Great Room with my mom."

She took the orange conch shell and thrust it against his chest. "You needed to talk to her."

He took the conch shell reluctantly from her hands and placed it around his neck. He whispered, "What I need to do is leave this place and stop the Inspector before he comes back and bombs the hell out of all of us. Otherwise goodbye Plymouth Incarnate or whatever the hell this place is called."

He rushed off to the dining hall where everyone was gathered for a prayer service to offer solemn remembrance for the fallen victims of the Common Good bombings.

Aurora grabbed him by the arm and ushered him to a far corner out of ear shot.

"I will go to Fawn and tell her what you are conspiring to do."

Boreas glared at her and for a second he resembled his evil side... the part of his personality that took over after he was given the Soul Extractor serum. Aurora had nearly forgotten that side of him was not extinguished with her power.

"Is that a threat?"

"Yes, it's a threat. I figured out that our birthday is the key. February 1st. We only have 2 months until the Geometric Storm. And we are leaving. We're going to Hyperborea with Otus."

Boreas rolled up his sleeve and pointed angrily at the green mark on his arm. "Look, Aurora! I can't be the God of the North Wind. Don't you understand that I am tainted? The only way to stop the storm is to stop Herald."

He jumped up and raced away from her just as the music began. The congregation's prayers had turned to songs of peace and understanding. The music was discordant to the dire situation Aurora was faced with. Boreas was falling deeper and deeper into Radar's hands and she ran faster, her concern fueling her speed.

Luckily a group of mourners walked through the curtain, blocking his exit. She managed to grab Boreas, whirling him around to face her. His black shirt sleeves were rolled up revealing that green mark that haunted him. "Let me use my powers. Let me try to heal you."

His piercing hazel eyes stared back at her. "There is no healing me, Aurora."

She pulled him behind the flap of the curtain out of sight with the glittering stone wall illuminating his eyes, his face, his lips. Before he could say another word, she kissed him. The goose bumps raced up her arms as he wrapped his arms around her, holding her close to him. A soft glow of light encircled their bodies as they were intertwined and she didn't want to let go of him. It was like their hearts were beating as one as he kissed her back with so much passion and love that Aurora felt lost in it, fearing it... the feelings she had repressed were now fueled, nearly lifting them into the air. It was the two of them, together, the way it was meant to be. She mussed his hair in her hands as she kissed him with all her being, the music sounding behind them, the words resonating in her heart. She could save him, she could heal him. If her kiss could do that, it was worth it.

Still deep in the kiss, she reached down, the light flowing from her fingers and she gently touched his arm with the green mark on it. He immediately pushed her away, extinguishing the light from his skin.

"What are you doing?" he grabbed his arm protectively.

She stared at him confused. "You said I could use my powers on you if I kissed you. That's what the bargain was yesterday, wasn't it?"

He raked his fingers through his hair. "So you just kissed me because you wanted to use your powers on me?"

Aurora nodded, unsure as to why he was getting upset. "I just wanted to help you!"

He shook his head in disbelief. "Keep your pity kisses, Aurora."

He barged through the curtain, back into the light of the world behind them. The people at the prayer service turned around at the disturbance and Aurora waved awkwardly at them as she was again in pursuit of Boreas, zigzagging through the crowd. Babs gave her a look like 'what the hell is going on?'

Otus stuck his foot out, blocking Boreas from exiting the room and put his finger to his lips to shush them as Fawn began speaking to the crowds about the people who passed away.

Boreas turned toward Aurora and whispered, "Look... you brought me back to the light with your powers, and I know I owe you my life... but that's not what I wanted, Aurora. I didn't want you to kiss me because of a bargain!"

"That wasn't the only reason. That mark is driving you mad, making you think you're evil, making you think you can kill Inspector Herald."

"I am going to kill him," he whispered fiercely, his eyes steeling. "He has to pay for what he's done."

"Killing Herald is not the answer."

"Isn't it?" he cried out, the man she had kissed a distant memory as the anger raged through him. His hand was on his arm like it was in pain, like he was fighting a side of himself that was screaming to be released.

The organist banged on his instrument, the keys pounding an ever louder and more chaotic symphony in her ears. And with each passing second, Aurora felt like she was losing Boreas even more. She had almost lost him to the Inspector before. She wasn't going to lose him again. He was going to be the God of the North Wind even if she had to drag him to Hyperborea herself.

Aurora felt her hands start to glow and Boreas's eyes grew wide.

"What the hell are you doing, Aurora?"

"I won't let you jeopardize your life...or our mission!"

Boreas stepped backwards toward the door, looking left and right and trying to get Otus's attention. "You can't force me to change my mind, Aurora."

"Try me!"

Aurora released her powers, aiming the stream of light at Boreas. He dove out of the way and she spun around and aimed again, but he zigzagged away from her, his tennis skills kicking into high gear. He was about to reach the door when instinct took over. She harnessed all the strength within her, creating a fire ball and flinging it at the door, the flames blocking Boreas's path and he fell backwards as the fire began to grow. Aurora stared in shock at what she had done when Otus scooped the two of them up in opposite hands and quickly stomped out the fire with his bare feet.

"What is the matter with you two?" he cried out as smoke wafted from below his hairy feet. "People are praying and crying for the people who perished yesterday, and you two are fighting! No more powers in the dining room, do you hear me, Aurora?"

Aurora stared at her hands… not believing this power that she possessed…that had nearly possessed her!

"I'm so sorry, Otus. I didn't mean to…"

Otus snorted. "Aurora, you are gonna hang up here with me for the rest of the service. Boreas, please get a team together to help clean up this mess."

"I'll take care of everything," Boreas said cryptically as Otus released him.

Aurora tried to protest, but Otus shushed her as Mother Hildebrand stepped up to say a prayer, and then introduced Babs who stepped up to the podium.

"As you know, I am no stranger to loss. My sister Eileen and my fiancé were killed at the hands of the Common Good Army when they destroyed Plymouth Tartarus, our home. I loved my little sister very much; Eileen was only 15 years old. I only wish I had a small fraction of the faith she had because it was so strong. I know for everyone who knew her, we miss her, but she never really left us. Her memory lives on."

The congregation said "Amen" and Aurora clutched the cross Eileen had given to her as she breathed her last breath. That cross that had given her strength. How she wished for that strength now.

Right when Babs stepped down, the loudspeaker sounded.

"This is not a drill. Everyone report to your rooms immediately."

The red lights flashed and the high piercing, screeching siren escalated throughout the room. Otus quickly put Aurora down to assist with the elderly and children to get them to safety.

Aurora spotted Jonathan at the door. She ran to him, screaming over the commotion, "Jonathan, what is it?"

Jonathan grabbed her and ushered her toward the missile room. "Boreas had another vision. He said that the patrol planes are coming right now."

Aurora turned to Jonathan in shock and then as understanding dawned, she cried out. "I am going to kill him!"

She ran out of the room with a confused Jonathan at her heels. She was entangled with a conglomerate of people who were running frenzied to their rooms, in fear of the supposedly imminent attack.

She turned to Jonathan and screamed to be heard over the commotion.

"Go find Otus. I am going to need his help to stop Boreas."

"Stop Boreas from what?"

"Just find Otus and bring him to the jail. And hurry!"

She tried to squeeze her way past the crowds and found a short cut through the altar room, the great books flashing by as she ran through. The Great Secretary spotted her and blocked her path.

"Even you need to retreat to your room, Miss Alvarez."

Aurora thought quickly, "I need to help escort the Professor to his room. He's in the infirmary."

The Great Secretary nodded saying, "Fine, but hurry."

She took off again. The scent of perspiration and fear filled the air as she pushed past the Great Secretary.

The alarm blared incessantly as she finally reached the jail. The guard was missing and she began to fear that Boreas had already gotten to him.

She made sure nobody saw her as she slipped through the open door and started down the dark narrow corridor. The green light shone eerily in front of her and she attempted to creep slowly around the light, her body scraping against the hard granite wall to avoid exposure. The light grazed her dress collar but she was nearly past it when out of nowhere a shadow grabbed her from the side and flung her into the green light. Immobilized, she saw the shadow that joined her in the light. Boreas's face stared down at her and she felt fear flow through her, the only thing that could move in her paralyzed frame.

"Let's see you stop me with your powers now, Aurora."

Aurora lay completely helpless as Radar joined Boreas, both of them glaring down at her as she struggled desperately to gain control of her body. The light's intensity was preventing her from even screaming for help. Not like anyone would hear her.

Boreas towered above her and said, "You and I have two different missions now. It's no longer just about the Geometric Storm. It's also about revenge, Aurora. It's about making the Inspector pay for what he did to me, what he has done to so many others. Nobody is even *trying* to stop him."

Radar cried out, "No more flirting with the enemy, Boreas! We can sneak out the back entrance now that everyone has retreated to their rooms."

Boreas fell to his knees, completely immersed in the green light...looking up at her as if he was struggling with something within himself. "I'm sorry, Aurora. I'm no hero, no God of the North Wind. Jonathan is more of a hero than I ever was."

Boreas gazed deeply into her eyes and before she knew what happened, he leaned down and kissed her softly on the lips.

"There was never a right time for us," he whispered.

And then he took off after Radar, down the back passageway. Aurora watched helplessly as his shadow vanished into darkness and cursed herself for not stopping him when she had the chance. She hoped someone would hurry and find her, but she knew it would be too late. Instead, she lay there gazing up at the green light, Boreas's farewell kiss lingering on her lips.

Chapter 11

Plan of Action

"The Inspector knows Boreas is David's son. He won't hesitate to kill him this time. He would probably even make a spectacle of it."

Fawn was pacing back and forth in Master Control. Once the prison guard awoke and freed Aurora from the light, he had led the others down the secret back passageway, but there was no sign of Radar or Boreas. They had escaped.

Otus punched a hole into the granite rock, smashing it to smithereens. Aurora wanted to do the same. She leaned against a bookshelf, tempted to throw the books across the room with all her force. But what would she accomplish by doing that? Throwing books or punching holes in the wall was not going to turn back time.

"I hear Boreas has escaped this nut house."

In entered Mrs. Xiomy, her blonde hair pulled back into a bun and dressed not in her typical orange and indigo colors, but instead a black tank top and jeans. She had bags under her eyes and her purple glasses hung crooked on her nose.

"Who sent for you, Rana?" Fawn cried out, not pleased to see her former friend there during this time of crisis.

"I did," Aurora spoke up, giving her teacher a hug. "Boreas is with the IDEAL."

Mrs. Xiomy's mouth hung open in disbelief. "Wait... the IDEAL has been here all this time?"

Fawn stared at them like they had two heads.

"What are you talking about? The IDEAL is not a person."

Aurora gasped, having forgotten that the IDEAL was still the mysterious ruler to Fawn and the others down here in Plymouth Incarnate. They never would have suspected Max Radar! Only her small group knew the prisoner's true identity from their chance encounter with him.

"Max Radar is the man behind the IDEAL. We met him when he captured us a few months ago in Peru. He had a secret base in Macchu Picchu. He wanted to recruit us to stop Inspector Herald so that he could once again be the ruler of the Common Good."

Mrs. Xiomy stared down Fawn. "I can't believe you had David's co-murderer in your grasp and you let him live."

Fawn stepped down from the altar, hands on her hips, confronting Mrs. Xiomy head on. "I can say the same thing about you when you were with him in Macchu Picchu. I didn't even know the IDEAL was a person until right now."

"This is not helping us!" Otus's big voice bellowed, causing everyone to nearly fall over. Aurora looked up and noticed Otus nervously carving something out of wood, a habit of his when he was worried. She realized he was carving a person, the hair spiked up slightly like Boreas wore his. She closed her eyes, thinking about

Boreas's goodbye kiss and her heart pulsed wildly at the memory. No bargains, no demands. It was on his terms. And it made her that much more furious that she couldn't tear him from Radar's clutches.

She began to understand how a man like Radar had manipulated a whole country — an angry 15 year old was a piece of cake compared to what he had accomplished. Radar convinced Boreas to help him escape — the man who spawned the Common Good Movement, the man who was the reason behind the death of so many people including Boreas's biological father, David Xiomy. Radar was even more dangerous than the Inspector and he had taken Boreas under his wing.

Aurora fiddled with her conch shell, wishing she could blow into it and summon Boreas back. She looked up at the two women who were their only hope in rescuing him and they couldn't even bear to look at each other. She coughed, catching their attention.

"Boreas and Radar are convinced that the only way to stop the storm is by killing Inspector Herald."

"But Radar tried to convert you to his plan at Macchu Picchu," Mrs. Xiomy recalled, "Boreas was against it then. What changed?"

"The Inspector changed Boreas' mind," Aurora said, seeing Boreas's tortured face in her mind. "Boreas is still haunted by what happened with the Soul Extractor serum. He now knows there is evil in him, an evil that could completely overtake him. He thinks he's not good enough to be the God of the North Wind. That he is 'tainted'. Those were his words."

There was a knock at the door and the Great Secretary and Jonathan entered. Aurora instantly stopped fiddling with her conch shell as a surge of guilt swept through her.

It was just a kiss, she told herself, fixing her hair and realizing how terrible she looked after the episodes of that day. She had dirt and mud all over her pants and her shirt was ripped on the side. She attempted to smile at Jonathan as he passed her but he didn't even look in her direction.

"Mom, the satellites have picked up Common Good patrol teams in the area. It also appears that a Common Good vehicle was commandeered and was heading due south toward where the planes are hidden."

The Great Secretary marched past the altar and pressed a button that revealed a screen with a digital map. A red dot blinked, indicating the vehicle's last known location. "Most likely Radar and Boreas were the ones who stole the vehicle, but it looks like the trail died around Ainsborough. The Common Good hit that town hard and are still patrolling the area. The car must have run out of gas or stalled and they are now on foot."

"We can cut them off before they reach the planes."

"Unless the Common Good gets there first."

Fawn turned pale as she realized the odds against her son reaching his destination.

Mrs. Xiomy pointed to a section of the woods on the map. "Jonathan, remember when we escaped from the Lake Champlain fort? Boreas advised you to disguise yourself as one of the officers... remember?"

Jonathan nodded. "Yes, and I pulled it off rather well, if I do say so, myself."

Mrs. Xiomy grimaced, "Yes, except for the part where we had to run for our lives and Boreas got captured... but regardless, if Boreas is on foot, I would bet money that he would disguise himself as one of the officers to blend in. He's probably in the heart of the encampment since he could blend in more and look for a chance to commandeer another vehicle."

Fawn stared at her, "If he's at Ainsborough, he will be seeing people hurt and killed by the Inspector's bomb raid."

Mrs. Xiomy nodded, now huddled next to Fawn. "He's smart like you, but his weakness is that he cares too deeply... like David. He could give himself away if he tries to help someone."

Otus pocketed his wood sculpture and said, "Then we need to stop him from revealing himself."

Fawn turned to Aurora and Otus and said, "We must continue with our plan from earlier. We need to evacuate Plymouth Incarnate and head toward Hyperborea."

"But that's where Boreas is supposed to get his powers." Aurora cried out.

"Exactly. We can create a diversion to give Boreas time to get to the planes, and then lure both the Inspector and Boreas to Hyperborea in order for things to play out according to the prophecy. What we'll need is a diversion."

Otus cracked his knuckles together and looked down at the others with determination. "And I know the perfect person to create this diversion. Me."

Chapter 12

The Survivors

Boreas and Radar were knee-deep in mud, in the outskirts of Ainsborough beneath a tangled wood of ivy and lotus blossoms when they heard the Common Good planes soaring above them. After their car stalled, Radar stole two Common Good uniforms and he and Boreas were forced to impersonate officers in order to continue on foot, trekking the 5 mile walk to where Fawn's planes were hidden. It felt odd wearing the dark indigo colored combat uniform, complete with the orange stripes on his arm where the badge read "IDEAL for Unity". Boreas pulled the heavy helmet already too big for his head further down over his forehead hoping no one would recognize him. A gun was in its holster along his waist belt and Boreas was afraid to even touch it, let alone use it. He wondered if that was the weapon he would use to kill Inspector Herald, but felt a little nauseous thinking about it.

"Just don't say a word," Radar whispered as they were surrounded by Common Good soldiers patrolling the area. "If they ask
you any questions just nod and let me do the talking."

The damage at Ainsborough was even worse than Boreas
imagined. Houses shattered, dust, and crumbled brick piled in the
streets. Lampposts had uprooted and slammed into cars and glass
and debris covered the pavement, breaking and shattering with
each footstep. Bodies were being lined up on the sidewalks, with
the living wailing and screaming over their lost loved ones.
Common Good Officers were interrogating the survivors, arrest-
ing most and not attending to any of the wounded, leaving them to
their fates. Dirt and blood was splattered on their faces and
Boreas's ears were witness to the shrieks of voices pleading for
help, for mercy. Boreas looked up into the gray blue sky, and for a
second he thought he saw a streak of blood orange, hidden ever so
slightly by the gusts of smoke flailing and encircling behind B52
Bomber plane.

"Help me," a young woman cried out, a bloody gash on her
forehead. Boreas was about to run to her aid when Radar grabbed
his shoulder, holding him back.

"A Common Good Officer shows no mercy," he whispered fer-
vently. "Unless you want to join that pile of bodies... move along."

A soldier patrolling the area stopped them, requesting identification. Boreas and Radar handed over their false documents that
they had stolen along with the uniforms. Boreas was relieved the
combat gear hid part of face and his neck scar to prevent being
recognized.

Radar sparked up a conversation with the soldier.

"So how long are we stationed here?" Radar asked pleasantly
patting the soldier on the back.

"Until the Inspector gets what he wants. That's the only orders
we have."

"Who's in charge here?" Radar took a bottle of water out of his stolen sack and handed it to his new ally.

"Sergeant Woolchuck. He's a jackass so stay on his good side. Are you and your partner new recruits?"

"Yes, we're from the Adirondacks. We were called down to offer assistance with the attack."

"Glad to have you on board. Keep your eyes peeled for that traitor, Boreas Stockington. If you hand him in alive there's a reward, I'm told. He's got a noticeable scar along his neck."

He imitated slicing his throat and Boreas quickly clutched the gun a little tighter in his hands.

Radar pushed him along and said, "Thanks, I gotta get this newbie situated. The IDEAL has spoken!"

The officer saluted, "The IDEAL has spoken."

Radar and Boreas hurried along and Boreas couldn't help but laugh. "You couldn't have come up with a better salute for yourself."

"Copywriters were in short supply on the campaign trail."

Once they confirmed that they were alone, Radar pushed him into a grove of trees. "Now stay put. We'll camp here tonight away from the guards. Once again, the Common Good fails to have any Common Sense!"

Boreas removed the backpack he had hidden under his combat gear and collapsed exhausted amongst the ivy and dirt. He took a look at the map that he had stolen from Plymouth Incarnate. They were about 100 miles from Candlewick and without Otus this trek was going to be more arduous and tumultuous especially since everyone in the Inspector's army was out looking for him.

At the thought of the Inspector, Boreas's blood began to boil with rage and he had to keep massaging his forearm where the Inspector had injected him. Memories of that day continued to haunt him, and it was a constant battle to fight the bitter angry person within him.

"Circumstances will ignite the good and evil in a person," Radar had told him. "And once the evil is ignited you can either hide from it or embrace it. If you choose to hide, it will haunt you till the day you die. And once you embrace it, there is no going back."

Boreas was already accepting his circumstances. And for him, there was no going back until he had the Inspector's head on a platter.

Radar dropped off some kindling for Boreas to start a fire and then ran off to try to collect more intel and provisions. Boreas slumped down, removing the helmet, combing his fingers through his sweaty hair. He took out a bottle of water and satiated his thirst. It was much colder than the last time he had been outside, now that they were in the heart of autumn with the wind chill gnawing at his bones. He lit a fire and started cooking pork and beans from the stash he had hidden in the cell the day he had planned his escape. He looked up to behold the Big Dipper constellation stretched out like a giant sparkling ladle across the sky.

The constellations brought him back to the nights he spent camping in the wilderness with Babs, Otus, Mrs. Xiomy…and Aurora. He leaned back, his head nestled in the soft grass, the fire crackling and he gazed up at the sky. He put his fingers against his lips, still in disbelief that he had kissed Aurora. Of course, the only reason she kissed him was over that bargain and to use her powers on him. But still, that kiss was unreal…like they were glowing! Did she not feel it too? Maybe that's why he had to kiss her before he left. To make sure the feelings and emotions between them were real and not just some figment of his imagination — just in case he didn't have the chance again.

But there was no going back to Aurora now. He had made his choice and Aurora would always despise him now, especially after how he had left her. She didn't understand that killing Herald was the only way to save her, to save everyone. And yet that kiss still haunted his mind…

He threw more kindling on the fire, igniting the flame so that the wood crackled and sparks burst out into the air before extinguishing themselves on the sand. There was no sign of Radar but he started eating anyway, his hunger beating out his manners. He heard voices approaching and froze in mid-bite. Without a second thought, he threw the rest of his water from his bottle onto the fire, extinguishing the flame. Boreas grabbed the helmet, shoved it back on his head and grabbed the gun that was stuffed in his holster. He hid behind a great oak tree and held his breath as the footsteps advanced, the voices louder and clearer.

"It'll be ok, Sansa." A man's baritone voice said soothingly. "It's going to be alright. Sing that last verse again for daddy, sweetheart."

A child whimpered in pain as she tried to sing a verse of a song Boreas remembered from his childhood called *The Open Window*.

"I ran to the open window
To behold my dreams there
To behold my daddy there
To behold my mommy there."

The child cried again with such anguish that Boreas's heart sunk. They continued to approach and he heard what appeared to be a strangled sob in the father's voice as he tried to be strong for his child. Boreas peeked out, still holding the gun close to his chest, his finger on the trigger. There was a man of about 6 foot 3 inches in height with broad shoulders that was holding a plank where a girl of about 5 years old rested. Her leg was bloody and a badly wrapped bandage secured it to the plank. A boy of about nine years old with a bandage covering his forehead held the other end of the wooden plank.

All of a sudden the boy whined, "Dad, I can't go any further."

"You have to, Steven. For Sansa's sake. She needs us now more than ever."

"Mom wouldn't make us walk this far."

"Your Mother can't help us now."

With that, the Father stopped walking, falling to his knees and throwing his arms around his daughter as pain erupted from him with a sob. The boy, Steven, couldn't watch and turned, spotting the lingering smoke and then the campsite. He ran over to the abandoned fire and saw the beans still cooking. He cried out to his Father who transformed instantly into a protective father and ran over to where his son was standing. Steven held up the beans excitedly, "They are still warm. Dad, can we eat them?"

"Odd that someone would be here in the middle of the woods at this time of night." The Father said suspiciously, clutching his knife, the elongated blade sparkled in the moonlight. Boreas held his breath to stop himself from giving away his location. For all these people knew, whoever abandoned the campsite had not lingered. Boreas now wished Radar hadn't run off into the wilderness. They could have eaten and been on their way by now.

After spying no enemy, the Father nodded to his son to distribute the beans. He went over to Sansa and tried to feed her. She ate a little and then shook her head that she couldn't eat anymore, she was in so much pain. Boreas kept staring at her leg, bleeding heavily and knew they must have been hit by the wave of bombs. These people were victims of the Inspector's wrath and his effort to try to smoke out the rebellion in the rocks. They were innocent and that young girl was never going to make it through the night — not without a doctor's care. Boreas quickly opened up the map in search of something within their proximity to provide them with medical care and shelter. The nearest hospital on the map was 20 miles away in a town called Hanover. The only other place to provide help was Plymouth Incarnate.

Boreas pulled the helmet down further over his head and took a deep breath, now cradling the gun in his arms. He entered the campsite and the man jumped up, brandishing the knife, ready to protect his family.

"Officer!" the father called out, shoving Steven behind him in a protective stance.

"What are you doing out here?" Boreas cried out, trying to sound authoritative. Are you coming from Ainsborough?"

"Yes… we didn't mean to run, but my children….please we can't go back there. Do you know of a hospital or a doctor nearby? My little girl needs help. She has lost a lot of blood."

Boreas cautiously peeked over at the little girl, dirt and blood streaked across her forehead and ash mixed with her light blond braids. Her eyes were the biggest eyes he had ever seen, with long lashes. She looked at him pleading and Boreas' heart sank. She was in too much pain, falling in and out of consciousness.

The Father eyed him curiously, seeing his uniform, but sensing his age.

"You're a little young to be an officer, aren't you?"

Boreas stammered, "Umm, I'm an officer in training." He fixed the helmet closer over his neck. "Look, the closest hospital is in Hanover and you are miles from there. But there's another place that can help. Do you know where Storm King Mountain is?"

The father's eyes grew wide as the moon reflected off his eyes. "Yes I know it. Who is there that can help us?"

Boreas couldn't believe what he was doing. The look of that child defeated all sense of reason. "It is imperative that I can trust you with this secret. Do you swear on the life of your children that you will not betray this trust?"

The Father nodded over and over again, "I swear, just please help my children!"

Boreas searched the desperate face of the father and finally said, "There is a safe haven within the mountain. There are people there with medical training who can help your children."

The Father started to thank him but Boreas didn't let him speak and instead said, "The problem is the entrance is hidden. I will need to come with you, give me a minute to collect my things."

Boreas ran to the opposite side of the clearing to grab his backpack. When he rounded the corner he was knocked off his feet by Radar.

"Boreas has a heart after all! I am truly touched by that scene there."

Boreas scrambled back to his feet, wiping the dirt from his hands, and exclaimed, "I have to help them."

Radar shook his head at him and said, "The Inspector will kill more children like that little girl if you turn back now. Do you seriously think that the High Magistrate is going to let you out of her sight after you return to the Safe Haven? This is your only chance to kill the Inspector. Think of the greater good."

Boreas closed his eyes and knew that Radar was right. All the hatred he had channeled was still there, burning strong in his veins. But at that moment the wind swept through the trees, and he stared as a leaf fluttered down from a nearby branch, and landed on Sansa's heart – so young and innocent, and on the brink of death. He watched as the leaf got swept up by the wind once again, taking flight, beckoning him back toward the safe haven.

"I can't let her fall victim to the Inspector. Not while I can still save her."

Radar's beady red eyes were mad with rage. "You can head back there alone, but one thing is clear. You are not ready to kill Herald. You have to make up your mind and go all in, because if you don't and you falter – then you will fail."

"I won't fail."

"You will… and remember this. When the Inspector finds you, and he will find you, he does not hesitate. He will execute you like he did your father."

Boreas glared at Radar. "I'm sure you'll be happy to stand by and watch."

Radar grimaced, reliving the memory of when David was executed. "You don't understand. It was because I stood by and watched that I am haunted by his death even today. His blood runs through yours. I made a pact that I'll help you and now I need to save you from yourself."

Before Boreas could react, Radar knocked the gun out of Boreas's hand and tackled him to the ground. Boreas's face was dug deep into the dirt, his helmet flying off his head. They fought for the weapon until Radar put Boreas in a head lock, pointing the weapon directly at Boreas's head.

"Now," he replied victoriously, "you are coming with me!"

Boreas was struggling to breathe and was about to give in when he heard a loud bump and Radar tumbled off him. Boreas quickly came up for air and there was Radar lying unconscious on the ground, and the Father stood towering over him with a branch in his hands.

The Father picked up the gun and pointed to Boreas's scar, exposed now that his helmet was off. "I know who you are."

Boreas couldn't talk his way out of this one with the evidence staring the man in the face. He wiped blood from his lip and said, "So, you're going to trade my life for your daughter's, I imagine."

The Father continued to point the gun and said, "Help me carry Sansa to your safe haven, like you promised me you would before this man stopped you. I won't give you up to the Inspector."

Boreas stared at him curiously, "Why would you do that?"

The stranger lowered his weapon and turned back to where his children were waiting. "I have my own motives for wanting to keep you alive, Boreas. And you can call me Sampson."

✬ ✬ ✬

Boreas nearly slipped on the muddy path near the creek as they trudged along back in the direction of the Safe Haven. Sampson looked back over his shoulder, still trying to figure Boreas out. It was bitterly cold and Sansa's bare hand was outstretched. Boreas took it in his and tried to warm it up.

"You'll be at the safe haven before you know it," Boreas smiled down at the angelic face. Her eyes fluttered open and she smiled back at him.

"What is it like?" she asked in her soft-spoken voice.

Boreas thought about Plymouth Incarnate, about living within Stone King Mountain, about the Great Books and the rebellion. But only one image shone out in his mind – a face. "Well, there is a girl there who can shoot fire and light out of her hands. She is the Goddess of Dawn and is on a quest with a boy and a 30 foot giant named Otus."

"A giant?" Sansa giggled.

"There are no such thing as giants," Steven countered, unimpressed.

Boreas laughed. "I didn't believe it at first either. But they are on a quest to stop the Geometric Storm. They are not your typical heroes or who you'd expect to save the world."

"I want to meet the giant," Sansa said with her eyes wide open. "I thought my daddy was a giant, but he's not 30 feet tall."

Sampson laughed, helping his daughter over a ledge. "No, I'm not that tall."

"What about the boy?" Steven asked. "What powers does he have?"

Boreas froze, looking up to the stars, but they were blocked by a veil of gray clouds overhead.

"The boy was supposed to be the God of the North Wind. But he wasn't cut out for the role."

Sampson interrupted, "I don't know about that."

Boreas turned to him curiously. "What do you mean?"

Sampson fixed a blanket around Sansa as they continued marching onwards through the sludge, putting a little ragdoll in her arms.

"I know someone else who denied his destiny. Said he wasn't meant to lead, that he wasn't strong enough to do any good in this world. He was waiting for someone else to stand up but no one did."

"So what happened?" Steven asked, holding onto his father's every word.

"Well, he didn't have any giants or powers or anything like that. But one day when the Inspector was speaking in Candlewick, this young man waited for the Inspector to finish speaking and while everyone else applauded and cheered, he climbed up onto a rock, standing opposite the Inspector. He just stood there. Not cheering, not clapping. He just stood there on that rock, taking a silent stand against the Common Good. And do you know what happened? People saw him. They saw him, and they watched and they wondered. And just from that solitary peaceful act, other people climbed on the rock with him. Others began to have strength to stand beside him and behind him. Before long, more than half of the audience was standing with this man who hadn't said a single word, hadn't shouted, hadn't fought and hadn't killed. He just made a statement that he would not stand with the Inspector."

"Who did this?" Sansa asked excitedly. "Was it you, Daddy?"

Sampson shook his head. "No, it wasn't me. It was your Uncle David who stood up against the Inspector. Your Uncle, David Xiomy."

Boreas stopped walking, thinking he misheard what Sampson had said. He put down Sansa and lifted his face, staring intently into Sampson's eyes that held his gaze, confirming the truth in his mind. Fear crept up Boreas's spine as he whispered, "You shouldn't have told me that!"

He ran as fast as he could, his heart feeling like it would burst out of his chest. He collapsed only when he hit the river blocking his path, the water rushing and tumbling over rocks and boulders, like his life that was tumbling out of control. He bent down and put his head between his legs. This wasn't happening. He had cousins. An uncle. All who the Inspector would destroy if they knew their identity… knew they were related. Boreas had turned on his friends and family once. What would happen if he did it again?

Sampson caught up to him, knelt down beside him and tried putting his arm around Boreas who immediately shrugged it off. "You just put yourself and your family in jeopardy." Boreas said, his fingers subconsciously rubbing the pain in his arm, that ever present reminder of the evil that lurked within him.

"You are my family, Boreas."

"No!" Boreas shouted. "Henry Stockington is my father. And if the Inspector finds out who you are…"

The water continued to rush on in front of them. The sun was beginning its ascent for the Awakened Hour. They were running out of time. Boreas looked up at Storm Mountain ahead of him, of the light reflecting reds and yellows off its towering peak.

"I ran away from the safe haven to kill Inspector Herald," Boreas admitted. "He forced me to betray my friends and I almost killed my brother. If it wasn't for Aurora…"

Boreas buried his face in his hands, trying to block out those devastating memories.

Sampson stood up and gazed outwards at the foaming swells of the river. "We've all done things we regret. But you have to forgive yourself and those who have wronged you in order to move forward."

Boreas looked up into the horizon… at Storm King Mountain that beckoned him onwards but his heart was clenched tight. He had no room for forgiveness.

Sampson held out his hand and Boreas took it, rising to his feet. They walked back to the kids in silence. Steven ran into his father's arms and Boreas checked on Sansa who was paler and more fragile than ever. He hoped he could save her. Why did he risk it all to save one life? Why didn't he listen to Radar and stay on their mission? Now he knew that he had more people who could suffer because of him. More people that the Inspector could use against him.

Sansa opened her eyes and smiled up at him, hero-worship in her eyes. She reached out her hand toward Boreas, and he clasped it tightly in his, protectively. He looked up at Storm King Mountain, her only hope. He was going to get her there. He had to.

Sampson watched this interaction with a smile and leaned down, kissing Sansa softly on the forehead. He picked Steven up and placed him swiftly on top of his shoulders.

"Sansa, Steven," he said. "I want you to meet your cousin, Boreas."

Chapter 13

Preparations

Plymouth Incarnate was in evacuation mode and no longer safe. Babs and Mrs. Xiomy were occupied with leading the colonists into the remaining submarines that were ready to take off to escape into the Atlantic Ocean. They would need to travel the "Golden Route" to San Francisco, journeying south around Cape Horn that would lead to the Pacific Ocean and ultimately to San Francisco Bay where the protest colony was located, led by Babs's parents.

Aurora had asked Babs why she and Eileen hadn't travelled with their parents out west and Babs had explained that, at the time, it had been too dangerous for her parents to travel with two young children. They believed their children would be safer at Plymouth Tartarus... unfortunately, they were wrong.

Babs hugged Aurora tightly, "I'm excited to see them again."

Aurora held her friend, a part of her wishing she too was going to be reunited with her parents. Aurora didn't know if she would ever see them again with her mom working as the ambassador for Inspector Herald and her father imprisoned somewhere out west. In the back of her mind, she wondered if her father was in a prison near where they were heading...near Hyperborea.

The last of 10 submarine doors was ready to be shut and Fawn said a blessing, wishing all her colonists a safe journey. She then turned to her group, the Red Herrings, which consisted of herself, Otus, Jonathan, Aurora, and the Professor. Though the Professor ranted and raved that he was too weak and blind and no longer needed on this mission, Fawn thought otherwise. She said that he was the only one who knew where Hyperborea was and since he had also outsmarted the Inspector before, he might come in handy to get through this alive.

Mrs. Xiomy smacked the dirt off of her hands after loading the last piece of equipment into the submarine, with Otus's help.

"Now you big oaf of a giant... you take care of my Aurora, you hear me?"

Otus nodded, looking teary-eyed that their group was separating. He bent down and Mrs. Xiomy gave him a kiss on the cheek. "Now, no tears, Otus. We'll see each other in Hyperborea. And I'll bring some crazy West Coast protestors along with me."

Fawn held out her hand to Mrs. Xiomy. "Until we meet in Hyperborea," she said solemnly.

Mrs. Xiomy took it and clutched it firmly. "I hate what you did, Fawn, and I don't know if I can ever forgive you...but on this quest Boreas has become like a son to me. I promise you that he will get his powers. The Inspector is not going to kill him like he did David."

Fawn smiled fondly at her old friend. "Since when did you become the optimistic one?"

Mrs. Xiomy smiled. "Since I started believing in magic."

Aurora, dressed in jeans, a black sweater and a woolen hat on top of her head, slid down from Otus's shoulders and hugged her beloved teacher.

"I can't believe I am going on this part of the journey without you," she said, hugging her teacher tightly. "I don't know if I can do this without you and Boreas."

Mrs. Xiomy kissed Aurora on the top of the head. "I believe in you, Aurora, but you need to be strong. I fear that there are dark days ahead of us. But you are the light in the darkness. Never forget that."

"But what if the darkness gets too great?" Aurora asked, clutching onto her backpack as fear settled in, recalling how she had nearly lost control when using her powers against Boreas. "What if I can't control my powers?"

The submarine engines revved up and Mrs. Xiomy raised her hand to signal to the Captain that she was coming. She turned back around, her blonde curls swishing against her face. She smiled at Aurora. "Remember, even a seedling needs some darkness to grow, Aurora. But it is through the warmth of the sun that it flourishes."

Mrs. Xiomy climbed down into the submarine and when she disappeared from sight, the hatch closed with a metallic bang as Aurora and the other Red Herrings waved to the colonists…all hoping that they would meet again in Hyperborea.

Fawn addressed the remaining group.

"Now that the submarines are set, Otus and our group will cause a diversion to lead the Common Good Army away from the safe haven and out west toward Hyperborea. The Great Secretary and a few other brave men have volunteered to stay behind to act as backup on the ground if Otus gets caught on the enemy's radar before we have a decent head start."

"Or the Common Good Army will blast us out of the sky," the Professor chimed in cheerfully.

"Well, that's why we have the Goddess of Dawn on our side," Jonathan said as his blue eyes beamed at Aurora. She gulped and tried to stop her hands from shaking. *No pressure*, she thought. She looked up at Otus who sensed her fear and winked at her encouragingly.

"At least we would go out with a bang."

Jonathan walked over, grabbed his jacket off the chair and covered his blond hair with a black wool hat. Aurora still felt strange being so near him and guilty about her kiss with Boreas. As if reading her thoughts, he asked, "Are you thinking about Boreas?"

Aurora shook her head. "No, I was actually thinking about you."

"That would be a first," Jonathan said, digging his hands into his pockets. "Ever since that kiss, I hadn't seen you away from him."

Alarmed, Aurora cried out, "Kiss...what kiss!?"

Jonathan stared at her, confused and hurt. "The kiss we shared after the trial...I didn't think you would have forgotten."

Aurora turned a deep shade of red, so embarrassed; she couldn't believe she almost gave away her secret. "No...no I haven't forgotten. I just thought you may have wanted to forget."

She picked up her backpack and hastily started looking for her gloves, trying to avoid eye contact.

"I don't want to forget," he said sweetly, taking the backpack out of her hands and placing it on the floor. She stared awe-struck as he took her hands in his and blew on them to keep them warm. "I'm sorry I ran away afterwards. You were the first girl I kissed since Hattie and I broke up. It just felt different."

Different? From Hattie? Of course he would compare their kisses. Hattie probably kissed him so perfectly while Aurora's kiss was sub-par.

"I can't wait to see you use your powers again."

His lips kissed her hands and she felt weak at the knees. Why did he always make her like this? She felt such a conglomerate of feelings...confused...nervous...nauseous...

The signal was given and Aurora was relieved for the distraction as everyone was lifted up into Otus's overall pockets. Jonathan of course choosing the pocket she was in...she felt such a weight on her shoulders. Why was she surprised that Jonathan compared her to Hattie? Hattie with the perfect body. Of course, Hattie's greatest pleasure was torturing Aurora in school, calling her Fatty Alvarez and throwing punch on her at the Spring Formal. Even after everything Aurora had been through, and even now that she was the Goddess of Dawn, she still couldn't measure up to Hattie in Jonathan's eyes.

She didn't have much time to dwell on that depressing thought as Otus shouted gleefully "Hang on, everyone!"

He burst like a bullet through the back corridor running as fast as he could and threw himself against the back of the wall, which crumbled like sawdust around them. He flew up into the bright morning sky and Aurora had to shield her eyes to adjust to the brightness of the sun. The crisp, cool wind hit Aurora's face like icicles piercing her flesh. She gripped the overall pocket rim tighter, since it had been a while since she had travelled by giant. She closed her eyes as vertigo overwhelmed her and she heard Fawn scream out, "Otus, continue forward."

The Great Secretary was giving her instructions through an ear piece, relaying the news that the Common Good Army were remobilizing and following their trail. The submarines were underway now that the Common Good were distracted, chasing after Otus. Everything was going as plan, but just when they were about to move past the mountain, Aurora sensed something was wrong. She opened her eyes and in the distance saw a large bird racing toward them. But it wasn't a bird, it was a F22 fighter plane.

"Otus, look out," she cried out frantically.

A fighter plane was narrowing in on Otus's southwest side. Otus did a summersault in mid-air and made a nose dive toward the ocean. He belly-flopped and everyone held on tight as they were submerged into the water. The bullets missing their aim as Otus dove to lower altitudes. Aurora and the others held their breath and then he jumped back up into the air, nearly face-to-face with the fighter plane. Otus snatched it and sent it sailing down into the water, the pilot parachuting out. More planes were speeding in their direction. Fawn screamed into the microphone that they were being surrounded.

"We need back-up!"

On command, Aurora spotted machine guns peeking out from the Storm Mountain bunker where the Great Secretary and his men were stationed. They hit two planes, nicking their wings and causing them to fly right into each other with a boom that caused Aurora's ears to ring. A third plane spun to avoid being hit by the onslaught of bullets. To Aurora's horror, it released a missile that raced straight toward the bunker and Otus was too far away to stop it.

The bunker exploded, flames appearing where machine guns and their friends once stood.

"Great Secretary! Great Secretary!" Fawn screamed into her ear piece. Only static echoed back.

Otus went into retreat mode, sailing high up into the sky but was met by another of the Common Good planes.

Jonathan screamed, "Aurora, use your powers!"

Aurora attempted to summon the power of Dawn but nothing happened! She was frozen stiff with fear as the plane headed toward them. It was aiming its missile at them, ready to strike. Aurora stood there, her hands outstretched – completely powerless.

✵ ✵ ✵

Boreas spotted the planes soaring above them and ordered Sampson and the children to hide in a grove of trees to avoid being seen. Sampson and Steven immediately followed suit and lowered Sansa down quickly, Steven huddling in his father's embrace. Jets whirled above them and they could hear the sounds of bullets shooting and then a huge explosion sounded.

"What the hell was that?" He asked as they ran, hunching close to the ground to avoid being seen.

Sampson pointed in the distance where smoke was curling into the sky.

Sampson stayed with the children while Boreas ran toward the explosion, recognizing the crevice in the side of Storm King Mountain where Plymouth Incarnate's bunker was located. The Jet plane's missile had a direct hit and one of the two machine guns was up in flames. He saw the Great Secretary who was brutally injured. Boreas ran to his side and dragged him away from the fire, staying hidden as Common Good officers infiltrated the bunker.

Boreas watched in anguish as the soldiers found two more bodies of men from Plymouth Incarnate who had also been manning the bunker. Then, none other than Inspector Herald's key henchman, Officer Woolchuck, entered the bunker. Boreas felt anger surge through him, a part of him wondering if the Inspector was there as well.

Officer Woolchuck kicked at one of the bodies to make sure the man was dead.

"Search for survivors. Bring the bodies back to the base for identification. Perhaps we can get their families to talk, if there are any."

"What about the giant?" Another officer asked.

"We'll have him down in a matter of minutes. Foolish of them to retreat the way they did, it is almost as if they wanted us to follow them."

Boreas felt his heart freeze in his chest. Otus was in trouble?

The Great Secretary was stirring, wincing in pain as he whispered, "High Magistrate is in trouble. Your friends are with her."

Another plane was swarming in to attack as Boreas looked up to see Otus high overhead, with a plane heading straight at him. Boreas watched helplessly as Otus turned and took the brunt of the bullets. Why wasn't Aurora using her powers?

Boreas's mind was racing, realizing he had to help them, but not knowing how. The soldiers were blocking the machine gun that was still operational. The Great Secretary, like he was reading his thoughts, pulled something out of his pocket.

"A decoy," he whispered. "Made by the Professor."

Boreas nodded in understanding. He took the ball and tossed it as far as he could. It exploded into the air with fireworks and Officer Woolchuck and the other soldiers ran toward the diversion with guns raised.

"Great Secretary," Boreas whispered. "It worked!"

The Great Secretary smiled, his eyes rolling backwards, breathing his last breath.

Boreas ran on instinct, jumped through fire and smoke to the one standing gun. He held his breath, putting his right eye through the view finder and pointed upwards, following the compass navigator as it zoomed in on the fighter plane. It was moving closer to Otus. Boreas pulled the trigger hard with his finger and an onslaught of bullets swarmed out of his gun, inching higher and higher into the sky toward the plane. It hit the wing but it was enough to set it off course and let Otus fling it wildly out of the sky. Otus took off due west and Boreas was shoved down by a strong hand that kept him down. Boreas attempted to fight but then realized it was Sampson who held him down.

"Stay down! Now listen to me. The Common Good soldiers are coming and if you want to stay alive and keep your friends alive, you do what I say. There's only one way."

Sampson took his knife out from his pocket and held it to Boreas's neck.

"There is one person the Inspector wants more than your giant."

He looked directly at Boreas, the blade glistening in the moonlight.

"And my daughter is running out of time."

Chapter 14

The Capture

Sampson held the knife against Boreas's throat as they were surrounded by Common Good soldiers, guns pointed at their heads. Officer Woolchuck strutted into the middle of the circle.

'"What is the meaning of this?" He cried out, wiping blood off his gloves. "Who are you?"

Sampson replied, "I just caught this young man with that machine gun. I believe he may be the one you are seeking."

Officer Woolchuck stared at the stranger and then his eyes lowered to Boreas, still dressed in Common Good attire.

"What young man? What are you talking about?"

Sampson's eyes sparkled, digging the knife a little deeper into Boreas's throat, exposing the scar that ran the length of his neck.

"David Xiomy's boy."

Woolchuck dropped the clipboard he was carrying. He immediately stepped forward and looked into the face of the boy who he had last seen in the dungeon where the Inspector had administered the Soul Extractor serum. It looked like the pain in the ass with the black hair and the cold eyes, but in the darkness it was hard to be 100% sure and the Inspector could not be disturbed for only a guess. The reward had been broadcasted that morning and already people were calling off the hook saying they spotted some poor kid who resembled the description. But there was one fool proof way to know.

"Show me his arm," he demanded, still holding the gun in his hand, pointed toward the stranger.

One of the militia men approached and rolled up Boreas's sleeve. The young man kicked the man in the shin and tried to struggle out of the head lock, but Sampson dug the knife further into his neck to stop him. The guard rubbed his leg and then irritably held up Boreas's arm where the green stain marked his vein.

A rush of adrenaline swept through his body as Woolchuck quickly called into the radio. "Inspector Herald. Are you there?"

The Inspector's voice cackled back, "You better have a good reason to interrupt this mission again."

"We have Boreas Stockington."

"You have who?"

Breathlessly, Woolchuck continued, "Boreas Stockington. It is confirmed. The other thing is a ruse. He's not with the giant. The boy is right here. He has the green mark on his arm."

The silence was palpable as they waited for the Inspector to respond. Officer Woolchuck held his breath, knowing this meant maybe a promotion for him or at least more credibility in the Inspector's eyes. He kept blinking to make sure that the young man in front of him was not just a mirage. Finally the Inspector spoke, "Bring Boreas Stockington to me immediately."

The Capture

Officer Woolchuck beamed and relayed the order to his men. They grabbed Boreas, handcuffed him and then he approached the strange man who had delivered this gift right to his doorstep.

"You have done a valiant and noble thing, sir," Woolchuck said shaking Sampson's hand. "You will be justly rewarded for this."

"I don't care about the money," Sampson declared frigidly. "I just want my daughter to be seen to right away. She is badly wounded."

"We will take care of her at the base. Show my men where she is and they will put you both in the helicopter. Everyone move out."

Officer Woolchuck dragged the handcuffed prisoner onto the helicopter, he was not going to let Boreas Stockington out of his sight. Nothing was going to go wrong on his watch this time. Sampson and his kids were also put onboard. Woolchuck signaled to the pilot to start the helicopter. He didn't remember the pilot having purplish/blue lips but then again, it was very cold in the mountains. They started their ascent toward the base...after all, the Inspector was waiting.

✮ ✮ ✮

Aurora watched the remaining planes turn and fly away from them, smoke trailing behind as the only evidence that a plane had been positioned to strike only a few seconds before.

"What happened?" Jonathan cried out. "Why are they retreating?"

Fawn looked down at the bunker, trying to still get a hold of the Great Secretary. "Someone helped us from the ground. It must have been one of our allies."

"Not just any ally," the Professor said slowly. "The Inspector would only have stopped the attack for one person."

"And who is that?!" Jonathan exclaimed, sick of riddles.

"Boreas," Fawn stammered, sinking down into the corner of the pocket.

"That's right. The Inspector wants him more than the rest of us right now. Boreas is the immediate threat, being the son of David Xiomy. He wants to make an example of him. The rest of us he knows he can deal with once Boreas is out of the picture."

Otus looked down at the others, his face distraught as he and all of them realized that their plan had backfired. The wind swirled around them as the sun loomed overhead. Aurora snapped out of her state of shock and couldn't believe her moment of weakness. Jonathan couldn't look her in the eye. She felt like such a failure. She was the one who was supposed to save them and she had acted like a scared child. Boreas was in the hands of the Inspector once again. And this time he wouldn't be coming out alive.

"We have to rescue him," she called out suddenly, finding her voice once again.

Fawn shook her head, "It's impossible. We don't have the manpower to take on their army. It would be a suicide mission and they are most likely watching us right now. They would be tracing our every move."

The Professor fixed his goggles, wiping the vapor off the lenses, and looked up at the giant. "I can see only one way. We have to move forward toward Hyperborea."

"But Boreas will be dead!" Aurora cried out. "Then there is no mission. The point of Hyperborea is for him to get his powers. What's the point of going without him?"

Aurora felt tears streaming out of her eyes. This was her fault. She had caused this.

Fawn held Aurora in her arms, "You have to have faith that Boreas will get out alive."

Aurora laughed at the implausibility of that. Faith that the Inspector would have a change of heart? Faith that some other being was going to help Boreas escape? Faith in who and in what? And then she looked down to see her cross dangling over her chest, sparkling in the sunlight. It reminded Aurora of Eileen and her undying faith. And then Aurora had that feeling again. That feeling that Eileen was still with them, though her body was leagues under the ocean. She clasped the golden necklace that still hung around her neck, and took a deep breath, the wind sounding through her ears like bells ringing. *I have faith in you, Boreas*, she thought, hoping that faith truly could move mountains. How she wished she had the same faith in herself.

Otus didn't wait for the others to make up their mind; he took a giant leap into the air, catching everyone off guard.

"Professor," he called out as they were up in the sky with their heads covered in the clouds, "we will need to make a stop first. At this point in the game, we will need all the help we can get. Even if that means a family reunion."

Chapter 15

The Ambassadors' High Summit

The helicopter landed in the backyard of a fancy castle that the Inspector had confiscated for his army base. It had once been a venue where marriage ceremonies had been held with beautiful views overlooking the cascading mountains and the sapphire Hudson River sparkling in the golden sun. Now it acted as an army base with the gardens the scene of make-shift obstacle courses and the castle as room and board for the forces. A thick black electrical fence had been built around the perimeter of the premises and the only way in and out was by air.

Boreas stared in awe at the magnificent structure on the eastern coastline of the United States of the Common Good. In his amazement, he nearly forgot that here housed his bitter enemy who had his life at his mercy.

Once the helicopter landed, a medic ran toward them and quickly saw to Sansa who was unconscious after losing a lot of blood. Boreas hoped that at least Sansa would survive, even if he didn't. Steven stared at Boreas from afar, wondering what was happening, and held onto his father's hand for courage. Boreas hoped that he could get some of that courage too, especially since what lay within that castle was anything but reassuring.

Boreas was thrust into the hands of a burly man with a wrestler physique and a long gnarly beard. He recognized the man as the former wrestler, Billy Goat. Boreas had to stop himself from gaping at the famous wrestler who used to be plastered on his walls when he was a kid.

"Billy Goat!" Boreas whispered, as he was dragged off the helicopter. "You retired early to join the Common Good Army?"

Billy Goat tugged on his beard, aggravated he had been recognized. "Recruited, kid. Glad to hear my fans still remember me. Even if it is protest scum like you."

Billy Goat led Boreas through a gated, gold-trimmed double door, entering a truly majestic setting with a huge crackling fire burning in an old fashioned brick fireplace and a glistening chandelier hung from a high paneled ceiling with each panel depicting a beautiful painting, similar to the Sistine Chapel. These paintings were not of biblical stories but instead scenes from the downfall of the Protest movement 15 years earlier. There was a panel showing the defeat of the Last Straw Protest and to Boreas's dismay, there was even a panel depicting the execution of David Xiomy...his real father. Boreas looked away with a knot in his stomach.

This place was not what Boreas would have imagined for an army base. It more resembled a resort with butlers and maids bustling around a nearby ballroom, tending to the needs of men and women dressed in their finery.

He looked up at Billy Goat and asked, "Who are all those people?"

The Goat laughed, saliva shooting out into Boreas's eye. "The World Ambassadors, of course. This is the high summit meeting."

Boreas wanted to wipe the man's spit off his face but couldn't since he was handcuffed. He peered into the ballroom, observing the World Ambassadors, and then his eyes rested on none other than Mrs. Alvarez, Aurora's mother. Her green eyes met his but quickly danced back to the people to whom she was conversing. Boreas had forgotten that Aurora's mom was now on the Inspector's side.

A trumpet sounded and suddenly at the top of the grand ruby-red staircase, stood none other than Inspector Herald. He was dressed in a tuxedo that covered his burned arms and neck. Boreas was completely thrown off guard because even his face looked like he had undergone plastic surgery to hide his deformities. His bald scalp was covered with a top hat. Boreas would hardly have recognized him except his familiar coal black eyes dug into his own with such hatred. He smiled down and waved as the group burst into applause. With a gesture, he quieted the crowd.

"Welcome to all our Common Good World Ambassadors! I am so pleased that you were able to join us for our annual world summit to discuss ways to continue the peace and prosperity that we have cultivated in the United States of the Common Good."

The room again erupted in applause as Boreas attempted to spot Mrs. Alvarez again in the crowd. She had retreated to the far corner of the room, her gloved hands clutching her green emerald dress, peering anxiously in his direction.

"Before our festivities begin, I wanted to first congratulate our own Officer Woolchuck for capturing the notorious rebel, Boreas Stockington."

Officer Woolchuck stepped forward, waving to cheers from the audience and nearly tripped over his own feet. Boreas had to stop himself from laughing at this ridiculous spectacle.

"We will work together to see what sentence this boy will receive, especially now that we have been informed of his actual lineage. He is a descendant of the notorious IMAM."

Boos erupted from the audience and Boreas just wished he could disappear. He stood firm and remembered what Sampson had told him about David Xiomy. He had stood strong against the Inspector.

If he's going to kill me, let me at least try to stand tall like my father, he thought, hoping for strength.

The Inspector put his hand up, silencing the crowd, and continued, "More updates will come from our Press Secretary, Analise Jones. She will be distributing room materials and conducting interviews throughout the course of the day. Thank you. The IDEAL has spoken."

"The IDEAL has spoken." The Public replied in unison.

As soon as the spectacle was over, several of the ambassadors came over to him to inspect him, like he was some inhuman monster in their midst. Some of the dignitaries yelled obscenities at him, jeering at him, calling him IMAM's bastard. He felt alone against the world and was about to retaliate and curse back when Billy Goat dragged Boreas into an elevator.

"Thanks Billy Goat," Boreas muttered.

The Goat snickered. "Don't thank me yet, kid. You got bigger problems than a mob of angry, rich ambassadors."

As they ascended to the second floor Boreas knew who would be waiting for him on the other side of that sliding door.

The door slithered open and Billy Goat threw Boreas down in a genuflect position, his face planted against the black suede shoes of the Inspector.

"So we meet again, Boreas Stockington." The Inspector's voice was the same cold and raspy voice from his nightmares.

Boreas felt the pain radiate in his arm as the hatred flowed through his veins. Despite his hatred, he needed to play for time. Sansa's and his own life depended on it.

He looked up and smiled. "Why, Inspector, you really shouldn't have gone to all this trouble. This is definitely an upgrade from the last time I had the pleasure of your company."

"I am so glad you like it," the Inspector laughed, playing along. "Come, walk with me. Everyone leave us."

"But, Inspector..." Billy Goat interceded.

"I said, leave us."

Billy Goat grabbed Boreas by the shoulders and lifted him in one swift motion to his feet. He looked up at the Inspector as if he was waiting for him to change his mind and then descended unwillingly down the stairs.

The Inspector sauntered down the hallway of the second floor and Boreas followed suit wishing he could get his hands out of those handcuffs and attack the Inspector like he had originally planned. How his plans had backfired. The hallway was lit by sconces hanging on the walls and in between each one was a painting that ran nearly the entire length of the wall and loomed from floor to ceiling. The ceiling gave the illusion of a night sky with stars glistening down on them and Boreas couldn't believe how real it appeared. The Inspector paused in front of a painting halfway down the red carpeted hall and Boreas stood beside him looking at the painting that stood before them. It was a painting of the Towers of Freedom, standing tall amidst a city skyline.

"They were a magnificent architectural accomplishment," he said somberly, putting his hand on the oil canvas. "Beautiful and majestic and representative of what our country stood for. And you know what happened, Boreas? They were destroyed by religious fanatics. Killing thousands of innocent people in the process."

He strolled to the next painting. "This subway car was blown up by a religious fanatic who had strapped a bomb to his chest, killing people during their morning commute. Two other bombs went off simultaneously that same day in different areas of the world."

He pointed to the next painting of a capital building. "That beautiful building was destroyed by people of the same religious sect. They believed in the same God but disagreed on one minute detail and ended up killing hundreds over it."

And then he paused in front of the final painting of the Last Straw Protest, "And this painting, well you know, is the Last Straw protest in St. Patrick's Cathedral in New York City. It was an honorable last stand by David Xiomy...a final 'peaceful' protest that still resulted in 15 people dead. Even he couldn't stop the violence. This act finally gave me the ammunition I needed to arrest him and stop him once and for all."

The Inspector turned to him and sneered, "Like father, like son."

Boreas bit his lip, staring at these pictures of his real father, awkwardly going down memory lane with the man who had killed him.

The Inspector smiled and licked his chipped front tooth. "I lived to witness all of these events, Boreas. Religion created so many hateful events, killing innocent people in the process. I was not the only one who demanded that something be done. Thousands of people turned to our side, to our political platform and we all agreed that something had to be done to stop the madness. Of course our methods may have been extreme, but it was for the benefit of the Common Good. And look at what we have now? Peace, prosperity, and all we ask is for people to obey us and the IDEAL. Ignorance is sometimes bliss, Boreas. You have to admit that there was a time that you didn't even question any of this. Not until you got thrown into this prophecy. Isn't that right?"

"You haven't mentioned all the horrific things you and your IDEAL have done these past 15 years," Boreas pointed out, "Like injecting people with the Soul Extractor serum to force them to do your bidding or blowing up hundreds of people in Plymouth Tartarus or imprisoning thousands so that you can keep your ignorant world alive. Very peaceful of you, Inspector."

The Inspector adjusted his tuxedo vest. He tilted his top hat ever so slightly to the side and looked at Boreas with respect. "You have changed a lot in two months."

"Well, I've gone through a lot in these past two months. Thanks to you."

The Inspector looked once more at the painting before proceeding down the hallway. Boreas took the cue and followed him reluctantly, not sure what else the Inspector wanted to show him as they advanced down a maze-like corridor to the final room. This one was barricaded with a code needed for entry. The Inspector entered in the code and the door swung open. Boreas took a deep breath, expecting a jail cell or sadistic torture chamber, but instead he walked into a giant library lined with shelves upon shelves of books. This room made the Candlewick library look like a child's bookshelf. Boreas had never seen so many books in his life and knew that Aurora would give her right hand to spend a day in this place.

"You see this section, Boreas," the Inspector pointed to the right where there were stacks of books in all different shades and colors and a fire blazing, beckoning visitors to curl up beside it with a book.

Boreas walked over and read the titles: "Robin Hood", "Moby Dick", "Ivanhoe", "To Kill a Mockingbird"...

"I don't believe these books were on the authorized reading list at school," Boreas sarcastically reminded the Inspector, since it was the Inspector's law that forbade the common person from reading books and frequenting libraries in the United States of the Common Good.

"These are stories about heroes." The Inspector said pulling one book out and coughing through a cloud of dust. "This one is Robin Hood. He would steal from the rich and give to the poor. Can you imagine a world like that?"

Boreas shrugged yet was intrigued to learn more about this man. Did he really exist?

The Inspector pulled the other one, "To Kill a Mockingbird. This one is about a man named Atticus Finch who was a lawyer and defended a black man in a time when there was widespread segregation and prejudice."

Boreas watched as the Inspector threw both of them into the fireplace.

"War and Peace...We don't need this one anymore. There is only peace for those who honor our cause."

He threw each book into the fireplace and Boreas watched horrified as the Inspector lit a match and held it up illuminating the red veins crisscrossed in his eyes.

"We don't need heroes in my world."

Boreas screamed out for him to stop but it fell on deaf ears as the Inspector flung the match into the fireplace, igniting the pages of the books and each and every one of them went up in flames. Boreas watched helpless as the fire grew bigger and bigger and the fire destroyed those pages, now lost forever.

The Inspector walked back toward Boreas and lifted his chin so that he was forced to look him in the eye.

"Heroes get burned, Boreas. Jesus died on the cross. Job lost his family and everything he had for God's graces. The Saints died and most suffered cruel and inhumane deaths. And your father was executed by my own hands. You don't have to be one of them."

Boreas looked defeated, the smoke encircling him as he stood in the hands of this madman.

"Do I have a choice, Inspector?"

The Inspector didn't answer, just turned and headed out of the library, his coat tails flailing behind him. Boreas took one last look at the fireplace, feeling like his own book was thrown into those flames. He closed his eyes tight and followed the Inspector out and away from the burning affront to heroes.

Chapter 16

Whispering Meadow

Otus made sure he was not being followed as he landed in Whispering Meadow. He put down his travelling companions who were desperately trying to muster up hope that Boreas would survive the Inspector's wrath. Aurora knew that their troubles were just brewing and that the Inspector and his army would eventually catch up to them.

Aurora collapsed onto the grass, still shaken from their run in with the fighter jets. She tried to forget about her powers, or lack thereof, when they were being attacked, but she couldn't forget her fear; the fear that had caused her to freeze up and not be able to help her friends. All of them would have suffered or died at the hand of the Common Good Army. If it hadn't been for Boreas getting captured... it was too much to think about.

They had been too close to death. All this talk of being a Goddess of Dawn had made Aurora nearly forget that she was still mortal. Despite the powers, she was still going to die. That fact had plagued her while they travelled over the countryside and still did when they finally landed in the middle of nowhere.

"Otus, can you explain why you took this detour away from Hyperborea?" The Professor asked, aggravated and swatted a mosquito that was sucking away at his neck. "Don't these damn insects ever hibernate?"

Otus was bouncing across the meadow as if he were doing a game of hopscotch. He looked to be searching for something in the tall thick grass. Aurora turned toward the Professor who merely shrugged and said, "Come on. This is not the weirdest thing he has ever done."

Aurora laughed, yanking a dandelion that has gone to seed out of the ground and blew on the white seeds that floated upwards, spiraling with the wind. The sun was rising in the East, in the direction they had fled from as they neared the Awakened Hour. Orange and yellow blotches bloomed across the sky as the moon emerged and darkness was fading ever more into the canvas.

The Professor's yelling brought Aurora back to their present predicament.

"You mad lunatic of a giant! Stop prancing around the meadow and tell us what you are looking for."

"I am looking for him," Otus finally cried out, twirling in gigantic circles forming crop circles in the meadow.

"Just tell us who 'he' is already!" Jonathan exclaimed, standing up and wiping the dirt off his pants.

Otus stared down at them and looked ashamed as he spit out, "I am looking for Ephialtes."

"Who is Ephialtes?" The Professor snickered, banging on the ground with his cane. "A groundhog?"

Otus shook his head and finally stuttered, "He is my brother."

Aurora couldn't believe her ears! She recalled Otus mentioning he had a brother, but all this time she thought he had died. She couldn't believe that Otus had never confided in her.

Fawn ran toward Otus and asked excitedly, "You have a brother? Another Giant lives on this planet?"

Tears fell from Otus's eyes that were like massive rain drops that plummeted toward the group. They dodged out of the way of the falling drops.

"Yes, I have a brother. But he is not like me at all. He is bad, like the giants you hear about in your fairytales. He is a troublemaker and doesn't want peace. But if you need to go against the army, then he is the giant that you should work with. He would know what to do."

Jonathan surveyed the meadow and finally asked the question that everyone was thinking. "Why are you looking in a meadow for a giant? Shouldn't he be in a forest or in caves or somewhere not as exposed?"

"After he made a big mess of things, Mrs. Taboo and I trapped him under the earth and put a great big boulder over the opening to keep him from starting trouble ever again. But I cannot find it."

Aurora dodged a falling tear, narrowly avoiding it. She reached into her bag and pulled out a scarf, to act as a tissue, and handed it to Otus. "Don't worry." She said, trying to comfort him and prevent getting flooded at the same time. "We'll help you find him, won't we?"

Everyone nodded enthusiastically and Otus thanked them, honking as he blew his nose into the scarf.

Aurora appeared confident as she comforted Otus, but really, she had no idea how they were going to locate one boulder in a huge meadow while the Common Good Army was so close behind them.

"We'll have to find this boulder quickly," Aurora said. "The Inspector always seems to be 10 steps ahead of us. We cannot take any chance of them catching us here with no chance of escape."

"Agreed," Fawn said. "Now Otus, what does this boulder look like?"

He scratched the stubble on his chin and looked up into the sky trying to trigger his memory. "It was a long time ago, but I believe it was a gray boulder with red spots. Mrs. Taboo said it looked like the rock had the chicken pox."

Fawn agreed to stay behind with the Professor and prepare camp while Jonathan teamed up with Aurora. Otus went solo. He could get the best perspective from high above so he jumped up high into the air to try to see the ground from a different angle.

Jonathan was walking at a brisk pace and Aurora was attempting to keep up with him while attempting to survey the ground in search of any large gray boulders with red spots. The grass was heavily over-grown with blades of grass and weeds up to their hips, making it difficult to tread through. If something was to be hidden, this was the place to ensure it never fell into the wrong hands.

"Why didn't he tell us sooner that he had a brother?" Jonathan exclaimed, aggravated and out of breath. "And not just any brother. A giant brother who could actually fight."

Aurora bent down seeing something with red spots, but then groaned when it was just a mushroom.

"Otus helped us fight the Inspector and took down those planes," Aurora said, coming to Otus's defense

"Yes, but imagine what a terrifying giant could do for us? He could help us overthrow the Inspector once and for all."

Aurora stared at him, dumbfounded. "I am not looking to over-throw anyone. I am just looking to get Otus to the Northern Lights and stop this Geometric Storm. That's all I plan to do."

"And you think that once you do that the Inspector will let you go back to your life the way it was? With your mom and dad all liv-ing happily ever after on Wishbone Avenue?"

Aurora stopped walking and wiped some sweat from her brow. Sadly, she stared out across the meadow, trying to picture Candlewick and her red and white house on Wishbone Avenue. She pictured her father reading his history magazines at the dining room table and quizzing her in the morning at breakfast on the Revolutionary War. How he loved Benjamin Franklin, George Washington and the founding fathers of the United States of America. It was like he was trying to instill those ideas of freedom of religion and speech in her at an early age, in direct contrast to the Common Good education which wanted everyone to conform to the IDEAL's beliefs.

"I know that I can't return to Wishbone Avenue." She finally said. "If we survive this and beat the Geometric Storm, I hope we can give people a choice again of what government they want. Almost like a new revolution. Nobody wants one person or the IDEAL telling them what to do or what to believe in. Isn't that what free will is all about, to have one's own ideas?"

Jonathan stood up beside her and looked into her eyes. "And what is your idea about me?"

Aurora paused, the tall grass tickling her arm. She yearned to tell him how she felt... how she had always felt about him. But that comment he made about being different from Hattie, she couldn't win.

"I think that we need to find this boulder." She quickly diverted her attention to the ground. Boulders were safer and easier to figure out than boys. She started to walk ahead of him when he took her hand in his and held her back.

"I think we need to re-ignite those powers of yours. And I think I know how to start."

He leaned in and pressed his lips against hers and she felt her body go numb and then warm all over. She put her arms around him, as he wrapped her in his embrace. She felt his tongue inside her mouth, massaging her own and she didn't want him to stop. All of a sudden his hands started to unzip her jacket and she pushed him off her.

"Um… what are you doing?"

He stared at her like she was being coy. "It's ok. In the tall grass no one will see us."

He leaned in again to kiss her and she couldn't forget what Boreas had said, about Jonathan just wanting her now that she was the Goddess of Dawn. Was that the only reason?

"Look Jonathan, you know I like you but I think with everything going on right now…"

"Yes," he said, kissing her neck. "Hattie always told me that you had a thing for me."

Hattie…again!

She pushed him off her, zipping up her jacket. "Jonathan, I can't do this."

She took off through the tall grass, wishing she could find this boulder and hide under it. She heard Jonathan calling out to her to stop.

She whirled around, "Tell me, Jonathan. If Hattie was here right now, would you even look at me, let alone kiss me?"

He stared at her dumbfounded, his hands in his pockets.

"But Hattie's not here…"

"It's a simple question."

Jonathan stared back, flabbergasted, and he touched her cheek lovingly, "Stop comparing yourself to Hattie. This strong, powerful side of you, that's what is attracting me to you."

He leaned in to kiss her again and she let him, though her heart was telling her that he was only attracted to her powers. What he truly loved was the goddess within her. At least that was something she had that Hattie didn't.

Just then a conch shell sounded, and she pushed away from Jonathan… a part of her believing it was Boreas calling to her. But the deep sonorous call she recognized as the music that resonated from Otus's shell. She looked down at her arm, no goose bumps visible as she looked back into Jonathan's confused blue eyes.

"What's the matter," he asked, looking to kiss her again.

She grabbed Jonathan's hand. "Come on. Otus found the boulder."

"How do you know...?"

She pulled him after her and together they ran through the grass, locating Otus in a small clearing where he was desperately attempting to lift the boulder, but without any success. He was red in the face, his cheeks bulging out trying to lift this little boulder that looked to be cemented to the terrain. Fawn and the Professor were already there with two cooked geese that they handed over to Jonathan and Aurora.

"Hope you like it Medium Rare," the Professor quipped. "Didn't have time to roast them too long once this giant grabbed us from camp."

Aurora plucked out a feather that was stuck in the meat and then bit into the goose, tearing the meat ravenously with her teeth, satiating her hunger.

Otus was grunting as he was pulling the boulder with all his strength. "It was not this hard putting the rock into the earth. Why won't it budge?"

"Well if you can't move that thing, then there's no hope for the rest of us," the Professor said, eying his meager muscles.

Otus finally gave up, collapsing onto the ground which caused a mini earthquake and made the others topple over like dominos. Here they were like sitting ducks waiting for the Inspector to strike and the one weapon they had hoped to acquire was hidden away near the Earth's crust.

Aurora exclaimed, "Otus, think. What did you and Mrs. Taboo do in order to trick Ephialtes to get into that hole to begin with?"

Otus scratched his head, biting his upper lip in deep thought. "We told him there was something down there. Yeah it was a bugger rat. He hated bugger rats and vowed he would destroy every last one of them."

"What are bugger rats?" Jonathan asked, giving Aurora a sly smile.

"Bugger rats... nasty looking things, like big rodents that I make my famous rodent soup with..."

"Let's get back to the story, why don't we?" The Professor cried out, exasperated, taking off his shoes and rubbing the soles of his calloused feet.

"Sorry. Well, my brother went down to destroy the bugger rats and that is when Mrs. Taboo said some sort of poem, and then she told me to put down the boulder. See, it was that simple."

He kicked the boulder frustrated and then cried out in pain and started hopping around on one foot as the others quickly darted out of the way to not get trampled.

Aurora quickly opened her knapsack and rummaged through until she located the prophecy book.

The Professor eyed her curiously. "Looking to do some light reading?"

"No, I think this Mrs. Taboo anticipated us coming back here," she cried out, scanning through the pages. "I think she knew we would need Ephialtes, just like she knew that Otus would find me and Boreas. I think the answer to this poem must lie in the prophecy book."

The professor shrugged, taking his cane and making marks in the dirt, "I have that book memorized and I cannot recall anything about getting a giant free from under a boulder. That is something I think I would remember."

Aurora wasn't about to give up and continued to scan carefully through the book. The binding was still intact but the pages were weathered and yellowed since it had stood the test of time at over 400 years old. The Professor's ancestor, Pierre Gassendi, had predicted the Geometric Storm all those years before. When he named the Northern Lights, Aurora Borealis, he had predicted there being the Goddess of Dawn as well as the God of the North Wind to help lead Otus to the Northern Lights. The secret to defeating the Geometric Storm was in that book, and so was hopefully this next clue on their journey.

The sun was blaring down on them and after several minutes she gave the book to Fawn to see if she had any better luck. Aurora turned around hastily, feeling like they were being watched, but all she saw were miles of long grass blowing in the wind, like they were participating in an interpretive dance routine. She couldn't shake that feeling but Fawn was preoccupied reading through the book to find anything to help them in this situation.

"Does anyone else think that the giant has gone mad?" Jonathan finally exclaimed, tossing the animal bones onto the grass.

"The giant has a name," Otus grumbled, shaking his head.

Jonathan continued, "I'm sorry Otus, but the Common Good Army could attack at any minute and we're sitting around this stupid boulder like it is magically going to move."

"Aurora's here," the Professor said, lying back and taking a bite of goose that Fawn had cooked up. "I think they should be more scared of us."

Jonathan's bright turquoise eyes stared intently into Aurora's. "Unfortunately we don't know if Aurora still has her powers."

Aurora's guilt surged back. "I didn't freeze up on purpose," she declared.

"And she can't just lose her powers," the Professor added in Aurora's defense. "She needs them for the Geometric Storm."

Jonathan kneeled down and patted her hands gently, blowing on them again even though it was warm out here in the meadow.

"Maybe now they will work," he said insistently, his face hidden by the shadows. "Will you try them for me?"

Once again she felt such pressure to perform, like she was some circus monkey. She pulled her hands away and stood up abruptly. Jonathan stared at her, waiting for her to create light and fire and she felt a huge weight on her shoulders. She pointed at a piece of timber but her mind went blank. This wasn't right. Something didn't feel right.

"I can't do it!"

She was about to run off when Fawn grabbed her and held the book up resolutely.

"Aurora was right! Here it is," Fawn declared resolutely. "I found Mrs. Taboo's poem. Otus, let me know if this rings a bell."

She cleared her throat and read,

> "From anger lead him from the land,
> It will be sealed by his brother's hand,
> Until a burst of light doth shine,
> And bring him forth to again reside
> And prove his worth."

"Yes," Otus recalled. "Yes, that's it! I remember because I thought that last part didn't rhyme and it still doesn't."

The Professor turned toward at Aurora and said, "Aurora, your light is what is needed to remove this boulder. Your powers. Mrs. Taboo knew that you would have them by the time you reached this destination."

Aurora felt her body go cold again thinking about her powers. They hadn't worked before to help her friends. Why would they work now?

"I don't think I can. I mean there has to be another way."

Jonathan pointed in the distance at little specks of light that were moving too fast to be stars. "It's Common Good planes," he shouted. "You have to do this now or we have to leave here immediately."

"Aurora," Fawn said, taking her hands in her own. "You can do this. You have been given a gift because you are worthy. You have to believe in yourself."

Aurora closed her eyes and said, "I don't know if I can."

"Think about something or someone that made you believe in yourself. Think about what you did for Boreas. Think about how you saved him."

"They are coming." Jonathan cried out. "There are four of them".

Aurora felt her hands sweating as she stared at the boulder and felt her heart palpitating, each second another second closer for the planes to find them.

Concentrate, she yelled at herself to try to get her mind to focus on making her powers work. But the fear again started seeping into her veins. She looked up at Otus who smiled down at her with no fear in his eyes. He trusted her and she became determined that she would and could do this.

She rubbed her hands together, cleared her mind and then heard Boreas's voice saying, "You always believed in me. You believed I would come back to you."

A ray of light illuminated from her fingertips and she felt a weight lifted off her shoulders as she aimed her light at the boulder and it lifted effortlessly into the air. Aurora held it levitated above them, the light enflamed from her fingertips as she held it there, her whole energy focused on keeping it in the air. It opened up a large crater in the ground and the roar of the planes was above them and bullets swarmed in their direction.

Otus quickly grabbed the boulder and swung it like a huge Frisbee. It went flying into the sky, colliding with one of the planes, hitting a wing, causing it to nose dive and explode too close to them in the meadow. The other three planes diverted from their course and made zigzags in the air preparing for a counterattack.

"Otus," Fawn cried out, "If you are going to reunite with your brother, now is the time."

Otus nodded and looked down into the giant crater and called out, "Ephialtes! It's your brother, Otus. We need your help."

"They're coming," Jonathan yelled, taking one of the Professor's contraptions and throwing it into the air, exploding a fog around them to help momentarily blind the attackers.

One of the pilots swerved off course and collided with another plane, both exploding. The blast knocked everyone off their feet and thrust Jonathan straight into the heart of the crater.

"Jonathan!!" Fawn cried out in horror as her boy fell into the suspending darkness. Aurora dove toward the crater, shining her light down but all she saw was spiraling darkness.

"Otus, do something!" she cried out, not believing Jonathan was dead. He couldn't be.

Otus stood up to his full height, grabbed the others and put them quickly into his overalls pocket as more gun fire came from the last remaining plane. The fog was lifting and Otus dodged the bullets but was out in the open with no covering or weapons left. They looked up as the fighter pilot aimed straight toward them and fired. Otus attempted to divert from its path, but the missile was locked on its target.

It was about to hit when all of a sudden a huge shadow emerged, grabbing the missile with its bare hands. It then swung the missile around like a disk and chucked it at the fighter plane, causing it to explode in the air like a firework.

A huge roar erupted from behind them followed by a deep raspy voice sounding out almost as if the mountains had come alive as a single voice.

"To think that could have been you!"

Otus whirled around and Aurora's eyes went wide as she stared into the face of Ephialtes.

His face was void of any friendliness or boyish innocence, he appeared to be the polar opposite of Otus. He had two bushy black eyebrows that were shaped over his sinister emerald eyes where a devil red pupil glared back at them. He had long, mangled raven black hair that cascaded down his broad shoulders and a braided beard that reached down over his bare chest that was covered in black, tangled chest hair. His muscles were massive, like a wrestler in build but with gigantic proportions. He wore tattered black pants, had no shoes for his feet and his toenails curled like claws. His hands were clenched in fists and a lone gold medallion hung around his neck.

"I should have let that missile kill you," Ephialtes cried out, his voice deep and maniacal.

Otus took a step back from his brother but then finally mustered enough courage to ask, "Why didn't you then?"

Ephialtes grinned, his two front teeth missing and the rest of them nearly rotted away.

"Because I want the honor of killing you myself."

He reached into his hair and held up none other than Jonathan wriggling like a worm at the end of a fish hook.

"But before I exact my revenge, why did you throw this puny human into my prison? Is he an offering or a light snack?"

"Put my son down!" Fawn cried out, elated at the sight of her son alive, but terrified that this new giant would eat him.

"And who might you be, pretty human?" Ephialtes spat, getting a little closer for a better look, his breath reeking like a dumpster filled with rotten eggs. His beard was swarming with flies and Aurora had to hold her nose to not pass out from the smell.

"My name is Fawn Stockington and I am the High Magistrate of Plymouth Incarnate. I am looking to enlist you into my army to help stop the Common Good from causing massive destruction to this

Earth. They are led by Inspector Herald and they are trying to stop Otus from reaching the Northern Lights since he is the only one who can prevent the Geometric Storm, along with Aurora Alvarez and my other son, Boreas Stockington."

Ephialtes burst out laughing, collapsed onto the ground rolling around uncontrollably. Jonathan managed to wrangle himself free, drop off of the giant and onto the ground and ran as quickly as he could to not be trampled by the gigantic monster rolling around like he was caught on fire.

"Otus is going to save the world. Now that's a good one. He locks me up for the past five years and now comes crawling back because he needs me. No, this pretty little human needs me. And then what? I am going to get cast aside again and thrown under the Earth again? Look, my quarrel isn't with you, High Magist…whatever your name is. For the past five years I haven't thought of anything else except revenge against my one living relative. And today I am going to have my revenge. So Otus, let those puny humans out of your pocket or I will destroy them and you together."

Otus turned to his brother and cleared his throat. "I am not going to fight you, Brother."

"Brother? You're not fit to be called my brother."

Otus reached in, took the others out of his pocket and told them to run for cover. Ephialtes cracked his knuckles and let out a huge roar into the Whispering Meadow, disrupting the birds nesting in the field who took off into the sky, flying for their life. Aurora grabbed Jonathan's hand, pulling him to his feet to get out of the line of fire.

Otus's eyes were close to tears as he said, "I had no choice, Ephialtes. You were killing people. Innocent people. You were the one who wanted to destroy them. I had no choice but to stop you."

"We have the right to destroy them. We are the ones on the top of the food chain. What are they but puny humans? We can't let them infest our home, tell us where to live. We deserve the right to be free."

"And you will be." Fawn said, standing on a tree stump to be heard over the uproar. "But right now, none of us have that right to be free. If you don't help us, everything will be destroyed."

Ephialtes looked down at Fawn as if he might acquiesce, but then the scowl returned to his beet red face.

"I don't believe you."

"It's true," Otus cried out, stomping next to Fawn like a united front.

Ephialtes roared. "I need to destroy you, Otus. You betrayed me! You betrayed your own brother to help these humans!"

Jonathan cried out, "Sometimes you have to betray the person you care about most in order to help them."

Ephialtes whirled around at the sound of the boy beneath him. "How dare you speak, light snack. You're lucky I didn't devour you when I got the chance."

"I am saying that I had to betray my brother once too. I thought I was doing what was right in order to help him."

"And where is your brother now?"

"He is taken by Inspector Herald. He will be killed unless we can stall for time and lure the Inspector to Hyperborea. We need the Inspector to meet us in battle there and we need you to fight with us."

Ephialtes listened intently and felt a battle brewing within himself. He looked down at the small human and said hesitantly, "It is nice to feel needed after all these years."

He glared at Otus with intense hatred, "you'd better sleep with one eye open, Brother. You never know when I'll be in the mood to get my revenge."

Otus walked up to him, giant standing beside giant. "So you will help us?"

Ephialtes roared again, this time shaking the earth so much that a huge crack formed in the ground. Aurora watched this spectacle in awe.

Fawn held out her hand to Ephialtes and he looked at her curiously. "Please shake my hand, Ephialtes."

His enormous hand wavered over hers and he tapped it slightly, afraid that if he put it in his grasp his strength would crush the little woman before him whose strength he admired.

"This is a pact that I am making with you. Today, human and giant are working for a single cause. Together we will save this place we both call our home."

Chapter 17

The Inspector's Warning

Boreas didn't understand anything anymore. He was the cleanest he had been in months, having showered with actual hot water and soap, and his hair was shampooed. He wore cotton pajamas and was resting in a big down comforter bed with silk sheets in the most beautiful suite in the Castle on the Hudson. Of course the windows were barred and the door was locked with two guards on the outside, yet he was living the life of luxury.

After the library book burning incident, the Inspector led him to this room, not the dungeon or the tallest tower which he thought would have been appropriate. The Inspector told him to rest here and think about what he had seen. He knew the Inspector was trying to manipulate him for his own personal gain. That much was obvious. Yet there was some truth in what the Inspector had showed him. Those paintings of events that had happened, they weren't fiction like those books of heroes. The heroes in those paintings were killed and for no reason except for religious fanaticism and hatred. He understood why the Inspector wanted to abolish religions, but then he remembered the prayer service in Plymouth Incarnate. Those people had proved that they could live together despite religious differences, but would that still remain true on a larger scale? Look what had happened before the days of the IDEAL. Do they take that chance? Would they return to the days of terrorism?

He closed his eyes on that comfortable pillow and wanted to clear his mind of everything related to the mission and the Inspector, but his mind wandered and he was with Otus and Aurora sailing through the sky heading toward the Northern Lights. But then there was a crash and ahead of them there was a massive explosion like an atomic bomb going off and shrapnel and colors streamed past destroying the trees, houses and all visible life forms around them. Until they were just there alone and looking at the Geometric Storm that they couldn't prevent. Then, out of nowhere, a giant gush of wind blew him off Otus's shoulder and into a tornado rolling around and around in a whirlwind.

Boreas awoke with a start and sprung out of the bed and out of the covers that now felt more confining than comforting. Boreas looked out through the window where he gazed upon the Hudson River, and then his eyes looked up into the horizon where he saw Antares staring straight back at him. His eyes wandered further north where his journey would ultimately lead – to the Northern Lights. And here he was, still without his powers, if he even was meant to get them, and held in the power of the enemy.

He looked down at the thirty foot drop into the Hudson River and knew that his only hope of escape lay in the hands of a man he just discovered to be his uncle. Sampson's priorities, of course, were Sansa and Steven, with Sansa's health his primary focus. Boreas knew escape was near impossible, especially during the World

Summit where security was at its tightest and the base was swarming with guards. Boreas wanted to throw himself out of that window because he knew that the odds of escaping were hopeless.

Boreas heard a key unlocking his door and he whirled around, fearfully expecting the Inspector or one of his cronies to come in. To his surprise, Mrs. Alvarez entered. The guard stood there beside her but she turned to him and said, "I just need five minutes alone with the prisoner."

The guard nodded and Mrs. Alvarez sauntered into the room alone. She was wearing a long white floral patterned gown that flowed down to her ankles and swayed in rhythm with her body as she walked. She had a silk scarf over her black curls. Boreas continued to lean against the window realizing this was a ploy by the Inspector to get information out of him.

She took a seat on a lounge chair and crossed her legs, still eyeing him curiously. And then she spoke. "So you're the one who started this mess."

Boreas glared at Mrs. Alvarez. "I didn't start any of this and neither did Aurora. Your BFF, the Inspector, is the one who started this 15 years ago."

"Let's not talk politics," Mrs. Alvarez cried out. "I'm here because I just wanted to make sure Aurora...that she's ok."

Boreas took a deep breath, "Aurora is strong and I am sure she is fine. She has Otus with her."

"The giant?" Mrs. Alvarez cringed, like Otus was some disease. Boreas laughed. "Yes, Otus is a giant."

Mrs. Alvarez stood up and paced back and forth. "I am glad to hear it. Aurora and I never saw eye to eye, but I love her. I have always loved her. I hope she...and you... know I am doing this to help. That maybe I can reason with Herald. Make him be more lenient on you."

She looked genuinely sad and Boreas realized that despite her motives, she was doing what she thought was best for her family.

Boreas turned away from the window and came close to Mrs. Alvarez in order to whisper, in fear that someone was eavesdropping outside the door.

"Is my father here?"

She looked at him like he had three heads. "Of course your father is here. Henry Stockington is second in command to the Inspector."

Boreas nearly fell backwards in disbelief but then again why was he surprised? His father had always been a man of power and wealth in the community and was friends with Inspector Herald. He froze thinking his Father must know that he was not his biological father. But he was the only father he had ever known. He took a deep breath before continuing. "So I guess he doesn't want to see me…"

Mrs. Alvarez put her hand on his shoulder. "I am sure it was quite a shock for you to find out who your father was. Henry took it really hard."

Boreas nervously chuckled. "I thought he would be relieved."

Mrs. Alvarez shook her head, "He loves you. That man has always loved you and Jonathan as both father and mother to you kids."

Boreas didn't know if that was true. His father had loved Jonathan surely. "He didn't stop the Inspector when he injected me with the Soul Extractor serum. You saw what he did to me. You were there in the fort when it happened."

She leaned in, her voice comforting. "And I know that he pleaded for the Inspector not to kill you. The Inspector cares about your father and you are still his son, whether by blood or not. You need to work with him. You need to forget this prophecy nonsense and tell Aurora to come back home."

Boreas listened to her siren song and he wanted to believe her. But Mrs. Alvarez was stuck in her daydream, not wanting to see the truth. She couldn't see it or she was oblivious to the fact that the fate of the world was in her daughter's hands. She had never seen

Aurora's potential, just like his own father never saw him as anything but a failure.

"I want to work with the Inspector," Boreas lied. "I want to swear off the prophecy, which is why I separated from the group. I want to tell Aurora, but the only way is to be interviewed so that she will see me, hear it from my own words. I am sure she'll come home, if she hears it from me."

Mrs. Alvarez smiled and gave Boreas a huge hug, her perfume so pungent that he almost choked.

"I knew you would see reason! I will speak with your father tomorrow and look to arrange an interview."

He smiled innocently and said, "I'm sure my father and the Inspector would love to hear what I have to say."

She gave him one last smile and knocked on the door. The guards opened it and she shimmied out the door, calling out 'good night' to him.

Boreas leaned back on his bed laughing internally and knowing Aurora was going to kill him for lying to her mother. But it was better than telling her the truth; that he wanted to kill the Inspector. And maybe he would get a chance to do something even worse — reveal to the world what a monster he really was.

✫ ✫ ✫

Boreas was led down a hidden secret passage by his favorite guard, Billy Goat. His beard appeared to have grown even longer in a day and Boreas felt rejuvenated even though he knew that his work was far from over. His encounter with Mrs. Alvarez proved to be a blessing. She would do anything now if she thought Boreas could convince her daughter to come home. He snickered at his cleverness.

The doors opened and he was led into a huge wine cellar that was converted into an office work space. Workers were frantically typing on their computers and he spotted reporters and other TV personalities who all were preoccupied with their work. As he advanced down the center aisle, he spotted one reporter he recognized, Analise Jones. She also had lived on Wishbone Avenue but was a few years older and had been a reporter for Candlewick Channel Five news. He recalled she had been close with Mary Fray's brother, Jake, before he was enlisted into the Common Good Army. She looked more beautiful in person than on the television screen. She had smooth, dark skin, short black hair and big intense eyes. His eyes noticed she was wearing a sparkling ruby necklace around her neck, but she kept tugging on her chain like it was irritating her skin. She looked up from her work and gave him a worried expression. "Be careful," she mouthed, as he passed. He didn't quite understand what she meant but then another woman who was at least 6 foot tall approached him and said with a British accent, "You are expected, Boreas Stockington. This way."

Boreas didn't know what paradise he had entered but though he was surrounded by beautiful women, none of them looked happy. And that made him worried.

The doors opened and there before him hung a huge painting of the slogan, "Religion Divides but the IDEAL Unites". Besides that painting, the walls were barren and there was only thick slabs of marble surrounding them, seemingly closing in on them. The doors slammed shut behind him, trapping him in that mausoleum-like room with the Inspector and none other than his father, Henry Stockington.

His Father had aged a bit since the last time Boreas had seen him, at the fort in Lake Champlain two months earlier. It felt like yesterday. His bleach blond hair was streaked with silver highlights and he still wore his thick eye glasses that were so out dated but he thought made him look more distinguished. He wore an expensive suit and a bright red tie that clashed with the Inspector who was still wearing his penguin suit, though this time he was not wearing the ridiculous top hat and was just exposing his bald scalp. The burn marks were once again visible so what he had seen yesterday was not plastic surgery, but a really fine makeup job. Everything about yesterday felt like an illusion and down here below the ground was more of where he would expect the Inspector to live.

The Inspector looked up and growled at Boreas, "Your father never told me that his son was such an extraordinary liar."

Boreas stood there, his mouth gaped open in surprise. The Inspector displayed a digital screen on the wall and played the conversation from the night before with Mrs. Alvarez. He felt his hands getting sweaty as against the iron chains.

"Why did you really separate from the giant and Aurora?"

Boreas smiled at them. "You are wasting your time. I know why you sent Mrs. Alvarez in to see me. I don't know where Aurora and Otus are going."

"Answer the question, Boreas." His father sternly cried out, the same stern voice he used when he got in trouble in his childhood.

Boreas took a seat though he wasn't invited to. "Let me see, Dad. Your wife arrested me. Tried me in front of the whole colony of Plymouth Incarnate for betraying my friends and my family. Because of this," he pointed at his arm, "that your Inspector injected me with. I was almost found guilty until Aurora came to my aid and by some luck figured out that my real father is David Xiomy. So yeah…what part of that would make me loyal to that cause?"

Mr. Stockington stood up abruptly, turned his back on Boreas and gazed intently at the digital screen.

The Inspector leaned back in his chair, digesting this information. "Don't mind Henry. He's still pretty shocked about the whole unveiling of your lineage. But Boreas…if you really have changed sides, I need you to convince me."

Boreas's eyes narrowed. Convince the Inspector that he changed sides? He wasn't that good of a liar.

"You'd better explain fast because with the press of this button I can put your precious Aurora's mom in prison for the rest of her life. Though I would hate to lose one of my most loyal ambassadors."

Boreas felt his legs getting weaker and he looked to his father for help but got none. His dad kept staring down at the screen at a map that he was scrutinizing.

Boreas stood up, his chains rattling. "Fine," he snapped. "I separated from the group because I wanted to kill you, Inspector. Fortunately for you, my plans changed."

The Inspector leaned back in his chair and fondled the button with the back of his hand like at any moment he would press it and destroy Mrs. Alvarez's life once and for all.

"Unfortunately for you, you didn't go through with it."

Boreas bit his lip. "I'm not as evil as you tried to make me out to be, I guess."

The Inspector laughed and said,"You have quite a son here, Henry."

"He is David's son." Henry muttered bitterly. Boreas slid back into his chair at those words.

The Inspector pretended to be surprised. "Oh, I've forgotten. I recall Boreas that was one of your reasons for turning. It was so easy with you. From your desperation to please your father, to your jealousy of your brother. It was as if I didn't even need to try so hard. So I commend you for coming back to the light…but you know as much as I do that your arm still aches when you get angry. Is it aching right now, seeing me, watching me?"

Boreas didn't answer, ignoring the pain escalating in his right arm. *Stay strong*, he urged himself.

"The only problem is," Herald continued, "Aurora's not around to save you again with her powers if you need that second dose. In fact, I know that they are going to Hyperborea."

Boreas shrugged, attempting to keep his poker face and said, "I've never heard of it."

The Inspector took a big bite out of a piece of raw steak and said, "Isn't that where you are supposed to gain your powers?"

Boreas bit his lip, having forgotten that there was a time that the Professor had worked with Inspector Herald. It was unnerving how much Herald knew about the prophecy.

"Well," the Inspector continued, chewing voraciously at the steak as Boreas's stomach growled, "I have a viable lead that there is a protest commune located near Alcatraz. A man by the name of Romero, who used to work for my former infuriating partner Max Radar, has changed sides. He is going to lead one of my men to infiltrate the San Francisco commune, where I believe Fawn and her protesting scum are headed. Romero will infiltrate this commune and lead us to Hyperborea, and that is where the battle will be held."

Henry laughed, "What battle?"

The Inspector whirled around in his chair to face his 2nd in command. "I want to crush Fawn at her game. She is gaining supporters with every step she takes and her goal is Hyperborea. That is where she will face off against our army."

"Fawn has been hiding like a gopher for the past 10 years. She has no intention of fighting again. That is against everything she believes."

The Inspector took a deep breath and said deviously, "Well, she has faith in her son. She believes that Boreas here is the God of the North Wind."

Mr. Stockington stood up and banged his fist against the desk, "He is not the god of anything! And when I get ahold of Fawn I am going to tear her apart for lying to me after all these years. I won't need a war to do that."

"Dad.... I..."

"You are not my son," He screamed, pointing his finger directly at Boreas's face and stormed out of the room, the door rattling behind him, knocking the picture off its hinges and crashed violently against the floor. Boreas stood there stunned and felt the room spinning around him. The Inspector watched him half humorously and said, "It was your DNA sample that helped us uncover the truth about your real father. I think Henry is still in shock, finding out the hard way. But, then again, you found out the hard way too, I imagine."

"In the court room," Boreas confessed, and then stopped himself not sure why he had just said that in front of his enemy.

The Inspector offered him the chair. "Look Boreas, I know you think I want to kill you, but that's just not the case. You see I have so many other plans for you. And you're not in Hyperborea right now getting your powers because a part of you doesn't believe that you are meant for this prophecy. But I see your potential. I always have. If we do go to battle with Fawn and the protestors, I want you fighting beside me. We're not so different, you and I. My parents were never there for me, lied to me, and I also never felt like I was ever good enough. But look at us now. Me, one of the most powerful men in the world and you, with the fate of the world on your shoulders. These things shouldn't happen to people like us. They are meant for stronger, more confident men. But here we are with our burdens...but we don't have to carry them alone."

Boreas stared into the pits of the Inspector's coal dark eyes. This snake was trying to get under his skin in order to manipulate him. He struggled with the wrist irons and wished that he *was* the God of the North Wind. He wished he already had the power to destroy this man before him.

The Inspector smiled, "Besides, you don't want me to inject you with another Soul Extractor serum."

Boreas felt his mind go blank, a vision popped in his head and he knew somehow that he was seeing through the Inspector's eyes. They were in Candlewick Prison and he was interrogating the First Lieutenant. A gun pointed at the Inspector about to fire but then the barrel was empty. The Inspector's voice spoke. "No. You are the traitor." And then he shot the gun, but he didn't kill the First Lieutenant. He killed a female prisoner instead. It was Mary Fray's mother! The Inspector had showed no mercy and caused such pain in the First Lieutenant. Controlling him now to do his bidding...forcing him to admit that he destroyed the rest of the Soul Extractor serum. There was none left for the Inspector to inflict any more pain with.

Boreas opened his eyes, still immersed in the pain and the power that the Inspector had felt. He stared into the manipulative eyes of the man he had just saw murder someone in cold blood.

Boreas stood up. "I am nothing like you. And you can't inject me with anymore Soul Extractor serum since you don't have anymore. You can't force me to fight with you."

The Inspector appeared taken aback by this revelation. He composed himself and out of his pocket he removed the small doll that Boreas recognized as Sansa's doll, the one she carried with her in the wilderness. The Inspector coddled it in his palm like it was a valued prize and hypnotically rolled it back and forth over his palm. "I will meet your mom in battle, Boreas. And it will be in Hyperborea. And I am going to win with or without your help. But I have a way of making people do what I want. You will speak at the World Summit or those children you came here with, Sansa and Steven, will die."

He closed his grip on Sansa's doll, covering it with darkness.

Chapter 18

Alcatraz

On the submarine, Mrs. Xiomy watched and listened as the worshippers of Islam knelt down on prayer rugs and prayed to Allah, even here as they escaped and ran for their lives to an unknown settlement in San Francisco. Rana remembered as a girl praying five times a day, no matter how busy or how hectic her day was, she would always kneel down on her prayer rug and pray with her family.

"Papa," she would call out to her father with the big rotund face and sparkling brown eyes, looking adoringly at his daughter. "It's time."

She would pull on his hand as they laid out their mats and prayed in the direction of Mecca, their religious homeland, and they would say their prayers together. Her father said that it was important to take time out of your day to have a conversation with God.

Those days felt a lifetime ago and though she still had her faith, after losing David, her beliefs were shaky with intense moments of doubt and grief. Her friends had abandoned her and her family disowned her years before when she had admitted to dating a man who was not Muslim. David was a mishmash of beliefs and heritage, one of the things that fascinated her about him, but her parents did not share that same fascination.

"Not praying?" the doctor asked, handing her a cup of water as they surveyed the group before them now chanting the prayer she still knew by heart, *Glory be to God, the highest.*

"Inwardly, I'm praying," she confessed. "It's like I have gone full circle," she said, sitting beside the doctor as they stared out at the Pacific Ocean water, murky with a cloudiness of doubt overshadowing her mind. "My husband David always used to start each protest with a prayer. And it's funny because I used to ask him which god he prayed to. And you know what he would say? He'd say, 'I'm praying to the God of my heart'. I used to ask, 'which god was that? Some ancient mystical god that I had never read about or heard of?' He would laugh and say, "why does God need a label? Is there one religion or god that is more powerful than the other? The only god that matters is the god of my heart and my mind and my soul. The one that brought me into this world to love you, Rana... the one that brought me into this world to try to save it."

"Your husband was a wise man," the doctor said, taking her hand comfortingly in his own.

Rana nodded, thinking of David with his soft blue eyes that had stared at her like she was the only woman in the world. Despite the troubles, the heartaches and the pain, he had loved her. But he had loved Fawn too and Fawn was the only one who carried on his legacy. She was the one who had carried his child.

The Captain called out to them and Mrs. Xiomy was grateful for the distraction. She carefully walked past the people deep in prayer. She hoped they had a prayer for them to enter the base unscathed. The Captain was with Babs in the control room, and utilizing a secret code similar to Morse code to communicate with the other 9 submarines. Screens flickered as the sonar radar was detecting the area for any Common Good submarines in the area. Babs was scribbling on a sheet of paper, interpreted the message and then looked up to Mrs. Xiomy. "We have a slight problem."

"What else is new," Mrs. Xiomy remarked, looking through the periscope at Alcatraz, the ancient jail of San Francisco that housed known criminals like Al Capone from the Prohibition era.

"The Common Good Army has infiltrated Alcatraz. We don't know where the rebel base is and if they have relocated."

"I thought the jail was abandoned."

"As per our last communication with my parents this was where they were setting up their base." Babs said, a worried frown on her face. "Unless they relocated and who knows where that could be."

Mrs. Xiomy leaned back and thought hard about what their next step should be. They couldn't just sit in the middle of the bay that was crawling with Common Good soldiers. Even the Professor's anti-detection sonar couldn't prevent another submarine from spotting them in the waters. They were lucky they had gotten this far undetected and they couldn't tempt fate.

"You said that they would have expected you at one point, Babs. Your parents, correct."

Babs nodded. "Yes, but for years there has been no way for them to reach us without risk of our communications getting intercepted. And once Plymouth Tartarus fell they had no way of reaching us even if they had relocated."

Mrs. Xiomy quickly looked back into the periscope at the Common Good flag raised high into the air. The interlocking swords for the IDEAL made her cringe, but she tried to think like Babs' parents.

"Babs, if your parents were going to leave a clue behind for you… Any idea what that would be? Did they mention anything in their last communication that would indicate a sign?"

Babs thought long and hard, closing her eyes tight to try to imagine the note that her parents had left her.

"They had mentioned something strange… About me and Eileen flying at a bird's eye view. I thought they were referencing a plane or something, but I never understood what they meant."

Mrs. Xiomy's heart danced in her chest. "I do. Look!"

She pointed the periscope upwards at the flag and Babs stuck her eye through to peer at it flailing wildly in the wind. On one side was the flag for the Common Good visible for all to see. And on the other side was a B.E. with an arrow pointing due south… almost like it was a compass but the other directions were faded.

"South! They are calling for us to go south. South of San Francisco?"

Mrs. Xiomy shook her head and turned to the Captain. "I think it is a lot closer than that. Captain, I remember reading that there could be an intricate fortress beneath Alcatraz… with hidden tunnels and a city. I doubt the Common Good is aware of this. I think we need to scout out the area."

"How?" The Captain asked, concerned.

Mrs. Xiomy turned to Babs. "Remember when I told you I used to Scuba Dive? I think it's time I take a lesson from Boreas and commandeer some scuba equipment."

✲ ✲ ✲

It was breezy along the deck of the San Francisco Pier at Fisherman's Wharf as Jake lowered his sunglasses, watching Rana Xiomy out of the corner of his eye exit the dive store, dressed in full dive gear and holding her flippers and mask in hand. Just as the Inspector's henchman, Officer Romero, had anticipated, Fawn's protestors had made their way to San Francisco by submarine, but they had been undetectable by the Common Good's technology. Jake quickly raised his sunglasses as Rana slipped past Romero, who was incognito and smoothly slipped a tracking device onto the suit she was wearing. He nodded to Jake peered out at the Golden-Gate Bridge almost completely covered in misty fog.

Officer Romero walked over to Jake, removed his blond wig, exposing his dark hair sticking to his forehead with sweat. He leaned against the railing and pulled the tracking monitor out of his pocket.

"It's just what I thought," he said in his brusque tone, watching the little red dot on the monitor. "She is submerging beneath the Golden Gate Bridge and heading toward Alcatraz. The protestors must be there."

"Good work, Romero," Jake said, coldly. His knuckles clutching the pier railing a little too hard, still in disbelief that he was here to infiltrate the protestor's organization.

"She knows me," Romero spoke frankly. "We met at Macchu Picchu."

"Does she know you changed sides?" Jake asked, adjusting his watch and waiting for the transmission from the Inspector.

Romero shook his head, "No. And neither does Molina. She thinks I was captured on our way here from Macchu Picchu."

The Inspector's face transmitted before Jake on his watch screen.

"Rana Xiomy is here," Jake replied, reporting to the man who held his puppet strings. "We're going to pursue her to see if she leads us to the protestor's safe haven entrance."

"Glad my little traitor is obeying my orders." Herald responded with a possessive tone in his voice.

Jake wanted to tear that smirk off the Inspector's face, but took a deep breath instead. "Do we have your permission to pursue?"

"Address me properly." Herald ordered, a slick smile crossing his face.

He waited and Jake loathed what he was making him do.

"Do we have your permission, Inspector Herald?"

"That's better," Herald was milking this for all it was worth, and Jake just stood there, his soul rotting away and turning more and more into the vile man he was...the man the Inspector had created. The Inspector peered into his eyes and replied firmly, "Keep me informed. And Jacob... do not fail."

Jake felt a coldness sweep through him as those words resonated. The transmission ended and without delay, Jake took off toward the dive shop, followed by Romero.

"Two dive suits," he commanded to the startled man behind the counter.

"Yo, man, what's your problem?" The dive store clerk shouted.

Jake raised his shirt sleeve to reveal the First Lieutenant tattoo. The man nearly fell out of his chair and immediately started rounding up two dive suits that would fit his prestigious customers.

Jake stared at himself in the mirror and knew Mrs. Xiomy would recognize him if he walked into Alcatraz like this, especially his eyes that were his most recognizable feature. He took a deep breath and slammed his right eye against one of the poles in the dive shop. He winced his pain but squinted in the mirror to observe his eye starting to swell. He then grabbed a white water-proof bandage and wrapped it around the left side of his face, covering his non-bruised eye.

"Are you done beating yourself up?" Romero asked, witnessing Jake's self-inflicted wounds.

"Rana Xiomy can't recognize me," he told Romero, ignoring he pain escalating from his right eye. "When we are down there I'm not the First Lieutenant."

Romero nodded, grabbing the dive suits out of the manager's hands. "Your secret is safe with me, Jake. I mean....Mark. Yeah, you could pass for a Mark."

Romero winked at Jake whose new alias had to work. Once they were in their dive suits they took off down a steep hill that led to a cove where they could submerge beneath the Pacific Ocean and then head toward Alcatraz. Jake looked down at his watch where the tracking device was following Mrs. Xiomy's movements. They stuck on their flippers and dive masks and Jake double checked that his knapsack was secured within an airtight package. Without another second to think, they jumped into the white foamy waves, leaving all hope behind and Jake took the plunge into his new identity - leaving his dignity and honor at the surface.

✦ ✦ ✦

It wasn't easy navigating through the blistery cold bay, even with the wet suit providing some additional warmth. Mrs. Xiomy dove deeper into the dark abyss, a helmet light illuminating the murky waters as she used the walls of Alcatraz as a guide. She kicked with her flipper legs to meander deeper into the depths. She had an earpiece which kept her in communication with the first submarine and an underwater camera connected to her mask. Babs was on the other end listening, watching the footage, and providing instruction back to the Captain.

"Don't get caught in any fishing nets." Babs warned.

"Fishing nets are the least of my problems," Mrs. Xiomy thought, breathing through the mouthpiece, the tank on her back giving her only enough air for an hour. Hopefully that would be enough time to find the entrance to the secret tunnels and return back to the submarine.

It was like a different world down here on the ocean floor and reminded her of when she used to scuba dive with David. He was the one who had taught her to begin with. They were so young and adventurous back then, searching the ocean floor for any sign of hidden treasure or just to take in the sea life. She recalled how envious Fawn was that they would go swimming together. Perhaps one of the reasons Fawn had chosen an underwater kingdom. Rana couldn't think of that now, she had to concentrate on the task at hand, and time was slipping away from her.

Just then she spotted something carved into the stone. She swam closer and put her hand over the inscription. She pointed through the camera at the mark and she heard the Captain call out excitedly on the other end of the radio.

"Babs, does this make sense to you? It looks like there's a code in the rock. A Celtic cross."

Babs's voice echoed back to her. "My sister Eileen used to wear one. Aurora has it now. Why?"

Mrs. Xiomy got excited and put her hand against it. She pressed in the wall began to shake.

"Something is happening!" Mrs. Xiomy heard Babs shout in her ear as a hidden drawbridge lowered and she quickly swam out of the way to avoid getting flattened. A cave-like entrance emerged and dozens of swimmers with spears swam toward her, holding the spears against her back. Mrs. Xiomy immediately put her hands up, showing that she was unarmed and one swimmer with cold dark eyes swam toward her, stopped and then signaled wildly to the others to not fire. She mimed something in the water that looked like sign language.... and it was!

"Hello, Rana Xiomy," the swimmer signaled to her.

Surprised but relieved to no longer have a spear against her back, she quickly signed to the swimmer that there were 9 submarines, one carrying Babs O'Hara. The swimmer nodded in understanding and signed back to Rana as she began to mobilize the others.

"Send them in. You are welcome!"

Mrs. Xiomy gave the thumbs up to Babs through the camera, who had been fearful of the radio silence.

"Affirmative," Babs echoed back. "We will proceed toward your location."

Mrs. Xiomy followed the divers into the massive cave and was led further into the underground tunnels of Alcatraz. When she submerged, Mrs. Xiomy removed her mask, able to breathe naturally again, and it was like she was transported back in time to the 1800's, standing within the confines of the hidden fortress that had been built to protect the San Francisco bay from enemy boats sailing from the west. During the Civil War era, the island fortress was partly used to store guns in order to keep as many firearms as possible out of the hands of Southern sympathizers. She lifted herself out of the water to behold a giant room, partly submerged underwater, with enough space to house the submarines that were following her lead. She lifted herself out of the water and onto a concrete floor. This room looked like a military hub that broke out into extensive tunnels that resembled dark giant sewers with intricate pathways leading to various enclaves. She wondered what embankments and other remnants of a military fortress were still preserved here beneath the floors of the Alcatraz prison. Mrs. Xiomy noticed the people around her were dressed in neoprene, the same waterproof fabric that was used for her wetsuit. The thermal insulation would definitely help keep them warm down here in this cold, damp base. Massive beams rose above her in a cross-shape holding up the modern Alcatraz, which was swarming with Common Good soldiers.

The submarines floated into the tunnel and were parked one behind the other within the massive water piazza... reminding Mrs. Xiomy of scenes she had seen of Venice, the sinking city, flooded. Babs and the doctor were busy helping transport people to safety, both children and those with motion sickness.

The swimmer who had recognized Mrs. Xiomy approached her, still holding the spear at her side. When the woman removed her mask, Mrs. Xiomy was shocked. It was none other than the bright brown eyes and tanned face of the protestor Molina from Macchu Picchu.

"Surprised to see me?" Molina laughed, shaking out her wet curls.

"Surprised is an understatement!" Mrs. Xiomy cried out, giving Molina a hug. "When they bombed Macchu Picchu and captured Radar I thought you and Romero had been killed."

"I nearly was," Molina responded, sadness sweeping over her expression. "A handful of us were able to escape. Romero was with me as we were advancing toward this settlement but was captured along the trail. I don't know if he is still alive, I am still hoping he will make it to this hidden fortress.

Babs came running over, shaking hands with Molina while eyeing her with distrust, given that their last encounter was when Radar had turned against them in Macchu Picchu.

"Where is Radar?" Molina asked, eyeing the various submarines for any sign of her old leader.

"That's why we are here," Mrs. Xiomy explained. "He manipulated Boreas to attempt to kill Inspector Herald. We are gathering protestors to meet Fawn, Aurora and Otus in Hyperborea."

At this news, Molina's expression changed to worry. "The situation is worse than you know."

"What do you mean?" Babs asked.

Just then, out of the shadows of one of the dark tunnels, emerged a woman who was the carbon copy of Babs's deceased sister, Eileen, with strikingly bright, wavy red hair and pale blue eyes. The man with her was strikingly handsome with messy dark black hair that hung down his shoulders and suspicious green eyes. They were both dressed in wet suits that were covered in mud. It appeared that they were fixing one of the leaking pipes that was spraying out water and mud above them. Mr. and Mrs. O'Hara did not come across as the leaders of this settlement. They seemed more like the hired help, working to keep the commune from falling apart.

Babs ran and threw herself in her parents' warm embrace. Tears were streaming down Mrs. O'Hara's eyes. She looked around, expecting another to run into her arms, but when there was no one else, she understood and her face fell.

"Eileen?"

Babs nodded against her mother's chest, choking up. "She… didn't make it."

Mr. and Mrs. O'Hara held Babs even tighter, but slowly they all regained their composure and Mrs. O'Hara reached a hand out to Mrs. Xiomy.

"Hello, Rana Xiomy," Mrs. O'Hara said curtly. "I know who you are."

"Doesn't everyone?" Mrs. Xiomy said, taking the woman's hand. "But I am happy to see you extend your hand in friendship."

"A friend of Babs is a friend of ours," Mr. O'Hara said, forcing a smile. "We have a lot to catch up on. Where is Fawn?"

"She's with Aurora Alvarez, the Goddess of Dawn, and the giant, Otus. They are heading to Hyperborea."

The two makeshift rulers took a step back, displeased by this news.

"What do you mean, she's not here?" Mr. O'Hara shouted. "How much longer must we stay here?"

Molina stepped forward. "Aurora and Otus are the ones that I told you about, those that the prophecy destined would prevent the Geometric Storm. Boreas Stockington is the other link... the boy the Inspector has captured."

Mrs. Xiomy and Babs gasped, stunned by this turn of events.

"What do you mean, he was captured?" Mrs. Xiomy cried out.

"I'll tell you all I know, but first let's help get the others situated. You've made a long journey."

Mrs. O'Hara instructed her people to get the visitors fresh food and water and to gather in the center of the fortress where a fire was already burning. Mrs. Xiomy welcomed the heat, but felt sick and not from the motion sickness. After how far they had come, Boreas was once again at the mercy of the Inspector. Down one of the tunnels Molina showed them a room that had once housed guns and ammunition that had been converted into a sleeping area lined with bunk beds. Molina handed the women some dry clothes and gave them some privacy to change.

When Molina was out of earshot, Mrs. Xiomy exclaimed to Babs, "Why the hell did Boreas leave to begin with?" She let out her frustration as she changed out of her wet suit and into dry clothes. "Did he really think he could kill Inspector Herald without his powers?"

"Boreas told me he wanted to make things right," Babs replied, anger still evident as she said his name. "By killing Inspector Herald he thinks he is protecting us. But he's not a murderer. He never was, despite what he did under the influence of the Soul Extractor serum. I fear his heart is his downfall."

"I thought you believed he was heartless."

Babs snickered bitterly. "He has a heart. And he knows how to break hearts too. I'll never put myself in that position to fall in love again. Not with anyone."

Mrs. Xiomy put her arm around her. "He wasn't the right man for you, Babs. Your warrior is out there."

Babs scoffed. "I prefer to be my own warrior."

Without another word they joined Babs's parents who were in an old cannon room, the artifacts still in decent condition. Mrs. Xiomy wanted to inspect them but before she could, Molina held out the article to her. Babs snatched it out of her hands, putting her fingers gently on Boreas's eyes staring back at her through the page. Mrs. Xiomy read the article over her shoulder and both held their breath till the last word.

"So, Herald is going to use him."

"Aye." Mrs. O'Hara said with her Irish brogue more prevalent than her daughters. "The interview is going to be live tonight."

"We need to get to Hyperborea," Mrs. Xiomy insisted. "Fawn needs us to help as they prepare for battle against the Inspector."

Mr. O'Hara shook his head. "It is a hopeless mission. We cannot take the risk of travel to Hyperborea now... let alone with the Common Good Army on high alert knowing that Fawn would be looking for reinforcements. We cannot put our peoples' lives in danger."

"But those are my friends," Babs cried out. "Aurora and Otus and Fawn...and the Professor. We can't abandon them."

Mrs. O'Hara put her arm around her daughter. "Fawn lost her way a long time ago, my darling. Plymouth Tartarus collapsed, Eileen was killed and many others. We need to look to our people now. The Geometric Storm is coming. We need to think about survival."

Mrs. Xiomy shook her head. "The only way for survival is for Boreas to get his powers in Hyperborea."

Mr. O'Hara cried out, "You think we are going to risk losing another daughter? We just got Babs back!"

Molina put her hands up and separated Mrs. Xiomy and Mr. O'Hara. "OK, let's calm down. Fighting isn't getting us anywhere."

Mr. O'Hara pointed around him at the crumbling edifice. "Look around you. This fortress is falling apart. Just like the rebellion."

He stormed off and slammed the dilapidated doors behind him.

Mrs. O'Hara clutched Babs's hand so hard that it turned red. "We've tried. Really we have. But your father and I were never meant to lead and there's no one else stepping forward to take over. So we just carry on, waiting. Waiting for the storm, for the Common Good to discover us… waiting for death…"

She burst into tears and ran off after her husband, her flaming red hair visible even as she headed further into the darkness of the underground tunnel.

Babs jumped down, splashing her feet into the puddles, debating whether to run after them or run away. She closed her eyes and whispered, "I remember them being braver."

Mrs. Xiomy put her hand on her shoulder. "They are brave. Braver than most. But fear is a tempting demon. Trust me. I faced it the day I turned the rebellion in to Inspector Herald in a desperate attempt to save David's life. Fear of losing those you love is the most powerful weapon."

Babs stared resolutely at Mrs. Xiomy, "Do not compare my parents to you. They would never turn on their people."

"Not even if they thought it would save you?" Mrs. Xiomy said sadly.

Molina jumped in, "OK, but despite all of that, I can tell you that those you brought with you are going to need a leader right now. Boreas is siding with the Inspector and Aurora and Otus are out there searching for a mysterious place in the middle of the desert."

"Fawn's the leader," Mrs. Xiomy said at last. "Not me."

Molina put her hands on her hips. "Well, this Fawn you keep complaining about… she's not here is she?"

Molina and Babs took off through the narrow tunnels in pursuit of Mrs. O'Hara, leaving Mrs. Xiomy to ponder over what in the hell she was going to do. Everyone else had gone to the fortress's central piazza for dinner but she wasn't hungry. She walked through the dark tunnels, her feet sloshing in the water that was flooding slightly due to the cracking concrete walls. A flickering torch hung on the wall every couple of feet to provide some light as it was just her and her shadow getting lost in this hidden historical gem. She thought misty-eyed that Aurora would love it here.

She lost track of time, wandering along the tunnel maze, and she found herself back in the submarine docking room. It was eerily quiet except for the soft lapping of the waves against the deck where the submarines were docked. Fawn needed reinforcements if she was going to take on Inspector Herald. But without a leader, these people were not going to abandon this safe place to head off into the unknown on a likely suicide mission.

"David... what the hell do I do now?"

Just then, the underwater sealed panels began to slide open, unlocked by someone pressing down on the Celtic cross on the other side of the undersea cave wall. Mrs. Xiomy stood there alone as the guards had disappeared back into the fortress. She was glued to the spot as the large panels slid, further and further apart. She searched frantically around her and spotted a spear hanging on the wall nearby. She quickly plucked it off the wall and held it firmly in her grasp. There was not enough time to call out and run for help, and she didn't know who was entering this hidden commune. Was it the Common Good? Did they follow her down there?

Two bodies in snorkeling gear swam through the panels and Mrs. Xiomy prepared herself for the kill, her hand steadfast on the trigger. As the bodies broke the surface for air, she stood on the deck, hovering above them, and pressed the point of the spear threateningly up against the larger man's head and cried out, "Don't move another muscle."

The two bodies froze, bobbing ever so slightly with the waves. Just then a deep voice laughed. "Looks like the shoes are on the other foot this time, Rana. Or do you just like to stab math teachers?"

Mrs. Xiomy dropped the spear and leaned down to pull off the man's mask, his voice... Molina said he had been captured and was presumed dead!

But the eyes of Romero stared back at her, and he was very much alive.

Chapter 19

Undercover

*J*ake was relieved Mrs. Xiomy was concentrating her efforts on Romero, going on and on about Molina telling her that he had been captured by the Common Good Army after they had escaped from Macchu Picchu.

"I managed to escape with my injured friend here," Romero said, pointing to Jake whose left eye was still swollen and the other half of his face bandaged up for the disguise. Mrs. Xiomy gave him a look, and it was almost as if she did a double take... trying to make out how she knew him.

"Who are you?" she asked. "Are you from Candlewick?"

He shrugged, pretending to check his bag that he removed from the sealed package to ensure there was no water damage. Jake quickly made sure that his upper arm was still covered by the wet suit, where the First Lieutenant tattoo was imprinted like an identity card.

Romero jumped in. "My friend doesn't like to talk and from what I can gather has been on the run for quite some time. His leg wound still hasn't healed properly. The Common Good Army that captured us really did a number on him, but luckily we were able to escape. As we fled, I remembered what Molina had said about reaching this commune beneath Alcatraz. When did you get here?"

"We just got here ourselves," she said, still eying Jake suspiciously. "Come with me and I'll take you to see the O'Hara's."

They carried on about Macchu Picchu and Max Radar while Jake hobbled along behind them, overemphasizing the limp in his leg. Jake feared his former neighbor and science teacher would identify him as the First Lieutenant, but she was just another person he had to fool or pay the consequences.

"This is for Mary," he reminded himself as he surveyed his surroundings. He realized if he were recognized that he was going to be killed in this underwater fortress. How many of these rebel's friends and family members had he tortured and killed? He tried not to think of it as he had to stay focused on his undercover mission. The tracker was still implanted in his arm and there was no way to get rid of it without cutting it out and raising the alarm.

They walked into a large piazza with cannons still intact from the 1800s lining the walls. It resembled a military base museum with countless artifacts and was nearly filled to capacity with a sea of rebels. The rebels were disorganized and chaos ensued as people were fighting to try to get a bite to eat. There was no system and no one standing up to take charge. The O'Hara's, who Mrs. Xiomy pointed out, were the leaders, were preoccupied doing some maintenance work. Mrs. O'Hara had rolled up her sleeves and was fixing one of the pipes that looked like it was about to burst.

"I need to fix this," Mrs. O'Hara kept saying to a girl who Jake recognized as Babs O'Hara, the travelling companion of Boreas and Aurora. She was more beautiful than her wanted poster.

"Can't that wait?" Babs cried out, aggravated, her auburn hair coming undone from the braid that hung loosely down her back. "The people need you to lead."

"The people can wait," Mrs. O'Hara cried out, twisting the knob with a screwdriver. "They've waited 5 years for a leader. At least they'll have water."

Babs stood up, eying the chaos around her and instinctively put two fingers in her mouth and let out a high screeching whistle that sounded over the entire forum. Everyone stopped in their tracks and turned in her direction.

"One at a time! No more fighting or you won't get any food. You hear me!"

She spotted Mrs. Xiomy and ran in her direction.

"Nicely done, Babs," Mrs. Xiomy said.

"If only we had Otus," she cried out in exasperation. She then spotted the two men behind her friend and her mouth hung open in shock as she stared at Romero.

"Wait... Is that...?"

"Romero!!!"

A woman with short thick hair and muscular arms zigzagged past masses of people huddled on the floor and threw her arms around Romero.

"Molina," he scolded. "Not a scene. I have a reputation."

"You Lucky Bastard, you escaped? I can't believe it!"

"Can my friend and I get in line for some food before the interrogation?"

Both Molina and Babs stared in Jake's direction and he forced a smile.

Molina inquired, "Friend? Who is this? I don't remember him escaping from Macchu Picchu with us."

"Do you want me to look at your eye?" Babs asked, starting to approach and Jake quickly held his hand up in defense.

"Hey, I'm not going to hurt you," she snickered.

Jake gave Romero a look with his one good eye that he'd better do something and fast or else they were both dead.

Romero whispered something in Molina's ear. Molina's face went pale and then she nodded. She approached Jake and said, "Sorry. Yes, let me get you a plate of food. Babs, can you help me?"

She pulled Babs after her toward the buffet line that was starting to get organized.

They headed back to the table and Jake whispered, "What the hell did you tell her?"

Romero shrugged, chugging the glass of wine. "I told her you lost your mother at the hand of Inspector Herald and you haven't spoken since then."

Jake clenched up thinking about his mother. "I didn't need you to tell her that."

"I had to tell her something and women get all sympathetic to things like that. Trust me, I did the right thing to get them off your back."

They scarfed down a small plate of beans and a half of a slice of bread and as Jake looked around, he realized that this rebel base was in worse shape than anyone would care to admit. The O'Haras were busy doing anything else except leading, with Molina stepping up in charge of the small militia that apparently she had trained in her short time at the base. Babs and Mrs. Xiomy were deep in conversation in the corner with the O'Hara's, and he strained his ears to overhear some of the conversation, picking up words such as Hyperborea, help, and Otus.

It wasn't difficult to piece together the dilemma. He understood that Mrs. Xiomy and Babs wanted these West Coast rebels to help provide reinforcements to Fawn and her people in Hyperborea. Jake swallowed bitterly, realizing that he would either have to convince them to go, or to convince Babs and Mrs. Xiomy to take him with them if they left separately. He needed to report in to Herald so he stood up and separated himself from the main hall, taking one of the tunnels leading deep into the fortress. He gazed sadly around at this place that could have been his refuge, but instead he was here as a spy.

After ensuring he was alone and not being followed, he ignited the watch with his tracker. Instantly he saw Inspector Herald's face glaring back at him.

"I'm in," Jake said curtly, hating himself with every word he shared. "Rana Xiomy and Babs O'Hara are here. They are trying to convince the commune to join them in Hyperborea."

"Good," the Inspector chimed back slowly, in deep thought. "You need to get to Hyperborea. We need to bring down Fawn and her rebels once and for all. Your job will be to convince Aurora to go with you to free her father."

Jake stood there hesitantly. "In the western prison?"

The Inspector smiled cunningly. "No, you are not going there to free him and your precious Mary. Your job will be to bring her to me."

Jake nodded like an automaton. "I'll bring you Aurora. But that's the end of my servitude. After that you will release Mary, unharmed and alive."

Herald smiled. "Yes, Mary will be alive. I assure you of that."

His face flickered off and Jake stood there, the Inspector's words resonating in his mind. Mary would be alive… but he didn't say he would free her. This endless cycle was driving him mad and he collapsed against the stone wall, hugging his chest to stay warm over his wet suit.

"I thought you didn't speak!"

Jake jumped to his feet, ready to attack when he came face-to-face with Babs O'Hara.

Jake relaxed his fists. "I never said I didn't speak. Romero said that."

Babs continued to stare at him, her arms filled with clothes. "Who were you speaking with? I heard voices but there's only you in here."

Jake felt his heart racing and he bit his lip realizing his charade would collapse unless he sold it.

"I was praying."

She stared at him, confused. "You sounded awfully angry to be praying."

"Let's just say me and God... we don't have the best relationship right now."

Babs nodded and handed him the clothes. "I thought you might need these. I was able to steal some from my dad's closet."

Jake stared at her questioningly, her bright eyes staring back at his. "Whatever made you do that?"

She looked taken aback and Jake realized that she was not always this charitable. "I... I heard you lost your mother, to Herald. I lost a sister in the Plymouth Tartarus bombing. I know what it's like to lose someone and thought you might need some clothes."

He felt his heart clench thinking about his mom and also about the bombing, which he had executed, under Herald's orders. That bombing that had killed this young woman's sister. And here he was risking more lives and causing more death and destruction... to save his own sister.

"Thank you," he stuttered, taking the clothes and holding them against his chest, the only nice thing anyone had done for him in a long time. "I have a sister too. That must have been hard for you to lose her."

She held out her hand. "I'm Babs O'Hara."

"I'm... Mark," he lied, using the alias he had agreed upon with Romero prior to arriving. He shook her hand that was warm yet calloused from her months out in the wilderness. Months he had been chasing her... but she had no idea he even knew who she was.

"Well, I'd better let you change," she said, her voice song-like and as she turned to go, she whirled back and said, "I'm singing later. Mrs. Xiomy insisted, saying it might give the people some hope if we have a concert... some semblance of normalcy. Will you come?"

He nodded, watching her as a small smile crept along her face. She then swung her braid around and took off down one of the tunnels.

Jake stared down at the clothes and he realized he had his way to get to Hyperborea. He just needed to win the heart of Babs O'Hara.

Chapter 20

The Khanda Sword

It was like a race between the two giants as they sprinted across the land during the Sacred Hour. Ephialtes trying to beat Otus and vice versa, living out their sibling rivalry. Aurora and Jonathan were in Otus's pocket while Babs, Fawn and the Professor were in Ephialtes's satchel. All humans were green in the face and praying that they would reach Hyperborea before dawn.

"Someone needs to teach these Giants the story of the tortoise and the hare," The Professor cried out right before Otus made another flying leap into the atmosphere.

"In their version, the hare probably eats the tortoise," Aurora said with a slight laugh while hanging on to the pocket rim for dear life.

Aurora looked out into the distance past the trees and the farm land patches. Somewhere out there Boreas was once again at the mercy of the Inspector. Nobody talked about the possibility that he could already be dead, especially with Fawn around. She was not giving up hope. Aurora felt deep within her that he was still alive. She couldn't describe the feeling and she couldn't tell the others in fear that they would think she was going crazy. She wanted to tell Jonathan to ease his worries but talking to Jonathan was another thing she was avoiding, especially after what had transpired in the Whispering Meadow.

Ephialtes and Otus landed with a screeching halt. Aurora shook her head to knock the vertigo sensation out of her and peered over the side of the pocket. There before her eyes was the most beautiful sight she had ever beheld.

It resembled a picture out of a storybook, with rolling hills, quaint cottages, beautiful trees in full bloom though they were in the middle of November. A picturesque lavender and blue mountain range surrounded them interspersed with a rolling river that cut deep into its sides and wound through the center until it emptied into a beautiful lake. The scent of lilac and honeysuckle filled her nostrils and she breathed in deeply the beautiful scents of nature. She looked over at Fawn and Jonathan who were both in awe with this vista before them and nobody dared disturb the beauty with their human voices.

Otus finally sang out, "We made it to Hyperborea."

Ephialtes stretched his muscles and cried out, "Even after five years of isolation, I can still beat you, Otus!"

"You didn't beat me. It was a tie."

Ephialtes picked up a stick and began to draw a line in the dirt showing where his feet tracks stopped and how it was barely half an inch ahead of where Otus's feet marks ended.

"Like they say in horse racing, I won by a toe."

"I think you mean a nose," The Professor said queasy and stumbling out of the satchel that was sprawled out onto the grass. He was followed by Jonathan and Fawn who both collapsed in a dizzy spell.

Ephialtes sneered at the Professor, apparently not happy to be corrected and ran off into the woods.

"Are you sure it was a good idea getting him involved?" The Professor asked, adjusting his goggles and making sure that they weren't broken.

Fawn was sprawled out on the thicket of grass and her long black hair was a tangled mess over her face that was starting to return to its normal color.

"He is reckless, but I think we need a little more reckless if we are going to fight the Inspector. He thinks like him."

"Just next time can I please drive?" Jonathan begged, looking like he was about to vomit.

"What do we do now?" Aurora asked, mesmerized by the beautiful place they had invaded and couldn't believe that this is where they were going to have to face the Inspector in battle. It looked too beautiful to be a burial ground.

"We find Mrs. Taboo," Otus said resolutely. He took out his conch shell and began to blow on it.

"Can she hear it?" Aurora asked her friend who looked down at her and doubt crossed his mind as well.

"I figured she gave it to me. I thought she would be able to hear it too."

"What is wrong with that conch shell anyway?" Jonathan asked, coming to sit beside Aurora.

Aurora felt tense with Jonathan sitting so close to her, his hair blowing across her shoulders and she turned to him and relayed the story of how only she and Boreas had been able to hear the conch shell back in Candlewick. That it was signaling them to help Otus out of the ruby-red house and begin their mission. He listened intently and with bitterness said, "Boreas can hear it and I can't?"

Aurora sighed thinking back to that day in Candlewick. It felt like so long ago.

"That's what got us in this mess to begin with."

Jonathan turned to Aurora and smiled. "At least this mess led me to you."

Before her mind could even grasp the words, he leaned in and kissed her on the lips.

When Aurora broke away she looked up to see Fawn staring at them with a smile on her face. "So, I see you two have been hitting it off." She said warmly. "I feel like I should be doing the mother thing, warning you about dating... using protection..."

"Mom, she's not the first girl I dated," Jonathan laughed, standing up and stretching. Once again, thoughts of Hattie popped into Aurora's head and she jumped to her feet to try to scavenge for some food, to try to block out jealous thoughts.

The Professor was pacing with his walking stick and tapping away until he threw the stick onto the ground and cried out, "So, is it not worrying anyone else that we are again ten steps behind the Inspector? He has Boreas and knows what he is capable of. And we are sitting here waiting for this Mrs. Taboo who we don't even know exists. Where is she? Where is anyone for that matter?"

Aurora realized that the Professor was correct. There was not a single soul outside or working. It was almost as if the town knew they were there and were biding their time and waiting. It was like a game of chess and each was watching the other's first move.

Aurora stood up and said, "I am going to take a walk to the lake."

Otus shook his head dismissively, the protective instincts taking hold. "You are not up to it. You need to rest."

Aurora shrugged off her friend and declared, "Boreas isn't getting any rest. I will not rest until we get the answers we need from

Mrs. Taboo. Everyone stay here and at the first sign of trouble, well, Otus you know what to do."

Otus nodded, though not condoning the ludicrous plan.

Aurora meandered her way down the steep slope toward the town and the glistening lake that was carved in the epicenter, surrounded by little reddish brown and orange cottages. She continued forward, the eerie silence unnerving as she advanced toward the lake. Sure enough, there was not a sign of anyone. All the shops had "Closed' signs hanging from their doors and she wondered if it was some sort of siesta or holiday that was causing everyone to be either inside their homes or away. She made it to the lake, taking a seat nearby to get a better perspective but all she saw was a ghost town. She took off her shoes and her feet were bruised and aching when she dipped them into the cool and refreshing water. She let them soak and then scooped up water in her palms and poured it over her bare arms. The sun was beating down on her with no shade and she welcomed the warmth on her skin, feeling as if it was being absorbed into her. She looked into the lake at her reflection, trying to smooth down hair that was now streaked with blond highlights. She wiped some of the grime from her cheeks and for a minute she admired the girl looking back at her, starting to see the goddess within her... what Jonathan was now seeing; what Boreas had always saw.

"Hello, Goddess of Dawn."

She whirled around at hearing the ghostly boy's voice, but, as before, there was no one there. She quickly looked back into the pool of water and there, staring back at her, was Swanson. He was the young boy who she had first met at Lake Champlain. He was some sort of mirage or spirit that could speak to her when she looked into the water. She leaned forward and whispered, "Swanson, what are you doing here?"

"I could ask you the same question," he said with a laugh, fixing the yellow fisherman rain hat over his eyes.

"Swanson, we are looking for a woman named Mrs. Taboo. Do you know where we can find her?"

Swanson looked left and right and made a motion like he was ushering her to come closer toward him. She got on her knees and leaned down into the water until her face was nearly resting on the surface. Swanson then said, "There is no looking for Mrs. Taboo. When she thinks you are ready, she will find you."

"Ready!" Aurora cried out. "Are you kidding me? I have done everything that has been asked of me. I have travelled across the country, been to jail, fought against the Common Good army, and oh yeah, got powers! And now Boreas is suffering at the hands of the Inspector and may die. And the Inspector is going to come here, fight and most likely kill me and my friends. So, tell Mrs. Taboo I am done waiting and I am ready to see her now."

Swanson was smiling, apparently amused at this tirade, and although Aurora splashed at the water, his reflection continued to stare back at her. After the splash rings dispersed, another face suddenly joined Swanson's in the water. Aurora gasped! The face that manifested was of an elderly woman with great big eyes and gray hair pulled back in a bun. Aurora was about to scream when a hand reached out of the water, grabbed her by the shirt and pulled her into the lake. Aurora hit the cold water and struggled to try to fight the apparition. Just then a voice spoke, "Don't struggle, Aurora or you will surely die. You said you were ready. Let's see how ready you really are."

Aurora was dragged deeper into the heart of the lake, afraid to heed the voice within her mind. She struggled, trying to summon powers that wouldn't ignite under the water.

"This is how I will die," she thought bitterly. "Not by the Common Good Army but by the hands of an old woman."

Aurora knew she had only been under water for a couple of seconds but it felt like an eternity as she continued to be dragged to her death.

To her astonishment, at the bottom of the lake was a table and chairs. "Of course," she thought at the absurdity of her life, "the old lady just wanted her over for tea and a rousing game of bridge… underwater!" The old woman released her grip on Aurora and seated herself in one of the chairs, ushering Aurora to take the seat opposite her. Instinctively Aurora tried to swim upwards, but with a clap of her hands, the old woman magically summoned bubbles that pulled Aurora onto the chair.

The old woman smiled and said, "You can breathe, child. The water is only an illusion to fool our enemies. This is actually liquid oxygen."

Aurora shook her head, not convinced, even though she had been through this situation before back at Lake Champlain. Her instinctual response was so strong. But the woman was clearly breathing – deep breaths too, no gurgles and she didn't appear to have gills. The old woman, Aurora realized, was Mrs. Taboo. She recognized her face from the painting in the ruby-red house back at Candlewick.

Mrs. Taboo said soothingly in her head, "Have faith, Aurora. Isn't that what your mission is all about? If you don't have faith, then you will surely drown."

Aurora froze thinking that this sounded ludicrous, but then again, this was the woman who befriended Otus and had saved him from the Common Good Army. If Aurora was going to put her faith in anyone, it should be in this woman. She closed her eyes and tried to clear her mind of everything she had ever been taught: that humans couldn't breathe under water, that there were no such thing as giants, that it was impossible for a teenager to have sunlight stream out of her fingertips.

And then she took a breath.

And Aurora was able to breathe normally. This defied not only logic, but science as well. She put her hand up in front of her as if it was wading in water and yet this was not water. It was an illusion.

"This is impossible," Aurora spoke, expecting water to go gushing into her mouth but the water merely floated in front of her lips.

Mrs. Taboo smiled, adjusting the shawl over her gray hair. "Anything is possible, Goddess of Dawn. You of all people should know that. I am so proud of how far you have come. I knew that Otus would find you. I foresaw this. The Inspector will be coming to fight. We will need both the Goddess of Dawn and the God of the North Wind to defeat them."

"Well, that could be a problem because… well, Boreas isn't here. And as far as I know he isn't the God of the North Wind yet."

Mrs. Taboo turned to Swanson who had been standing beside her and they exchanged a look of dismay.

"Well, then I am afraid there isn't much hope for success."

A feeling of foreboding overwhelmed Aurora as Mrs. Taboo's words sunk in. They had come so far for answers and all Mrs. Taboo confirmed her greatest fear — they would die in Hyperborea.

"Then it has been all for nothing?" she stammered. "We are just going to fail and the Geometric Storm is going to cause death and destruction on an unfathomable scale and the Inspector will win! I can't believe that. I can't believe that we have come so far just to give up now."

Swanson walked over to Aurora, his big brown eyes shining and said, "That was what I was hoping you would say."

Mrs. Taboo nodded at him and Aurora didn't understand what was transpiring around her.

"So you are saying you are going to help us fight?"

Mrs. Taboo laughed and said, "Aurora, we have been fighting for the past 15 years. My religion, when I was free to practice, was Sikhism and what that means is that I believe I possess the qualities of a Sant-Sipāhī or a saint-soldier. We have a duty to defend the rights of all people who are persecuted due to their religious beliefs.

We are all one, Aurora, and in time you will understand how important your role is in this fight."

Aurora turned to Swanson and stammered, "I am not a soldier. I thought all I needed to do was get Otus to the Northern Lights. I am not a killer. The reason I received my powers of dawn was not because I took a life, but because I saved a life. I saved Boreas's life."

Swanson put his youthful hand onto her shoulder and gave it a reassuring squeeze. Aurora looked into the big brown eyes of the young child spirit before her and felt comforted by having his presence near her.

Mrs. Taboo's eyes looked troubled. "You know some of the old history. You know that sometimes to gain liberty the people need to rise up to make change a possibility."

Aurora remembered her father's words and his obsession with the United States of America's Revolutionary War. Fighting the British for freedom and to create a new democratic country, freeing themselves from the reign of an oppressor. They were outnumbered and the odds were against them, but they possessed a spirit with hope of a better tomorrow.

"What do I need to do?" she asked.

Instantly a school of fish swarmed around them, causing the sand at the bottom of the lake to spin into a tornado. Aurora shielded her eyes as she spotted in the center of the tornado was a double edged sword with hole in the center of the handle. Swanson reached into the sand tornado and pulled out the sword. Immediately the tornado ceased and the sand collapsed again onto the bottom of the lake. Swanson held up the magnificent sword and then to Aurora's surprise, he held it out offering it to her.

"This is my gift to you Aurora, Goddess of Dawn."

Aurora gazed upon the beautiful sword, the blade glistening before her. "What kind of sword is this?"

Mrs. Taboo smiled. "This is the Khanda, a symbol from the Sikh belief that it is wisdom cutting through ignorance. The right edge symbolizes freedom. The left edge symbolizes divine justice that punishes the oppressors. There needs to be a balance between the two and the Chakra (the centers of spiritual power in the body), which is symbolized by the hole here in the center, emphasizes this balance. This sword is a symbol of justice, unity, humanity and morality. Swanson gives this gift to you to either use in battle yourself or to bestow upon the one person who you believe will use this sword to help create this balance. Just know that once you give this gift away, you cannot take it back or use it yourself, no matter the cost."

Tentatively, Aurora held out her hand and grasped the handle, accepting the gift. The sword was light in her grasp as she studied the blade closely.

"Thank you, Swanson. I will try to choose wisely how best to use this sword."

Mrs. Taboo came closer to Aurora and said, "It is time to return to the surface or else I fear your friends will think you have drowned. Take my hand. Swanson, if you wouldn't mind a little push?"

"Not at all," Swanson said grinning from ear to ear as he rubbed his hands together. A huge burst of pressure propelled Aurora and Mrs. Taboo upwards toward the surface. Aurora grasped the hilt of the sword with all her strength in order to not let go as she was flying like an out of control rocket. She broke through the surface, coughing as her body adjusted to the oxygen now pumping into her lungs. Before she could open her eyes a huge hand grabbed her out of the water.

"Otus," Aurora cried out, afraid she might accidentally cut Otus with the sword. "Put me down. I am fine!"

"I thought you were dead!" his green eyes were glazed with tears. "You were underwater for the past 5 minutes."

"Otus! It's Mrs. Taboo!"

"And just because now you are the Goddess of Dawn don't think that... what did you say?"

Aurora laughed and pointed down toward the dripping wet woman standing at Otus's feet.

Otus nearly dropped Aurora as he recognized his long lost friend.

"It's nice to see you too, Otus," she said, squeezing the water out of her shawl and then placing it over her head. "I told you that when you were ready, you would find me again."

A woman's heart wrenching scream interrupted this reunion, followed by running footsteps. More screams ensued and Otus strained his neck to try to see what the commotion was.

"Otus, what is it? What do you see?" Fawn exclaimed as Jonathan held up a gun he had found, preparing for an attack.

A flood of people were running in their direction, some tripping over each other's feet as they scrambled down the hill toward where Mrs. Taboo was standing. A huge shadow was towering over them as they ran and Aurora's throat went dry thinking it was a fighter plane above them... that the fight was already beginning.

The shadowy form of Ephialtes stomped out from behind the mountain chasing after the people and yelling at them, "Come on, move faster. We have army training and you are all invited. Now hurry up!"

Otus collapsed onto the ground stupefied that his brother was the cause behind this commotion and mass hysteria.

Mrs. Taboo glared up at Otus and exclaimed, "You freed your brother!"

Tongue-tied, Otus attempted to come up with an explanation. Aurora shone her light into Ephilates's eyes, forcing him to freeze in his tracks.

"You puny human, get your light out of my eyes before I permanently put them out."

Mrs. Taboo stared at the hysterical people congregating around her in fear and she put her hands up and shouted, "Ephialtes, that is enough!"

Ephialtes looked down, stunned silent upon hearing the voice of Mrs. Taboo. Aurora ceased shining her light in his eyes.

"I was just finding the people," he declared defensively. "And besides, can't a giant have a little fun?"

Chapter 21

The Broadcast

A make-up artist applied more powder to Boreas's face as he sat in front of the World Summit Ambassadors waiting for his monumental interview. The cameras were set-up in a half-moon around Boreas as he sat nervously waiting for the director to signal the start of the broadcast. The Inspector told Boreas that if he obeyed and read the speech word for word that Sansa and Steven would be spared. Boreas glanced over at the first row where the children were sitting. Sampson sat beside them, unaware of the danger his children were in. Sansa, to Boreas's relief, was looking well. She did have a bandage on her leg, but the color had returned to her cheeks and her big brown eyes were staring at him with such love that he had to turn away. He could be risking their lives, unless he adhered to the Inspector's demands. How he wished he could get word to Sampson to get his kids out of there, but there was nothing he could do. He wished Mrs. Alvarez would approach him so he could maybe give her some kind of message, but they were purposely keeping her at a distance.

The beautiful reporter from Channel Five news approached the stage wearing an orange dress and indigo high heels. The ruby necklace adorning her neck sparkled in the limelight. She sat down across from him and crossed her legs. "I will be the one interviewing you today, Boreas. My name is Analise Jones."

"I know who you are," he said, half-listening, his mind preoccupied. How was he going to get himself out of this mess?

"I have been dying to interview you," she said, her eyes glued on her notes. "Especially since you are here to stop the Geometric Storm."

Boreas's eyes immediately shot up and he turned to the reporter who was playing with the necklace, like it was strangling her. She leaned toward him, pretending to show him something on her cue cards and whispered, "I know that the Inspector wants you to read what's on the teleprompter. I helped write it. I know what that means and you can't do it. Too many people are counting on you."

He shook his head, his eyes darting toward Sansa and Steven. Analise followed his eyes and understood.

"I will take care of it. Radar is ready with the helicopter."

"Radar's here?" he asked stunned, and then, catching himself, resumed looking at the cue cards.

"Yes," she said, fixing a strand of hair behind his ear. "Sampson and the children, we will have to leave them behind. You are too valuable to the cause."

"No," was all Boreas said, looking intently at the reporter who couldn't understand. He was not about to let the Inspector kill two innocent children...his cousins...because of him.

"More children will die unless you stop the Geometric Storm."

"You sound like Radar."

"Radar knows what he's talking about."

Boreas glared at the reporter and watched as the final ambassadors were filing into their seats in the great ballroom. He saw Mrs. Alvarez enter the room wearing a floral suit concoction with a large brimmed hat with a pink feather sticking out at the top. The paparazzi took her picture and while she pretended to not notice, she gave a different pose for each one. A teenager about his own age came right up to Boreas, snapped a picture, nodded his thanks and then retreated back off the stage before he could get caught by one of the guards. Though he wasn't handcuffed, Boreas had an electric bracelet on his wrist to track him in case he tried to run. The Inspector had said clearly, "If your heart beat rises above 100 beats per minute, I will tell my sniper to take out the kids immediately so that you can watch them massacred."

Boreas closed his eyes, trying to regulate his heart rate. What would Aurora do in this situation?

The moderator was going to be the famous comedian, Harold Humpnick, who starred in a popular show called "Bringing up Humpnick". He had a very red complexion in real life and orange hair that clashed with his polka dot outfit. He looked more like a clown than a television star. He stepped onto the stage to resounding applause, took a bow and nearly slipped on the stage, to which the audience burst into laughter. He took the microphone to warm up the crowd, saying, "Any ambassadors in the house?"

More laughter. Boreas felt his heartbeat racing and eyed the bracelet with contempt and fear. Analise was saying something into her microphone, probably talking to the director. The makeup artist came up to put more powder on his face. He thought he was going to look like a girl before they were through with him, adding to the humiliation for what he was about to do. The makeup artist opened the powder, but instead of the foundation, there were tools. He took out two little screwdrivers and before Boreas had a chance to react, he swapped his electrical bracelet for the one that the makeup

artist had on his wrist. He put Boreas's sleeve down while simultaneously combing his hair and then retreated off the stage. Boreas
turned to Analise, but she didn't make eye contact. Boreas felt for
the first time that he wasn't the only one trying to fight against the
Inspector. There were spies inside and they wanted him to make the
speech he had intended all along.

Chapter 22

Pro-IDEAL

urora turned on the television set in Mrs. Taboo's house and felt horrified as the commercials ended and the program began.

Boreas sat wearing a suit and tie with his hair combed over the left side of his forehead, as opposed to the front and spiked upwards. His skin looked so smooth and he seemed to be taking in all of the prestigious guests since he appeared to look at everything but the camera while Harold Humpnick was doing his opening monologue.

Aurora thought about how much her mother loved the "Bringing up Humpnick" show on television. She never missed an episode, rushing home from work in order to catch it. She said laughter was contagious, but Aurora never knew what was so funny about this clown, though she had enjoyed spending alone time with her mom. She felt her eyes water a bit as she watched the television set, trying to get a glimpse of her mom as the new Ambassador of the Common Good. She thought she saw her in the back and wondered if she had a chance to speak with Boreas. What would she even have said? She was probably just excited to see Harold Humpnick in person.

Otus knocked on the door and peeked his eye into the house. He looked exhausted, his eyes drooped as if he would pass out in any minute.

"Ephialtes is finally asleep," Otus yawned, stretching his arms high above him. "Did I miss Boreas?"

Aurora shook her head, "No, but he doesn't look hurt. In fact, it's the best I've seen him in a while."

Otus stared intently at the screen and shook his head, "He looks good, but his eyes can't hide the truth. He is scared."

Aurora turned back to the screen and sure enough, while he now looked at the camera confidently, there was something in his eyes that made him nervous. She wondered what the Inspector was doing to Boreas to make him participate in this charade.

Jonathan humphed, "Please, my brother is probably thrilled that he is going to be on national television. He always wanted something to gloat about."

Aurora gave Jonathan a nasty look. "Your brother could be killed and you think he's doing this to one up you?"

Jonathan shrugged, "Why not? I would."

He put his arm around her shoulders but Aurora pushed it off, making up some excuse that she felt warm. She felt guilty sitting here with Jonathan while Boreas was all alone. A part of her wished she was with him...wished that she could help him.

"I feel so helpless," she confided, her hands clenched together, prayer-like.

Jonathan was about to say something when Fawn entered the room looking disheveled. She had spent a long day of working with

Mrs. Taboo to rally the forces. Fawn just stared at the screen without speaking and Aurora knew how painful this must be for her.

Harold Humpnick made another crude joke and then slipped once again on his large shoes doing a backflip into the air. The audience laughed and applauded. Harold stood up, dusted himself off and bowed. Aurora was just glad he was finished with his stupid act.

The host announced a commercial break and said, "Stay tuned! When we come back, Boreas Stockington, son of David Xiomy, will speak out to the Common Good for the first time since his arrest. The IDEAL has spoken."

Aurora groaned as an image popped up on the screen of Boreas holding up the logo for the IDEAL.

"They are trying to paint him as Pro-IDEAL." Mrs. Taboo said, rocking gently in her chair in deep thought. "This could be detrimental to our cause."

Aurora jumped up, maneuvered through the crowd of people in that room and pushed through the door that led outside. She stood in Otus's shadow and he hastily put his foot in front of her to block her exit.

Otus stared at her, perplexed that she was walking out on the interview. "Where are you going?"

Aurora combed her fingers through her hair. "I just needed to get some air."

He didn't buy that excuse and patted her on the head, comfortingly. "He's going to be alright," he said.

"No, that's not it," Aurora said, wanting to pull her hair out. "Before, it was the Soul Extractor Serum, but now... is he willingly siding with the Inspector Herald against us?"

Otus scooped her up with his hand and lifted her eyelevel with him.

"What happened to having faith in him?" Otus raised his eyebrow. Aurora had to look away, ashamed.

"I want to have faith in him," she said slowly.

Otus put her back down on the ground, facing the television program that was about to come back from commercial break. "He needs you, Aurora. He needs you to believe in him."

The camera panned down from the top of the beautiful castle ceiling that reflected sunlight off the stained glass windows and zoomed in on the former Channel Five news reporter, Analise Jones. She looked radiant as she calmly looked into the camera and began the interview.

"Hello, fellow members of the Common Good. He was seen as a threat, with everyone in the nation searching for him once his true identity became known. And here today, as promised, Inspector Herald and the IDEAL have captured Boreas Stockington, the biological son of infamous conspirator and anti-government protestor, David Xiomy."

The audience gasped and the camera did a cut to the World Ambassadors and for a split second Aurora thought she saw a glimmer of her mom in a floral print suit in the back row.

Analise held up her hand and said, "Hello Boreas, or would you prefer Mr. Stockington?"

Boreas cleared his throat, and played nervously with his tie, tying the end of it into knots and looked over and over again at the front row. He then swallowed and said, "I've been Boreas Stockington all my life, but recently I discovered I have David Xiomy's blood flowing through my veins."

Analise smiled, "So how do you feel about your newly found lineage?"

Boreas looked directly at the front row and said, "I wish I could protect this new lineage, but it is out of my control. Other things have a hold on me."

The reporter didn't understand what he meant by that statement so she deftly changed the subject.

"So Boreas, is it true that you were conspiring against the Common Good and following in your father's footprints?"

Boreas tugged on his tie and shifted his body to face the camera but his eyes rolled from left to right like a typewriter. "No, I have no intention of turning against the Common Good. The Inspector is everyone's friend and IMAM, I mean, my biological father, was a fool to have turned against him. Religion is the root of all evil as everyone knows."

He closed his eyes as if fighting some unknown demon within him and Aurora couldn't believe the words coming out of his mouth, almost as if he was possessed.

He turned toward Analise and then back to the front row, and then directly at the cameras again. "If any of you are thinking of fighting against the IDEAL, you will be crushed in Hyperborea. Surrender now or else you will suffer the fate of my father and fall to the will of the Common Good."

Aurora faced Fawn but she didn't respond, her face pale and Aurora felt her heart beating wildly as if it would explode.

Analise was smiling a little too brightly as she said, "Great advice, Boreas. What should the rest of us do in order to ensure peace in our country?"

Boreas strained his eyes, staring once again into the camera, and it looked as if he was shaking his head no. But she had no idea who he was shaking his head to.

His voice was shaking like he was freezing as he said, "Peace will only be sustained if you follow the IDEAL. There is no other way."

He paused and bit his lip, fidgeting even more with his tie. Suddenly he yanked his tie from his shirt and threw it down on the ground viciously and pointed directly at the camera.

"No, I can't do it. Everything I have said here today is due to the Inspector threatening to kill people I care about. There is NO IDEAL. The Inspector is the only one who holds the power and keeps you all in his clutches. The Geometric Storm is coming and he wants nothing more than to let it destroy each and every one of you to keep you in his control. Don't let him. We need to rise up together. We need to…"

A gunshot rang out and the lights went to black instantly. The television screen cut to a still frame of colorful barcodes that stood stationary as a loud, high pitched beep reverberated from the audio track, indicating a test of the national broadcasting system.

Aurora prayed that gunshot had not struck Boreas's heart and she clutched her own to make sure it was still, in fact, beating. What had he risked to say those words? Aurora held her ears, blocking out the noise, but it couldn't block out the fear that Boreas had perished at the hand of the Inspector once and for all.

Chapter 23

A Rush of Chaos

Boreas couldn't see in the dark. He thought he was dead, with the bang of the gunshot ringing in his ear, but he didn't feel any pain. Then his mind raced thinking it was Sansa or Steven who had been shot. How he hoped Sampson had understood what was at stake after Boreas's warning during the interview about his lineage.

Boreas had no time to think. Analise grabbed his arm and urged him to follow her through the massive chaos that was ensuing beneath them. The guards were rushing in with guns drawn and lights shining from sniper rifles. Boreas ran, lost in the shuffle of people, hoping he could escape that room before the workers had a chance to restore power.

Analise hit a dead end and Boreas collided against her as more people ran past them to get out of the line of fire. Analise pressed a button on the side of the painting and it slid open, revealing a secret passageway. He followed her into the dark tunnel, closing the painting swiftly behind him. There was a long, narrow, brick corridor that smelled like a mildewed rug. He tried holding his breath as he ran through the pitch dark corridor following Analise's lead. Boreas spotted a light up ahead - one of the lights from the sniper rifle - but before he could signal to Analise, she grabbed his hand and pulled him hastily out of the soldier's line of sight. They hid silently behind a large obstruction against the wall that resembled a treasure chest as the heavy prodding of footsteps ran past.

Once the coast was clear, Analise flung open the lid of the treasure chest and pulled out a guard uniform and a pair of jeans, a shirt and sneakers.

"Quick, put these on," she commanded, throwing the uniform at him.

"How did you know I wouldn't say the speech?" He asked, still so confused by the turn of events as he stuffed himself into the uniform.

"Wishful thinking," she said, quickly snapping the jeans on, kicking off her heels and replacing them with the sneakers.

Analise cupped her hand over her ear and listened intently into her earpiece to the person who Boreas had assumed was the Director, but now realized was another spy helping them to escape.

"It's not safe yet to make a run for the helicopter," she said.

"What about Sansa & Steven?" Boreas whispered frantically. "Were they shot?"

Analise put her hand up to signal Boreas to wait, covered her ear again and then shook her head in the negative. "No, they are safe. Their father, Sampson, is the one who fired the gun. He informed my source that he is going to try to get his children to Radar's helicopter too."

Boreas nodded, adrenaline pumping through his veins and his heart racing. He couldn't believe what he had done merely 5 minutes ago. He had told everyone on national television that the IDEAL was a fraud. He had told them all about the Geometric Storm.

He didn't have a chance to dwell on his impromptu speech because Analise received word that they could proceed. She opened the wall panel that led them into a vacant conservatory on the main floor. There was no one in the room but they proceeded cautiously, knowing that there could be danger anywhere.

"You will pretend that you captured me if we get caught," Analise explained as she checked to make sure the coast was clear before advancing toward the back entrance.

Her spy was trying to help configure where the armed guards were to prevent a confrontation, but there were too many. Analise and Boreas needed to be prepared for the worst. A chance encounter would affect many more lives than just Boreas now that he wasn't working alone.

They snaked their way through long hallways and Boreas felt like they were stuck in a corn maze where each door led to another room. It was an endless labyrinth. He caught his reflection in one of the mirrors in the lounge and hardly recognized himself dressed in the Common Good fatigues. He hoped his disguise would fool more people than just himself. They were nearing the back entrance where Radar's helicopter was waiting for them when a group of soldiers headed their way. Billy Goat was one of them. Boreas's stomach churned. If any of the guards would recognize him, it would be Billy Goat. He tried to remain calm and focused as the guard approached, with three other big burly men behind him.

"Where do you think you are going, guard?" Billy Goat's husky voice demanded.

Boreas gulped, trying to disguise his voice. "Bringing the prisoner here to the Inspector for questioning."

Billy inspected him thoroughly and asked suspiciously, "Why didn't you call it in? That's the first protocol."

Boreas felt his forehead sweating in the gladiator-like helmet.

"I lost my radio. Besides, I think the Inspector would rather I bring the prisoner to him personally."

Boreas grabbed Analise tighter and started to inch forward when Billy grabbed him by the helmet, yanking it off.

"I think the Inspector wants me to bring *you* to him personally, Boreas."

Boreas tried to duck but Billy Goat was too quick, grabbing him in one of his famous wrestler headlocks. The other guards attempted to seize Analise, but she executed a masterful karate kick that knocked the second guard into the first, causing them to lose their balance. She disarmed the first guard and turned it on Billy Goat just as Billy Goat held his own gun against Boreas's temple.

"Nice try Analise, but one more kick out of you and the kid here is going to get a bullet lodged in his brain."

Analise stared at the gun and then back at Boreas. Unwillingly, she put her hands up in surrender.

Billy Goat snickered, "That's better. Now let's start walking. The Inspector doesn't like to be kept waiting."

Boreas felt all hope begin to drain from his body. Before he could completely give himself over to despair there was a crash and Billy Goat loosened his hold on Boreas and slumped to the ground, unconscious. Glass fragments sprinkled around his prone form as Boreas untangled himself from the wrestler's hold. He quickly looked up to see Sampson smiling down at him with a half broken vase in his hand. He threw the remains of his weapon and held his hand out to Boreas.

"Sampson, I'm so happy to see you," Boreas said, grabbing onto Sampson's hand.

He smiled, helping Boreas to his feet. "I told you we'd find a way to escape."

Sansa peaked out from Sampson's back, her arms wrapped tightly around his neck. Steven was looking frazzled beside his father and cried out, "Dad, I can't run much farther."

Boreas offered his back to the youth and Steven reluctantly jumped on and they proceeded down the most dangerous corridor yet. It led to the barricaded courtyard where Radar's helicopter was waiting for them.

"Miss Thompson said we need to turn back," Analise cried out, after listening to her contact through her earpiece. "There are more guards stationed outside the perimeter."

"There's no time to turn back," Sampson called back, leading the charge and picking up speed. "We need to get to the helicopter now."

"The Inspector is calling it a terrorist attack. He's claiming that we have reinforcements coming to take the ambassadors hostage."

"Let them think that," Boreas cried out, running as fast as his legs could go carrying Steven on his back.

Despite the warning, it seemed like they were leaving the action behind them in the castle. They could hear the sounds of the chopper more and more with each frantic step. It was almost too silent as they ran as fast as they could toward the helicopter. They burst through the corridor into the courtyard and saw the copter with the engine running and the propellers turning in an incessant circular motion, waiting impatiently for its passengers. Boreas could almost make out the shape of Radar's head in the cockpit, when all of a sudden gunshots rang out from above. Sampson put Sansa in Analise's arms so that he could reload his gun. He pointed his gun upwards toward the gunman in the tower and shot back, all of them ducking behind an Osprey plane for cover.

"I'll hold them off," Sampson screamed out to Boreas.

"No," Boreas cried out. "We're not leaving without you."

Sampson grabbed Boreas and looked him straight in the eye. "Get my children to Hyperborea. God willing I will find you there."

Boreas nodded reluctantly, knowing the priority was the children's safety. They had to get them into the helicopter.

Analise cried out, "On your right. Incoming!"

Sure enough, an influx of armed soldiers were approaching, having realized they were hiding behind the Osprey plane.

Sampson shot at the influx of soldiers heading in their direction. He shouted at them, "Go!"

Boreas and Analise, with the children on their backs, took off running. They didn't stop running, they couldn't.

"We can't leave my dad!," Steven exclaimed, trying to fight Boreas to put him down, but Boreas wouldn't relent, knowing full well that Sampson was sacrificing himself to save his children.

He turned back to see that Sampson had gotten into the Osprey and aimed the machine gun at the Common Good soldiers. The Osprey's machine gun rang out, shooting and making the soldiers run for cover, giving Boreas and Analise a clear path to the helicopter.

The chopper's propellers were flailing wildly at full speed, ready for takeoff. The wind it created nearly blew Boreas off balance as he ducked low under the blades and nearly crawled to the entrance. Radar was there and yelled, "Get in or I swear I am leaving without you!"

Analise helped Sansa in and Boreas ignored Steven hitting him on the back and demanding they go back for his father. Boreas slammed the door shut and yelled to Radar, "Go, Now!"

Radar didn't hesitate and lifted the helicopter up off the ground. Sampson was still shooting to save them time, each bullet another second that would help his children get off the ground safe and away from the onslaught of the Inspector and his army. Boreas looked out the window at the bravest man he had ever known, as they flew farther away from the castle overlooking the Hudson, the grounds now stained with blood.

Boreas went to help Analise who was attempting to wrap her bleeding arm where a bullet had grazed her skin. He found her a first aid kit and she applied gauze and antiseptic to help treat the wound.

"You were brave down there," Analise said, her eyes staring intently at Boreas while she administered to her wound. "For the first time, the world knows the truth."

Boreas looked out the window regretfully. "Yes, but at what cost?" He turned to see Sansa huddled against Steven. She was crying and he looked numb. Boreas didn't have anything comforting to say to them. He distracted himself by applying pressure to Analise's wound. "The Inspector will be heading to Hyperborea. I need to get there before he does."

Analise nodded in understanding, digging through the back of the helicopter for some provisions and found a water bottle that she passed to Steven and Sansa who drank gratefully.

The helicopter flew into the sunset, blood-red streaks staining the blue canvas. Sansa crawled up beside Boreas and rested her head on his shoulder. Boreas put his arm around the young girl, glad at least she had survived and was safe. He let her cuddle with him as she fell asleep, her dark brown bangs nearly covering her sleeping eyes, trusting him with all her heart to keep her safe. Guilt consumed him as he looked at the little girl, dirt smeared across her face, her leg still in a bandage. She may be fatherless because of him. It was all his fault....

But it wasn't his fault, Boreas reminded himself. Boreas was just a teenager trying to stop the Geometric Storm and causing a heap load of trouble along the way. This was the world's fault... a world who had let a man like Inspector Herald become powerful. A world that stood by and watched from the sidelines, not believing the pain and injustice would impact them. From the ambassadors to the media to countless thousands, no millions, of people who stood by and let him rise to power. It was time they heard the conch shell sound, waking them up to the injustice in this world. Boreas had taken a stand, like his father David Xiomy, did before him. Maybe he wasn't so different from his father after all.

Boreas was dozing off and turned to see Steven was still wide awake.

"Steven, are you ok?" He asked gently.

Steven didn't answer as he stared out the window, searching for some trace of his father; still hoping that his father would meet them in Hyperborea.

Chapter 24

True Intentions

Jake fixed the bandage around his eye as he sat in the back of the Alcatraz subterranean commune, held to his promise to hear Babs sing. It was eerily quiet in the fortress square surrounded by splashes of candlelight, the dripping wax landing in the ever-present pools of water at his feet. Jake peered up at the water falling like rain drops from the leaking pipes. This dilapidated fort needed structural fortification if it was going to hold for another month, let alone longer. The makeshift plumbing work that the O'Hara's were doing in a desperate effort to hold this place together was not going to last. He peered up at the steel pipes and exposed wooden beams that were holding up Alcatraz, where the Common Good was stationed. Jake was still in disbelief that these protesters had set-up right under the Inspector's nose - first Fawn's commune in the Atlantic Ocean near Candlewick and now this one beneath Alcatraz. He wondered how many more there were out there, and how detrimental it could be if they all joined forces together.

He didn't dwell on that thought as a hush fell over the commune as Babs walked onto a makeshift stage. She looked absolutely angelic, wearing a white flowing shirt that resembled wings with her hair tied back in a braid. She took a deep breath and said, "This song is for all of us who have lost someone we love. They are always in our hearts."

Jake thought she was staring right into his own eyes and he tried to fight the trance as she began to sing. Her beautiful voice echoed in the room and even Jake had to sit back as the words and the melody sunk in.

"Something is missing in my heart
Ever since you've gone away,
I only wish I found the words
To help ease your pain.
And now I pray I'll find you
In your home amongst the stars,
I'll always be your family
Our love can erase any scars."

Jake felt himself transported back to Candlewick... to Passover dinner where he, his parents and Mary were all sitting around the table...to the hymns his family would sing, always trying to coax him to sing with them, but he always chose not to. He would listen to his sister singing, off-key and over-dramatic, but singing just the same. He would laugh as she took his hand in his, smiling at him and offering him the next course, the next prayer. And then his father would sing and then his mother. His mother's beautiful voice he remembered so vividly, like she was still singing there beside him. Still saying a prayer for him, like she told him each year, even after he was drafted into the Army... each year she would pray for him... and wait for him to come back home.

He stood up abruptly, walking swiftly to the back of the room, to escape Babs' song... this song of peace and love. He didn't deserve to hear something so beautiful, especially when he felt the darkness consuming him, digging deeper and deeper into his soul. He was becoming the First Lieutenant once again.

Applause sounded in the commune, but Jake didn't go back in, preferring to sit in the darkness where he could do no harm. Where he couldn't try to manipulate Babs O'Hara.

Hidden in the shadows, he watched as the O'Hara's exited the commune's hall, their footsteps sloshing through the puddles towards him with their toolbox in tow. Rana Xiomy looked disheveled, flushed and agitated as she chased after them toward one of the leaking pipes.

Mr. O'Hara removed a wrench from the toolbox and attempted to fix the broken pipe. Jake was about to come out of the shadows and offer to help when Mrs. Xiomy urged, "You need to listen to me! Fawn is running out of time. You heard Boreas's broadcast. Inspector Herald is going to attack with everything he's got in Hyperborea."

"No," Mr. O'Hara cried out. "It's a suicide mission. I can't in good faith send my people to the slaughter."

"I agree with my husband. This is not our fight." Mrs. O'Hara agreed, clutching onto her husband's elbow protectively.

Jake listened curiously, still watching this confrontation from the shadows.

In a rage, Mrs. Xiomy grabbed the tool box flung it and the tools shattering onto the pavement, "If you aren't willing to lead, then I will!"

"Good Luck," Mrs. O'Hara laughed.

"You think it's so easy?," Mr. O'Hara snapped, his eyes glaring at Rana, searching for his precious tools in the puddles and tossing them back into the toolbox. "Besides, no one is going to follow you, Rana... you're the woman who gave up the rebellion."

Rana looked like she might punch him, but just then Molina came running out of the Hall and summoned the O'Haras. There was a family disturbance in the south tunnel.

"You see," Mr. O'Hara pointed around him. "We are needed here."

They took off running and Mrs. Xiomy whirled around to where Jake was standing.

"You don't have to hide. I know you are there."

Jake folded his arms over his chest and stepped forward into the light. "I didn't mean to eavesdrop."

Mrs. Xiomy's feet walked rapidly through the puddles toward him. "Sure you did." She stood across from him and asked abruptly. "How do I know you? Are you sure you've never been to Candlewick?"

Jake swallowed and tried out a charming smile, "I had a field trip to the Candlewick Government building when I was in middle school. Perhaps you recognize me from then."

"Perhaps," Mrs. Xiomy said, fixing her purple glasses, eying him suspiciously.

Jake turned so that a shadow rested on his face to prevent Mrs. Xiomy from recognizing him. He played with the watch on his wrist but quickly stopped when he realized what could happen if he pressed the watch the wrong way.

"The O'Hara's don't realize that this is a losing game," he said. "The Inspector will find them and except for maybe Molina, they are not prepared for a fight. You are better off going to Hyperborea without them."

Mrs. Xiomy listened to him but shook her head. "I am not leading anyone to Hyperborea.

Especially not you, since I don't trust you. Besides, I'm not fit to lead. I'm the one who turned against the rebellion 15 years ago, remember?"

Jake took a deep breath, thinking about Mary. Thinking about his mother. "You did it to save the person you love. Do you ever regret it?"

The melancholy drip-drip of the water in the background sounded like the heartbeat of a metronome that kept pushing time forward. Nothing could turn back time. "Let's just say that regret is something I've had to deal with." Mrs. Xiomy said slowly. "But what do you regret, Mark? If that is your real name?"

"There you are!" Babs cried out, entering the tunnel.

Jake was relieved she had entered at that crucial moment, whereas Mrs. Xiomy didn't seem happy her interrogation was interrupted.

"Your friend Mark and I were just having a little chat," Mrs. Xiomy said a little too brightly. "I'm going to go find Romero."

She took off back into the commune, glancing behind her once. Jake feared she was getting close to putting the final pieces together of the puzzle, and if she recognized him, it was over, his cover would be blown. He would hate to have to hurt her, but he may not have a choice.

Babs eyed him curiously, "What did I just walk in on?"

Jake shrugged, playing innocent. "Nothing."

The lights were about to be shut off to conserve energy, so Jake volunteered to walk Babs back to her room. She gratefully accepted. They walked in silence through the dank tunnel, listening to the ominous sounds of the pipes creaking. Pitter-patter of feet raced past them and splashed them as they ran, so Babs started running too.

"Come on, I'll race you to that next tunnel!"

Jake laughed and started to chase after her, feeling like a kid again as they splashed through puddles and he nearly caught up to her when a sharp pain shot up his left leg. He fell to his knee and held it close against his body, biting his lip to not call out. Babs whirled around and ran back, realizing he was hurt. She bent down to take a look at his leg and Jake reluctantly gave in.

Babs scrutinized the injury, slowly bending his leg while Jake winced in pain. Her eyes were wide. "The bone didn't heal properly. How on earth did this happen?"

Jake didn't answer and she didn't pressure him. Instead, she had him apply his weight to his one good leg and she helped him back up, letting him lean on her as she guided him back to his room and placed him on his bed. She raced to her dormitory and returned with a first aid kid which consisted of some pain killers, bandages and ointments for the leg.

"Here, take this. It will help ease the pain," she handed him one of the pain killers and Jake took it, swallowing it eagerly. He leaned back down on the bed, angry at himself for the turn of events, hating himself for not being the same man he was. His leg was a constant reminder of what happened that night at Candlewick Prison.

"You should go," he said, fearing the Inspector would want him to check in that night. The last thing he needed was for the Inspector to dial-in while Babs was in the room and ruin his plan of getting to Hyperborea.

Babs shook her head, digging into her bag for a bandage. "Let me wrap it and get it in a better position to heal properly. I really should break it and re-set the bone, but I doubt you want another broken bone to deal with."

Jake shook his head, feeling frustrated yet grateful that this woman was taking an interest to help him. He watched her as she bandaged up his leg with such care that he realized she must have bandaged up many protestors... many hurt or injured by his command.

She was nearly done bandaging up his leg when she asked, "Mark... I saw you leave during my song earlier. Did you not like it for some reason?"

Jake bit his lip, not realizing that his rude exit from the commune had offended her. "I'm sorry," he said slowly. "Your song...it just brought back some repressed memories. It had nothing to do with you."

She gave him a slight smile, playing with the ends of her hair. "I wrote that song not for my sister, but for that boy Boreas... the one on the broadcast tonight. I don't know if you heard a lot of the commotion and rumors earlier... but he was my boyfriend for a while."

Jake studied her. It seemed like this confession was something she needed to get off her chest. He rubbed the stubble on his chin, not realizing that Boreas and Babs had actually dated. For some reason he had thought that Boreas would be with Aurora.

"Do you still care about him?" he asked.

She took a deep breath, leaning on the side of the bed. "I'll always care about him, but I don't love him anymore. I know he was injected with the Soul Extractor serum, but a part of me thinks that if he truly loved me he would have fought the serum... that I could have saved him."

"We can't save everyone," Jake said slowly... wincing in pain as she finished clipping and securing the bandage into place. It was already putting a strain on his bone but the pain relievers were helping to numb the pain.

"He attacked me one day," she said, lowering her eyes. "Thankfully he didn't really hurt me, but that's why I swore I wouldn't get mixed up with anyone again."

She tilted her head to look at Jake and he took a deep breath, realizing where this conversation was heading. This was exactly what he had wanted, for Babs to fall for him, but Jake couldn't reciprocate those emotions. He had to play the part, continue the charade no matter who he hurt in the process, even if it was the fragile heart of the young girl mending him back to health.

"I'll tell you what," he said taking her hand in his. "If you continue helping me with my leg, I'll train you to protect yourself. I know a thing or two about self-defense and weapons."

Babs' bright blue eyes lit up. "That would be great! We'll have to do it somewhere that my parents can't see though."

"I can be discreet," Jake smiled. "So, do we have a deal?"

Babs nodded.

Just then the lights flickered and Babs stood up quickly, dropping his hand. "I'd better go."

Jake nodded. "Will you be ok getting back to your room?"

Babs nodded with a laugh, "Listen, I may not have much experience with self-defense like you, but I've survived worse than this."

And without another word she took off into the darkness singing as she ran and Jake leaned back, smiling, listening to her beautiful voice until it faded in the distance.

☆ ☆ ☆

Rana desperately tried to bring order amidst the chaos within the Alcatraz commune, but she wasn't having much success.

"This is not a playground!" she cried out, nearly toppling over two young kids playing tag around the dining hall. She was infuriated. It felt like they had been in the commune for a month, even though it had only been a couple of days. She had made no headway with the O'Hara's and feared they would need to leave this commune and head to Hyperborea without the Alcatraz commune's help.

Rana spotted Romero who had just finished his shift guarding the secret entrance into the commune. She grabbed him a tray that consisted of some salty spam and a glop of instant mashed potatoes. She felt sick just looking at it, but it was either eat this or starve. There weren't many provisions here in the commune or ways to bring it in without risk of getting captured by the Common Good, so they were stuck with the meager artificial and processed food supply.

She slumped down in one of the tables next to Romero and he handed her a flask of whisky as she handed him the tray of food. Both were grateful for the exchange.

Rana took a swig and then put her head down on the table. "My students behaved better than these hooligans. And they were better listeners than the O'Haras."

Romero stared off at the chaos ensuing around them, fondling the fork in his calloused hands. "Times like this you'd almost want to be the Inspector... or the IDEAL. No one would question their authority."

'Yeah, why don't I murder one of the useless O'Haras," Mrs. Xiomy snickered, taking another swig of the flask, "that'll show the rest of them who's boss."

Romero patted her briskly on the back. "Now you're talking!"

They both laughed. Rana heard some commotion transpiring outside the commune dining hall and out of the corner of her eye she caught of glimpse of Babs' auburn hair flailing wildly as the stranger, Mark, was attacking her with a sword!

She was about to jump up and save her when she caught sight of Babs laughing, the stranger wrapping his arms around her neck and staring intently into her eyes.

"What the hell is going on over there?" she cried out, grabbing Romero's head and turning it in that direction.

"Oh, that," Romero said, biting down on the rubbery spam entrée. "Babs wanted to learn how to defend herself, so Mark is training her."

Rana's mouth hung open in shock. "And you didn't think to mention it to me?"

Romero laughed, shaking his head at her. "Rana, since when are you overprotective? Babs is old enough to make her own decisions and if she wants to learn how to fight, she's learning from the best."

"The best?" she asked, perplexed. "So he was a soldier. I thought you said he was a farmer suffering at the hands of the Common Good."

Romero took a swig of his whisky, drops of the brown liquid landing on his scruffy beard. "He was suffering, beaten by the Common Good, you've seen his leg," He stammered. "I helped him escape, so he's kind of in my debt."

Rana could tell Romero was lying and observed the stranger, the bandage covering nearly both of his eyes as he appeared to be showing Babs how to fence with a sword. His left eye was still swollen but was healing rapidly now and she could swear she recognized him from somewhere. She also observed the attention he was giving Babs, and that was a little unnerving since she didn't trust him.

She stood up, determined to confront them and Romero cleared a path for them to squeeze through the huddled masses of confused people. Many stopped her, asking her questions she didn't want to hear: Where should they go? When would they be seeing Fawn? Did Fawn know they were alive? Was Fawn even alive?

Rana considered tearing her ears off. If she heard Fawn's name one more time! Fawn who everyone adored! Fawn who slept with David! Fawn who was her best friend and broke her heart!

"Fawn this, and Fawn that," she thought angrily, wanting to bang her head against the wall as she reached Babs. Babs was occupied, executing a self-defense move that Mark had shown her, wrapping her arms around his neck. Rana noticed a smile on Babs's face as she held him close against her.

"Uh hem," she cleared her throat. "Hope we're not interrupting anything."

Babs quickly released her hold on Mark and her face turned beet red. "Rana. Thank God it's you and not my parents. Mark here is teaching..."

"Teaching you how to fight," Rana interrupted, giving Mark the evil eye. "Romero already filled me in. I wish you would have told me."

Babs held out the sword, practicing her stance and exclaimed, "I would have, but you were constantly harassing my parents. Figured you were too busy to care."

"I wasn't harassing your parents…"

Babs ignored her and cried out, "Wait till you see this new move that Mark showed me."

She lunged forward, meeting Mark's sword halfway, she pivoted and lunged again, this time to the right, nearly disarming him.

"You're a fast learner," Mark admired, patting her on the shoulder. His hand lingered a little too long on her shoulder for Rana's taste, her overprotective instincts kicking in.

"Your parents still will not agree to help us in Hyperborea." Rana said, walking in between them, breaking up their little moment and picking up one of the swords from the table. Though it had been a while since she held one, it felt familiar in her grasp.

Babs sat down on a bench, taking a sip of water. "Then what do we do now?"

Rana cringed. "Don't ask me. I am not the leader, as your parents and everyone else here likes to remind me. I'm the one who betrayed the rebellion, remember."

"Hey," Romero said, grabbing her arm. "If you want to lead, I can help you. I used to work for the IDEAL, remember. And the Inspector. I am sure I can help you lead… and Mark here…"

The stranger stared Romero down with his one good eye, causing Romero to nearly fall backwards into a chair. Rana observed this exchange curiously. If she didn't know any better, she would say that Romero was scared of Mark, but why?

Babs picked up one of the knives off of the table and was steadily rotating it in her hands, deep in thought. "The only leader the rebellion truly has is Fawn. We need to find out who is still loyal to her. From Plymouth Incarnate and from this commune."

Mark leaned against the wall, grimacing like his leg was causing him pain. "You'll need a way to get to Hyperborea. You can't get all the way there by submarine."

Rana eyed him curiously. "And what makes you a Hyperborea expert?"

He smiled slyly. "Babs said you need a train to get to this mystical place. Let's just say I know a way to get you a train... if you are interested."

Babs jumped up, excited, "You really could get us a train to take us to Hyperborea."

He nodded and Rana felt even more certain something wasn't right.

"What's the catch?" she asked. "Do you think you are coming with us?"

Mark put his arm around Babs and pulled her close to him in a bear hug. "If that's where Babs is going, I don't want to be left behind."

He kissed her and Rana's blood boiled as his cunning mouth covered Babs's lips.

"You are not going anywhere near Hyperborea!" Rana cried out, grabbing the sword off of the weapon stand, the blade held up against the stranger's cheek. "If you value your good eye, I think you should back away... and quickly."

Mark removed his arms from around Babs and held them up as if in surrender, but said menacingly, "You're lucky I'm not armed."

"And you're lucky I'm not in a murderous mood. I was captain of my fencing team in High School, so don't tempt fate because my moods can change rather rapidly."

He took a step back and Rana lowered the weapon. He turned to Babs and said, "I'll get the train for you, Babs. Start rounding up Fawn's supporters and plan to leave by the Sacred Hour. If you need a leader, I'll lead you to Hyperborea."

He took off with Romero down one of the tunnels and Rana felt relieved that they were leaving, although the stranger's face was nearly registering in her memory.

Babs threw her sword and knife back down on the table, aggravated, as water dripped onto her head in that underground mausoleum.

"Why did you give Mark the third degree?" Babs sputtered, wiping her hair and tugging furiously on her braid.

Rana stared at the love-sick teenager, "I'd tell you, but you're not thinking clearly."

"What?" Babs's eyes burst open in shock. "You're the one who acted crazy and attacked him and I'm the one who's not thinking clearly?"

"I think you were fooling yourself when you told me you wouldn't fall for someone again."

Babs's mouth dropped open, "I didn't fall for anyone... and even if I did, that's NOT affecting my judgment. If Mark can get us a train, that's more than what we have now to get us to Hyperborea. We don't have Otus to fly us there."

Rana crossed her arms over her chest. "I just don't trust him and I don't want you to get hurt again."

"Like with Boreas?" Babs sneered. "I don't need you to be my mother. I have a mother and a father. And despite their cowardice, they are still stronger than you'll ever be and you know it!"

Babs ran off, wiping tears from her eyes as she raced down the dark corridor; her feet splashing through the puddles and fading in the distance.

Rana felt her strength diminishing, like she was drowning in that young girl's tears. She collapsed into the water, her body drenched as she pulled out the ponytail clip, releasing her curls and letting them hang loose and wild across her face.

"David, what have you made me?" she yelled out angrily, her voice echoing in that barren tunnel. "What have I got left to lose?"

She looked down at her reflection in the water, at the woman she was... the woman who had betrayed her people to save the man she loved.

"I tried to save you David and I failed," she whispered, her words vibrating off her trembling lips. "Now there's only one person left to save."

She looked down at the feeble woman's reflection in the water and splashed at it angrily until the ripples subsided and in its place was a transformed face staring back at her with eyes both beautiful and deadly, with no fear trapped behind them... only power.

✮ ✮ ✮

Jake recited the account of his "dangerous" mission to attain the train. His tale consisted of fighting off two Common Good guards, incapacitating them, snatching the key to the train, and just barely making it back through the secret entrance in time before the electricity shutdown. Of course what really happened was that he had made a simple call to the Inspector to set aside a train for him in San Francisco.

Babs was on the edge of her seat as he lied to her face. She took a hold of his hand and squeezed it lovingly, so impressed with his bravery that Jake felt a twinge of guilt deceiving her. But his lie was justly rewarded as she said that of course he would accompany them to Hyperborea, and best of all, help drive the train. *Things were turning out just as he planned.*

Babs had rounded up Fawn's supporters and ran off to ensure that everyone was ready to leave immediately to sneak to one of the submarines that would lead back to the mainland where the train was waiting. Jake kissed her and said he would meet her and the rest of Fawn's supporters in the main hall but needed to gather his belongings first. He rounded the corner to his room and was about to grab his backpack and check in with the Inspector when he froze. His bag had been tampered with! He frantically dumped the contents of his bag onto the bed, searching frantically for one object.

"Looking for this?"

Jake whirled around to behold Rana Xiomy standing there, the orange tinted conch shell in the palm of her hand.

Jake took a heavy breath. "I was hoping you wouldn't figure it out."

Mrs. Xiomy smiled slyly, "I was fooled at first, Jake Fray. Why would the First Lieutenant be stupid enough to try to spy on our little brigade? But once I saw how you reacted to commandeering the train, wanting so desperately to get to Hyperborea… I realized why. You want to get to Aurora and are working with the Inspector. And this conch shell… well, this is proof that you have Boreas."

"Had Boreas," Jake corrected, slowly easing his hand down toward the pack of belongings, looking to reach for his knife. "The Inspector confirmed he has escaped."

Mrs. Xiomy grimaced, "Making you and Herald more desperate, I imagine. Oh, if you are reaching for your knife, it's just the holder I left in your sack."

Crestfallen, Jake watched as she held up the sparkling blade, holding it like a toy in her hand, taunting him.

He sat down on the bed, out of options. "So are you going to turn me in to the O'Hara's? They would wet their pants in fear that the First Lieutenant infiltrated their base."

Rana slowly advanced toward him, the blade outstretched, a crazy, wildness in her eyes like a tiger ready to devour its prey. Jake kept his arms folded but was ready to attack and overpower this woman if necessary.

She pointed the knife at his watch. "Put me in contact with Herald."

He pretended to play dumb. "I'm not in contact with..."

"Don't play games with me, Jake. I know that watch can communicate with the outside. It just wasn't until today that I understood why you were so keen on wearing it."

Jake stared at her and his face slowly drained of color. Fear settled in at the thought of his cover being blown... of what Inspector Herald would do now that Jake was no longer useful to him.

"If you contact Herald," he said pleadingly, "then my sister Mary will be killed."

She watched him carefully, the blade now grazing his skin, like she could sense the tracking device that lay within his arm.

"I don't wish to contact Herald to turn against you, Jake." Her eyes danced wildly. "I'm here to work with you."

She stared at Jake's shocked expression, expecting this reaction, and then clicked on the watch, transmitting and waiting for the signal.

He looked up at his former teacher and said, "You surprise me, Rana. I thought you were on the side of good."

She laughed bitterly. "There aren't any true sides, Jake. It's about beliefs and I need Herald to believe that I want Fawn to suffer for what she did to me. How dare she be the one to rule, the only true leader. I should rule and what is more fitting than to rise above her and take over the one role Herald has yet to fill since Max Radar."

Jake stared at her like she had gone mad. "You can't be serious."

Her amethyst eyes reflected off of the knife blade as she held it up against Jake's throat. "I am very serious. Contact Herald and tell him that together we will bring Fawn down."

✿ ✿ ✿

The train whizzed onwards as Jake was again dressed in the Common Good uniform, so strange to be wearing the colors again like he was once again who he was meant to be... but not quite. He drove the train onwards, relieved to see some soot stain the fabric. Babs huddled next to him in the tight compartment, a gun glued to her side and he was glad he had trained her on the weapon back in Alcatraz.

"I don't understand why Rana insisted on staying behind. My parents won't change their minds about helping at Hyperborea."

"She's persistent," Jake kept his eyes glued to the track ahead, as the desert sun beamed down on them. He wiped the sweat from his forehead, trying not to divulge the fact that he knew why Rana was really staying behind.

"I wish we were already there," she continued talking nervously, and he shared her fear as they were approaching another check point. He was able to talk the guards out of checking the train cars at the prior stops. It was risky, though, if they checked out the cargo, they would behold humans, not food cargo within the confines of the train cars.

Another check point and Jake told Babs to stay down.

"Where are you headed?" the guard said, staring at Jake's papers that he had stolen.

"We are heading to the mountains. Inspector Herald's orders."

The guard grunted, scrutinizing the papers and Jake knew this was going to be more difficult than the last ones.

"I knew a guard named Henry Peterson. Stationed at Alcatraz. You don't look like him."

Damn! Jake swallowed and put on his best smile, Babs huddled near him, the gun outstretched and her finger on the trigger.

"Look, I'm not Henry Peterson."

"Right you are, you're not. Step out of the car," he cried out, extending his weapon. Jake pointed Babs's gun down.

"Look, soldier," Jake commanded. "I can explain everything. Let me show you."

Jake put his hands up and stepped out of the train car, ensuring Babs was not seen from below him. The soldier kept his gun glued on Jake's head.

Once they were out of earshot, Jake whispered, "I am under-cover for Inspector Herald. I am the First Lieutenant."

"Bull," the guard laughed, his gun still pointed at the imposter. "Like I haven't heard that one before."

"This time it's true."

Jake lifted up his sleeve where the branded symbol for the first lieutenant was visible. The soldier stared at it and then scoffed. "Anyone can get a tattoo."

"This is a special brand that was made by Inspector Herald him-self when he appointed me. Do you want me to summon him?" Jake pointed down to his watch and this time the soldier took a step back, the reaction Jake was waiting for. The soldier did not want him to summon the Inspector.

"That won't be necessary," he cried out in a panic.

Jake removed his hand from the watch. "There now. So let us pass and do not give my position away, you understand me?"

The soldier nodded, putting down his weapon. "This train is clean," he cried out, waving them off to the other soldiers.

Jake stepped back onto the train and started the ignition, it roared and the train chugged forward as the soldier saluted him. Jake wanted to shoot the bastard as Babs watched the salute with shock and then suspicion in her eyes as the wheels trudged forward along the track.

"What the hell just happened and why did he salute you?" Babs questioned, the gun still resting in her fingers, the safety still not on. "Who are you, Mark?"

"It's who I was," Jake admitted, his hands on the wheel. "I'm a friend, Babs. Though I may not always have been."

"Then who were you?"

He didn't answer. His eyes were glued on the track as the large cascading mountain range loomed before them. Based on Babs's coordinates, the mysterious Hyperborea should be located in the valley on the other side.

Before he could stop her, Babs grabbed his sleeve and rolled it up, revealing the tattoo. She pressed the gun firmly against his temple. He clutched onto the wheel tighter and sighed.

"You'd better put that gun down, Babs, because your friend Aurora is going to want to hear what I have to say."

Chapter 25

Giant vs. Aurora

"**D**o any of you puny humans know how to fight?" Ephialtes kicked a boulder and it went sailing into the lake, water gushing out like a tidal wave and splashing the last line in formation. Women and men now drenched were trying to hold up their weapons and follow Ephialtes's instructions as their Sergeant.

"Let's try this again, shall we?" He took a deep breath, blew on his whistle and watched his battalion of disorderly recruits march with their guns drawn, preparing for battle. It had been an exhausting 4 days with training from dusk till dawn since every person able to hold a gun, meaning even elderly women and stubborn teenagers, were enlisted into the rebel army. In total, there were about 500 people on the Protesting side and Mrs. Taboo promised that scores more would join now that the word was out that there was to be a battle.

Aurora wondered if Mrs. Xiomy and Babs were able to recruit more members of the San Francisco commune to help them. However, even if they were able to convince the whole commune to join their cause, the reinforcements most likely would not get there in time. Mrs. Taboo's spies were reporting that the Inspector had deployed about two-thousand armed and specially trained soldiers to take them down by the end of the week. There was a media campaign demoralizing Boreas Stockington, painting him as a traitor. The Common Good was looking to bring the country back to the old ways with terror campaigns. Boreas's face was on TV every five minutes. It gave Aurora hope that he had indeed escaped. That explained why the Inspector was going to do whatever was in his power to discredit Boreas amongst those who had watched the broadcast. She hoped that people could see through the Inspector's brainwashing tactics and start to see the truth.

The protesting army was slowly starting to look like a real army, with many of the soldiers actually shooting and hitting their targets. Mrs. Taboo and her people had gathered plenty of guns and ammunition, but they hardly had any explosives or bombs that could work to their benefit against the Fighter jets. So Fawn had asked the Professor to help them devise a strategy. They had amateur fighting skills and primitive weapons, but they could at least outsmart their opponent. They had knowledge of the terrain and the element of surprise.

On the Professor's orders, Jonathan was busy setting traps throughout the mountain that would act as their base. The Professor was busy making bombs and other chemical warfare products, including the hypnotizing, paralyzing light.

Aurora sat down by the lake with the Khanda sword in her lap. She stared down at the blade, her gift from Swanson. She could not stop thinking about whether she should keep it for herself during the battle or present it as a gift to the person she believed would uphold the balance. The person she wanted to give it to was Otus, but it was so small that it would not be a weapon, but a toy in his humongous grasp. She realized that Otus was not meant to have a human weapon. She watched him during the combat practice and Ephialtes's voice was getting hoarse yelling at his brother. Otus seemed unable to fight or even throw a boulder with accuracy. Ephialtes definitely was the one with all of the fighting genes in that family.

She overheard Ephialtes berating Otus yet again. She ran over to the training yard and watched as a glum Otus threw a boulder over his head and smashed a tree 100 yards away.

"I threw the rock. Are you happy now?"

Ephialtes stomped onto the ground and cried out, "No, Otus. You didn't throw the rock. You tossed it like it was a bubble to be played with. I want you to get mad, use your force and knock that tree down with all your strength."

Otus turned toward Aurora for help, but she just shrugged. She was definitely not going to get in the middle of this family squabble. Besides, who was Aurora to train on fighting tactics?

Jonathan called out, "Ephialtes, he's not used to fighting. Give him a break."

Ephialtes snorted and angrily brushed past Otus. He peered down at Jonathan who appeared so small and frail compared to the giant looming above him. Jonathan stood firm with his shoulders pulled back defiantly, staring up at Ephialtes without flinching. Ephialtes stomped right next to Jonathan causing a mini earthquake, but Jonathan managed to stay on his feet and not break position. Ephialtes nodded his consent and then yelled out, "Very good, Jonathan. I am impressed." Aurora could see the smug look on Jonathan's face when suddenly Ephialtes grabbed Jonathan like he was a doll and turned him upside down. Jonathan's shirt fell over his face and before Aurora could use her powers to stop him, Ephialtes dropped Jonathan head first into the lake. Aurora ran to the edge of the lake and searched frantically for any sign of him. Five seconds later Jonathan re-submerged and was gasping and coughing for air. Aurora held out her hand to help him, but he brushed it aside, scampering out of the water and back on his feet.

"Why the hell did you do that?" Jonathan cried out, fuming and spitting out water.

"That's the last time you talk out of turn to your commanding Sergeant." Ephialtes barked.

Aurora couldn't take this anymore and exclaimed, "Ephialtes, you are more of a bully than a commanding officer. You have yelled at Otus 10 times in the past half hour. 10 times!"

"The little lightning bug speaks," Ephialtes yawned. "I don't see you fighting. Let's see you actually put that sword to good use instead of babysitting it."

Aurora gulped, but then composed herself and lifted the sword up, the blade glistening in the sunlight.

"Fine. You want me to fight you?"

Ephlates roared with laughter that echoed in the mountains and caused a mini rockslide.

"I would squish you like the bug you are."

Aurora felt the sun rays absorbing into her skin, her powers growing and beckoning to be used. She played off Ephialtes's ego. "You seem pretty confident in yourself or are you afraid you will be beaten by a puny human?"

Ephialtes laughed humorously at this spectacle. "If you fight me, little lightning bug, you fight for real. I will fight you like you were my own enemy. Are you up for that challenge?"

Aurora heard the doubts in her mind and was about to step down, when out of nowhere she heard another voice inside her head saying that she had to fight. She had to prove herself somehow and this was the time.

"Fine, I'll fight you," Aurora agreed. Jonathan and Otus both started yelling at once, but Ephialtes lifted up his hand and said, "My opponent has agreed to fight me, so we shall fight."

Otus grabbed Ephialtes by the shoulders and yelled, "I swear, if you hurt her…"

Ephialtes grinned. "Glad to see there is some anger in that fatty mass of yours."

Aurora put the sword in its hilt around her waist and thought insanity must have possessed her to say yes to this crazy fight. What was she doing? But then again, if she couldn't fight one giant how could she fight the Inspector and the whole Common Good Army? She took a deep breath and went to the far right corner. She watched as Ephialtes took his place in the far left corner of the square, heckling her and calling her names to try to get her aggravated.

Jonathan ran over and put his hands on her shoulders. "Tell Ephialtes you are not fighting."

"I am fighting."

He turned to survey the crowd of onlookers who had gathered and whispered, "Aurora, listen to me. No one will think any less of you if you don't fight. You don't have to show off for me."

Aurora laughed and cried out, "I am doing this for myself, Jonathan, not you. All week you have been yelling at me to practice fighting. Well look… I'm practicing."

"I didn't say with a giant! Aurora, you are not strong enough to fight him!"

Aurora pushed Jonathan's arms off her shoulders, staring at the face of the man she cared for and yet he didn't believe in her. She recalled him blowing on her fingers, like he was the one giving her the powers of dawn. Like he was the one controlling her powers!

"I am strong enough, Jonathan. And I will fight him. Because I am the Goddess of Dawn! Do you even believe in me?"

"Aurora..." he swiped the hair out of his face. "It's not that I don't believe in you..."

"No, that's exactly what it is. Boreas would believe in me. Why can't you?"

Aurora brushed past Jonathan, marched further onto the field and stabbed the sword into the ground as she fixed her hair up into a ponytail, fuming at her confrontation with Jonathan. She had stood up for herself in front of him. She couldn't believe she had finally done that. She was already feeling stronger. For all those weeks, she had gotten lost in her infatuation of him... cared too much what he thought, even worried too much to eat in front of him. He was just a man. She was something more. She looked into the sunlight, grasping onto the hilt of the sword, pulling it from the ground, measuring its weight in her hands and then holding it firm in her grasp. For the first time in a long time she felt powerful.

"Never thought I'd see Aurora Alvarez holding a sword," she heard a voice cry out from the sidelines. Aurora recognized that voice!

She turned and saw Babs on the side of the field with a group of people from Plymouth Incarnate behind her. Aurora couldn't believe her eyes and ran over to her friend and the reinforcements they had been hoping for.

"Babs, I don't believe it!" Aurora cried out, running and hugging her friend tightly. "And you brought the reinforcements."

"Mostly the people from Plymouth Incarnate, but Mrs. Xiomy is still trying to convince my parents to bring even more reinforcements. I have a lot to fill you in on."

Aurora felt fear overwhelm her as she realized that the additional reinforcements would never get there in time — even if they were coming. She felt dizzy and was about to exit the ring, when

Ephialtes yelled out, "I'm getting hungry waiting for you, little fire-fly. I think I'm going to eat your friend as a little snack."

Aurora gulped and said, "Fill me in after I beat Ephialtes. Otus's brother."

Babs stared upwards, "That's Otus's brother? And you are fighting him?"

Aurora sized up her opponent, straining her neck as she did so. She adjusted the sword in her hand. It felt heavy all of a sudden, almost like she couldn't lift it. Or perhaps fear was settling in. Her legs felt like Jell-O too. She really should have eaten something that day.

"Aim for his legs."

She whirled around at the sound of a man's voice. It was the injured man who had been standing beside Babs. His left eye was bruised and a bandage covered the right side of his face. He was dressed in a long-sleeved orange shirt and indigo pants. It was like he had been dressed in the Common Good uniform, but lost the jacket. His hands were bound with thick rope and Aurora wondered if he was a prisoner.

"He's strong, but he relies too much on his brute strength," he continued. "You'll need to outsmart him. Get the legs and then use those powers of yours that everyone is talking about."

She eyed him curiously, not remembering him from Plymouth Incarnate. "Do I know you? You sound familiar…"

Babs removed the bandage, revealing the other half of his face.

"This is one of the things I needed to talk to you about."

Those eyes… how could she forget? Seeing him brought back the night at Candlewick Prison so many months ago. It was the First Lieutenant!

"Jake Fray!" She gasped.

Jake smiled. "I think you have bigger things to worry about, Aurora Alvarez."

Before she could react, a large shadow appeared overhead and Aurora jumped out of the way right before a giant foot smashed down on the spot she had been standing in a second earlier. The crowd gasped from the sidelines as Aurora found herself face-down in a pile of mud. She used a clean part of her arm to clear her eyes, spotted the sword, grabbed it and leapt deftly to her feet. Ephialtes looked menacingly down at her, upset he hadn't smooshed Aurora like a bug. Before he could react, she ran through his legs and managed to slash both of his ankles with the sword. He yelled out in pain as blood trickled down to his feet.

"Ow, that hurt!" He cried out.

"That's what you get for cheating!" Aurora yelled back, admiring the courage in her own voice.

"You're going to pay for that!" He stomped toward her and she stood her ground, even though Otus was yelling at her to get out of the way.

"I think you underestimate who you are fighting."

She held up her right hand and released a flood of sunlight into Ephialtes' eyes. Blinded, he tripped over his own feet, tumbling down toward the ground like a giant torpedo. Once again, Aurora barely managed to get out of the way in time. The crowd broke out in thunderous applause and Babs was whistling one of her high piercing whistles too. Aurora felt a flood of relief rush through her, but then she heard, "Look out!"

She turned around to see a giant shoe gunning right for her. It knocked her off her feet and she landed hard onto the ground. A shoe, of all things!

She opened her eyes, discombobulated, and saw Ephialtes yelling, "Anything can be used as a weapon!"

"Yeah, but you didn't have to stink up the place!" Aurora goaded him, holding her nose as the stinky waft was coming from the shoe.

"Just think, that's going to be the last thing you smell," Ephialtes laughed. "Now I'm going to finish you off."

Aurora couldn't find her sword and she struggled to her feet. Her head was pounding after her fall. She dodged his blows and his attempts to snatch her up. Aurora knew once she was caught that she was done for. She spotted the sword halfway down the perimeter and knew she had to make a run for it. She made it appear as if she was going to run to the left and then did a quick turn, silently thanking Boreas for teaching her his tennis moves, and she ran as fast as she could toward the sword while Ephialtes took time to figure out what happened and readjust. Her heart was beating out of her chest and her hair was flailing wildly, now out of its ponytail. Nearly there, she dove as if she was sliding to home base and scooped up the sword just before Ephialtes had his hand over her. She stabbed with all of her might and sliced through his palm and he yelped again at the sting of her sword.

Without another thought, she headed toward his ankles again and this time with her adrenaline pumping and the sun scorching her skin, her fingers easily exuded a flame that ignited the grass beneath his bare foot. The flames grew and Ephialtes looked dumbfounded, sniffing the scorching scent of flesh before realizing it was his foot that was burning. He shrieked and hopped up and down to extinguish the flame. Otus and the others were laughing at the sight. Aurora started to laugh too until Ephialtes got behind the fire, struck the ground with his foot and sent a wave of wind brushing the fire in Aurora's direction. She held out her hands attempting to use her powers to keep the fire from hitting her, but the fire had a mind of its own and was not adhering to her powers. A bonfire was heading right toward her and she braced herself for the painful impact.

The next thing she knew, a force hit her from the side and she was thrown onto the ground. She rolled over to see Jake Fray tearing off his shirt sleeve that was enflamed. He threw it onto the ground and stomped on it a few times to extinguish the fire. Aurora stood up, her mouth gaping as he turned to her, unharmed. He held out his hand to help her up. Ephialtes was fuming and cried out, "No one was to interfere!"

"I am no one, so it doesn't matter," Jake wittily said. "I didn't know you really intended to kill her."

Ephialtes bit his lip and cried out, "She lit me on fire!"

"I did not," Aurora cried back. "I lit the grass on fire. You just stood on it, that's all."

Ephialtes cracked his massive knuckles and started to head toward them when Otus jumped out from the sidelines and stood in his way.

"You had your fight. It's over. You won."

Ephialtes at first looked as if he would tear Otus apart but then a big toothy grin stretched across his face. "The way you feel right now, Brother? That is how I want you to feel when the Inspector gets here. Picture the Inspector is me attacking your precious Firefly."

"I can't believe you almost killed her!"

"This was a battle, not a game. Remember that."

With that Ephialtes stomped away and Otus humphed, gusts blowing out of his nostrils that blew back the hair of many of those in the audience.

Aurora turned to the First Lieutenant who had just saved her life. Her eyes took in his muscular arm showing through his ripped sleeve where his flesh was branded with the infamous tattoo. An elaborate letter "I" with an orange and indigo circle around it was etched into his skin. He looked up to see her staring at it and rage manifested in his pale blue eyes.

Babs put a gun to Jake's back and said, "He used the jagged edge of the fence to cut the rope that was binding him while we were distracted watching the fight. Surprised he saved you and didn't run off."

He smiled slyly, "I wanted to witness your powers in person, Aurora. The Inspector does have reason to worry."

"Jake Fray," Aurora stated, staring at the man she had known since childhood, but didn't feel like she knew so well anymore. "What are you doing here?"

Babs stared at her, dumbfounded. "Wait, you know him?"

She nodded. "He's the brother of my best friend, Mary, from Candlewick. He's the one who warned me at the prison that Boreas had turned against us."

Jake closed his eyes and replied, "Unfortunately, that didn't work out so well for me. I was stripped of my title and cast out by the Inspector. I am lucky to be alive. I headed out west to join you at Hyperborea."

Aurora felt fear ignite within her at the thought of the First Lieutenant there, even if his story was true.

"Let's take him to Mrs. Taboo."

Chapter 26

The Skinwalker

The sun was setting to the west as an eagle soared wildly in the storm, beckoning Boreas forward into the desert. He followed the eagle until he saw Hyperborea, the fields stained with blood. One sword clashed with another in the distance as he strained to see two shadows fighting, the wind encircling them like a typhoon. While he watched the battle, one of the figures was struck down. Suddenly the eagle was back and transformed before his eyes into the form of Inspector Herald. His coal black eyes stared straight at Boreas, smiling victoriously.

"The woman you love has fallen!" he declared.

Boreas awoke with a start. Steven was next to him, shaking him out of his nightmare. Boreas sat up, breathing heavily and realized he had been dreaming, though the image of Inspector Herald had seemed so vivid, way too real. He turned toward Steven who was staring at him, concern in his eyes.

"Steven, what is it?"

He pointed to the intercom and said, "The pilot keeps calling you."

Boreas wiped the sweat from his brow and sure enough Radar's voice was coming through loud and clear.

"Boreas, where the hell are you? Wake up, damn it!"

Boreas jumped to his feet and grabbed the intercom, "Radar, it's me. What's the matter?"

"Sorry to wake you, sleeping beauty, but I'm landing the chopper."

Boreas was now wide awake and screamed into the intercom, "What do you mean 'landing the chopper'?"

"Unless you have more gasoline in your pocket, then we have to land now. I think I found a place on the map that we can land that shouldn't cause too much suspicion."

Boreas closed his eyes. He had not realized that they would have an indirect route to Hyperborea. Suspicion was something that would follow them wherever they landed. Here he was, a fugitive, with two kids, a news reporter and a former IDEAL. What story could he come up with that would not arise suspicion?

"Where are you landing?"

Static answered back, along with two words that Boreas managed to hear, "Monument Valley."

Boreas already felt the chopper descending as he shook Analise. She awoke with a start and with a right hook to his jaw.

"Oww," Boreas yelled out as pain escalated from his face and Analise sat up in shock.

"Sorry," she stammered.

"Next time use your right hook on the enemy, not me," Boreas winced in pain, rubbing his jaw.

"Why are we landing?"

"Radar said we're running out of gas. He's landing in Monument Valley."

Analise's eyes bulged out. "Is that safe? I am sure every person and their mother saw that broadcast. They will recognize you and me."

"I don't think we have a choice. Gather as many supplies as you can carry."

Sansa rubbed her eyes, coming out of her deep slumber and asked loudly, "Is Daddy here?"

Boreas felt a knot in his throat as he shook his head, staring at the angelic face staring back at him... so innocent and so unaware of the evil that was brewing outside these helicopter doors.

"He said he will find us so you need to be brave and do what Analise and I tell you, you understand?"

Sansa nodded, courage shining forth in her eyes.

He turned to Steven who was looking at him with doubt. "You need to disguise yourself," Steven said and offered his hat to Boreas.

Boreas took it and ruffled Steven's soft wavy brown hair in thanks. He placed the hat on top of his head. He found some sunglasses and put them on as well.

"Do I look like me?" Boreas asked modeling the new look.

Sansa giggled slightly and Analise shook her head, calling out, "You look ridiculous."

Boreas grabbed his backpack and stuffed it with blankets and anything else he could fit from the helicopter. He found a flashlight, a medical kit and cans of food and stuffed them into the backpack as well.

Boreas looked out the window at Monument Valley unfolding before his eyes, the big naturally formed sandstone carvings stood tall before him. He hoped that there were no Common Good soldiers occupying this part of the desert, but there was no way to tell from this height.

He felt a tap on his back and turned to see Steven looking up at him. He whispered, "You may lie to my sister but don't lie to me. Dad may have told me to go with you but I don't have to listen to you."

"Steven, I am going to keep you and your sister safe. I promise."

"And why should I believe you?" Steven crossed his arms and looked at him with such animosity. Boreas couldn't understand where this was stemming from.

"Steven, did I do something to you?"

Steven glared at him and said, "My father thought your life more important than his own. He died to save you."

"First of all, we don't know if he died and second, he stayed behind to save you and Sansa."

"No, he died to save you. He told me that you are on an important mission and that you needed to escape."

Boreas put his hand on Steven's shoulder, knowing anything he told this boy was not going to bring his father back. So he had to stick with the truth. "Your father was right. I am on an important mission and I am just realizing how important it really is. But we will find your father. If he survived, I promise I will find him."

Radar's voice boomed from the intercom again. "Brace yourselves for impact. I haven't landed a chopper in ten years, so it might be a little bumpy, that is if we survive at all."

Boreas grabbed Steven by the hand, pulled him down and strapped on his seat belt. He then ensured that Sansa's was fastened. Analise grabbed him and pulled him down into his own chair and snapped on his belt just as the chopper hit the ground. It bumped over the sandy desert and Radar maneuvered the chopper to a sliding stop. The propeller slowed and finally stopped entirely. Boreas felt like his stomach was in his throat and his knuckles were white from clutching on to the sides of the seat. The door swung open and Radar's grinning face was before them.

"Hope you all enjoyed your flight. Tipping is expected."

Boreas unsnapped his belt and then helped the kids. He grabbed his pack and left the helicopter, pushing Radar on his way out. "Were you the one who gave away Plymouth Incarnate's location?"

Radar removed the helmet over his head and started slathering his albino body with sunscreen. "I should be the one mad at you for deserting me in the middle of Common Good territory. I awoke to find you and that stranger who hit me over the head gone. I followed your footsteps and that's when I saw they arrested you. I impersonated the helicopter pilot so that I could save your sorry ass."

"You'll get no apology or thank you from me," Boreas sneered. "You were the one who wanted me to desert those kids and let Sansa die."

Radar grabbed Boreas by the shirt and pulled him in so that his words hissed into his ear, "And if you had done what you're told and listened to me, you could have avoided this whole mess and the Inspector would be dead."

Sansa was crying at the fighting happening in front of her and immediately Radar released Boreas. Boreas brushed past him, ran to Sansa, lifted her up in his arms, and reassured her that they were alright.

The sun was sweltering in the desert and Radar was staring at the map to try to gauge where they needed to go to get to civilization. Steven was off in a distance, sulking. Boreas stared up at the hot sun and felt like he was losing control. He rubbed his left arm where the green mark was still evident and was throbbing as he had lost his temper. He took a deep breath to try to calm himself down and stay focused on the task at hand. He had to get to Hyperborea. He looked at Sansa and Steven, fearing once again for their safety. He had to warn them to keep their family relationship with him a secret, for their own safety. If that information got into the Inspector's hands it would be detrimental. Boreas pulled down the baseball hat over his forehead and put the sunglasses over his eyes. His finger traced the scar on his neck and he knew that despite his efforts that the scar wasn't hidden and without that, he might as well not be wearing a disguise. They needed to find a way out of that desert before they got caught. They were not an inconspicuous group and if the local precincts were notified, then there was no hope of getting out of Monument Valley alive.

The scorching sun was beating down on them as they made their way across the desert. Sansa was on Boreas's back and Steven was still giving Boreas the cold shoulder. Despite the sunscreen, Radar's face was turning bright red from the sun beating down on them. Boreas gave Steven's hat to Sansa to try to protect her face from the heat but knew that it couldn't be helping too much. How did he get himself into this mess? He thought about Aurora and Otus and wondered if they were safe. He wondered if Aurora had seen his interview and what she thought of him. Most likely she thought he was out of his mind, but maybe she would think him brave. Boreas tried to get his mind off of Aurora. She was with Jonathan and probably very happy with him. Jonathan was who she wanted after all.

Boreas wiped a bead of sweat out of his eyes and knew that they would need to find more water soon or they wouldn't get very far. He put Sansa down and sat on the hot sand to catch his breath. Analise unzipped the backpack that she had been carrying, and handed a bottle of water to Boreas. He took a quick drink and then handed it over to Sansa who drank from it heartily.

"Make sure you save some for your brother," Boreas said, staring at the young girl, trying to discern some part of himself in her features, but he couldn't identify anything remotely like him. She was too delicate a creature to be related to him.

Red sand had stained his socks, pants and shoes and white cumulous clouds were sprinkled across the baby blue canvas. He looked up at the monuments that loomed before his eyes, of the red rock statues that resembled a city of nature's handiwork. In one direction were three rock figurines shaped like three women. Another structure resembled a lion standing tall and statuesque; a witness to this ever changing earth for thousands of years. Boreas felt so small compared to these natural wonders, but his mission was not small, it was to preserve this and more for generations to come. If he could get out of this desert alive, that is.

"I think we should go north," Analise pointed at the map she had confiscated from the helicopter. "It should lead us to this town here where we can maybe rent a car."

"And use what for identification?" Radar shook his head. "If we are going to get transportation, we are going to need to steal it. We can't just go up to someone and say, 'Hi, we are running from the government. Can you please let me borrow your car? We'll make sure it comes back in one piece'."

Analise shoved the map into Radar's chest. "Fine, what do you suggest?"

Radar wrinkled his nose and pointed abrasively at a section on the map.

"We are on Native American territory. If memory serves me correctly, we are under the Navajo jurisdiction, not the government."

"The IDEAL has eradicated a lot of those past laws, you know that," Analise reminded him. "You should know that since you were the IDEAL, correct?"

Radar shot her a glance. "And how would you know that?"

Analise smiled shrewdly. "It is my job to know these things. The First Lieutenant had confided in me who you were after you were arrested in Machu Picchu. And I want a complete interview once we get out of this mess."

Radar sniggered, bending down to rest his legs. "A complete interview! Well, how about I start with this. You don't know the

Inspector like I know him. I know that as much as he wants to preserve this Earth and his subjects, he knows he is losing control. Many are starting to doubt and question his methods and the IDEAL itself. Seeing is believing and no one has seen the IDEAL. And now, after Boreas's interview, more people will start to question, which will make him desperate. He will make sure this Geometric Storm happens and that it destroys much of what we hold dear. But in the end, he will survive. He will be the savior, the one who will rebuild this world, the way he wants it. And people will flock to him as their leader. Do you see where I am going with this?"

Analise shook her head, not wanting to believe it. Radar turned to Boreas, shuffling his feet so that the red sand rose into the air, spiraling like a storm.

"The Geometric Storm is coming, whether we want it to or not. No technology or weapons will be able to destroy it. Only those from the prophecy can prevent it – I have known that for a while, so has the Inspector. We've known this day would come. At a point in my life I would have welcomed it. If I was the one still left standing once it was all over."

"That's why you wanted me to kill the Inspector?" Boreas's voice rang out. "So that you could once again become the IDEAL?"

Radar cracked his knuckles and said, "Tsk tsk, Boreas. I thought you were smarter than that."

Boreas grabbed his backpack, sand sifting off the fabric. "I don't have time for this."

He grabbed Sansa's hand and called out to Steven saying that they were moving. "We are going west."

Analise grabbed the map and exclaimed, "Why west?"

Boreas didn't answer and didn't know why he knew that was the direction they needed to head toward. Radar eyed him suspiciously, but picked up his things and followed obediently.

Analise repeated, "We need to talk about this. You don't know what we will find that way. It could be leading us straight back into the hands of the Inspector."

Boreas turned toward the beautiful reporter standing behind him and didn't know what to say. "I feel like I have been here before, in a dream. And I remember I saw the sunset ahead of me. I can't explain it."

Analise stared at him trying to read the truth in his eyes. She scooped up Sansa who was falling asleep standing up and carried her in her arms. "I'll trust you, Boreas. After all, you are the god God of the North Wind."

Steven came forward and asked if he could help pick out a camp site before the sun set.

Boreas nodded, ruffling Steven's hair and his young cousin ran forward to take the map from Radar. Eager to be of help, he surveyed the map to try to find something within their path suitable for a campsite.

Radar pulled Boreas aside, his red eyes glaring like a viper and whispered, "What else happened in your dream?"

Boreas shrugged saying, "I don't remember."

"Or you don't want to tell me is more like it. I know you Boreas, and I know something bad is going to find us out here in the desert. I see it in your eyes. Just as Analise saw it. I think it's about time you trust me."

Boreas felt a shiver run up and down his spine as Radar continued to wait for him to respond.

"Radar, let's not fool ourselves thinking we are friends," Boreas whispered coldly. "You authorized the killing of David Xiomy... my father. I'm sorry, but I can never trust you."

Boreas stormed off after the others seeing the sun beginning its descent in the distance. He fought himself to stay strong. He needed all the strength he could muster to keep walking and prayed that he would not have to face the nightmare from his dream.

Radar continued to follow obediently, checking his jacket pocket to ensure that the gun he had commandeered after taking the helicopter was still properly hidden. Before the night was over, he would surely use it.

✿ ✿ ✿

They walked another two miles until they reached the West Mitten butte, one of the rock structures that had a small cave crawl-in space where they could huddle together for the night. Boreas took out the blankets he had packed in his knapsack and spread them out over Steven and Sansa to keep them warm and used one that he rolled up as a pillow to let them rest their heads against it. They fell swiftly to sleep. It was freezing with nighttime upon them but the stars and the moon were illuminated above them. Radar took off to search for water and Boreas collected some loose twigs from a Juniper Tree that was not far from their campsite and set-up a fire. He struck at the flint waiting for an ember to catch. Once it caught, he blew on it, watching the fire grow and then spread it quickly onto the other twigs and plant life. He patiently tended to the fire, watching it grow, remembering how Aurora had taught him this when they were out in the wilderness together. How he wished Aurora was here and could light this fire with one point of her finger.

Analise opened one of the cans of food and was trying to eat the beans delicately, one at a time with her fingers.

"To think I used to take silverware for granted," she chided herself, eating another bean and swallowing it, disgusted. "I have been on long shoots and stakeouts, but nothing that compares to this."

"Try living like this for the past 6 months," Boreas stretched his muscles, exhausted. "However, it was a lot easier in the woods where there was food and water to drink. And of course, a giant who could provide shade."

"Speaking of water, we are down to half a bottle," Analise reminded him. Boreas nodded, knowing that they were still a good half day's walk away from the closest town. They hadn't seen any cacti or any other bodies of water in this barren wasteland but he hoped Radar would have some luck and uncover something they had missed.

"I miss my cellphone... and Google... and technology," Boreas said, eating beans from the can and trying to picture it as a steak and savoring the juices.

He lay his back down against the sand, the flames crackling near his feet and he stole a glance at the kids sleeping soundly in the cave, glad the fire was providing them warmth. Analise lay down beside him and looked up at the stars glittering above them.

"I have never seen the stars so clear before," she admitted. She pointed up into the night sky at the Big Dipper.

"My dad used to tell me the stories behind the constellations. He loved the stories of the Greek heroes and their battles; of Hercules and Orion. He used to tell me the stories to try to get me to go to sleep, but they enraptured me and I wanted to hear more. It went against his plan of getting me to fall asleep, but they are some of the best memories I have of him."

Boreas turned to face her. "What happened to him? Your dad?"

Analise took a deep breath as the fire crackled. "He was caught conducting a secret religious ceremony. When the Common Good tried to arrest the bride and groom, he intervened and was shot."

"I'm sorry," Boreas said.

"I couldn't even bury his body. The Inspector called him an enemy of the state and never gave him a proper burial. I think that was the worst part - not being able to say goodbye."

Boreas nodded, remembering when he thought his mother had died when he was 5 years old. How confused he had been at that age, thinking he could have stopped it; that he could have saved her.

He got up abruptly and put his face in his hands, the monuments now seeming like big shadows lurking over the valley. He felt his mind racing as he thought about his mother and everything she had done to hurt him. Faking her death, leaving him and his family in order to create Plymouth Tartarus. Lying to him about his real father. Nearly committing him to a lifetime of imprisonment. And here was Analise who had truly lost a parent, a father who anybody would be proud to call their own. Boreas felt such hatred in his heart. The green mark began to burn and he gasped in pain as he reached for it, but the pain escalated. He collapsed down onto the sand and Analise was immediately at his side.

"Boreas, are you alright?"

He pushed her away and got back to his feet. "I'm fine. I just need to be left alone."

Analise stared at him, her brown eyes concerned and a little hurt, but she backed up and said, "I am sorry if I upset you. I don't like to talk about my father and..."

"It's not that. It's just, I have been through so much and I don't understand it. I don't understand how there could be so much pain, for you and for me. These Monuments are the only things that haven't felt pain in this world. What am I doing protecting it? What am I doing protecting a world that just wants to hurt one another?"

He collapsed to his knees and just stared up at the stars, so high above him, so majestic and intimidating. Analise wrapped her arms around Boreas who froze at her gesture and then accepted it, burying his face in her shoulder. She said soothingly, "There's a passage my father would quote from the book called The Bible. In it, God said, 'My grace is sufficient for you, for my power is made perfect in weakness'."

Boreas wiped a tear from his eye, looked up into Analise's face and whispered, "But what does it mean?"

Analise kissed him on the cheek, soft and sweet and smiled saying, "That the Lord will give you strength to get through this. Maybe through your weakest times, you will find the strength and the power to overcome them."

Boreas felt his arm stop burning as he looked deep into Analise's eyes, but these eyes were not the ones he wanted staring back at him. The eyes he wanted to stare back at him were in love with another.

She fell asleep in his arms in the middle of the desert. He carefully removed himself from her embrace to check on the fire that was nearly out, the wood charred black. The only light was from the moon and the stars twinkling above them.

Boreas stretched and started walking toward the cave when he thought he spotted Radar hovering near the cave, but then he froze. It was not a human shadow that lurked near the cave opening, it was more beastly, more animalistic.

He screamed out, "Get away from there!"

The figure howled like a coyote and turned abruptly toward Boreas. In the light, Boreas could see that it was like a human in a coyote's clothing staring at him with its sharp teeth salivating at the sight of new prey. Boreas grabbed one of the sticks from the fire, the flame still glowing on its tip. He waved the torch frantically at the creature to distract it from the kids and it stared at him both amused and bewitched. Boreas called out to Analise to wake up and she jumped to her feet.

"Get the kids and run! Go!" He shouted.

Analise ran toward the cave and awoke the children, whispering for them to follow her. Boreas tried to stab the stick at the creature, but it moved swiftly, snarling at him and snapping its sharp teeth. The fire was nearly out when Boreas snuck a peek back to make sure that the kids and Analise were out of harm's way. That distraction was all the beast needed. It clawed at Boreas and knocked the stick out of his right hand. Boreas backed away from the beast quickly, knowing he was unarmed.

"What are you?" Boreas cried out. "What do you want?"

The beast continued to stalk him. Boreas spotted a narrow opening up higher onto the West Mitten butte. He lunged away from the beast's attempt to claw him again and made a running leap toward the butte, cutting his hand against a jagged rock, but he held on. The creature snarled at Boreas as he quickly pulled himself up, despite the pain escalating from his injured hand. He ran up the narrow slope, his sneakers sliding, but he didn't dare look backwards. He slipped and fell once in his desperate attempt to claw his way upwards, but he jumped back onto his feet with the desperation of a man running for his life. He reached the narrow steep ledge hanging 20 feet above the ground. He heard the creature's footsteps behind him as he hung on to the red sandstone rock and tried to get a good grip with his sneakers to not slip and fall over the side. He spotted a small crevice in the rock. He ran past it and then backtracked and snuck quickly into the cramped opening. The creature continued to follow his scent and its head made the turn onto the narrow ledge. It was searching wildly, sniffing and looking for a sign of Boreas who lay cramped and hidden in the dark crevice. He hoped it took the bait to continue walking forward onto the ledge. The creature stopped in front of the hole and Boreas held his breath knowing that he was trapped and that there was nowhere else to go. Just then there was a shot from below and the creature howled into the night. It took a gigantic leap off the Butte and Boreas heard a human scream from below followed by another shot. The creature howled in agony and then there was silence.

Boreas cautiously stuck his head out of the hole and looked over the edge. There was the creature dead on its side, and next to it, lay the motionless body of Radar.

Boreas retraced his footsteps and found himself slipping and sliding until he was back on the desert floor. He ran to Radar's side and pulled him away from the creature's body. Radar lay unconscious.

"Radar, wake up! Come on, don't die on me."

He checked him for a wound but found none. He shouted for Analise to help him, but he didn't know where she had gone to with the kids. He ran to the cave to retrieve the first aid kit from his knapsack and when he returned, the mysterious creature that had been lying next to Radar had vanished into thin air.

In its place stood a man that was glowing, dressed in white with long black hair that seemed to sway with an invisible wind. He turned to Boreas and spoke in a deep, somber voice, "No human medicines will heal your friend. He needs the work of a medicine man. He was attacked by a skinwalker. He has touched corpse powder which will cause death if not treated immediately."

"Who are you?" Boreas cried out. "How do you know all this?"

The man didn't answer, but instead pointed in the direction of the Juniper tree. "The Medicine Man lives beneath that tree. Knock on the trunk three times. He will be expecting you."

"How could he be expecting me?"

Before he even finished his sentence, the man vanished right before his eyes. Boreas blinked twice not believing what he had just seen. He shook his head to snap himself out of his stupor and heard someone approaching from behind. He stood up ready to fight, but relaxed at seeing Analise with Steven and Sansa close at her heels.

She ran up to him and held him tightly. He thought he might suffocate from her hug. "Are you alright?"

"I am, but Radar's not. Help me carry him to the Juniper Tree. Someone there should be able to help."

"How do you know this?"

"Don't ask, just help me, please!"

She nodded, sensing the urgency. She told Steven to hold her knapsack and to stay close to Sansa. She lifted Radar's legs and Boreas picked him up under the armpits. Together they managed to lift him and carry him to the Juniper Tree. Radar was barely breathing, fighting death. Boreas didn't know what he was doing, but quickly knocked three times on the trunk of the Juniper tree anyway. At first nothing happened as he stared at the tree expecting it to open up or something to happen. He realized he must have gone mad. The man in the desert could only be a mirage! But then out of nowhere the tree trunk slowly rotated upwards, the momentum pressing them downwards. They huddled together as the ground descended and the tree was pulling them beneath its roots.

"Hold on," Boreas told them as Sansa screamed and Steven held onto Boreas's bad wrist a little too hard.

Analise gave Boreas a dubious look, but did as he said. Boreas held onto Steven's hand with all his might, hoping they weren't all being buried alive.

Chapter 27

Question of Life or Death

The ground stopped moving and above them the tree disappeared from view, replaced with a layer of sand. They stood in a tomb-like room, surrounded by ancient drawings that glowed in the dark.

"What is this place?" Boreas asked, gingerly touching the drawings.

Analise looked at it and said, "It looks like a story."

She traced it with her hand and said, "It shows a boy, a girl and a tall person, like a giant. They are travelling over the miles and here is the sun. And this drawing, this is the wind. And this looks like a battle with many people dying. And then this... is the giant flying. And here he is, like he is killed in the sky."

Boreas listened in disbelief. It was Boreas's quest being told before his eyes through ancient drawings.

"And the girl?" Boreas asked urgently. "What happens to the girl?"

Analise traced her hand on the last panel and there was the girl with fire coming out of her fingertips.

"It looks like she's part of the battle." Analise said, reading the drawing. "But it doesn't show who wins."

Boreas looked at the figure of Aurora facing off against the Common Good Army... Against the Inspector. She was facing him alone. Boreas was nowhere to be found, unable to help her.

"Where am I in this story?"

"That is still to be determined, God of the North Wind."

They all whirled around in unison. Where the story had begun now stood a doorway into a hidden room where an old Native American man was standing. His long grayish-white hair reached down to his backside, his face was wrinkled like a prune from years of sun damage, and he wore a red bandana with white feathers hanging from the sides of his head. He wore a white fringed vest and a turquoise beaded necklace.

Boreas stood there with his mouth open in bewilderment. "How did you know...?"

"I know many things and I know that you have been attacked by the skinwalker."

"Skinwalker?" Steven asked amazed. "Like a werewolf?"

Analise shushed him but the Medicine Man smiled at the boy and said, "Similar. It is a cursed man or woman who preys upon the Navajo people and causes fear and harm to those who are not prepared for their evil ways. Like your poor friend here. He has been cursed by the corpse powder."

"Can you help him?" Boreas exclaimed, looking down at Radar who was looking more like a corpse now than even before.

The Medicine Man looked deeply into Boreas's eyes and said, "It will depend on you."

Boreas didn't know what that cryptic answer meant but suddenly two men with guns charged into the tomb behind the Medicine Man. Boreas and Analise stepped in front of the children, guarding them from harm as the Medicine Man held up his hands and said something in his native tongue to the men. The men lowered their weapons, then walked forward to lift Radar and bring him into their chamber. Boreas and Analise exchanged glances and then followed suit.

Steven looked at Boreas and asked, "That giant in the story... Is he the one you told us about?"

Boreas looked down at him and said sorrowfully, "Yes, that's Otus. He's my friend."

They were led into a large chamber that was set-up like a living room. There were Oak wood chairs and a table, beautiful hand woven rugs with intricate patterns and colors were hung on the walls. Dream catchers dangled from the ceiling and animal skin rugs lay on the dirt ground. Standing in the room was a Native American woman with black hair woven into two long braids and dressed in black military gear. The only bit of color she wore was from her dangling turquoise earrings. She smiled at Sansa and handed her a feather headdress which she giddily put on. The woman addressed the group saying, "You are safe here. My father will make sure to protect you. We offer you a hand of friendship."

Analise thanked her, and said tentatively, "We haven't eaten much in three days. And the children here have had little water. Do you have anything that could help them?"

The woman kindly nodded and ushered the two male guards to get some food for the children who sat down on a soft bear rug. Sansa rested her head on her brother's shoulder.

"My name is Yanaba. Please rest here with me. There is nothing more you can do to help your friend. He is in a dark place and my father will try to bring him back to the light."

Boreas peeked his eye through the beaded doorway where the male guards and Medicine Man were attending to Radar. Boreas recalled his last words to Radar coming back to haunt him, saying he could never trust him. Then Radar had saved his life.

He yearned to be anywhere but here, leaning his head against a patterned rug. He pictured himself in Plymouth Incarnate with Aurora holding him, kissing him. He was not alone. He felt her hand on his shoulder and saw her eyes staring back at him. Her eyes so tender and beautiful. "We are in this together," she had told him.

She needed him now more than ever. Aurora could not fall to the Inspector. Not if he could help it.

"Boreas", the Medicine Man's voice called from the other room. He snapped out of his daydream and walked through the beaded walkway to behold the Medicine Man wearing a large feathered hat and shaking some sort of musical instrument.

"I have removed most of the evil spirits from his mind and am driving them elsewhere, but there is something evil down here that is preventing me from saving him."

"What is that?" Boreas asked, confused.

"You, God of the North Wind. You are the evil force. You have ill sentiments toward this man. He is not a good man."

Boreas felt so exposed, his internal thoughts like an open book to this strange man. He put his hand on his bandaged arm fixing it tighter around his wrist as he said, "Max Radar is not a good man. He is responsible for the death of my real father, but he also saved my life tonight. He is not entirely evil, but I cannot stop myself from hating him for what he did."

"Forgiveness is the only way for you to save this man."

Boreas shook his head and declared, "You are not going to blame me for his death."

The Medicine Man held out the beaded necklace and put it around Radar's neck. "The choice is yours, God of the North Wind.

You have a lot of anger inside you. Anger toward him, anger toward your mother, anger toward your brother."

Boreas couldn't believe he had entered a therapy session while Radar lay dying before him. "What do you want me to say? That I forgive him? Then yes, I do. Just save him already!"

The Medicine Man shook his head at Boreas and said, "The choice is yours. You must learn to forgive in order to move forward toward Hyperborea. Without forgiveness you will never achieve your powers."

The Medicine Man exited the room leaving Boreas standing there in disbelief. He collapsed in the chair and stared at Radar's albino face that was even paler now, still lost to this world. Boreas was still consumed by his demons and now those demons would literally kill a man. He looked down at the green mark on his arm, wanting to scream.

Yanaba entered the room with a plate of food and a glass of water for Boreas. She handed it to him and he took it gratefully. He chewed on the bread not realizing how completely famished he was and drank the water which reinvigorated his senses. She eyed his arm and asked, "Do you want me to treat that?"

Boreas quickly pulled the sleeve down over the green mark on his arm and said sadly, "There's no treating that."

She smiled sweetly, pointing not at his mark from the Soul Extractor serum but at the cut on his hand.

"I meant treat that wound."

He looked up at her and before he could even respond she opened the bandage and stared at his hand. The blood had dried but the gashes were deep. She applied an ointment to the wound and sang sweetly as she closed it up again with a clean bandage. He watched her meticulous work and felt himself drifting to sleep, lulled by her song.

"All wounds can heal," she said softly, as he closed his eyes.

"I need to help my friend," he said drowsily, fighting to try to stay awake.

"You will," she said, then continued humming the tune. "But now you need your sleep."

Boreas succumbed to sleep. Soon he found himself in his house in Candlewick. He was in his room watching from a corner as his five-year-old self lay sleeping in bed. His mother sat at the edge of the bed, combing her fingers through his thick black hair and singing a lullaby to him. He remembered the melody as she sang; her voice was like a nightingale. She looked so much younger and yet had such sadness in her eyes, as if she had been crying. Young Boreas woke up and looked at his mother but she said, "It's time to go to sleep, Boreas."

"I want you to keep singing." he said, throwing his arms around her lovingly, resting his head against her shoulder.

"You want me to sing to you all night?"

He nodded, smiling up at her and she gave him a big hug and a kiss on the cheek.

"I love you," she said, looking deep into his eyes.

"I love you too, Mom."

"I know it will be hard. And I know you will not understand. But one day Boreas, you will know that I am doing this for you. And for Jonathan. To make a better world for you. Though it is the hardest thing I have ever done in my life."

"What is?"

She held him again close to her heart and started singing the song again. The song he had sometimes hummed without knowing why. His mom continued singing even after Boreas had fallen asleep. Holding his hand until the morning sun shone through the window.

Boreas awoke with a start, tears in his eyes. Yanaba was sitting across from him, nodding slightly as if she had also been inside his dream. He turned abruptly toward Radar who was still unconscious. Yanaba handed him a drink and smiled saying, "This is real water. The other drink was a sleeping potion I mixed up for you. I hope you had sweet dreams."

Boreas snapped to reality and stared at this witch before him. "What magic is this? What did you do to me?"

"You relived a memory that you had repressed for so long. A memory that could help you remember how much your mother loved you. It is through that love that you will be able to be the man you were born to be."

Boreas shook his head and tried to get to his feet, but was still wobbly after the sleeping draft. "I need to get out of here. Where are Sansa and Steven? And Analise. What have you done to them?"

Yanaba banged her hands on the table, her dangling earrings hypnotically swinging back and forth. "You think we have tricked you to come down here? That we are the Common Good? We are not the enemy, Boreas. We want the same thing you do. We want the freedom to believe without fear of repercussions. And you are the one that can grant that. You have crossed our path for a reason. You need us in order to move on and help your friends, the giant and the Goddess of Dawn."

"How do you know that? How could you know that unless you are working with the Inspector?"

She exclaimed angrily, "We are no friend of the Inspector or the IDEAL. They took away our land, our rights, and our freedom. Hundreds of years ago my ancestors were granted the right to practice our way of life on this land without interference by the government. The Inspector and the IDEAL broke that pact. Here we are, reduced to live beneath the trees and wait for a young foolish boy to save us when he cannot even save his friend who is dying before his eyes."

She grabbed the tray and threw it against the wall, a clay cup and saucer smashing into pieces on the floor. She started to cry as she picked up the smashed pieces and piled them onto the tray.

Boreas bent down to help her. "Yanaba, I'm sorry," he said slowly. "I have been lied to so much and betrayed by the people I care about the most. It is so hard for me to trust anyone. I couldn't even trust Radar and he saved my life."

He paused and said slowly, "I want to find forgiveness, but I don't know how."

She dumped the pieces back onto the floor and turned to him resolutely saying, "Pick up these pieces and put them back together."

He looked at her confused, staring down at the broken pieces lying on the floor. "Excuse me?"

She repeated the statement and pointed again at the pieces. He bent down and started to pick them up. "I don't understand."

"Just do it."

He picked up all the pieces, cracked and broken with jagged edges sticking out. He sorted them into different piles, discerning which pieces were the cup and which were the saucer. He was getting frustrated and stammered, "I think I need glue or tape or something to mend this."

"No you don't."

Boreas looked up at the crazy woman who towered over him as he tried to put the pieces together without anything to bind them to one another. He would put them together like a jigsaw puzzle, but they would soon topple onto the tray again since there was nothing to hold them together.

"This is impossible," he thought bitterly.

He had about four pieces of the saucer together and then proceeded to mend the cup. He had held up nearly all of the pieces of the cup but could not hold the piece that was the handle too. He was thinking of anything that could hold it for him but there was nothing. He was frustrated and angry with himself for not being able to figure out this stupid riddle. Yanaba sat down across from him, watching him, expecting him to fail.

He was about to drop the pieces and give up when he paused and thought about what Analise had told him out in the desert, what her father used to tell her: 'My grace is sufficient for you, for my power is made perfect in weakness'.

Still holding the shattered pieces together in his hands, he looked up at Yanaba and said, "Will you help me?"

Yanaba smiled at the young teenager before her, picked up the handle and put it against his hand to form a full cup.

"There's an ancient Navajo folktale called "Ch'al To' Yini'lo'", translated as "Frog Brings Rain". In this tale there is a huge fire ablaze on a mountain that is heading toward a village. Many animals refuse to put it out. Some try to put it out alone and fail. But it is through the crane and the frog cooperating, that they are able to succeed and save their friends and their homes. Humility is the first step toward forgiveness, God of the North Wind. Sometimes you need to step back to see the full picture and realize that sometimes there's more to the story than you know and it's normal to not have all the answers."

Boreas stared at the face of Radar before him. In Radar's mind he had been doing what he thought was right. He thought killing David Xiomy was the only way to prevent more destruction and war. He didn't realize the consequences of his actions until afterwards and now grappled with the fact that he had killed an innocent man.

"Radar thinks helping me is his penance." Boreas said out loud. "By helping me, he is trying to make amends for killing my father."

The door flung open and the Medicine Man entered; his eyes cross-eyed and possessed, seeming to glow in that dim room. Yanaba grabbed Boreas's hand and pulled him to the far corner of the room as the ground shook and the pictures and dream catchers plummeted to the ground with a bang. Radar took a deep breath and the Medicine Man stomped the earth with his stick three times. Boreas stood was pinned against the wall waiting for the earthquake to cease.

The glow in the Medicine Man's eyes faded and he looked at Boreas with a smile exposing his crooked front teeth. "The evil has left this room. Your friend is going to survive."

Boreas stood up, weak and off balance, trying to get his footing. He stepped toward the bed and saw that the color had returned to Radar's face and he was breathing normally. Yanaba was already dapping water on his lips and putting a cold compress on his forehead.

Boreas stepped outside. He felt numb, but also as light as a feather, as if a great weight had been lifted from his shoulders. Analise ran to his side and exclaimed, "What happened in there? I tried to get to you, but the guards warned us to not interfere."

Boreas found the clearness of mind to utter, "Radar is going to survive."

Analise wrapped her arms around him in a big bear hug and Steven and Sansa both shouted for joy at hearing the good news.

Sansa tugged on Boreas's shirt, looking up at him curiously.

"You look different," she said in her sweet voice.

Boreas didn't understand. "What do you mean?"

The Medicine Man patted him on the back and said, "The child sees a glow around you, like a halo."

Analise looked Boreas up and down and replied, "He looks the same to me."

The Medicine Man smiled, rubbing his crinkled forehead. "You are not a child, my dear. Only innocence and lovers can see one's true soul."

Analise blushed and the Medicine Man ushered her and Boreas to follow him into a separate chamber that was lined with paintings of great Native American warriors and Chiefs. They sat in a circle on the floor. He asked them to tell him the story of how they came to

Monument Valley and about the war that was brewing in Hyperborea. Boreas confided in this man who had saved his friend's life, sharing their story and telling the Medicine Man that he needed to find a way to get to Hyperborea to help his friends who would face the Inspector in battle.

"And what is to happen in Hyperborea?" the Medicine Man asked. "Why did they choose that peaceful part of the mountain for their battle?"

Boreas spoke of the prophecy and about how Aurora received the powers of dawn and how he was now meant to become the God of the North Wind. Boreas clasped his hands together and hung his head, doubt plaguing his mind. "Hyperborea is supposedly the key to receiving my powers. At least that is what the prophecy says. But who knows if I will get them! And my friends may be dying and I'm not there to help them!"

The Medicine Man stood up and slammed his staff down onto the ground, making Boreas sit back down.

"The prophecy has been right thus far, Boreas. If you start doubting yourself now then you will fail. We will grant you safe passage to Hyperborea."

Boreas shook his head. "No, you have already done so much. I cannot ask you to risk your life for me."

"But it is you who risk your life to save us. Whatever my people can do to help, we will. There is a secret underground passage that can take you under the desert and lead you to the Rocky Mountains. You will need to cross the mountains by horseback, down an old road that is no longer used for travel due to the highway that was built around it. This road will take you over the mountains and straight to the valley where Hyperborea is located."

At the thought of horses Boreas shuddered and remembered being thrown from a horse when he was a child. Horses hated him for some reason and never allowed him to ride them. There had to be another way into Hyperborea but he was not about to admit his fear of horses in front of the Medicine Man.

Analise looked torn and pulled on her hair anxiously. "What about the children? We cannot take them with us."

Boreas forgot all about his fear of horses and now another fear brewed within him. "Analise, I can't abandon Sansa and Steven."

"You want us to take them into battle? It is too dangerous."

"I made a promise to their father. I will keep them safe."

"You are keeping them safe by not taking them to Hyperborea."

"But the Inspector will kill them if he knows who they are."

Analise stared at him, dumbfounded. "What are you talking about?"

Boreas bit his lip, almost revealing that Sansa and Steven were his cousins. He had to keep that a secret, even from Analise and the Medicine Man. Nobody could know of their connection.

"I mean that the Inspector knows they escaped with us. If they were found..."

"They will not be," The Medicine Man promised. "I will keep them safe here with me until the battle is won. You will know how to find us again."

There was a knock at the door and Yanaba entered, smoothing the ends of her braids that cascaded down her shoulders. "Your friend is awake," she said brightly.

Boreas and Analise jumped up and ran through the beaded doorway, but they were too late, already hearing Radar yelling at the kids to get off the bed.

"Come on, none of this mushy stuff. Get off the bed. You'd think I nearly died!"

Sure enough, Sansa had her arms wrapped around Radar's neck and Steven was trying to help him drink water, but was splashing more of it on Radar's shirt than into his mouth.

"And to think it used to be quiet in this room," Boreas laughed.

Radar turned at the sound of Boreas's voice and broke into a smile. "Glad to see you still in one piece."

"Thanks to you."

Radar sniffed. "Will take more than a wild half human, half animal monster to defeat me. I've seen worse."

"Yes, Boreas in the morning," Analise jibed. Boreas swatted at her playfully but she shifted away, just missing contact. She stooped down and gave Radar a kiss on the cheek. "What you did was very brave."

She wrestled with the kids and they climbed onto her back, all three skedaddling out of the room, leaving Boreas to speak to Radar alone.

Radar stretched his arms over his head, his fingers touching his slightly less pale cheek. "She is something. She can kick both of our asses with her eyes shut."

Boreas nodded and sat down, fidgeting. He could see the cup and saucer he had put back together with Yanaba's help... the pieces that helped him realize there was room for forgiveness in his heart.

He took a deep breath and said, "I should have trusted you, Max."

"Oh no, you didn't just call me by my first name." Radar chided, taking a drink of water.

Boreas laughed, "Don't worry, it won't happen again."

Radar rose to his feet, looking at himself in the water cup's reflection and cringed. He wiped his face with a wet towel and pulled his platinum blond hair back behind his ears. "Just so you know, I heard what transpired between you and Yanaba."

Boreas sat up straighter. "You heard what I said?"

Radar nodded. "You were right. I never forgave myself for aiding in the execution of David Xiomy. I hoped helping you on this quest would bring me peace. Your Father was a good man. You're a lot like him."

Boreas fidgeted with his hands and stared long and hard at the dirt congealed beneath his fingernails as if it was the most fascinating thing in the world. Anything to prevent himself from tearing up.

"Thanks, Radar."

"OK, enough of this. When do we leave this pottery museum? Last I heard we still need to get to Hyperborea."

Chapter 28

Aurora's Quandary

Otus nearly tore Jake's head off after hearing that he was part of the Common Good Army. Instead he clutched Jake in his grasp, slowly squeezing the life out of him.

"If you kill me," Jake sputtered, "I won't be able to tell you what I know about Boreas!"

Otus froze, releasing his grasp and Jake plummeted to the ground, roughly rolling in the dirt.

Babs had a gun against his head before Jake could move another muscle.

"He deceived me at Alcatraz." She said coldly, the barrel pressed harder against his temple. "I didn't learn of his real identity until we were almost here in Hyperborea."

Aurora studied him, like she was trying to read him, her golden waves even brighter as the sun shone on her. So different from the little girl who used to run around Jake's house with Mary all those years ago.

She took a deep breath. "If he wanted me dead, he wouldn't have saved my life. Let's take him to Mrs. Taboo. She will know what to do."

They bound him and led him along the perimeter of the lake toward the south side of the valley where a magnificent structure manifested before his eyes. He had to blink twice to behold a medieval castle carved into the natural wonder, its reflection now cast off the shimmering lake. It resembled an Antoni Gaudi architectural masterpiece with huge circular spires intertwined into the natural trees and boulders. A large drawbridge, camouflaged with ivy and moss, was slowly let down over the lake to grant them passage into this mysterious edifice. Unless someone was looking for it, they would never find it. Hyperborea was immersed with magic and Jake swallowed hard, knowing what was at stake if he failed his mission.

The drawbridge lowered as young men and women stood watch, their guns drawn. He realized he had been like them once when he was first recruited into the Common Good Army, young and inexperienced. However, they were not trained as efficiently as he had been. Their guns were drawn but their trigger fingers would be unsteady, likely missing him the first time they tried. Fear of his own death had been eradicated in him at an early age, but here he was with that emotion coursing through his veins – fear. Fear of losing someone he loved. Fear of losing Mary.

He glanced over at Aurora, remembering a time earlier that spring when he had a fight with Mary over her. Mary had come home crying, slamming the door to her room. Jake was home for the day, gathering intel about his family's friend who owned the Laundromat on Main Street. The Inspector had reason to believe that man was practicing religious ceremonies and wanted Jake to gather proof to arrest him. Jake hadn't been home in some time and his family of course were overjoyed that he was back for the weekend.

He opened the door to Mary's room and at seeing his sister crying, he felt compassionate for her, despite the Inspector's indoctrination that the Common Good was now his family. He asked Mary what was wrong, and she looked up at him, her black bangs nearly covering her eyes completely, desperately needing a haircut.

"Like you care?" She swiped the bangs out of her teary eyes, upset that she was caught crying in front of her brother.

"I'm asking, aren't I?" he replied coldly, dropping his gun and backpack onto the floor.

"Well," she wiped her eyes with the back of her hand, "I heard Aurora got made fun of by Hattie Pearlton again at the Spring Formal. And I wasn't there to help her."

"Aurora needs to stand up for herself," Jake answered abruptly, wondering why his sister was even friends with that girl on their street. "You should stop hanging out with weak people like that."

"Aurora is my friend!" Mary shouted, throwing a book at Jake who was caught off guard by the attack. "And she's strong. She just doesn't know it yet."

Jake swallowed bitterly, recalling that conversation and realizing how wise his sister had been. Mary had seen the strength and inner goddess in Aurora when she hadn't even seen it in herself. It made him miss his sister even more.

A fire was burning in the corner and Fawn Stockington, the famous protest leader, stepped forward, dressed in red like a phoenix risen from the ashes. Her eyes bore into him, recognizing him immediately without even glancing at the tattoo.

"Jake Fray. Or should I call you 'First Lieutenant'?"

Jake was about to respond when Babs interjected, "He claims he is no longer the First Lieutenant."

Fawn stared at him doubtfully. "Really? And what could Herald's young protégé have done that was so deplorable as to get him demoted?"

Jake smiled coyly. "That's for me to know."

Aurora whispered something to Fawn who looked taken aback. She fixed the shell that was fastened to her hair and then said, "I hope the news you have about Boreas is worth risking your life for, Jake. Mrs. Taboo has jurisdiction over Hyperborea and she will not be happy to see you."

Jake cracked his neck, "I guess you have to convince her to keep me alive... since I know you are dying to find out what I know about your son."

She stepped forward, a murderous look in her eyes, reminiscent of Boreas when he was first injected with the Soul Extractor serum. Jake took a step back, nearly banging into Aurora who also looked taken aback by this transformation. She grabbed his shirt and dug her nails into the tattoo until his arm bled. He grimaced, biting his lip to not give her the satisfaction of seeing him in pain.

She smiled down at him. "Just wanted to make sure you still bled, Jake Fray. You are human after all."

She released her nails from his skin and stared into his eyes from so close that he could see her blood vessels. "I have killed for my son before. Don't think I won't do it again."

She released her hold on him and whirled around, ushering one of the soldiers to fetch Mrs. Taboo immediately.

Jake caught his breath as blood slowly streamed down his arm. The assembly stood in silence until the double doors of the hallway burst open and Mrs. Taboo entered, followed by Jonathan Stockington. Mrs. Taboo walked up to Jake, her eyes wide as she recognized him.

"You were the last person I expected to see here, First Lieutenant," Mrs. Taboo said, her voice expressionless and monotone.

"Ex-First Lieutenant," Jake replied, realizing more guards had emerged from behind the double doors, their guns pointed straight at him.

"How many of my people have you killed in the name of the IDEAL, Lieutenant? And what do you hope to achieve by coming here, beside your death, of course."

Jake looked into the eyes of this enigma, the mysterious protest leader that the Inspector had warned him about. He hadn't believed she actually existed. The woman who had hidden a giant.

"I have information regarding Boreas Stockington."

The whole room went silent and no one dared to breathe. Jake felt for the first time like he was not a sitting duck; he had the room at his mercy.

He started to remove something from his bag but Babs quickly pressed the gun against the back of his head. "Easy!" Jake cried out. "I don't have a weapon."

"We'll be the judge of that," Aurora cried out, grabbing the bag from him and pulling out the orange conch shell that belonged to Boreas.

Aurora gasped, recognizing the shell immediately. Without a word, she walked over and handed it to Fawn who cradled it in her palm like it was a piece of Boreas that she had back again.

"So... he's alive?"

Jake nodded. "Yes, Boreas is alive. The Inspector tracked him after the TV broadcast incident out west, not too far from here, in Monument Valley. He found their abandoned helicopter, but no sign of him. The Inspector is still out there searching with the Common Good Army but soon they are going to come here – to Hyperborea – to fight you all. And from what I can see, they will win that battle."

"Thank you for your vote of confidence," Mrs. Taboo said sarcastically. "But it doesn't explain what prompted you to come and tell me this yourself."

Jake took a deep breath, "They killed my mom."

He stared into Babs' eyes, who said hesitantly, "So, that wasn't a lie?"

He nodded. "That was true." He continued. "I realized I couldn't fight for the Inspector any longer and came here to warn you. He must be stopped."

The room went silent until Jonathan cried out, "What a load of crap! I believe you are still loyal to the Inspector. Did he tell you to spy on us?"

"Jonathan, please," Fawn interrupted him as she stood quietly thinking. "We don't have time to waste figuring out if you are a spy or not. Jonathan, go to the Professor. We'll need to tighten up our security immediately if the Inspector is almost here."

He nodded and ran off with two men to assist him.

Mrs. Taboo eyed the young soldier curiously and then directed Babs, "Put him in the jail cell until we can figure out what to do with him."

Babs nodded and forced Jake to walk toward the back end of the castle.

Jake smiled inwardly. He was in.

Once the door was shut behind Jake, Mrs. Taboo said, "I cannot sense if he is lying. The Inspector has trained some of the best spies, especially with them young like he was and easily manipulated. Aurora, what do you make of this?"

Aurora felt sick. Mary's mother was dead. "How could he have just let his mother die?" she wondered out loud. "There must be more to the story."

Fawn put her arms around Aurora. "He is not the same boy we once knew from Wishbone Avenue. He was enlisted so young into the Common Good Army. They brainwashed him, Aurora. You saw it yourself. They arrested Mary and her parents."

"But Jake saved my life. He either did it to gain my trust or he truly has changed."

Mrs. Taboo laughed, "You always want to see the good in people, Aurora. Some people are just evil. That boy may be one of them. And the Common Good Army is at our doorstep."

Fawn put her hand on the large brick fireplace mantle, thinking. She spotted an open toolbox lying on the floor and found a piece of string inside. She cut and wrapped the string around the orange conch shell. She pulled the ends around her neck and knotted them together to create a necklace. Fawn looked at the orange conch shell for a long time as Aurora watched her. She was protecting the conch shell for her son. *Could it be a sign from Boreas that he was on his way? That he would find a way to get to them?*

Fawn took a deep breath. "If what Jacob Fray said is correct, then Boreas is within one or two days journey from here. He could get his powers when he gets here and help us win this war."

Mrs. Taboo shook her head, "Don't put too much value on what he says. He could be giving us false hope."

"I think any hope right now is better than none. God knows we need it."

Fawn spun and stormed out of the room, banging the double doors behind her.

The room felt like it was spinning. Aurora knew they needed all the hope and any help they could get at this point. Even if it was from a soldier with strange motives.

"I need him to teach me everything he knows," Aurora said finally. "Ephialtes proved to me that I am no match for the Inspector, especially since I am still learning my powers. Jake knows how the Common Good Army fights. We can use this to our advantage."

Mrs. Taboo started going into a trance, rocking with her eyes shut tight. Suddenly they opened wide and her pupils were dilated. "He wants something from you, Aurora. He is going to test you, I sense it. I sense that he saved your life because he needs you."

Aurora stared at the wise old face before her, marveling at the many years she had lived, and the pain and agony of many battles prior to this one that she had experienced. She understood human nature and how far people would go to get what they truly wanted.

Aurora nodded and then headed through the double doors and to the back of the castle where the dungeon was located. As she walked down the hallway, she stared at the grey brick walls lined with shelves upon shelves of books that had been confiscated, collected and hidden here for prosperity. She wished she had time to read these books, these traitorous artifacts stored here. There would be severe consequences if they were found. *Were stories so dangerous?* She wondered if anyone would write a story about their adventure. Perhaps she was the one meant to write it, once their journey was over… that is, if she survived the battle.

She pulled on the rusty latch that opened the rickety door at the end of the long hallway revealing a dark, windy staircase that led down into the dungeon. A shadow appeared on the wall, enlarging with each step causing Aurora to pause until she realized the shadowy figure was Babs. As she came into view, Babs looked deep in thought, like she was losing her own internal battle. When she spotted Aurora, she gave her a hug.

"I fell for him, Aurora; though I swore to myself that I wouldn't like anyone else. Why do I always go for the guy that has the Inspector after him? I think I need my head examined."

Aurora smiled, taking her friend's hands in her own. "Jake has always been charming. Believe me, I've known him most of my life. Though, I still can't figure him out."

"Do you trust him?"

Aurora shrugged. "He is going to help us, whether I trust him or not."

Babs nodded. "Figured you would say that."

"Did he tell you anything else when you brought him down to the dungeon?"

Babs blushed slightly. "He said that I was the best female soldier he has ever met."

Aurora nodded in agreement and told Babs to go get some food and rest. Babs handed her the cell key, then expressed concern over leaving Aurora alone with Jake, but Aurora reminded her that she won't need weapons with the First Lieutenant. She was one.

Babs took off down the hallway as Aurora opened the rickety door, no longer delaying the task at hand. She slowly descended the old termite infested wooden steps leading into the dank cellar where rows of jail cells were lined up. It brought back the memory of when she had been in the Plymouth Incarnate prison with both Boreas and Radar. It had been the last time she had seen Boreas... when she laid paralyzed in that mysterious green light... when he had kissed her.

Jake sat at the end of one of the jail cells, hidden in the shadows. A lone window illuminated a single ray of moonlight onto his arm where the cursed tattoo beamed at her. He looked up with those mysterious eyes of his. "Didn't expect to see you so soon."

"Well, time is something we don't have a lot of around here."

She opened the cell door with the key, weaponless except for her powers as he sized her up and down, sensing the same. Aurora knew he was notorious at deception, recalling how he had spared her life at Candlewick Prison and revealed to her that Boreas had been injected with the Soul Extractor serum. He had deceived the Inspector then. Was he deceiving her now?

Aurora leaned back, the bars pressing against her spine. "Whose side are you really on, Jake Fray?"

His fingers tapped nervously on his watch, the movement rattling the metal shackle that bound his hands. "It's complicated."

Aurora could not make heads or tails out of that answer. "Everything about you is complicated. I'm here to find out the truth. What's the true story... how could you let your mother die?"

He looked up at Aurora angrily, tapping on the watch like a ticking clock about to go off. "I didn't let her die. You don't know what the Inspector is capable of."

Aurora stood up and clutched onto the cold iron bars. "I know what he's capable of. That's why Boreas, Otus and I need to stop him and the Geometric Storm."

He struggled to his feet and it was then that Aurora noticed the slight limp in his left leg. His chains clinked as he stood, bitterness in his face as he clenched his fists.

"Yes, stopping the Geometric Storm. I remember when you first warned me about it. Getting on the elevator to take you to see Inspector Herald. Do you remember?"

Aurora shuddered, recalling that nightmare. "Of course I remember. You saved Boreas and my life that day."

"No," he said, reaching toward his watch and pressing onto it. A face flickered onto the screen and Aurora stepped back, unsure what was happening before her eyes.

"Your father, Aurora. Your father saved you."

She leaned over and flickering on the screen was a picture of her father, broken and beaten and lying in a cell. It was video footage and she started screaming into it, yelling her father's name, but he didn't hear her. He was just lying there, looking out into space, all hope lost.

Jake clicked on the watch and her father's face vanished and she felt tears streaming down her face.

"Bring him back! I need to speak to him!" she cried out.

Jake laughed mercilessly, leaning back against the wall smugly, like this was exactly what he bargained for. "I see I have gotten the Goddess of Dawn's attention. Now I have a deal to make with you, Aurora. If you don't fight in the battle here at Hyperborea, then your father will go free."

Aurora felt such anger and anguish running through her as she clumsily wiped the tears from her face, the love of her father igniting her hands. "Tell me where he is! I want the truth."

She shone her light at Jake, illuminating his body and he cried out, shielding his eyes. He appeared to be fighting the light, but Aurora shone it stronger. "Where is he?"

"In a jail in Bryce Canyon. 15 miles from here."

She continued shining her light at him, and exclaimed, "Is Mary alive?"

He stared up at her, now at her mercy. "Yes, she is alive. Herald is going to kill her like he killed my mom! He is forcing me to help him."

Aurora released the light and Jake collapsed, his chains clinking on the concrete floor. He held his head into his hands, angry at himself for being so weak. He looked up at her with a mixture of awe and fear. "How did you do that? How did you force me to confide in you? I couldn't fight it."

Aurora took a deep breath, "It's how I got Boreas to see the light. My powers can bring out the good in a person."

Jake swallowed and looked up at her. "Aurora, if you reveal that I am a spy, Mary's life is over. I tried to end this, to kill Herald. After the Candlewick breakout I tried to shoot him, but I didn't succeed. That's why I'm no longer the First Lieutenant."

Aurora stared down at his feeble frame, the soul of Jake still clear in her mind, the horrors he had seen, but also the love he still felt for his sister. There was too much at stake if she revealed him. That much was clear. She had to play along, until she could figure out what to do.

"So here's what's going to happen. You are going to help us Jake… or I will tell Mrs. Taboo and the others that you lied and they won't be as forgiving as I am. You are going to be in charge of our army."

Jake shook his head, "Your army, except for you and your giant friends, don't have what it takes to take on the Inspector. Even if I did train them…"

"Which you will."

He glared at her. "Fine. I will train them. But if you care about Mary and your father, you can't fight in the battle."

"You have got to be crazy if you think that I'm not going to fight in this battle."

Jake started pacing and then turned, smiling deviously to himself. He knelt down toward her and whispered, "I think I just discovered a loophole in Herald's plot. He never anticipated us teaming up. We can use Herald's terms to our advantage. With your powers we can save them. My sister and your father. We can rescue them from the prison."

Aurora was about to rebuke it but then she thought about that video of her father. Sickly and suffering in that cell. She couldn't let him suffer. Jake knew where he was being held and she could help fight to release him.

But then what about Otus, Babs… and Fawn? Could she abandon them on this foolish mission? And could Jake be trusted? Just because she shone her light on him didn't mean he wasn't still working with the Inspector.

She shook her head wildly, "No. I can't leave. What if the Inspector attacks tomorrow? I have to help my friends."

"The Inspector won't attack for another two days. He's still readying his troops to take on a giant. I'll get you back in time for the battle and we will have the leverage that the Inspector is holding over us. My sister and your father. You'll finally be able to kill the Inspector, once and for all."

She stood there frozen. "I don't want to kill him."

Jake stared at her in shock. "You're probably the only person who could try to kill him and succeed."

"My powers are to save a life. Not take a life."

Jake took a deep breath, grasping her hands in his. "Aurora, here's some free training advice. The Inspector wants to kill you. What do you hope to accomplish by going into battle if not to end this once and for all?"

Aurora shook her head fiercely. "I can't kill him. I don't want to kill anybody."

Jake's eyes looked troubled as they peered into her own. "Then he'll win."

Aurora pulled away from him and quickly opened the cell door, slamming it shut behind her. She ran up the stairs and nearly tripped over the last step, swiftly closing the prison door behind her. Even with the door closed, Jake's words haunted her mind.

She stared at the book shelf, at the stories and thinking of her own story unfolding before her. Aurora the murderer. Aurora the fierce. Aurora the brave. Or Aurora who lost it all.

And for the first time in a long time, she fell to her knees- and prayed.

Chapter 29

The Calm Before the Storm

The Awakened hour had barely begun but Jake was already standing with Ephialtes, lining up the men and women to begin their training session. Aurora had not slept the night before. She had wandered the halls like a zombie trying to wrap her mind around what had transpired in that jail cell with Jake.

Memories streamed back, knowing that her love of her parents was her weakness. Boreas had preyed on it when he was injected with the Soul Extractor serum, concocting the lie that they were locked in Candlewick Prison. Of course it wasn't true. Boreas was just under the influence of the Inspector. Jake's plan, or 'loophole' as he called it, could be another lie, preying upon her weakness to remove her from the battle, ensuring the Inspector's triumph. Fawn had confirmed that Aurora's father was in a prison out west, but who was to say that he was in the one at Bryce Canyon? Aurora wouldn't even know it existed without Jake and she certainly wouldn't know where to find it without him.

She shivered slightly as Jonathan ran up to her. He handed her a piece of bread and a hot cup of coffee.

"I was looking for you. Breakfast?"

Aurora took the food gratefully. The hot coffee warmed her ice-cold fingers in her flimsy gloves.

"Thanks, Jonathan. I had a rough night."

"Because of Jake Fray?" he asked, straightening his coat, and putting his hands in his pockets to keep them warm.

Aurora nodded. "He made me second guess why I am fighting. What do I hope we will achieve?"

Jonathan stared longingly into her eyes. "Aurora, have you even spoken to any of these protestors...their conditions, what they were put through these past 15 years? You are giving these people hope. And as much as you think I don't believe in you, I really am trying to."

She looked at that beautiful face she had always fantasized about, longed for. Here he was and yet she still felt cold. Like something was missing.

She forced a reassuring smile. "Thank you, Jonathan. Now we just need Boreas. I hope he will make it here in time."

"Boreas." Jonathan threw his plastic cup into the garbage can and looked disgusted. "I don't know why we can't have a conversation without you bringing him up."

"Stop pretending like you don't care about him. I know you were just as relieved as the rest of us when Jake said he was alive."

"Relieved? More like a thorn in my side that I can't get rid of."

Aurora wanted to throw the coffee into his face to get him to wake up. "Why can't you just admit that you care about him? If you don't, I might just have to go find another boyfriend."

Jonathan smiled and wrapped his arms around Aurora. "So, you forgive me for not believing that you could fight Ephialtes?"

Aurora kissed him on the lips. "Just make sure it doesn't happen again. I am the Goddess of Dawn, remember."

Jonathan pressed his hand against her face. "Well, Boreas might have the glory, but at least I have something he'll never have."

He kissed her and she fell into his kiss and nothing seemed to matter while that kiss tied them together. It also didn't seem to be the right time to confess to him that Boreas had kissed her back at Plymouth Incarnate. Some things were better left unsaid.

"Uh Hem."

Aurora quickly released herself from Jonathan's arms. Jake stood staring at them with a wry smile plastered on his face, his lips as red as fire, though she knew how cold blooded he really was.

"Didn't mean to interrupt," he smirked, "but Jonathan, you need to get in formation."

Jonathan looked aghast and then raced over to Ephialtes who was chugging a jug of beer. "You demoted me?"

Ephialtes towered above Jonathan and grinned like a school boy. Spit dripped down his face and splashed onto Jonathan's shoulder.

"Yep, you're demoted. That Jake actually knows how to fight so he will be my 2nd in command today."

Ephialtes wiped the drool from his mouth and exclaimed, "Now, you pathetic love birds go run the perimeter, twice. You pansies need to learn discipline!"

Aurora smiled sheepishly at Jonathan and they both ran around the lake perimeter abiding by the giant dictator's command. Aurora was secretly pleased to get the blood flowing in her veins. Since when did it get so cold in Hyperborea? She looked up and grey clouds were hovering overhead. It was almost as if Jake had brought the winter with him to their spring sanctuary, foreshadowing a cold front drifting in from the East.

While running the second time around, they heard gun fire in the training field and then surprised gasps from the troops. Jake had made two bulls eyes in a row.

"What a show off," Jonathan muttered. Aurora pretended not to hear, but secretly was amused, knowing Boreas would have a field day knowing someone was actually better than Jonathan in something. Of course it had to be Jake. She was tempted to confide in Jonathan about Jake's proposition, but something warned her against it. If Jonathan knew, he would surely go straight to Fawn and they would arrest Jake. She knew that she couldn't abandon the troops, her friends, but she couldn't risk losing Mary and her father again, especially if there was a chance she could save them.

Even though he had been made to train the troops against his will, Jake was a very good trainer. He taught them maneuvers and took them through training drills that Ephialtes could never have heard of since so much had changed in technology over the past 5 years. There were new satellite and radar sensors and too many automatic weapons. Just hearing about them made your blood curl and heart convulse. The Professor listened and was able to suggest ways that his chemical weapons could be used to counter the Common Good's efforts. Jake was impressed with his work, especially the hypnotic paralysis that the Professor had invented and that had been used in Plymouth Incarnate. Jake said it would slow down the Common Good, but it would not stop them.

While Aurora was practicing with the Khanda sword, Jake approached and started playfully fighting with her. He soon turned serious, calling out sword fighting tips while their blades crashed against each other. He parried masterfully, the only sign of his effort was his brown hair blowing into his eyes. With a loud 'clang', her sword flew out of her hands.

He gazed at her humorously. "I think your powers are stronger than your sword skills."

"Very funny," she said, rushing to pick up the sword, but he beat her to it.

"Beautiful sword," he admired, his hand tracing the hilt of it. "Where did you get it?"

He ogled the sword and put his fingers against the blade.

Aurora bit her lip remembering what Swanson had told her. This sword had to be a gift to a person who would uphold balance. Jake was surely not that person.

"It was a gift from a friend. Only the person who can restore balance can wield its power. Apparently I need to find that person and give him or her the sword."

Jake appeared caught in a trance while holding the weapon, but he soon snapped out of it and reluctantly handed the sword back to Aurora. Aurora took it quickly and put it in the sword holster around her waist.

"Have you considered my proposal?" he whispered, checking to make sure no one was eavesdropping. "Will you come with me to the prison to rescue Mary and your father?"

Aurora stared out into the sunset, shaking her head. "I need more time."

Jake whispered into her ear. "I'm leaving tomorrow night at midnight. Stop me if you dare, but I have to try to save Mary. And no Khanda sword or superpowers are going to stop me."

He stormed off down the hill toward where Babs was waiting for him. He put his arm around her as they headed off toward the castle.

✫ ✫ ✫

The following night everyone gathered in the castle for dinner like they always did, but this evening felt different. People appeared afraid with the battle near at hand. Husbands and wives were holding onto each other a little tighter and even the children were less rowdy and more somber, as if they too understood what was at stake. Aurora had more pressing matters on her mind, like Jake and the Sacred Hour deadline he had given her. She watched him out of the corner of her eye talking to Babs. Jake was showing her a more precise way to shoot that would nearly guarantee accuracy. Babs smiled up at him and he smiled back. It was like Babs had a way to soften that hard exterior that Aurora couldn't break through.

Aurora leaned back in her chair as Otus dropped down beside her.

"A penny for your thoughts?"

"Otus, if you had the chance to save two people you love, but you knew there was a possibility of causing more people to die in the process, what would you do?"

Otus scratched his head and pondered this. "I believe that sometimes one life makes all the difference. Look at you and Boreas. With one of you out of the equation, the prophecy wouldn't exist."

"And you too, Otus." Aurora said, smiling up at her friend. "Where would we be without you? Remember when Boreas and I first met you in the ruby-red house you and you had him eat the rat stew?"

"What's wrong with my stew?"

Aurora imitated Boreas's face like she was gagging. "I wish I had captured that moment on camera!"

"I still don't know what was wrong with my stew. Rat is a delicacy."

Aurora smiled up at Otus and rested her back against his hairy leg. "I wonder if we are going to see him again."

"Of course we will, Aurora. You have to have faith."

Aurora closed her eyes, trying to think positively but was distracted by Ephialtes. He was swaying clumsily with a gigantic jug of gin, spilling most of the drink out from the top. He sang along with the music, completely off key, but no one dared to tell him to stop at the risk of starting a fight with him at this hour.

Ephialtes sang, "We are all going to die tomorrow...ya ya ya... drink another bottle of gin... and send me home... ya ya ya..."

"What am I going to do with him?" Otus wrinkled his nose and buried his face in his hand as he reached onto the table to pick up a small piece of chicken. He started to raise it toward his mouth but stopped when he saw a little girl sitting by herself. He handed the chicken to her and she took it gratefully. There was hardly any food left since they had sealed off the borders and though they wanted to make sure that the giants were fed, Otus could not eat when others were starving.

He then pointed to Babs and said, "Glad to see her smiling again. It's been a while."

Aurora nodded. Seeing Babs smiling was definitely not something she had seen in a long while.

"Boreas will have to find another girl, I'm afraid," he bellowed and stood up to try to stop Ephialtes from making more of a fool of himself.

Fawn looked radiant with her hair pulled back in a loose bun and the conch shell necklace around her neck. She clanged on her goblet and the music stopped. Even Ephialtes stopped his rambling and looked over to where Fawn was standing. Her voice lifted over the entire castle chamber and she said, "Before the Last Straw Protest, our world consisted of fighting – one religion fighting the other in an endless battle. We ignored the wisdom of our religions and focused instead on hating each other. It sadly took the Last Straw and the Common Good party to make us realize that our religious freedom could be taken away. And it was taken away, with many of us also losing our homes, our jobs, our friends and our families. It was through this suffering that we soon realized that we are all one. As David Xiomy said, "We may believe in different gods, different beliefs and different customs, but we are all one people on this earth. We have to breathe, we have to eat, and we all will one day die. We want the same things, just in different ways. We want to understand why we are here. We need the freedom to be able to think and to understand and to have faith, even if it is just to have faith in ourselves." She paused before continuing. "David died hoping that we would have this day; that we would rise up as one voice and declare that we will not let our freedom be taken away from us. Religion does not need to divide. We as a united people can fight together for the same cause – our freedom. We can see the light ahead of us. If we die, at least we know that we died for a cause greater than us. We fight for our friends, our family, our children and their children. May our faith in whatever our hearts believe in, keep us strong and forever bless us!"

The crowd erupted in Huzzah's and cheers. Aurora could not believe that only a moment ago this group of 500 souls had looked as if they had already thrown in the towel. Now they were all one voice, screaming for one cause and for one hope – to not have to live in fear any longer.

Aurora suddenly felt sick to her stomach and ran outside to the lake to get some air. It was all too real now. Everything was happening so quickly and she couldn't stop it. She was risking so much and she felt so torn and scared. She was only 15 years old. Was this where her life was destined to end? Why were some able to accomplish so much and others so little? Why did Eileen have to die and her friend Mary be captured and why did David Xiomy have to be killed? And why was she, Aurora Alvarez – a nobody – the one with the powers?

"Why?" She screamed out into the night sky, yelling at the stars and whatever was up there that could hear her cry. "Why me?"

She collapsed onto the ground, her tears falling like rain drops onto the glassy lake surface. She held her fur coat closer around her neck as the temperature had dropped.

"Why not you?" A boy's voice echoed back.

She looked down and there was Swanson staring back at her, concerned and frightened.

"Swanson, I don't want to hear it. I want to cry and yell and vent like any other normal teenage girl. I don't want you or anyone else to stop me. I'm allowed a good cry, especially if it is the last one I will ever have."

Swanson nodded and just stared up at her silently until she was all cried out. Then he said, "Can I speak now?"

She sniffed and wiped her nose with her sleeve. "Fine."

"You have been chosen for this mission for a reason, Aurora Alvarez. Never forget that."

"But why me? I mean, I get why Boreas is involved. I mean, his father was David Xiomy so I completely get it. But my parents are just my parents. I am not from some special lineage. I've said it before, but I think you have the wrong Aurora."

"I don't think Boreas would think that."

"Well Boreas isn't here."

Suddenly, Swanson splashed her and she cried out in surprise as the cold water hit her in the face. "What was that for?"

"That's what you get!"

He splashed her again.

"Cut it out!"

"That's what you get!"

"That's what I get for what?"

Swanson glared at her and exclaimed, "That's what you get for giving up on yourself. And us."

"I didn't give up. I just don't think I can... kill anyone. Even the Inspector."

Swanson stared at her doe-eyed and said, "Maybe you can help him see the light with your powers!"

Aurora shook her head, trying to dry off where Swanson had splashed her. "What do you mean?"

He fixed his hat over his head. "Maybe you need the Inspector to get to the Northern Lights. Maybe there are more than 3 pieces in this puzzle."

He vanished into the water and though Aurora cried out for him to come back, he didn't reappear. Aurora pulled the coat closer around her as cold air was seeping into her skin and making her ice cold. Aurora looked into the water, but it was only her reflection that stared back at her now. She knew what she had to do, even though the world may never forgive her. She looked around her at Hyperborea and felt like it knew she was going to betray them. There was no choice in the matter and there could be no second guessing. She had already made up her mind. It was like Otus said; sometimes one life is worth saving.

Chapter 30

The Sacred Hour

Aurora headed back toward the castle and knew that soon they would be in lockdown. The festivities were starting to end and the fire was nearly out in the main dining room. Rats were scurrying across the floor as they searched for scraps left over, but nothing was wasted tonight. She felt exhausted as she headed up to her room. Jake had said he would find her at the Sacred Hour so she figured she would start getting ready. She opened the door and walked in to find Jake dressed in a black leather jacket and jeans, some dirt still congealed on his face from the day's training. He was sitting at the edge of her bed, the Khanda sword in his hand.

Aurora shut the door behind her, startling Jake. He put down the sword and asked, "Are you ready to come with me?"

Before Aurora could respond, Jake held up his wrist where another video of her father was displayed. He was so frail and beaten down that she hardly recognized him. His hair had been shaved off and he wore an orange jumpsuit, like he was a criminal. Her eyes brimmed with tears.

"Yes," she said resolutely, as the video flickered to black. "I have to save him."

Jake stood up, grabbing a backpack and tossing it to her. "I already packed us everything we need."

Aurora stared at him startled. "How did you know I would come with you?"

He smiled slyly, "We're more alike than you know, Aurora. Let's go."

They snuck out the back entrance and Aurora knew the way to avoid the Professor's traps. The guards on duty were searching due west where the Inspector was to be advancing the following day. Aurora gulped as they headed up a steep incline and through thick shrubbery. Except for the pale moonlight, there was no other light guiding their path. She wished she could illuminate the path for them, but it was too risky. She followed Jake's lithe movements as she tried to keep up with him. Even though he had a slight limp, he was still in extremely good shape. He was able to maneuver like a tiger through the night, advancing stealthily up the mountain. She realized then what a force he was to be reckoned with.

They paused to catch their breath and Jake looked anxiously due north as if expecting someone to have followed them.

To their dismay, snowflakes trickled down from the gray misty sky. It wasn't supposed to snow in Hyperborea. It was considered the land of eternal spring, after all. It was almost like a forewarning of what was to come.

"Come on," Jake ordered, grabbing her hand. "The snow will leave tracks and we can't risk being followed."

Aurora jumped to her feet, glad she dressed for the cold with a wool hat, dark red thermal jacket and hiking boots. The Khanda sword she had secured in the sword belt around her waist. She scrambled after Jake, her glutes already sore from running up that steep terrain. She was actually glad Ephilates had trained them as intense as he did or just getting up this mountain would have caused her to collapse.

The snow was falling faster now and Aurora was blinded as they kept trudging forward. Jake said that they could commandeer the same train that had taken him there from San Francisco.

He looked at his watch as they continued running forward.

Aurora peered down at the castle, feeling guilty about abandoning her friends in the night, looking down at the dots of houses below her, little lights flickering in the windows. "I'm doing this for you, Dad," she reminded herself. "I promised I would save you and this is my chance."

The slope was steep with a 1,000 foot drop and Aurora began to feel panicky looking down at the valley beneath her. Jake had reached the top and was holding his hand out to her when Aurora's feet began to slide on the gravel. She reached up to grab the ledge and Jake grabbed her hand as the rock slide ensued beneath, her body flailing in mid-air.

"Quick... give me the sword!" Jake cried out.

Aurora stared up at the man who had her life in his hands. "The what?"

"The sword. It's weighing you down."

Frantically, Aurora unhooked the sword with her free hand and passed it up to Jake who grabbed it.

He stared at the sword, again in a trance, and Aurora cried out, "Jake!" to try to snap him out of it.

Aurora grabbed his wrist with her now freed hand and looked at the face of the watch. Instead of numbers on a clock, there were words illuminated on the screen: *We are in position. Bring her to me.*

Jake pulled her up and over the ledge roughly and she landed face-first into the snow. She wiped the snowflakes from her eyes, looking at Jake in a new light as he was holding onto her sword... the sword she had given to him freely.

"Give me the Khanda sword," she demanded, standing tall.

He shook his head at her. "I'm sorry, Aurora, but this played out better than I had anticipated."

"Who is that message on your watch from? The Inspector?" She cried, so mad at herself for being so naïve!

Before he could respond, a huge explosion sounded outside the castle walls. Horrified, Aurora gazed at the Northern side of the Hyperborean mountains. It was one of the Professor's traps. He had set it up to catch anyone trying to sneak in without their knowledge. The alarm blared, echoing across the valley. Aurora stood there aghast, staring at Jake.

"You just wanted to get me away. You knew they would attack tonight."

"Aurora, I had no choice. I needed you to give me the Khanda."

"To give it to the Inspector? We were going to save Mary... together. You don't have to do this."

He held the sword up, the blade shimmering in the breath of dawn. "I AM saving Mary!"

Aurora's hands glowed in fury and she aimed her light at him. Anticipating this, Jake moved the sword to protect himself from the rays, the light reflected off the blade and bounced back at Aurora, knocking her off her feet. Aurora's body was flung backwards, landing roughly against a tree stump. Jake sprung over to her and held her body down in the snow.

"Never underestimate your opponent, Aurora. Or did you not learn anything from me?"

She struggled to get up but he held the blade against her throat.

"Now, if you even think about raising those hands of yours, I swear I will end this prophecy once and for all. Unlike you, Aurora, I know how to kill."

Chapter 31

A Warrior Manifested

"**M**rs. Taboo, what is it?"
Fawn ran into the security base where Mrs. Taboo was already working with her men and women to survey the damage and the threat to the North Wall.

"Security picked up motion near the Northern Border. The Inspector and his men fed incorrect information to our spies. They are not attacking tomorrow. They are here now!"

Fawn felt anger surge through her veins, realizing the Inspector was going to fight during the Sacred Hour. He was breaking his own mandatory curfew. Fawn took charge, mobilizing the men and women in the Courtyard, and everyone rushed to change into their uniforms and grab their weapons off the shelf.

"Just like we practiced," Fawn was yelling to be heard over the commotion. "They may have the element of surprise, but we know this terrain better than they do. It is our advantage and we're going to use it."

Hundreds of the Protesting army were already lined up inside of the castle and the drawbridge had been raised to keep the enemy out. Outside the safety of their walls, Jonathan could hear what sounded like firecrackers popping on the Independence Day of the Last Straw, but they weren't firecrackers. They were the sounds of gunfire coming from planes overhead from the enemy that wanted to kill them. The battle had begun.

Babs rushed to her position with Otus and Ephialtes and Otus placed her in his overalls pocket.

"It's about time we do some real fighting!" Ephialtes cried out in glee. "I'm ready to kill these puny humans."

"Where's Aurora?" Babs shouted to be heard over the uproar.

Otus stared at her. "I thought she was with you!"

Babs shook her head, staring down to try to find her friend amongst the masses scurrying below them.

There wasn't time to waste as the two giants ran through the dungeon and crawled through the tunnel they had built this past week. Mrs. Taboo spoke in the earpiece so that Otus could hear what was going on above ground. From the central surveillance room she was recounting the enemy's play by play.

"They are coming down from the Northern side. At least a thousand troops. I can see a helicopter at about 50 yards north, coming in fast. Otus, Ephialtes you will need to take aim at 45 degrees exactly on my mark. Let me know when you are in position.

They stepped through a crude hole covered by algae and moss and slipped beneath the still waters that led them onto the bottom of the lake. Due to the lake being filled with liquid oxygen, they were all able to breathe normally under the water. Rooted at the bottom of the lake were boulders prepped and ready for the attack.

The two giants picked up a boulder each and Otus called out to his brother, "Ephialtes, be careful."

Ephialtes grinned. "I'm the reckless one, remember? And the better fighter and the..."

"We're in position," Babs cried out and the giants froze, waiting for the cue.

"Ready in... crap! We just lost our visual feed. Abort the mission! Abort."

Otus was about to drop the boulder when Ephialtes shouted, "No! Otus, don't fail me now! On my cue."

Otus followed obediently and Babs watched in amazement as Ephialtes dropped to the lake floor and put his ear against the soil. He was hearing the vibrations of the helicopter approaching! Suddenly he cried out, "Now!"

Otus, remembering the hatred and the fear that he had felt for his brother the days before, channeled that same power and threw the boulder up with all his strength. It burst out of the water. Babs clutched Otus's pocket, fearful that the boulder hadn't made contact; waiting desperately for some sort of sign. It felt like forever before Mrs. Taboo cried into the ear piece, "Our visual signal is back up! It was a direct hit! The chopper is down!"

Ephialtes patted Otus on the back, but now that their presence was known, the two giants jumped out from under the lake and landed on two Humvees that were speeding toward the castle.

Immediately the drawbridge opened and the Protesting soldiers ran forward to join the giants. Ephialtes and Otus held up the massive metal shields that they had constructed and blocked the onslaught of bullets coming at them from the Northern border. Guns fired as the massive wave of Common Good soldiers rushed down the side of the mountain. There were thousands of them.

Jonathan cried out, "Don't break your position!"

The front line were in formation, bent down on one knee with their rifles aimed at the incoming army, waiting for Jonathan's cue.

"Fire!" he cried out. Bullets exploded out of the gun barrels, striking the bodies of the Common Good soldiers, knocking them down, one by one. Jonathan and his soldiers reloaded as Otus advanced toward the top of the mountain. The snow was falling harder now, blocking their vision. Otus slipped and slid as he climbed. While some soldiers pointed their guns at him, Otus quickly snatched them up and dropped them into the frozen lake below.

Babs jumped out of Otus's pocket and landed on her feet at one of the machine guns near where a fallen soldier lay. She gave the thumbs up to Otus and started firing away at the Common Good Army. Being a sure shot, she was hitting her marks when Otus yelled to her, "If you run out of bullets, whistle!"

Babs didn't respond, just continued to shoot as Otus climbed to higher altitudes. He peered around at the people fighting, but the one person he searched for was still missing. *Where the hell is Aurora?*

✡ ✡ ✡

Aurora watched the scene unfold below while she was incapacitated by the paralyzing light. Jake had vanished with the sword and had forced her to watch her friends getting attacked. She saw some of the Common Good falling but more bodies with the brown and green colors of her allies were lying still. And more soldiers were coming over the mountain. How could she have been so foolish as to trust Jake Fray? Not only had he had betrayed her, but he was also now in possession of the Khanda sword. Swanson was going to kill her for giving it away so freely.

She heard the sound of an approaching fighter jet. It was aimed right for Ephialtes. He picked up a boulder and tossed it at the incoming plane but the pilot dodged it, doing whirlies in the sky. The snow was accumulating beneath their feet and as the jet rushed in, she knew that the pilot's vision was already obstructed by the storm. She remembered what it was like to get a sun glare when driving in the snow. He aimed right for Ephialtes, shooting a torpedo at him. Ephialtes jumped high into the air, but while the torpedo missed its mark, it was heading right toward the Castle door!

"Look out!" Aurora tried to call out but her lips were still frozen and her body completely helpless.

Otus made a flying leap over the side of the mountain, tossed his shield at the torpedo, managing to knock it just enough that instead of hitting the Castle door, it barreled into the side of the mountain. Instead of bursting through the door, it caused a massive rock slide that raced down and crushed the soldiers standing beneath it. She spotted Fawn rallying the troops behind her. With snowflakes resting on her hair she looked like an angel hovering above the fallen bodies. She gave her people hope and the strength to continue to rush forward, drawing their sabers as bombs exploded around them.

"Boreas, where are you?" Aurora thought frantically, believing in him, having to believe that Boreas would come before it was too late.

She fought the Paralysis Light with all of her being, her hands, to her astonishment, flickering with light. She managed to slowly turn her head upwards, just when a plane circled overhead, spotting Aurora huddled in the Paralysis Light. Her mind went blank as bullets raced towards her paralyzed frame. She closed her eyes, creating a bubble of light around her and the bullets bounced off of the light. She couldn't hold it forever and the protective layer of light faded. The plane came back for a second pass, the pilot took his time, setting his target right for her.

Out of nowhere, Ephialtes leapt into the air, grabbed the plane, spun it around and tossed it like a discus into the lake. He scooped up Aurora and plopped her onto his shoulder — breaking the effect of the green light, freeing her at last!

"There you are, Little Firefly," Ephialtes roared, jumping and smashing down onto the bottom of the valley floor.

"Ephialtes, how did you find me?" Aurora called out, so relieved to see the rabble-rousing giant.

"Jake told me last night that if you went missing that I'd find you on the northwest corner of the mountain trying to run from all the fun," he looked down at her scornfully.

Aurora created a fireball in her hands and watched it grow in the air, the anger of Jake's betrayal still reverberating deep inside her. "No. Jake betrayed me and it's time for payback."

Aurora extended her hands, flinging the fireball at the incoming army, causing a wall of fire to block their path. Ephialtes cried out in amazement, "Whatever Jake did, he made you a warrior, Aurora."

Aurora continued to control the rising fire as Ephialtes landed beside Otus.

Ephialtes shouted, "Quit your moping, Otus, and keep fighting. Your Little Firefly is in one piece."

Otus's eyes lit up when he saw Aurora. "Where were you?" he asked, a worried expression on his face.

Aurora yelled, "No time to chat."

She instructed Otus to pick up a tree trunk, and he yanked it out of the grounds by the roots.

"Let's startle the Inspector," she said, emblazoning a fire ball in her hands. "Let's show him he couldn't stop this goddess from fighting."

Remembering the baseball skills that Boreas taught him, Otus got his footing and Aurora pitched him the fire ball. Otus struck it with the tree trunk like he just hit a Home Run. The fire ball went sailing like a comet over the battle and into the Northern side close to where the Inspector was watching the spectacle.

"I think that woke the Inspector up!" Otus cried out, grinning.

Chapter 32

The IDEAL Has Spoken

Inspector Herald surveyed the damage made by Aurora's fireball, 10 men blown asunder and a fire ablaze near his compound. Aggravated by this minor setback, he watched as Officer Pelican ordered her battalion to put the fire out. Soldiers rushed toward the billowing flames to extinguish them with water, the scent of charred flesh resonating in the air; that scent which reminded him too well of his own encounter with fire when the Candlewick Government building burned 10 year earlier. He stomped hastily over the muddied terrain, trying to stomp out that bitter memory encapsulated in his mind. Instead, he chose to focus on the unfortunate turn of events involving Jake Fray.

Henry Stockington, his now second in command, joined him on the edge of the mountain, white snowflakes blending into his white hair. His Common Good uniform was wrinkled, torn and covered in soot from the battle. The Inspector was relieved his old friend was still alive, Henry being his last remaining confidant despite his sons being traitors to their cause.

"Jake's tracker is showing that he is heading this way," Henry Stockington spoke brusquely.

The Inspector nodded, wiping some dirt from his mouth, leaving a lingering aftertaste on his chapped lips. Aurora had either escaped from Jake's clutches or he had let her go. Either way, Jake was going to suffer for his insubordination.

Through the smoke, the Inspector spotted his young protégé advancing toward him, a strange sword outstretched in his hand. As he walked through the snow, Herald could have sworn he could see the semblance of victory in Jake's expression, though Herald had no clue as to what he had to be victorious about.

"You have two seconds to explain how Aurora is fighting in this battle before I give the order to kill your sister."

Jake threw the sword at the Inspector's feet. Herald stared at it, confused, as Jake smiled.

"That sword is all you need to defeat Fawn once and for all."

Herald picked up the mystical double edged sword and examined it. He admired the design-work of the sword and the circle carved into its engraved hilt. "It's the Khanda sword," he replied impressed. "But how did you get it?"

Jake stared at him, hatred fervent in his eyes. "You taught me well how to be deceptive."

Herald held the blade out toward Jake's neck. "Sword or not, Fawn's army now has a goddess on their side," Herald signaled to the guards who seized Jake. "We made a deal. Aurora was not supposed to fight in this battle."

"I'm telling you that there doesn't have to be a battle," Jake explained. He turned to Henry Stockington. "Don't you want to spare your son?"

Henry Stockington took a step forward, his eyes wide, "Jonathan? You saw him? Is he alright?"

Jake shrugged, "I don't know. I know he's a tough fighter. I trained him and the others in the short time I was down there. He doesn't need to die."

Henry Stockington peered down at the fighting ensuing beneath them, trying to make out his son's blond head amidst the chaos.

"What do you propose?" he asked.

"Don't humor him," the Inspector put his arm around Henry. "Jacob likes to toy with our emotions. Believe me, we don't need a Khanda sword to win. We have guns, bombs and an army 4 times their size..."

Jake pushed the guards off him, advancing toward Herald. "You told me you are losing control. This is your time to make a statement. Show the world that you will fight for them. They will rally behind you and the IDEAL. Not Fawn, not Aurora, not a giant! They need an IDEAL."

Herald stared into the young man's eyes, the man who was like a son to him for all those years. His relationship with Jake had nearly repaired the hole in his heart left when his real son was torn from him. He paced back and forth, turning to the north where his IDEAL was sitting, waiting. This could be their time.

"And you would swear on Mary's life that we can't lose." He stared into Jake's eyes.

Jake nodded. "Whoever wields that sword cannot lose. I just need to willingly hand it to the one who will fight."

The Inspector licked his front tooth in thought.

"Our IDEAL will fight for justice. Let's see if Fawn is willing to fight and die for her cause."

Chapter 33

Running Out Of Time

"**D**on't breathe," Radar warned. "They are right above us."

Boreas cautiously looked up through a grate, saw the orange and indigo colors standing over their heads and shrunk back to avoid being seen. They had just reached the end of the underground tunnel and had found themselves directly beneath the hidden road that would lead into the mountains. To their dismay, two Common Good soldiers were at the dilapidated train station, using it as a makeshift gas station. The trains were now running again on this forgotten train line and being used to drop off supplies to the armies in the desolate Hyperborea region, especially now that the snow had made it more difficult to travel up the narrow and unpaved mountain roads. The guards were talking softly about the battle that had already begun in Hyperborea. Boreas strained his ears to hear the conversation.

"Yeah, who would have expected they would put up such a fight."

"Did you see the giants? Never would have believed it."

"Me too. Shame we'll blow them up before the night is through."

"The bomb flying in?"

"Yeah, the Inspector placed the order. He preferred to not use it, but it's a last resort."

"Yeah, I know what you mean."

"I hear the IDEAL is here for the victory."

"No, you don't say?"

There was a new IDEAL? Boreas turned toward Radar with a look of shock on his face but to his dismay, Radar opened the latch. Boreas tried to stop him, but it was too late.

The Common Good soldiers jumped back in surprise and quickly raised their weapons.

"Woo wee, it's hot down there," Radar called out, pulling himself up and landing right beside the men. "Picked a bad day to fix that damn gas pipeline."

The first soldier raised his rifle and ordered, "Stop and put your hands up!"

"Why, hello there. Didn't know you were here! Did you get everything you needed? I've volunteered to help run this depot for the Common Good effort. Some gasoline just got dropped off not too long ago and we can fill your tank and get you going in a jiffy. I also have a Common Good discount, 10% off each gallon..."

"Where did you come from?" The second soldier squealed, looking down and seeing Boreas, Analise and Yanaba who were pretending to fix the gas pipeline.

"Need another wrench... just dropped one," Boreas cried out.

Radar wiped his forehead, "So hard to find decent assistants now-a-days... you know what I mean?" He slapped one soldier on the back hard enough that he nearly dropped the gun right out of his hands.

"So where you boys off to?" Radar asked.

"No business of yours." The first soldier grimaced. "You get your assistants out of there and help us fill this tank."

"Why didn't you just say so? Butch, Sally and Missy get your butts out of that hole and help these nice men, will ya?"

Boreas and Yanaba scrambled out of the hole and nodded sheepishly toward Radar like they were in trouble and ran to the gas pump to start filling up the tank. Radar continued talking and Analise grabbed Boreas behind the tank and whispered frantically, "Your friend has lost his mind."

"No he hasn't," Boreas replied, picking up the gas nozzle and smiling at Analise, who finally understood what they were doing. "On my cue."

She picked up the other one and winked at him, as they advanced toward the soldiers. Radar was rambling on and on about gas prices soaring and the men looked as if they were going to shoot him in order to stop him from talking. Boreas made eye contact with Radar who nodded.

"Hey Boss, what do these things do?"

The two soldiers whirled around just to be caught in the chest with a heavy stream of gasoline. Boreas and Analise continued to hold down the triggers as Yanaba and Radar snatched the men's weapons and held them up against the backs of their heads as the soldiers struggled to clear the gasoline out of their mouths.

"Now," Radar said. "I think we are going to need a lift to Hyperborea."

The two men reluctantly relented and they all piled into the tank. Since only the officer knew how to drive a tank, they put him behind the wheel and the other next to him, keeping their guns trained on both. The snow was falling with more ferocity as they drove down the hidden path, and thankfully the tank's wheels were able to gain traction against the unpaved road up the mountain.

"This weather is strange," Yanaba said uneasily. "Hyperborea was rumored to be the land of eternal spring. This snow is against nature."

Boreas sighed nervously, recalling the passage from the book that Professor Gassendi had read to him about the prophecy. "The God of the North Wind will inherit his powers by fighting against death and riding a black stallion to the tallest point in Hyperborea, a land of eternal spring, which on this day will be touched by a cold wind. He will conjure up a gust of wind that will save the person he loves most. Many will perish beneath the mountain of snow."

Boreas was relieved he wouldn't have to ride any black stallions up the mountain, especially since horses disliked him since he was a boy. Yet, everything else about this prophecy was unimaginably coming to life. He needed to get to the tallest point in Hyperborea. Aurora was running out of time.

"What are we going to do once we get to the army base?" Analise asked, acting as the voice of reason.

"How do I know?" Radar asked, bemused. "I'm winging this."

"Well your 'winging it' has nearly gotten us killed multiple times so I would prefer we had some kind of plan."

"Patience," Yanaba said softly. "It will all make sense."

"Nothing makes sense," Analise grumbled, shifting her position as they sat cramped in the backseat.

Boreas spotted smoke and fire in the distance and he felt his heart beating knowing that his friends were fighting and were possibly already killed in the battle. He thought about Aurora, Otus, Jonathan, Babs and his mother and didn't know if he would ever see them again.

"Can you go any faster?" he yelled at the first soldier frantically.

"What do you hope to achieve?" The man snarled. "There is no chance of victory for your side. The bomb is coming that will destroy them all."

"Not if we can help it!!"

The road started to get more wet and slippery. Snowflakes fell around them as they continued to travel higher in elevation. The smoke was building as they got closer to the battle. In no time they saw the checkpoint. An Officer stood guard and flagged down the tank.

"You mention us and this bullet will be lodged in your back," Radar spoke menacingly and the first soldier nodded as he pulled over and opened the tank hatch.

"Sergeant Hilt and Private Lyons on our way to the North post."

He showed his credentials to the officer who nodded. "Inspector Herald expected you 15 minutes ago. Where have you been?"

"We were ordered to unload the gasoline at the train depot. One of the barrels leaked and we were detained fixing it."

"Any sighting of the rebel, Boreas Stockington?"

Boreas held his breath as Sergeant Hilt paused. Radar jabbed him in the leg with the barrel of the gun and the Sergeant tensed up, spitting out, "No, no sighting of him. Can we pass now? It's freaking cold out here."

"Yeah, well you're the lucky one in the tank. Move along."

Sergeant Hilt sealed the top hatch as Private Lyons started the ignition, moving toward the northern point of the mountain.

"So," Private Lyons said, "we have the honor of having Boreas Stockington in our tank."

Boreas sat up straight but Analise sharply snapped, "It's no concern of yours who is in your tank."

"I just wanted to know before I had the honor of killing him!"

Lyons made a sharp right with the wheel and everyone fell over, Boreas hit the side sharply, knocking the breath out of him. Sergeant Hilt pounced on Radar and struggled to grab one of the guns as Private Lyons drove straight off the road and toward the cliff. Boreas lunged at Lyons and grabbed at the wheel, fighting to turn it in the opposite direction. The cliff was getting closer and they were all going to plunge to their death when a gunshot exploded in the tank. The Lyon's hand went limp and Boreas's ears were ringing, but he pulled the wheel as far left as he could, using all of his energy, praying for the tank to find traction and turn in time, and then the tank jammed against tree after tree, slowing them down and jerked suddenly to a stop.

Boreas fell on top of the lifeless body of Private Lyons but quickly jumped off of him. He looked behind him and the officer had been knocked unconscious. Yanaba held a gun in her hand, the barrel still smoking.

"I feared the bullet would hit you," she said softly. "But then I remembered who you are and fired."

She sang a brief chant, praying over this enemy, as Boreas watched, not knowing what to say.

Boreas unlocked the hatch and they looked out at the tree that had saved them. The tank's gun turret was hanging out over cliff, turned at a right angle to the body of the tank. The tank itself was lodged into one of the perimeter trees, with a sea of fallen trees in its path. They were less than a foot from the edge and there was a 1,000 foot drop that would have been the end for them all. He slowly maneuvered himself out of the tank and carefully helped the others out, fearful that any added weight to the right side would cause the tank to slide straight down into the abyss below. Once they had all safely landed on the snow (even the unconscious body of the Sergeant), they analyzed their situation. They no longer were able to ride into the Inspector's camp unobserved. They were sitting ducks, with two guns amongst them and the Inspector was expecting this tank that would not show up – and would act as a beacon for any in the Common Good Army. Boreas and his team had no time to lose, they had to get out of there.

"What do we do now?" Radar asked, turning to Boreas for guidance. Boreas felt lost as he stood amidst the mountains of Hyperborea. Below them in the valley he could make out the bodies of fallen men and women lying lifeless on the battlefield, covered in blood and snow.

"What have we done?" He knelt down, put his hand over the snow and watched it melt beneath his palm. He put his cold, wet hand over his eyes, but it couldn't erase the destruction and death that transpired below them. "How did this happen?"

Yanaba put her hand on his shoulder and whispered, "Wars have been fought amongst mankind for as long as our species have lived on this planet. No one understands why we fight. We just know that we do."

"I need to stop this."

"Yes," Yanaba nodded. "Yes, you do."

Boreas stood up, a light flickering in his eyes though the rest of him was frozen. "I need to go to the northern most tip of the mountain. That is where the prophecy said I am supposed to be to get my powers, so that I can save the person I love most. Unfortunately that section of the mountain is where the army is situated. I can't ask you to come with me."

"You don't need to ask," Radar answered firmly. "I will do whatever I can to protect you."

Yanaba didn't respond, just walked to Boreas's side. Analise tied a slumped Sergeant Hilt to the tree and then stood up, pacing back and forth to try to keep warmth in her body. She finally rested her eyes on Boreas and asked, "You said that in order to get your powers, you need to save the person you love most. Is the one you love down there?"

Boreas looked down at the fighting below and pictured Aurora's face. "Yes, she is."

Analise nodded and ripped the ruby necklace, the gift from the Inspector, off her neck and flung it over the cliff. "Time to defeat Herald once and for all."

Chapter 34

The Meeting

When Aurora turned around and saw the bodies sprawled across the field, she felt her heart in her throat and her body convulsing in shock and disgust. She leaned heavily on Jonathan as it all started sinking in. People she had just shared a meal with, trained with, laughed with were no more. Was it all worth it? What were they fighting for?

Babs walked solemnly over to Aurora, holding something close to her heart. It was then that Aurora realized what they were - the Professor's goggles.

Babs wrapped her arms around Aurora and said slowly. "The Professor told me he was glad he got to die this way, helping you and Boreas fulfill the prophecy."

Aurora just stared at those lifeless goggles that had belonged to the man who had told her about the prophecy and how she and

Boreas would stop the Geometric Storm. Now, there was just another fallen body and a pair of goggles that should have had a pair of bright blue eyes behind them.

They helped carry the wounded back inside the castle where the doctor and Mrs. Taboo were shouting instructions in the hallway. Rows upon rows of men, women, teenagers and children crying out for help. Mrs. Taboo and her medical students were rushing to aid them, but there were too many.

"Where is Rana with the reinforcements?" Fawn shouted, but Aurora and Otus didn't have the answer.

Otus stood guard at a nearby window as Aurora slumped down against the wall, completely drained. She felt as if hope had fled with her strength, her powers. The sword was in the Inspector's hands and they were completely outnumbered. The reinforcements they had hoped Mrs. Xiomy would bring must have been ambushed. No help was coming.

"What are they waiting for?" She asked out loud.

Otus replied, "I think they are waiting for us to surrender."

Aurora feared this was the truth, but they would never surrender. They couldn't surrender or retreat. They were trapped in the castle and the Inspector held all the cards.

"Look, they are retreating!" Jonathan screamed out triumphantly. Sure enough, the soldiers were retreating back to the Northern side of the mountain.

Aurora shook her head at Jonathan and said, "He's playing with us. He wants us to think they are retreating. I fear something else is coming."

Sure enough 3 horses stood at the top of the mountain with the Khanda sword held high into the sky, the silver blade shimmering. Aurora felt sick at the sight of the sword in enemy hands. Jake was still with the Inspector. He had never changed.

One rider held up a white flag and charged down the mountain.

Mrs. Taboo joined them and said scornfully, "Now they want to talk?"

Fawn wiped blood off her face and declared, "That's not the Inspector's style."

"Whose style is it?" Jonathan asked.

Fawn took a deep breath. "Your father's."

The solitary rider waited at the brink of the lake near the mouth of a small cave. Fawn gave the order for Otus to lift the drawbridge and she approached the cave followed by Aurora and Jonathan. The lone rider unsheathed his gun and left it with men waiting with the horses. He strode toward the tent where he would meet with Fawn. Aurora and Jonathan approached cautiously. Ephialtes and Otus were not far behind in case they needed back-up. The snow was falling heavier now and they left footprints as they tread forward slowly. Aurora adjusted her red jacket that kept her body insulated, her boots moving forward over this winter wonderland stained with blood.

The rider removed his helmet and sure enough Mr. Stockington stood silently at the entrance of the cave, waiting for Fawn, Jonathan and Aurora to enter before him. Jonathan's hand was clasped in Aurora's and she felt his pulse quickening as his eyes met his father's as if he didn't recognize him. Mr. Stockington's golden blond hair was now streaked with gray and long enough to cascade down his shoulders. It was wet with sweat and a few loose strands covered his bearded face that was covered in soot. Aurora still pictured Mr. Stockington as the proper, well-groomed notable in the city of Candlewick. How much he had changed since the Independence Day of the Last Straw barbeque. Now he stood before them looking as if he had passed through the gates of Hell.

Aurora lit two of the torches that hung on the wall of the cave to illuminate the dark and dismal meeting place. Fawn poured Mr. Stockington a glass of water from her canteen, but he didn't accept the offering.

"Never accept gifts from the enemy," he replied darkly, his tone menacing and Fawn leaned back in her chair, adjusting the maroon fur cape around her shoulders. Aurora felt her blood go cold as she stared into the face of this man before her. He wiped the lenses of his glasses and affixed them once again over his mesmerizing blue eyes. He stared at Fawn as if he was staring at a ghost. Before she could speak, he grabbed a hold of Fawn's hand and held it firmly in his grasp. Jonathan was about to spring forward when Fawn gave him a warning to back off.

Mr. Stockington continued to hold her and said, "I had to make sure that you were real. Not a ghost come back to haunt me."

Fawn wrapped her fingers over his hand and she whispered, "I am real, Henry."

They stared at each other for a long time until Henry's eyes rested on Jonathan.

"Jonathan, get your things. The Inspector has allowed me to come and bring you to safe keeping."

Jonathan stood there, flabbergasted. He turned to his mother, but Mr. Stockington stood up and declared, "I am your father, Jonathan. You will do what I say."

Jonathan shook his head. "But Dad, what about Mom and Aurora?"

"Your Mom is a traitor to this country. She has betrayed the IDEAL. You are being granted clemency, which is more than I can say for the others here. You have a chance to make things right and have a future."

His father's hands grasped Jonathan's shoulders and Aurora could now see the Jonathan she had forgot existed. The obedient one, the one who always did his father's bidding. The perfect son in everyone's eyes.

Aurora gulped and turned toward Fawn who still stared at Henry.

"It's not like the Inspector to negotiate," Fawn sternly said. "Why are you really here?"

"I don't recall addressing you!" he snapped, anger flashing in his eyes. He took a shaky breath, trying to calm his nerves. "But since you're so eager for my attention, Fawn, you have it now. You have wronged your country and put my son in danger. You have committed the ultimate betrayal to a country that has done nothing but try to create a safer and better world. And you have led these kids astray with all those people that you aimed to protect. Their blood is on your hands."

Fawn closed her eyes and said, "It is fear that leads this country of yours. Fear and hate are your weapons of mass destruction. You have deprived the people of the freedoms of religion and speech, the foundation of what the United States were originally built on."

"You have brought war to this country again! You have forced me to fight against my son. What did I ever do to you to deserve this? All I ever did was love you and this family that you ran away from 10 years ago!"

He collapsed down into a chair, his face worn and beaten as he put his face against his fist, his knuckles digging into his chin.

"I'm sorry," Fawn whispered, her voice hoarse and the flame danced eerily on its wick. "I was doing what I thought was right."

"And now? You are using my son against me," Henry said antagonistically.

"Dad, I..."

"Enough, Jonathan." Henry snapped. "This is between me and your mother. Fawn, first you turn Boreas against me and now Jonathan. I cannot begin to tell you how angry I am at you."

"Henry, you have every right to be angry at me, but I couldn't just sit back and watch the injustice happen. I had to do something about it."

"Yes, I know very well what you did about it. And who you did it with." He spat out bitterly.

Fawn bit her lip and swiped a strand of hair out of her eyes. She rose to her feet and tried to regain her composure. Aurora looked at Jonathan, but he was awe struck. Despite the fighting, he couldn't believe that his parents were in the same room. It was a sight he hadn't seen for so long.

"This is not the time or place to talk about my relationship with David. Boreas may not be your son by blood, but you are the only father he has ever known."

Mr. Stockington bolted up, threw the chair across the cave, it echoing loudly as it clanged against the wall. He shouted, "Boreas is not my son! He is that fanatic's offspring and he will be made an example of." He stared intensely at Fawn. "I have never been so disgraced in my life. Why couldn't you have stayed dead and let your secrets die with you?"

Jonathan lunged at his father, knocking him off his feet and sending him sailing against the cave wall.

"That's my brother you are talking about, Dad! How dare you turn your back on him? I won't go with you, ever!"

Mr. Stockington grimaced as if he was stabbed in the heart. He swallowed hard, rose, picked up his helmet and put it back on his head.

"Don't judge me, Jonathan. I am just trying to keep my family together in a world that's falling apart. And right now you are the only family I have left! I am not going to lose you too!"

He turned to Fawn and said, "The Inspector is a fair man and I work for a just and even fairer IDEAL. Our leader has asked for the opportunity to save lives on both sides and have leader fight leader in a battle to the death. No interference from either side. It will be broadcasted live around the world to show that the sacrifice of one is better than the sacrifice of all. You have until the Sacred Hour to decide. If you do not acquiesce, we will bomb you until there is no one left. Is that what you want, Fawn, total annihilation of your people? Choose wisely. The IDEAL has spoken!"

He reached into his pocket, his face stoic, though his hand was shaking as he held out a photo. It was a picture of the four of them, smiling and happy at Candlewick Park. Jonathan and Boreas were young kids posing for the camera. Boreas was in desperate need of a haircut and was smiling bigger than Aurora even knew he could smile, sitting on his mother's knee. Jonathan was about 7, his arms wrapped lovingly around his father's neck in a big bear hug. Henry and Fawn looked as if they didn't have a care in the world.

"It was a nice life," he said slowly.

"Yes it was," Fawn said trying to hold back tears. "Henry, you must know that I always cared for you…"

"But you never loved me," he said, taking her hand and putting his lips against it, kissing it tenderly. "I guess I always believed you did. At least, I wanted to believe that you did. But like all things, love is an illusion. The Inspector is right. All that is real is power."

He lit the side of the family picture as tears streamed down Fawn's face. They watched as the picture was shriveled up, eaten by the flame. He stormed out of the cave and Jonathan and Aurora watched as he lifted himself into the saddle and galloped back up the mountain to the Northern side where the Inspector was waiting for him. The eye of the storm had passed. The family photograph continued to burn, until all that remained were ashes.

Chapter 35

The Choice

Silence ensued as all eyes turned toward Fawn. She wiped her tears, exited the tent and looked out over the dead. At first sad, her expression soon steeled and became determined. Aurora watched her in horror, finding strength in her voice to exclaim, "Fawn, you cannot do this!"

Fawn said, "Not here, Aurora."

"They all have a right to hear this. If you give in to this fight, it is exactly what the Inspector wants. Do you think he would broadcast to everyone a fight where he expects to lose?"

"It will be a chance for us to show that we will not give up! That I will risk my life to help my people continue to stand and to continue to fight for a better tomorrow."

"The Inspector will kill you and all of us anyway. Don't you see that?"

"I have to believe that Boreas will come! That if I fight, I can buy him some time to get to us!"

"He may already be dead!"

Aurora ran out of the tent with Jonathan close at her heels. She didn't turn back until she was under a weeping willow tree, where she collapsed onto the snow-draped ground and started to cry. Jonathan tried to put his arm around her, but she pushed him away.

"She will listen to you!" she cried out in between sobs. "You have to tell her not to fight!"

"I can't," he said softly.

"Why? Why can't you?"

"Because I believe that Boreas will come."

She wiped her eyes and stared at the man before her. She put her head on his shoulder and let him hold her. "I have seen things today that I never thought possible," she said softly. "I have done things... I killed people... how did this happen? What have I done? What have I become?"

"We have to finish what we started or else all those who have died, died in vain. We have to hope that my mom wins this fight."

"She won't win against that sword."

Jonathan shook his head, in denial. He wiped a strand of hair nervously behind his pierced ear, the silver pendant smeared with mud and grime from battle. He took a deep breath and said, "If my mom doesn't win, then we all will die." He wrapped his arms tightly around her. "If this really is the end, I just want to remember this moment. Me kissing you."

He kissed her hard and Aurora didn't want this moment to end. She wanted him to hold her and to continue kissing her forever to eradicate the anger and the fear that was living in her heart. How could love exist simultaneously with hate? How could two such strong emotions ever co-exist?

They heard someone call out their names and Jonathan's lips pulled away from hers, his arms dropped from around her waist. Aurora wiped the tears from her eyes and turned to see Fawn. Fawn cleared her throat and said, "I want you both to be in my corner during the fight. I want you to be close to me in case I don't... in case I need you."

Jonathan stood up abruptly and replied, "I will be at your side when you win, Mom."

She wrapped her arms around her son and held him close, kissing him gently on the forehead. "Did I ever tell you how proud I am of you? Of the man you have become?"

He choked back tears and said, "No need for that. You will win. I know you will."

She then turned toward Aurora with the question in her eyes. Aurora's eyes shined brightly as she said, "You know I will be there, Fawn. You didn't even have to ask."

"Everyone has a choice, Aurora. Some are easy, but most of them are hard. This is my choice and mine alone. I will show the Inspector that people of all religions can stand together against oppression. David Xiomy's dream lives on."

✭ ✭ ✭

Boreas continued to trudge through knee-deep snow. He couldn't feel his toes and feared he was suffering from frost bite. They had stolen coats and boots from the soldiers and Yanaba had her Native American fleece wrapped around her body. Analise tried not to look down at the blood stained on the coat that had belonged to Private Lyons. Radar said he never felt the cold, though they caught him shivering and his teeth chattering more than once. They had travelled over a mile up the mountain toward the north peak when they heard silence below them in the valley. The shooting had stopped for some reason and they were fearful that the bomb was still coming. Boreas was moving as fast as he could, but was still far from his destination.

"We will never get there in time," he cried out, kicking at the snow in frustration.

Radar's teeth chattered as he said, "Stop your complaining. You need to keep walking."

"Think warm thoughts," Analise said. "Like fire and the sun."

The sun - Aurora.

Boreas took another step and his foot sunk again into a mound of snow. He picked up the pace and was nearly running – as much as one could in deep snow. He could not let them down. All the players were in position, except him.

There was an opening ahead of them and Boreas peered over the edge to see a circle of light illuminated in the center of the plateau. He could make out three small figures standing there. Even at this distance, he knew who they were and he wanted to scream out to them, let them know he was there, but his voice wouldn't carry from that altitude. If only he had his conch shell! He pulled the fur jacket closer around his shoulders and it was then that he heard the sound of a horse neighing behind them. They all whirled around to see none other than the burly form of Officer Woolchuck on a majestic black stallion, gun pointing directly at Boreas.

"Throw your weapons toward me slowly or else I will kill your precious leader."

Yanaba and Radar had no choice but to abide by the officer's wishes. They tossed their guns toward Woolchuck and stood holding their breath for what would happen next.

He slowly dismounted from the horse, gun still pointing directly at Boreas with a glimmer of retribution in his eye.

"How fortunate that I am the one to capture you again, Boreas Stockington. But don't think you will get any closer to helping your friends. You are going to wait here and watch your mother die."

Chapter 36

Fight to the Death

The Khanda sword glistened as the IDEAL rode down the mountain on a beautiful stallion, the color of the snow, its mane flowing in the wind. The IDEAL was followed by two other riders in black. Fawn stood waiting in the center of the plateau, her sword held tightly in her hand as Jonathan and Aurora stood behind her. Despite the circle of flame torches surrounding them, Aurora felt it was too dark since the moon was hidden by the gray clouds above. Though she didn't see them, she knew that there were cameras broadcasting this event for all the world to see.

The IDEAL stepped down from the horse, dressed in an orange and indigo suit of armor, a knight's helmet covering his face from view. Though shorter than Aurora had pictured in her mind, the

IDEAL was a menacing presence that stood before them, like a figment of her nightmares come to life.

He stepped foot into the circle, keeping the Khanda sword in the hilt of the belt and one of the figures in black spoke out like a game show announcer.

"Here the IDEAL will face off against the rebel leader, Fawn Stockington. This is a fight to the death using only their swords and bare hands to finish the job. There will be no interference from outside the circle. If there is interference, the deal to have the victor of this battle determine the victor of the war will be null and void. Is that understood?"

Both Fawn and the IDEAL nodded, in addition to the other witnesses. Aurora held her breath and clutched Jonathan's hand hard as the whistle blew and the fighting commenced.

Fawn held up the blade of her sword and her opponent followed suit. The Khanda sword looked so mighty in his grasp. Aurora continued to blame herself for allowing it to fall into enemy hands. It clanged against Fawn's sword as they danced around each other in the circle. Fawn swung bravely, making full contact with the opposing blade. Both appeared to be very skilled swordsmen. As Fawn maneuvered around the circle perimeter, the IDEAL swung, and she threw herself down to the ground, the Khanda just grazing her arm. She quickly jumped to her feet, her silver shield blocking the blade just in the nick of time. Blade struck against shield and then blade clashed against blade - back and forth. Aurora clutched onto Jonathan's hand too forcefully, fearing with each thrust that it would be the last. Fawn tripped the IDEAL, causing him to fly backwards and lose hold of his shield. Fawn plunged her sword down into the IDEAL's left arm causing it to splice through the armor and cause a wound. The IDEAL yelled out in pain and it was then that Aurora realized that the IDEAL was not a man, but a woman!

Fawn was struck by that realization as well as the IDEAL struck again, rolling out of the line of fire and jumping back to her feet.

"Who are you?" Fawn demanded. "Reveal yourself!"

"Wouldn't you like that?" The IDEAL shot back, the voice unidentifiable. "You can't talk yourself out of this one, Fawn."

The IDEAL parried again with the Khanda sword, this time penetrating through Fawn's armor, slashing her waist. Fawn dropped her shield as she reached toward her wound and the IDEAL took advantage of the opportunity, crashing the sword with stroke after stroke. Fawn finally spun away to the far side of the circle, clutching at her side where she had been injured. Fawn seized her shield and held it up just in time to receive another blow from the IDEAL who was getting frustrated that Fawn was still standing.

"Give up now, Fawn; tell the people that the IDEAL is victorious!"

"Never!" Fawn struck again and again, pivoting and hitting the sword against its mark, until the IDEAL's sword flew out of her hand and landed inches away. Fawn held the sword up to the IDEAL's throat and declared, "Now let's see who you are!"

Fawn grabbed a hold of the IDEAL's helmet and ripped it off her head. She immediately dropped it as blond hair trickled down. Mrs. Xiomy's face stared back, her eyes glazed with hate. Fawn backed up, her sword shaking in her grasp as both she and Aurora stood staring in disbelief. *It wasn't true. This couldn't be real!* Aurora feverishly thought, her eyes planted on the IDEAL's face, hoping the image would change if she stared long enough.

"It's over, Fawn!" Mrs. Xiomy spoke maliciously.

Before Fawn had a second to think, she heard a noise and looked up to see a plane flying in, giving Mrs. Xiomy a chance to get to her feet. Aurora was about to try to stop the plane with her powers when one of the two black figures seized her and held her down while the other held a gun against Jonathan's head. The figure bound Aurora's hands together with an electrical cord. Aurora screamed out in frustration, but her attacker whispered in her ear, "Trust me."

It was Jake!

Mrs. Xiomy laughed with the Khanda sword again in her grasp. "I have been waiting for this moment for a long time!"

Fawn kept shaking her head, her sword getting heavy in her hands as the betrayal washed over her. "Rana, why are you doing this? You could have killed me back at Plymouth Incarnate. Why wait until now?"

"After what you did to me, it wasn't enough to just kill you. I had to kill everything you believed in! After you left for Hyperborea, I contacted Herald and told him everything. Once he gave me the role of the IDEAL, I told him that I wanted the chance to kill you myself. And in turn, he agreed to destroy all of your protestors, once and for all."

Fawn looked up into the sky, at the plane hovering overhead, and then North, hope still beating in her heart that Boreas would come, a hope that had never diminished. "I believe in something greater than all this, Rana. Greater than the Common Good and you, and me." She tossed her sword outside of the circle and stared into the eyes of her friend. "Rana, I will not fight you."

Fawn faced the camera, shouting into it, "All of you out there! I am Fawn Stockington. I will not give in to the hate and the fear that the Inspector is inflicting on all of us. People of all religious backgrounds are here fighting to preserve our fundamental rights to be free. Join us… stand with us and together we shall rise!"

Mrs. Xiomy swung and the Khanda sword found its mark. Fawn went down as the sword glistened red above her, preparing for the final blow.

✡ ✡ ✡

Boreas gasped as his mother was wounded again. He heard Officer Woolchuck chuckle behind him, knowing that this was it. Boreas's mother was about to die.

Boreas didn't care that a gun was pointed at him. He had nothing to lose. He swung around and head butted a stunned Officer Woolchuck whose corpulent body fell backwards. Radar didn't waste any time and jumped on him to hold him down while Analise grabbed a hold of the gun.

Boreas took off, following his instincts. He grabbed a hold of the black stallion's mane and threw himself onto its back. The horse reared up, trying to toss the invader, but Boreas held on and yelled, "Go!" The horse obeyed instantly and galloped to the Northern tip of the mountain. Boreas prayed he wouldn't be too late - that he could save his mom. He had to!

The wind whipped against his face as they raced up to the tip of the mountain. He heard the heavy grunting of the mare as his hooves collided against the slippery slope, but he never wavered. They reached the edge of the mountain and Boreas cried out to the stallion to *Stop*, and he came to a skidding halt. Boreas released his hold of the horse's mane and jumped off its back, surrounded by a misty fog that blinded his vision of the valley below. As soon as his feet landed on the snowy ledge, the gray clouds instantly opened up to reveal the battle scene, with one ray of light illuminating his mother's nearly lifeless body with the Khanda sword about to strike her again. He closed his eyes, retrieving a memory from the far reaches of his mind of his mother's love for him. And he realized that his love for her had never disappeared, that it was always present and that love made him who he was.

He held up his hands and shouted, "I am the God of the North Wind!"

Instantly the north wind obeyed him sending one mad gust down into the valley, knocking Mrs. Xiomy off her feet sending the

Khanda sword flying up in a tornado, spiraling upwards and landing in the hands of Boreas. Everyone down below looked up, including Aurora. There they saw Boreas standing tall, stationary as the tornado encircled him and the Khanda sword shone brightly in his grasp. Aurora watched him in awe as hope was restored in her.

Just then, there was the roar of new incoming planes heading straight toward Boreas. Jake cut Aurora's bounds, releasing her wrists as the sun beams absorbed into her skin, her powers renewed. The other guard, seeing her free aimed his gun at her, but Jake knocked it out of his hand and knocked him to the ground in a full out brawl.

Aurora lifted her hands to the sky sending a huge ray of light from her fingertips, aimed right at the incoming planes, blinding the pilots. Boreas instructed the wind to knock them off course and the planes spun wildly out of control, diving into the base of the mountain.

The bomb was released from the plane still hovering above the battle, sailing down toward Hyperborea. Otus was about to jump up when Ephialtes knocked him to the ground, shouting, "This is mine, brother!"

He shot up like a rocket, pulling the bomb into his arms and continuing to sail upwards into the sky until it exploded, bursting into the air.

Otus let out an agonizing yell at seeing his brother's last courageous act. Furious, he yanked trees out from their roots and launched them at the army, sailing through despite the winds. The enemy soldiers were rapidly dispersing, fleeing to avoid getting sucked up into the tornado or crushed by Otus's wrath. The Inspector cried out for the army to keep fighting, but Henry Stockington grabbed his arm, instructing him to retreat. The Inspector couldn't believe that despite all his efforts, Boreas had reached Hyperborea.

Avalanches erupted caused by the winds and loosened rocks coming from Aurora throwing her fire balls into the air and Otus smacking them at the fleeing soldiers. The winds spread the fire faster than ever before until the Inspector ran too, retreating with the rest of his men on the opposite side of the mountain.

Mrs. Xiomy jumped back on her stallion, attempting to ride back up the mountain when an avalanche nearly crushed her and her horse. She was saved when Otus grabbed her, desperately trying not to crush her in his furious grasp.

And then as suddenly and as fiercely as they began, the winds ceased.

Aurora let the fire dissipate from her fingers as Boreas galloped down the mountain on the back of the black stallion. He didn't stop until he was in the center of the circle. He jumped down off the steed and ran to his mother who was lying nearly lifeless in Jonathan's arms. He knelt down at her side and Fawn turned weakly toward him, gazing into her son's eyes.

"I knew you would come!"

He took her hand and held it against his heart. "I am so sorry…"

"No," she interrupted, coughing up blood, clutching her side where the mortal wound was draining life from her. "No time for regrets. Your journey continues. That's what I prayed for. I never stopped hoping you would come."

"I'm here, Mom. I'm here."

Boreas buried his face into her shoulder and started to cry. She caressed his hair with her hand and said to both of her sons, "Please forgive your father. For me. He loves you both so much. Just like my love for you, it has no beginning and no end. It will always be."

Just then a beam of sunlight streamed through the clouds, resting softly on Fawn's face. She looked up into the sky and smiled as Boreas pulled his head off her shoulder to look at her.

"I remember how the clouds opened up, letting David see the sun one last time on the morning he died. Seeing the sun shining down now is a sign that he is still with me. With all of us."

She pulled off the orange conch shell and handed it to Boreas. He took it from her and placed it around his neck. She grasped Jonathan's hand and her free hand went to Boreas' face, wiping a tear from his cheek. "I will always be with you."

And with that, Fawn Stockington breathed her last breath.

Chapter 37

And the Snow Melts

Overnight the cold front passed, melting the snow and producing tumbling rivers that flowed down the crevices of the mountain and emptied into the heart of the lake. The plateau was cleared of bodies with rocks left in their place as tombstones. Blades of grass peeked their heads out of the snow and crocuses burst forth, reborn in the place of death and destruction. The only remnants of the battle were in the memories of those who had lived through it and whose lives were changed forever.

With Fawn's death, Mrs. Taboo took over as leader. After the funeral for all those who had fallen, she instructed all Protestors able to make the journey to prepare to leave Hyperborea. The Inspector had lost the battle, but he would return with even more reinforcements and a new plan of attack. Babs stepped forward to close out the funeral and her voice lifted out over the tearful cries within the castle walls. She sang for the men, women and children who were no longer with them, but whose memories would live on.

Aurora tried to close her mind to Babs' memorial hymn, the same song her friend had sung 6 months earlier at the funeral procession for the fallen loved ones at Plymouth Tartarus when Eileen had been killed. And now, Babs was singing for too many others who had died: for the Professor, Ephialtes, Fawn and countless others who perished during the battle. Aurora ran out of the funeral service with tears streaming down her face, spotting Otus creating a massive gravestone for Ephialtes, carving it with his knife out of wood, labeling it "for my brother". Aurora wanted to comfort her giant friend, but couldn't find the words and so took off running across the broken drawbridge until she slumped down at the edge of the lake. Her sorrowful eyes drifted over to the mausoleum in the rocks where Fawn was to be buried.

"It was never supposed to end like this," Aurora whispered, feeling an emptiness overwhelm her as she buried her face in her hands.

"It's not the end yet," Swanson's boyish voice responded. Aurora glanced down to see Swanson's reflection in the water, his rain hat off in solemn mourning.

She stared down into his child-like face, seeing an undying hope, but Aurora felt only guilt and anger.

"Swanson, you should never have given me the Khanda sword," she yelled down at the manifestation in the water. "Without that sword, Fawn would still be alive!"

"The sword ended up exactly where it was meant to be," he replied cryptically.

"What the hell does that mean?" Aurora cried out. "Fawn's dead because of that sword and without her I feel so lost and alone."

"You have me."

She whirled around and there stood Boreas. She had avoided him that entire day, knowing he and Jonathan needed to mourn the death of their mother. He stepped toward her looking older, and stronger, a halo illuminated around his body as the orange conch shell dangled around his neck. His hair was whimsically swirling in the hands of the wind as he stared down at Aurora with a veil of sadness in his eyes.

Boreas sat down beside Aurora and stared down at Swanson. "So you're the famous Swanson."

Swanson nodded back at him. "The one and only."

Startled by this revelation, Aurora cried out, "You can see him?"

Boreas nodded. "Yeah, I can see him."

Swanson said, "I think I'll leave you two. Boreas, please leave the Khanda sword in the tomb with your mother. Some power doesn't belong in human hands."

With that he vanished, leaving only ripples in the water. Music sounded from within the castle, echoing throughout Hyperborea and reverberating off the mountains, like the voices of the fallen heroes. Boreas sat beside Aurora and took her hand in his. They just sat there in silence, staring out at the sun drifting down beneath the mountains, creating purplish, golden hues amongst the shadows in the hills. Together they gazed sadly at the beautiful view before them that only a day ago had been swarming with soldiers and stained with blood and death. Now spring had returned to Hyperborea, like it had also been waiting for Boreas to return. Aurora dipped her fingers into the water as birds chirped nearby at a tree that dripped snow from its branches like tears. She looked up at Boreas who was gazing deeply into her eyes.

"I don't know what to say," he said.

Aurora took a deep breath, resting her head against his chest, listening to his heart beating. "Don't say anything. I'm just glad you're here."

"Did you ever doubt that I would come?"

She nodded slowly. "Yes. And I doubted myself too. The only one who never doubted was Fawn. She always knew you would save us."

He touched her hair gently and took a deep breath, "I am glad I was able to save you, even though I couldn't save my mom."

The wind grew, encircling them and pushing them closer together. Aurora felt like the part of her that had been missing had been returned as she gazed into his eyes, those hazel eyes that she had prayed to see one more time.

"Did you summon the wind?" Aurora asked, the sun shining brightly down upon them as she lifted her face from his chest to look up at him.

He smiled down at her, the sun shining in his eyes. "It's like the sun and the wind want us to be together."

He leaned in like he was about to kiss her, but Aurora snapped out of the spell, pulling back and opening her eyes wide.

"Boreas... we can't."

The wind died down and the sunlight was blocked by the shifting clouds.

"I'm sorry," he said, standing up and clutching onto the Khanda sword for support. "I know you're with Jonathan. But you need to know that I care about you, Aurora. I always have."

Aurora found herself fighting the feelings within her, fighting the goose bumps prickling on her neck and on her arm. But then she thought about Jonathan. She couldn't leave him... not now that he lost his mother.

"Boreas, you know I care about you, but..."

"You don't have to say anything," he jumped in, avoiding her gaze. "I just made a promise to myself that I would tell you."

He brushed a strand of hair from his eyes and gazed across the shimmering lake where Fawn's tomb was lurking in the shadows, waiting for him to say his final goodbye. "I'd better return the Khanda sword."

"You don't have to go alone," Aurora said, offering her hand. "We're in this together."

He smiled slightly, like he was remembering the countless times she had told him that phrase. This time though, when he looked into her eyes, it appeared that he believed it. He enclosed his hand around hers and, like a whisper in the wind, said... "Always."

Together they walked along the slippery path adjacent to the lake and faced the circular cave where Fawn's body had been buried. It was a peaceful sanctuary, with crickets chirping as they entered the abyss, dark except for one lone candle lit at the entrance. Fawn lay there seeming like she was sleeping, with a white cloth blanketing her body leaving only her face exposed. She was so serene with her long black hair draped down over her shoulders, a lone conch shell clip in her hair. Boreas walked slowly toward her and after a pause, placed the hilt of the Khanda sword into her hands.

"She looks like a warrior," Aurora said admirably, staring down at her leader with a mixture of sorrow and pride.

Boreas held his orange conch shell close to his heart. "She looks like my mom."

Boreas bent down and kissed his mom one last time on the cheek. "I love you," he whispered.

Aurora took his hand and together they walked out of the cave. With a wave of Boreas's hand, the wind rolled a massive rock over the entrance, sealing it shut behind them.

✫ ✫ ✫

Aurora maneuvered through the crumbling edifice that had been the Hyperborea castle, reaching the steps that led into the dungeon. She was glad to be indoors so that she didn't have to feel the presence of the wind, like a constant nagging reminder of her conversation with Boreas; his confession earlier that he had always cared for her. Those words continued to haunt her but she had made her choice and it was Jonathan. Why did it feel like she was always fighting and trying to convince her own heart that she had made the right choice?

Aurora treaded carefully down the spiral staircase where she found Mrs. Taboo guarding the cell where Mrs. Xiomy sat in a cathartic state. The maniacal IDEAL who had killed Fawn had vanished and in her place sat a scared little girl, playing with her hair and rocking back and forth.

"Is she playing us?" Aurora asked slowly.

Mrs. Taboo shook her head, exhausted from the lack of answers from her interrogation. "I think she is suffering from manic-depression. We won't know for sure what else she knows until we can get her back to Alcatraz and under medical supervision. She must know more of the Inspector's plan, what he intends to do now in retaliation."

Aurora nodded, sorrowfully looking into the face of the woman she had loved like a second mother. Mrs. Xiomy had truly lost everything and had given into her anger to side with the Inspector against them. She faced her former teacher and friend and said, "How could you turn against us?"

Mrs. Xiomy didn't respond just continued rocking back and forth, her hair drizzling down her face. Aurora couldn't bear to watch her in that state of isolation, lost in her memories, under the powerful control of the mind and heart.

Aurora retreated up the stairs feeling frazzled and frail after that encounter and entered the castle courtyard which was now being used as an infirmary. Babs and the doctor were busy attending to the sick and wounded. Aurora took a deep breath and snapped out of her stupor to lend a hand where needed. She headed over to Babs who was looking after Jake Fray who was still recuperating.

After having freed Aurora from her bonds allowing her to use the powers of dawn, he tackled the guard before being picked up by the cyclone. He had been flung against the rocks, knocking him unconscious. He looked pale, but he was breathing deeply as Babs took a cold compress and held it against his forehead. She turned to Aurora and with hope in her voice said, "He should wake up soon. The doctor says it is only mild head trauma, thankfully."

Babs pointed down at his arm where a bandage was wrapped around a fresh wound. Babs had caused that one by cutting out the tracking device from deep in his arm. The remnants of the Inspector's metal device were on the side table, barely recognizable after Babs had smashed it. Aurora remembered Jake's words - *you don't realize what the Inspector is capable of*. Aurora had a better idea now of how far the Inspector was willing to go.

"So, was he on our side the whole time?"

Babs shook her head, "I don't know, Aurora. But what I do know is that if he didn't free you and risk his life to stop that guard, you wouldn't have been able to use your powers to help Boreas defeat the Common Good Army."

Aurora nodded, knowing she was right.

Babs continued to massage Jake's hand. There was such love that shone through her eyes, that Aurora was envious of that emotion.

She put her hand on Babs's shoulder and said, "When Jake wakes up, tell him I will honor my promise. I will free Mary and my father. That will be the first thing we do before heading to the lights."

"Does Boreas know that?" Babs asked, concerned.

Aurora shook her head. "No, but I have to do this. After all, if we are going to save this world, I need to believe it is worth saving."

Aurora proceeded back toward the castle drawbridge where she saw Otus, tossing rose petals into the sky.

"Ephialtes regained his goodness at the very end. I am proud to be his brother."

Aurora took a hold of Otus's hand as he cried tears the size of giant tree ornaments and Aurora had to dodge them to not get wet.

Aurora then spotted Boreas speaking with the beautiful reporter, Analise Jones, in the corner and a part of her wished she knew what he was saying. She shook that idea from her head. She was with Jonathan, not Boreas, but that part of her heart was wishing she had chosen the latter. Like Boreas had told her when he gave her that farewell kiss in Plymouth Incarnate – there was never the right time.

✫ ✫ ✫

Analise grabbed Boreas and took him under a tree that was still dripping from the melted snow on its branches. It was like there was a circular waterfall surrounding them and they were in the center, away from the world.

She raised an eyebrow at him and asked, "So did you tell her?"

Boreas pretended to be playing with the tree bark and responded, "Tell her what?"

Analise wanted to smack some sense into the teen who just became the God of the North Wind. "Aurora. Did you tell her how you feel?"

He looked at Aurora standing with a backdrop of eternal spring, a light resonating from her while consoling Otus. She looked so beautiful that he wished he had kissed her when he had the chance… but she had done the right thing. She was dating his brother. Boreas watched uneasily as Jonathan walked over to her and kissed her tenderly on the lips; Boreas quickly looked the other way, wishing he truly was invisible beneath this tree.

"She made her choice." He said, fixing his jacket over his chest.

Analise looked over her shoulder and spotted Aurora gazing at them while in Jonathan's embrace. "If she made her choice, then why can't she stop looking at you?"

Boreas was about to look up when Analise grabbed him and kissed him hard against the lips. Boreas took a step back, thinking his ears were ringing and then realized the sound of Aurora's conch shell was resounding in his ear. He smiled wide, thankful for Analise's bold gesture and hinted, "Maybe she hasn't made her choice after all."

Analise stared at him in confusion as Boreas raced over to where Aurora was standing, blowing into the conch shell, her eyes penetrating his own.

"I'm right here, Aurora!" he cried out, indignantly.

"I didn't want to interrupt," Aurora chided, raising her eyebrow in Analise's direction. "Isn't she out of your league?"

Boreas crossed his arms. "Last time I checked I was single and the God of the North Wind. Apparently that makes me a catch."

"And a modest one," Otus chuckled, ruffling Boreas's hair, causing him to laugh.

Aurora took a deep breath. "I just wanted to tell you that I know where they are holding my father and my best friend Mary. I made a promise that I would save them before heading to the Northern Lights."

Otus looked down at her, his big green eyes glowing. "Whatever you need, Aurora, you know I will follow."

She turned to Boreas who sat down, shaking his head as he contemplated her plan. "I maybe gained us a day or two with the Inspector by knocking out the electrical wires in the area, but won't he suspect that you will head there from Hyperborea?"

"He'll suspect, but if he gets there first they will die."

Boreas hugged his knees, realizing how close they had been to losing everything the day before to the Inspector. Boreas had lost his mother. He couldn't let Aurora lose her father too.

"OK." He said quickly, rising to his feet. "We will save them."

Aurora looked like she was about to hug him, when Jonathan approached, having overheard their conversation and said sharply, "I'll come too. You'll need someone who can figure out how to overcome their prison defenses."

Boreas felt a coldness sweep through him at the thought of his brother coming along with them on this mission, but was not about to counter his decision. Aurora forced a smile, looking trapped in a corner as she agreed for Jonathan to accompany them.

"I'll come too," Analise said, joining their circle. "And you'll need Jake Fray. Only he knows where the prison is located."

"Not a chance," Jonathan shouted, pointing at the prison. "He needs to suffer for turning against us. If he didn't take the sword from Aurora, my mom would still be alive."

"You don't know that," Aurora said quickly.

Otus held up his hands up as a peace offering, "If it wasn't for that sword then Boreas wouldn't have gotten his powers. Like the Professor had said, he needed to save the person he loved most."

Jonathan glared at Boreas. "But he didn't save her."

Aurora tried to hold Jonathan back but he escaped her clutch and took off toward the castle. Boreas stared after him, sending a cool breeze after him. Trying to soothe his grief. Trying to make peace with his brother.

Radar and Yanaba, who had been watching this spectacle unfold, walked forward, breaking the uneasy silence.

"Well, my friends," Radar began, "as much as I am going to miss all of this drama, I am sure you are not going to miss me. I am returning with Yanaba to Monument Valley to try to recruit more followers for our cause. We will rally the people to follow you and stand up to the Common Good."

Radar turned to Boreas and said solemnly, "I think my debt is paid, God of the North Wind."

"Thank you, Radar," Boreas said, shaking his hand warmly. "For everything."

Yanaba gave him a kiss on the cheek and told him that he must always remember to keep forgiveness in his heart. "Don't forget the pottery pieces and how you put them back together."

Boreas promised he would remember.

Analise and Jonathan went to prepare two horses for the travelers while Radar paraded through the streets, waving at everyone like he was the mayor of the town making his grand exit.

Boreas took this momentary distraction to pull Yanaba aside and he whispered, "You cannot tell anyone, but Steven and Sansa are my cousins. No one can ever know this because if the Inspector finds out this could be detrimental to them and me."

Yanaba nodded, realizing the severity of the situation. "I will protect them with everything I am. You have bigger struggles ahead of you, God of the North Wind. Now that the Inspector knows you have your power, he will stop at nothing to destroy you and Aurora. He needs you to fail."

Radar came trotting over on his horse, followed by the beautiful black stallion. He handed the reigns over to Yanaba who mounted and Boreas took a moment to pat the mane of the horse that had helped him reach that final destination on the mountain to fulfill the prophecy. And with a final wave, Yanaba and Radar took off galloping up the mountain in the direction of Monument Valley. Boreas stood watching them as the dust settled in their wake, wondering if he would ever see his friends again.

After they left, Boreas rejoined Otus and Aurora who were standing on the outskirts of the lake, the tomb where his mother was buried reflected in the shimmering water.

"I know the Inspector," Boreas said, looking uneasily at the others. "He is going to come at us with everything he has."

Otus reached up toward the sky, "He may have everything else, but he doesn't have a giant."

Aurora smiled, her hand smoothing the side of the conch shell around her neck. "That's right. Or the Goddess of Dawn or the God of the North Wind."

Otus held out his hand. "A pact. We are in this together. To the lights."

Aurora put her hand over giant's and they waited as Boreas looked at his two friends. He placed his hand over there's.

"To the lights," he replied, bringing the trio back together again.

Aurora laughed, putting her arm through his. "Now don't you dare run off again or I will have Otus force-feed you dinner. He has new rat stews that he created that I am sure you are going to love."

"Of course he will like my stews!" Otus said placing both of them on his shoulder as they headed toward the castle. "I can make us the Rat Stew ala mode tonight!"

"No!" they shouted in unison as the sun was setting behind them.

Boreas smiled dexterously, gazing at Aurora out of the corner of his eye. "And now I am stuck with you again."

✵ ✵ ✵

Later that Evening

Jake snuck down into the depths of the prison, taking the key he had confiscated from Babs and opened the lock. The guards were snoring lightly as he had snuck a sleeping draft in their water before their shift.

Mrs. Xiomy lay pretending to sleep, her hair a mess of curls around her head. She sat up and smiled at Jake. "About time."

Jake didn't answer. "You're lucky they didn't kill you."

Mrs. Xiomy shrugged shrewdly. "I don't believe in luck, Jake Fray. I believe in knowing your enemy."

They snuck upstairs and through the graveyard, realizing as they passed that their scheming had spared more lives than lost. It was still difficult to bear as they advanced cautiously along the perimeter of the lake. A cool breeze felt restorative to Mrs. Xiomy who was stuck in her cell with her secrets those past 2 days. In solemn procession they advanced towards the cave where Fawn was buried.

"The Khanda sword was a nice twist of fate."

Jake nodded, his gaze intent on the stone. "When you revealed your plan about making Fawn a martyr, I knew that sword was the key."

"Do you think the Inspector knows?"

Jake shook his head as the moon illuminated the stone. They stood there beneath the moonlight during the Awakened Hour, the sun nearing its ascent. It was nearly time. He was getting agitated and was about to push the stone aside when all at once the ground shook, causing the large tomb stone to get knocked off its hinge. Jake grabbed Mrs. Xiomy and they scrambled out of the way as the massive stone rolled past, narrowly missing them before crashing against the side of the mountain. Silence ensued, except for the eerie whistling of the wind in their ears. Suddenly the sun streamed down breaking up the darkness and footsteps could be heard coming from the tomb. And then a hand reached out, the light illuminating the Khanda sword.

Mrs. Xiomy's amethyst eyes gleamed brightly toward the Northern Hemisphere. "It's time this world believed in magic."

The adventure continues with

The Integration

The Fourth Book in **The Hypothesis of Giants** series

Acknowledgments

Every journey has its challenges. Some are massive like a Geometric Storm, whereas others are smaller challenges like getting out of bed in the morning. These past 2 years writing "The Control" were challenging years for me. I had become a mom, was working full-time and was trying to scrounge time out of my new crazy life to write this novel. And then I found out I had developed an illness. It made the little challenges like getting out of bed in the morning difficult. The last thing I wanted to do was write, and in fact, it was the last thing I wanted to do. I doubted myself and my series, to a point I thought this book would remain unfinished and Aurora and Boreas's journey would remain in limbo...

And then I heard the conch shell sound!

The conch shell was in the form of many different things, but especially people. It was from the support of a good friend, Angela Barbara, who over lunch asked me when the 3rd book would be finished. Her support helped me remember how much I loved writing this series and how invested I was in the characters' stories. I had to return to the United States of the Common Good. It was time.

The conch shell was in the form of my amazing editor, Theresa Goncalves! Despite becoming a new parent herself, she embarked once again on this journey with me and it was through her edits, and love of the series, that this story is as strong as it is. I couldn't have done this without her and it truly is wonderful to work with not only such a talented editor, but an amazing friend. Also a shout-out to her father Tom Brennan for passing his army and air force knowledge down to Theresa to help make the battle scenes much more believable!

And, of course, the conch shell sounded from my amazing family. Thank you to my sisters, Erin and Cassandra, and my brother-in-law Louie. You never cease to support me and be my number one fans and your love of the series and the characters continue to inspire me to write. To my dad who always tells me to reach for the stars. I'm reaching farther than I ever have before and loving every minute of being a dreamer. To my darling husband Mike who has stood by me every step of the way. This journey wouldn't be possible without you in my corner and I am so blessed to have you in my life. And to my little goddess, Lily. I love you so much and you are my reason for the reason. And to my beautiful mother, who this book is dedicated too. I am so proud to be your daughter and thank you for teaching me the power of faith and love.

Lastly, the conch shell that sounded was the love and support of all of my friends, fans and readers of this story who continue to show your support and reach out and express your love of *The Hypothesis of Giants*. I am touched that this story inspires all of you, and that inspires me to continue to write. There is one more story to be written for this series, "The Integration", and I can't wait to share it with all of you. This series is more powerful than anything I could have imagined when I started "The Assumption" 7 years ago. Thank you for being on this journey with me and I hope my story helps inspire you to hear your own conch shell sound and follow your passions in life, no matter what obstacles come your way. May you all find magic in your life and always believe!

About the Author

Melissa Kuch is the author of **The Hypothesis of Giants** series. She currently resides on Long Island, NY with her husband Mike and their daughter Lily. For more updates about this series and other works by Melissa Kuch, please visit her website at www.melissakuch.com, or follow her on Facebook (https://www.facebook.com/the-hypothesisofgiants/) and Twitter @kuchmelissa

Proof

87097358R00226

Made in the USA
Columbia, SC
09 January 2018